Cindi Myers is the author When she's not crafting new skiing, gardening, cooking lover of small-town life, she lives with her husband and two spoiled dogs in the Colorado mountains.

Nicole Helm grew up with her nose in a book and the dream of one day becoming a writer. Luckily, after a few failed career choices, she gets to follow that dream—writing down-to-earth contemporary romance and romantic suspense. From farmers to cowboys, Midwest to *the* West, Nicole writes stories about people finding themselves and finding love in the process. She lives in Missouri with her husband and two sons and dreams of someday owning a barn.

DANGER ON DAKOTA RIDGE

CINDI MYERS

WYOMING COWBOY JUSTICE

NICOLE HELM

MIX
Paper from
responsible sources
FSC
FSC C007454

This book is produced from independently certified FSC™
paper to ensure responsible forest management.

For more information visit: www.harpercollins.co.uk/green

Printed and bound in Spain
by CPI, Barcelona

MILLS & BOON

First Published in Great Britain 2018
by Mills & Boon, an imprint of HarperCollins*Publishers*
1 London Bridge Street, London, SE1 9GF

Danger on Dakota Ridge © 2018 Cynthia Myers
Wyoming Cowboy Justice © 2018 Nicole Helm

ISBN 978-0-263-26598-9

1018

DANGER ON
DAKOTA RIDGE

CINDI MYERS

For Susan

Chapter One

What she was planning wasn't illegal, Paige Riddell told herself as she hiked up the trail to Dakota Ridge. Her friend Deputy Gage Walker might not agree, but she hadn't asked his opinion. The mayor of Eagle Mountain, Larry Rowe, would object, but Larry always took the side of corporations and businesses over people like Paige—especially Paige. But she knew she was right. CNG Development was the one breaking the law, and she had a copy of a court order in her pocket to prove it.

The tools she carried clanked as she made her way up the forest trail. She had borrowed the hacksaw from a neighbor, telling him she needed to cut up an old folding table to put out for recycling. The bolt cutters were new, purchased at a hardware store out of town. Planning for this expedition had been exciting, she had to admit—a nice break from her routine life of managing the Bear's Den Bed and Breakfast Inn and volunteering for various causes.

She stopped to catch her breath and readjust the straps on her pack. A chill breeze sent a swirl of dried aspen leaves across her path, bringing with it the scent of pine. In another week or two, snow would dust the top of Dakota Ridge, rising in the distance on her right. In another month, people would be taking to the trail with snowshoes instead of hiking boots. Thanks to Paige, they would be able to make their way all the way up and along the top of the ridge, their progress unimpeded by CNG's illegal gate.

She set out again, walking faster as she neared her destination, a mixture of nerves and excitement humming through her. She planned to leave the copy of the court order at the gate after she cut off the locks, so that whichever CNG employee discovered the damage would know this wasn't a random act of vandalism, but an effort to enforce the court's ruling that CNG couldn't block access to a public trail that had been in use across this land since the late nineteenth century.

The trail turned and followed alongside an eight-foot fence of welded iron and fine-mesh wire. Snarls of razor wire adorned the top of the fence. Paige was sure the razor wire hadn't been there when she had last hiked up this way about ten days ago. What was so important on the other side of that fence that CNG felt the need to protect it with razor wire?

She quickened her pace. CNG had the right to protect its property however it saw fit, but if the management wanted to keep out hikers, they needed to reroute their fence. Maybe wrecking their gate would encourage them to do so. Waiting for them to comply with the court ruling hadn't worked, so it was time for action.

She had considered asking other members of the Eagle Mountain Environmental Action Group to join her. The local hiking club, which had evolved into the closest thing Rayford County had to a political action committee, had a diverse membership of active people, most of whom were already up in arms about the gate over one of the most popular trails in the area. With more people and more tools, they probably could have dismantled the obstruction. But more people involved meant a greater chance of discovery. Someone would shoot off their mouth in a bar or to the wrong friend, and the next thing Paige knew, CNG would have filed a countersuit or criminal charges or something. Better to do this by herself—less chance of getting caught. CNG might suspect her of having something to do with the messed-up gate, since she was head of the EMEAG and one of its most vocal members, but they would never be able to prove it.

She quickened her pace as the offending gate came into view. Welded of black iron, four feet wide and at least six feet tall, topped with pointed spikes, it sported a massive padlock and the kind of chain Paige associated with cargo ships, each link easily three inches across. She stopped a few feet away, slipped the pack from her back and dropped it onto the ground beside the trail, where it settled with an audible *clank*.

She moved closer, inspecting the setup. The lock was new, made of heavy brass. She had heard Gage had shot the old one off when he and his girlfriend, Maya, were up here searching for her missing niece. Paige grabbed the lock—which was bigger than her hand—and tugged. Not that she expected it to be open, but she would have felt really foolish if she went to the trouble to cut it off, then found out it hadn't even been fastened.

The lock weighed several pounds. The hasp was thick, too. She returned to her pack and fished out the cutters and the hacksaw. Some videos she had watched online had showed people slicing through locks with portable grinders, but that approach had struck her as noisy and likely to attract attention. Better to snip the lock off with the bolt cutters, or saw through the hasp.

She tried the bolt cutters first, gripping the hasp of the lock between the jaws of the cutters and bearing down with all her might.

Nothing. They didn't even make a dent in the metal. She gritted her teeth and tried again, grunting with the effort. Nothing, save for a faint scratch. A little out of breath, she straightened, scowling at the recalcitrant lock. Fine. Time to get the hacksaw. Her neighbor had assured her it would cut through metal.

Sawing the blade was hard, tiring work, but after half a dozen strong strokes, she had succeeded in making a dent in the hasp. Another half hour or so of work and she might sever the hasp—provided her arm didn't fall off first. But hey—she wasn't a quitter. She bore down and sawed faster.

She was concentrating so hard on the work she didn't hear the voices until they were almost on her. "Over here!" a man shouted, and Paige bit back a yelp and almost dropped the saw.

She recovered quickly, gathered her tools and raced into the underbrush, heart hammering painfully. She waited for the voices to come closer, for someone to notice the damage to the lock and complain. Had they seen her?

Her pack! Feeling sick to her stomach, she shifted her gaze to the dark blue backpack clearly visible by the side of the trail. Did she dare retrieve it? But moving would surely attract attention.

She held her breath as two men in forest camo parkas, watch caps pulled down low on their foreheads, emerged from the woods on CNG's side of the gate and tramped down the trail toward her. She shrank farther back into the underbrush, sharp thorns from wild roses catching on the nylon of her jacket and scratching the backs of her hands. Her eyes widened and her heart beat even faster as the men drew nearer and she could make out semiautomatic weapons slung across their backs. Since when did a real-estate development company equip their security guards with guns like that?

Talk about overkill! Anger took the place of some of her fear. If those big bullies thought they could intimidate her, they had another think coming. She had every right to be here, on a public trail, and if they didn't like it, they could take it up with the sheriff's department, but she was in the right.

She had about decided to emerge from her hiding place and tell them so when they reached the gate. But instead of stopping and opening it, or yelling out at her, the two men walked past, along the fence line. Now Paige could see they carried something between them. Something heavy, in a large wooden packing crate. She shuddered as they passed. Though the shape wasn't exactly right, the big box reminded her of a coffin. What the heck were these two doing with that out here in the middle of nowhere? After all, there was a perfectly good road leading right onto the property, which had once been planned as a luxury resort. Last she had heard, CNG wanted to turn the abandoned resort into a high-altitude research laboratory. So why sneak through the woods carrying a heavy box instead of just driving it to wherever they needed it? And why carry guns along with the box?

As soon as the men had passed her hiding place and moved out of sight, Paige emerged. She shoved the tools and the pack out of sight under some bearberry bushes, then hurried down the trail after the men. The former Eagle Mountain Resort had been the site of plenty of shady activity lately—maybe this was more of the same. It was her duty as a citizen to find out. Besides, who could resist a mystery like this?

She didn't have any trouble tracking the two men. They crashed through the underbrush like a pair of bull elk. They probably didn't expect anyone else to be up here. Word had gotten out around town that the trail was blocked, and no one lived on the abandoned mining claims that surrounded CNG's property, except Ed Roberts, who was practically a hermit and made a point of keeping to himself. Paige had counted on that same privacy to help her get away with cutting the lock off the gate. She'd have to make another attempt at that. Next time, she would bring more muscle, and maybe power tools.

Wherever the two guys with guns were headed, they weren't wasting any time. Paige had to trot to keep up with them. Fortunately, the trail paralleling the fence made movement easy, and her lightweight hiking boots made little noise on the soft ground. She stayed far enough behind that the men would have to turn all the way around to see her, but she could still keep them in her sights.

A few hundred yards from the gate, they turned away from the trail. Paige stopped and crouched down. She watched through an opening in the underbrush as they carried the box about fifty feet, then stopped and set down their burden. The man in the lead bent and felt for something in the drying grass. The sound of metal scraping against metal carried clearly in the still air. The man turned around, then descended into the ground. The second man shoved the box toward the spot where his companion had disappeared and tipped it up, then slid it in. Then he disappeared after it.

Paige straightened, her mind racing to solve this puzzle. She looked around, noting her surroundings. Gage and Maya had been trapped in an underground chamber on the resort property. Maya's niece, Casey, had climbed out and run for help. That must be the same chamber where the two men had disappeared just now. What were they doing in there? What was in that box? And why did they have to carry it through the woods instead of driving it to the storage bunker that led to the chamber?

She would definitely be paying Maya and Gage a visit to find out their take on all this. Of course, she had no proof anything at all illegal was going on, but given the property's history, it might be worth watching. She turned and made her way back down the trail and collected her pack and tools. She checked the lock again, but all her efforts had barely marked it. She would have to come up with a better plan.

Shouldering the pack once more, she started back down the trail. She needed to get back to the B and B. She had a new guest checking in this afternoon. Some government worker, Robert Allen. His secretary had made the reservation, and the credit card information she had given Paige had checked out. He had reserved her best suite for a week, a real bonus, considering this was her slow time of year—past prime summer tourist season, too late for fall leaf-peepers and too early for the Thanksgiving and Christmas holidays.

These thoughts occupied her until she reached the spot where the two men had turned away from the fence.

She couldn't resist taking another peek, to see if she could make out anything else distinctive about the site. She bent over and wormed her way into the opening in the undergrowth, a more difficult task while wearing the pack. But she managed to wedge herself in there and look through—just in time to see the second man join the first up top. He bent and slid whatever cover was over the opening back in place. Then both men started straight toward her.

Paige quickly backed out of her hiding place, fighting the branches that snagged on her clothing and tangled in her pack. She swatted a vine out of her way and a thorn pricked her thumb, a bead of bright red blood welling against her white flesh. The tools in her backpack clanged like out-of-tune wind chimes as she pushed her way back toward the trail.

"Hey!" a man yelled.

Something whistled through the air past her and struck a tree to her left, sending splinters flying. A second gunshot followed the first. Paige yelped and ran, heart racing and legs pumping. Those maniacs were shooting at her! You couldn't shoot at someone on a public trail! Gage was definitely going to hear about this.

They weren't shooting anymore. They probably couldn't get a clear view of her. The trail was downhill and Paige ran fast. The two men would have to fight through heavy underbrush and get over or around that fence to pursue her. She had left her car parked at the trailhead and she was sure she could get to it before they could.

Idiots! In what universe did they think they could get away with something like this? You could bet she would be filing charges. She'd call the papers, too. CNG would get plenty of bad publicity from this fiasco. And when the corporate lawyers came calling to apologize and persuade her to settle out of court, she'd use that leverage to have them remove that gate over the trail. In fact, she'd make sure they donated some of their high-value ridgetop property as a conservation easement. They would have to if they had any hope of recovering their precious reputation.

Buoyed by these plans, she jogged down the trail, head bent, watching for roots and other obstacles that might trip her up. She didn't see the big man in the dark coat who stepped out in front of her—didn't register his presence at all until she crashed into him and his arms wrapped around her, holding her tight.

Chapter Two

As a DEA agent for the past fifteen years, Rob Allerton had faced down his share of men and women who wanted to kill him, but none had outright tried to run him over. The sound of gunfire had sent him charging up the trail, only to be almost mowed down by a female hiker who fought like a tornado when he grabbed hold of her to steady them both. He managed to pin her on the ground, then satisfied himself that she wasn't armed—and therefore probably not the source of the shots he had heard.

"I'm not going to hurt you," he said, speaking slowly and distinctly in her ear, ignoring the alluring floral fragrance that rose from the soft skin of her neck. "I'm a law enforcement officer. I only want to help." Carefully, he eased back and released his hold on her.

She sat up and swept a fall of straight honey-blond hair out of her eyes, and he felt the angry look she lasered at him in the pit of his stomach—and farther south, to tell the truth. He hadn't seen Paige Riddell in almost two years, but she wasn't the kind of woman a man forgot easily.

"Agent Allerton." She pronounced his name as if it was a particularly distasteful disease. He had figured out the first day they met that she seldom bothered masking her feelings or suppressing her passions. Feeling the heat of her hatred only made him wonder what it would be like to be on the receiving end of her love.

"What are you doing here?" she demanded, standing and dusting dirt from the knees of her jeans.

He rose also. "I heard gunshots. Was someone shooting at you?"

"*I* certainly wasn't shooting at *them*." She adjusted her pack, which clanked as she shifted her weight.

He frowned at the dark blue backpack. "Is that a *saw* you're carrying?" He walked around her to get a better look. "And a pair of bolt cutters?" He moved back in front of her. "What have you been up to?"

"None of your business." She tried to walk past him, but he blocked her way. She glared up at him, with those clear gray eyes that still had the power to mesmerize.

"It's my business if someone was shooting at you." He touched her upper arm, wary of startling her. "Are you okay? Are you hurt?" He should have asked the questions earlier, but he was so surprised to find her here he had forgotten himself.

"I'm fine." She shrugged off his hand, but he recognized the pallor beneath her tan.

"Who fired those shots?" he asked. "It sounded like a semiautomatic."

She glanced over her shoulder, in the direction she had run from. "I'm not going to stand here, waiting for them to come back," she said. "If you want to talk, you can come with me."

He let her move past him this time, and fell into step just behind her on the narrow trail. "Did you get a look at the shooters?" he asked. "Was it anyone you know?"

"I don't know who they were—two men up at the

old Eagle Mountain Resort." She gestured toward the property to their left. The trail had turned away from the fence line and descended away from the property. "I spotted them carrying a big wooden crate through the woods. They lowered it into an underground chamber of some kind. At least, they both disappeared through some kind of trapdoor in the ground, and came out without the crate. I guess they saw me watching and fired. I took off running. They were on the other side of that big fence, so they couldn't chase me."

"Maybe they thought you were trying to break in," he said. "Were you using those bolt cutters on their fence?" He wished he could see her face, but she didn't look at him, and walked fast enough so that he had to work to keep up with her.

"No, I was not trying to break through their fence," she said.

"What were you doing? Bolt cutters and a saw aren't typical hiking gear."

"I was going to cut the illegal lock off their illegal gate over a legal public hiking trail," she said. "I have a copy of a court order instructing them to remove the lock and open the gate, which they haven't done."

"So you decided to take matters into your own hands," he said.

"The lock was too tough," she said. "I'll have to get someone up here with power tools or a torch or something." She might have been discussing her plans to build a community playground or something equally as virtuous. Then again, Paige Riddell probably saw opening up a public trail as just as worthy an enterprise. This was the Paige he remembered, absolutely certain in her definitions of right and wrong, and that she, of course, was in the right.

"You're not worried someone is going to shoot at you again?" he asked. "Next time they might not miss."

She glanced back at him. "I'm going to report this to the sheriff. I was on a public trail. They had no right to fire on me. Even if I'd been trespassing—which I was not—they had no right to try to shoot me."

"You aren't the first person who's been fired on up here," Rob said. "Someone tried to shoot the sheriff and his deputies when they visited the property months ago."

"So there's a pattern of unlawful behavior," she said. "It's time to put a stop to it."

"Except no one can ever identify the shooters," Rob said.

"I could identify these men." She bent to duck under a low-hanging branch, then glanced back once more. "What are you doing here?" she asked. "I doubt you just decided it was a nice day for a hike."

"I'm staying in town for a few days—a little vacation time." Long practice made him reluctant to share his plans with anyone, especially a woman he didn't know that well, who had made no secret of her dislike of him. "I heard a new company had taken over this property and I wanted to check out what they were doing here."

"You didn't find anything illegal when you were there last month, did you?" she asked.

"No." He had overseen an investigation into an underground laboratory that had been discovered on the property, but his team had found no signs of illegal activity.

"The new owners say they're going to use the property to build a high-altitude research facility," she said. "Did you know that?"

"I heard something to that effect," he said. "What do you think of that idea?" Paige headed up the local environmental group that had gotten the injunction that stopped development at the resort years ago.

"It's better than a resort that only gets used half the year," she said. "Depending on what they research, that kind of facility might actually do some good, and I wouldn't expect a lot of traffic or other stressors on the environment. We'll wait and see what they plan to do, and we'll definitely have some of our members at their permit hearings."

"Do you ever worry you'll get on the wrong side of the wrong person?" he asked.

She stopped so suddenly he almost collided with her. She turned to face him. "No, I'm not afraid," she said. "The kinds of people we do battle with—people or companies who want to do harmful things for their own gain, without thought for others—they want us to be afraid. They count on it, even. I'm not going to give them that satisfaction." She turned and started walking again.

"You don't think that's foolhardy sometimes?" he asked, picking up his pace and squeezing in beside her. "Not everyone plays by the rules. Some of them can be downright nasty." He had met his share of the second type in his years in drug enforcement.

"I try to be smart and careful, but I'm not going to back down when I'm in the right."

There was that passion again, practically sparking from her eyes. He couldn't help but admire that about her, even when they had been sparring on opposite sides of a battle. "Tell the sheriff what you saw," he said. "Then let him and his deputies handle this. Don't go up there by yourself again."

"I told you I try to be smart," she said. "Next time I'll go up there with other people. I might even have a reporter with me." She smiled. "Yes, I think that would be a great idea. Companies like CNG hate bad publicity."

They reached the trailhead, where his black pickup truck was parked beside her red Prius. She studied the truck. "Is that yours?" she asked.

"Yes. It's my personal vehicle. I told you, I'm on vacation."

She turned to him again. "I just realized I've never seen you when you weren't wearing a suit." Her gaze swept over his hiking boots and jeans, over the blue plaid flannel shirt, up to his hair, which he hadn't found time to get cut lately. He felt self-conscious under that piercing gaze, wondering if he measured up. Did Paige like what she saw? Was he vain, hoping the answer was yes?

But her expression was impossible to decipher. He half expected her to say something derogatory, or at least mocking. Instead, she said, "I guess the truck suits you."

What was that supposed to mean? But before he could ask her, she stashed the pack in the back seat of the Prius, climbed into the driver's seat and sped away, leaving him standing beside his truck, feeling that, once again, Paige had gotten the upper hand.

OF THE PEOPLE she might have expected to encounter on the trail that morning, Paige had to admit that DEA agent Rob Allerton was probably five hundredth on the list of possibilities. Sure, he had ended up in Eagle Mountain a month ago, leading an investigation into that underground lab, but she had managed to avoid crossing paths with him. Once he had wrapped that up and gone back to live and work in Denver, she had comforted herself that she would never have to see the man again.

Now that she was alone, and the full impact of what had happened up on Dakota Ridge was making her break out in a cold sweat, she could admit that she had been relieved to see him, once she realized he wasn't a friend of the shooters. Rob Allerton might be a coldhearted pain in the behind, but he had probably been armed, and he knew how to handle criminals. For all her talk of not letting fear make her back down, she had been relieved not to have to face those two men and their guns by herself.

She gripped the steering wheel more tightly and glanced in the rearview mirror, to see Rob's Ford pickup behind her. She might have known he would drive a truck. He had always had a bit of a cowboy swagger—something she might have admired if they hadn't been adversaries.

And they were adversaries, she reminded herself. Rob Allerton was the reason her brother, Parker, had ended up in jail, instead of in a rehab program where he belonged. She had fought like a mama bear—and spent most of her savings—to get her little brother into a program that would help him, and to get the sentence deferred if he completed all the requirements of his parole. Allerton hadn't lifted a finger to help her, and had in fact spoken out against any leniency for Parker. She was never going to forgive him for that.

Remembering how she had won that battle, and that Parker was all right now and well on his way to putting his life back together, calmed her. She rubbed her shoulder, where it ached from carrying the pack and tools, and slid her hand around to massage the back of her neck, then froze. Her fingers groped around her collar, then back to the front of her throat, under her T-shirt. Her necklace was gone—the thin gold chain from which hung the gold charm of a bird in flight. She had purchased the necklace shortly after her divorce, as a symbol that she was free as a bird. She never took it off—but it was gone now. She swore to herself. The chain must have caught in the bushes when she pushed through them to get a better look at those two men. Or maybe when she had retreated.

She would have to go back up there later and look for it. But she wouldn't go alone. She would take plenty of friends with her, and she would make sure they were armed with more than bolt cutters and saws.

By the time she parked the Prius in front of the Rayford County Sheriff's Department, she felt ready to relate her story calmly. She headed up the walkway, only to meet Rob Allerton at the front door.

He held the door open for her. "After you."

"Are you following me?" she asked.

"I needed to check in with the sheriff anyway," he said.

"Why? I thought you said you were here on vacation."

"Just professional courtesy, to let him know I'm in town." He followed her into the reception area. "Besides, I can add my account of the shooting to yours."

"Agent Allerton! What a nice surprise!" Adelaide Kinkaid, the sixtysomething administrator for the sheriff's department, greeted Rob with a wide smile. She didn't exactly flutter her eyelashes at him, but the implication was there.

"Ms. Kinkaid. Nice to see you again." Rob clasped her hand and flashed a smile of his own, and Adelaide looked as if she might swoon. Paige crossed her arms

over her chest and looked away. Honestly! It wasn't as
if Rob Allerton was the only good-looking man on the
planet. Yes, he had that young Jake Gyllenhaal charm
going on that probably appealed to Adelaide's generation, but Paige had always liked men who were a little
rougher around the edges. Less glib. Less deceptive.

"I just stopped by to say hello to the sheriff," Rob said.
"Ms. Riddell needs to make a report of an incident up
on Dakota Ridge, though."

"Oh, hello, Paige," Adelaide said. "I didn't see you
standing there."

"No, I don't imagine you did," Paige muttered.

"Did you say an incident? On Dakota Ridge?" Sheriff
Travis Walker, Gage's brother, joined them in the reception area. Clean-shaven and spit polished, Travis could
have been a law enforcement poster boy. The fact that
he was smarter than most and full of grit had made him
a local hero, and at twenty-nine, the youngest sheriff in
Rayford County history.

"It's Paige's story to tell," Rob said. "I only happened
upon the tail end of things."

"Come into my office." Travis led them down the hall
to his office and shut the door behind them. Paige sat
in the chair in front of the battered wooden desk, while
Travis took the black leather chair behind it. Rob sta-
tioned himself by the door. "Tell me what happened,"
Travis said.

"I hiked up the Dakota Ridge Trail this morning,"
Paige said. "I wanted to see if CNG Development had
complied with the court order to remove the gate over
the trail. They hadn't."

She glanced at Rob, daring him to reveal her plans
to remove the lock, but he said nothing. "While I was

up there, I saw two men on the other side of the gate, on the old Eagle Mountain Resort property. They didn't see me. They were carrying a large wooden crate between them—about the size of a coffin, though I don't think it was a coffin. It looked heavy. I thought it was really odd that they would be carrying something like that through the woods, instead of driving up to wherever they needed to be. The second thing that was odd was that both of the men had semiautomatic rifles slung over their backs. I'm no expert, but I think they were AR-15s."

Travis's brow wrinkled, and he pulled a pad of paper toward him and began making notes. "Can you describe these men?"

"Muscular—big shoulders. They were wearing forest camo parkas and black knit watch caps. I didn't get a really good look at their faces through the trees, but I didn't recognize them."

"What happened next?" Travis asked.

"They continued through the woods, on the other side of the fence. I went back down the trail, but I was curious to know what they were up to, so I followed them. They stopped and one of them bent down and I heard the scrape of metal on metal. I think they opened a trapdoor or something. Then one of them climbed down into the ground. The other one pushed the box in and climbed down after it."

"So they went underground?" Travis asked. "Out of sight?"

She nodded. "I wondered if they were going into that same chamber where Gage and Maya were trapped this summer. But then I wondered again why they hadn't just driven up to it. Isn't it connected to that underground lab you found?" She looked to Rob for confirmation. "That's what Maya told me."

"It is," Rob said. "But we didn't find any sign that that chamber had been used for anything in a long time."

"That chamber is farther from the fence line," Travis said. "I don't think you could see the opening at the top from the fence."

"I don't think so, either," Rob said.

"Maybe it's just underground storage of some kind," Travis said.

"Fine, but why sneak through the woods, especially carrying something heavy?" she asked. "And why were those guys armed? And why did they shoot at me when they saw me watching them?"

"Did they say anything?" Travis asked.

"No. They just yelled 'Hey!' or something like that, and started firing. I couldn't get out of there fast enough."

"Did they try to follow you?" Travis asked.

"I don't know. I just ran." Her heart raced, remembering. "I knew they were on the other side of the fence and they'd have a hard time catching up to me. I figured I could make it to my car before they did. Then I ran into Agent Allerton." No sense elaborating on how he had pinned her to the ground. Though she had to admit that was after she did her best to knee him in the crotch.

"I heard the gunshots and came running up the trail," Rob said. "I met Paige coming down."

"What were you doing up there?" Travis asked.

Paige watched his face, not hiding her curiosity. Would he give the sheriff his story about a vacation? He shifted his weight. "I took some personal time to do a favor for my aunt."

"What kind of favor?" Travis asked.

Rob glanced at Paige. Was he going to ask her to leave the room, or suggest that he and Travis talk later? "I didn't ask you to leave while I told my story," she said. "I think I can hear yours."

"It's not exactly a secret," he said. "My aunt by marriage is Henry Hake's older sister. She asked me to look into his death a little more, see what I could find out."

"We're still investigating Henry Hake's death," Travis said. The man behind the Eagle Mountain Resort development had disappeared earlier in the summer. His body had been discovered on the property last month, but so far no one had been able to determine either how he had died or why.

"I'm not trying to step on any toes," Rob said. "But she's been worried sick since Hake disappeared early this summer. When he was found dead in that bunker on what had been his own property, it left her with more questions than answers. I told her I didn't expect to find anything you hadn't already learned, but she begged me to try." He shrugged. "I had some time off coming, and it's not exactly a hardship to spend a few days hanging around Eagle Mountain."

"Does your aunt have any ideas about what might have happened to her brother?" Travis asked.

"He had heart trouble, but she doesn't think he died of a heart attack," Rob said. "She's sure he was murdered. He was definitely afraid of someone in the weeks before he died. I'd like to find out who."

Chapter Three

Rob gave Travis credit—the sheriff didn't even blink when he learned Rob's reason for a return to Eagle Mountain. Paige, however, was gaping at him as if he had revealed a secret identity as a circus clown. "You're related to Henry Hake?" she asked.

"Not exactly," he said. "My uncle's second wife is Hake's sister. I never met the man." He turned to Travis. "And it's not my intention to interfere with your investigation. I just promised my aunt I would see what I could find out. I hiked up that trail this morning thinking I would start by getting another look at the place where his body was found—or as close as I could get, since the gates to the compound were locked up."

Travis nodded and turned back to Paige. "I'll go up to the resort property and take a look around. Do you think you could identify either of the men who shot at you if you saw them again?"

"Yes," she said.

"Good. I'll be in touch." He stood, and Paige rose also.

"While you're up there, would you look for my necklace?" she asked. "It's a gold chain, with a charm of a bird in flight. I was wearing it this morning and I don't have it now. I think it must have snagged on the bushes near where I was watching those two men."

"Sure, we can look for it," Travis said.

"Thank you, Sheriff," she said, and turned toward the door.

"Paige?"

"Yes, Sheriff?"

"Don't go up there by yourself anymore," Travis said. "At least until we get this settled. And tell the other hikers you know the same."

"All right." She turned toward Rob and acted as if she wanted to say something, then closed her mouth and left the room.

"Stay a minute," Travis said to Rob.

He nodded, and waited until they heard the front door close behind Paige before he took the seat she had vacated.

"Did you see either of the men she described?" Travis asked.

"No. I wasn't that far up the trail before she came barreling down." He chuckled. "I didn't recognize her at first, and I'm sure she didn't recognize me. When I took hold of her to try to calm her down, she fought like a tiger." He rubbed the side of his face, where she had scratched him.

"You knew each other before?" Travis asked.

Rob nodded. "Yes. And it's safe to say I am not one of her favorite people."

Travis waited, silent. He was probably a good interrogator, using silence to his benefit. "I'm the one who arrested her brother," Rob said.

"For possession of meth?" Travis asked.

"Yes. And for trying to sell stolen property. He was

part of a group of addicts who were robbing apartment complexes in Denver. I was part of a joint drug task force working that case. We had already determined the thefts were linked to drugs."

"There was no doubt of his guilt?"

"None." He sighed, all the frustration of those days coming back to him. "Paige wanted an adjudicated sentence, with her brother, Parker, allowed to go to rehab instead of prison. I didn't agree."

"From what I've seen, she can be a little protective of Parker," Travis said.

"I get it. As far as I know, he's the only family she has. But the fact that part of my job was to help see that he was punished for his crimes made me the enemy. Her opinions about right and wrong tend to be very black-and-white."

"She went up there today to cut off that lock, didn't she?" Travis asked.

Rob grinned. "I didn't see a thing. Though she was carrying a hacksaw and a pair of bolt cutters with her."

Travis shook his head. "When Paige believes she's in the right, there's no changing her mind."

"I certainly learned that." Though he would have preferred she didn't see him as the bad guy. Still, she wasn't his chief concern at the moment. "As long as I'm here, maybe I could help you out with Henry Hake's case," he said. "Is there anything you'd like me to look into? Unofficially, of course."

"Did your aunt say who her brother was afraid of?"

"No. Except she thinks it had something to do with his business."

"So not necessarily Eagle Mountain Resort. He had other real-estate holdings, didn't he?"

"A few apartment complexes and some office build-ings," Rob said. "Eagle Mountain Resort was definitely his most ambitious project. When the court ordered him to stop development, I gather it put him in a financial bind."

Travis nodded. "That's what I've learned, also."

"What can you tell me about the property's new own-ers—CNG Development?" Rob asked.

"They're another real-estate development company, out of Utah. They're much larger than Hake Develop-ment, with projects all over the United States. I wondered why they even bothered with Hake—he was pretty small potatoes, compared to them."

"Maybe they're one of these companies that special-izes in finding small firms in financial straits and buy-ing them for bargain prices," Rob said.

"Maybe so."

"Paige says they want to build a research facility up there."

"So they've said. They haven't presented anything concrete to the town for approval. The couple of times I've been up there since Hake's body was found, the place has been deserted."

"It wasn't deserted today," Rob said. "I'd sure like to know why those two were going around armed—and what was in that box. And why they reacted the way they did when they caught Paige watching them."

"Want to go up there with me to check it out?" Tra-vis asked.

"You know I'm not officially on duty," Rob said. "My boss doesn't even know where I am."

"You wouldn't be participating in any official capac-ity," Travis said. "I just want someone to watch my back."

"I can do that." And maybe he would get lucky and discover something he could tell his aunt. He couldn't bring her brother back to her, but finding out what had really happened to him might ease her suffering a little bit.

THOUGH PAIGE VOWED to put Rob Allerton firmly out of her mind and focus on work at the bed-and-breakfast where she both lived and worked, she couldn't stop thinking about the man. He was always so aggravatingly calm and sure of himself. Having him here in town annoyed her, like walking around with a pebble in her shoe. Those days following Parker's arrest had been among the worst in recent memory. Her brother had needed help and men like Rob were preventing her from helping him. Yes, Parker had broken the law, but he wasn't a bad person. His addiction had led him to do things he never would have done otherwise. Instead of punishing him, why not treat his addiction and give him another chance?

Rob Allerton had made it clear he didn't believe in second chances. No thanks to him, Parker had at least gotten a chance to get clean, though he had had to serve time, too. But he was clean now, going to school and staying out of trouble. Another year and the charges would be wiped from his record.

But he was in that position only because Paige had fought for him. Other people weren't so lucky. They had to deal with the Rob Allertons of the world without anyone on their side.

She sat down at her desk off the kitchen and tried to put Rob out of her mind. His vacation wouldn't last forever, and she had more than enough to keep her occupied in the meantime. She was working there a little later when the back door opened and Parker entered. He dropped his backpack on the bench by the door and pushed his sunglasses on top of his head. To some of the more conservative people here in Eagle Mountain, he probably looked like trouble, with his full-sleeve tattoos and often sullen expression. But Paige saw past all that to the little boy she had read stories to and made macaroni and cheese for more times than she could remember. "How was class?" she asked.

"Okay." He opened the refrigerator. "What did you do today?"

Attempted vandalism and ended up getting shot at by two thugs, she thought. "I was up on the Dakota Ridge Trail and you'll never guess who I ran into."

He took out a block of cheese and a plate of leftover ham. "I don't have to guess," he said. "You always tell me anyway."

"Rob Allerton is in town."

"Who?" He took a loaf of bread from the box on the counter and began making a sandwich.

"Rob Allerton. Agent Allerton? The DEA guy who arrested you?"

"What's he doing here?"

"He says he's on vacation." He hadn't told the sheriff about her attempt to cut the lock from the gate up on the trail, so she figured she could keep quiet about Rob's aunt and Henry Hake. Parker wouldn't care about any of that anyway.

"Maybe he wanted to see you," Parker said.

"Me?" She blew out a breath. "I'm sure I'm the last person he would ever want to see. Don't you remember how we clashed at your trial?"

"I remember sparks." He shot her a sideways look. "He thought you were hot."

"He did not!"

"You thought he was hot, too."

"You're delusional."

He turned back to his sandwich. "I'm not the one blushing."

"I'm not blushing. This room is too warm." She opened the refrigerator and began putting away the items he had removed. "Are you volunteering at the museum this afternoon?" she asked. She had talked Parker into volunteering at the local history museum. Her friend Brenda Stenson, who ran the museum, needed the help, and it was a good way for Parker to keep busy. Everything she had read had said that having too much free time could be a problem for a recovering addict.

"No." He took a bite of the sandwich.

Paige tore off a paper towel and handed it to him. "What time does your shift at Peggy's start?" She had found him the job as a delivery driver at Peggy's Pizza as another way to keep him out of trouble.

"I'm off tonight," he said, then took another bite of sandwich.

"Oh. Well, I guess you can use the time to study." He was enrolled in classes at a nearby community college. Another condition of his parole.

"I'm going out," he said.

"With who?"

"A friend."

"Do I know this friend?"

"I doubt it."

"Parker, we are not going to do this."

"Do what?" He didn't bother trying to look innocent. If anything, he was annoyed.

"Don't make me give you the third degree," she said. "Just tell me who you're going out with. I don't think that's too much to ask."

"And it's not too much for me to ask that you give me a little privacy."

A flood of words came to mind, beginning with the notion that he had violated his right to privacy when he had gotten hooked on drugs, broken the law and gone to prison. But she had vowed when she took him in that she wasn't going to throw his mistakes back in his face. Her husband had done that and she knew how miserable and degraded it made her feel. So she swallowed back most of what she wanted to say.

"Be careful, and be quiet when you come in," she said.

"I will." Carrying the rest of his sandwich, he retreated to his room off the kitchen. Paige sagged against the counter. She was exhausted and it wasn't even one o'clock yet. Big guys with guns, Rob Allerton and her troublesome baby brother—maybe what she really needed was a vacation from men.

WHEN ROB AND Travis arrived at the entrance to the former Eagle Mountain Resort, Rob wasn't surprised to find the gates shut tight. "This is how they were this morning when I stopped here," he said. He peered through the iron bars at what had once been the resort's main street. Weeds sprouted in holes in the asphalt, and in places the paving had disappeared altogether, the road little more than a gravel wash. A weathered sign still proclaimed that this was the future site of Eagle Mountain Resort, a Luxury Property from Hake Development. No sign of luxury remained in the crumbling foundations and sun-bleached wood of the few structures scattered about the property. Rocks ranging from those the size of a man's head to boulders as big as small cars spilled down from the ridge above at the site of a major rock slide where two men had been killed earlier in the year.

"It doesn't look any different than it did when I was here a month ago," Rob said.

"I'm guessing if CNG does plan to develop the place—for a research facility or anything else—they'll wait until spring," Travis said. "In another few months there will be eight to ten feet of snow up here. The county doesn't plow the road up this far and there's always a danger of avalanches on the ridge. It's one reason the judge agreed with Paige's group that a housing development up here was a bad idea."

Rob looked again at the deserted street. "What do we do now?" he asked.

"Let's hike up the trail a ways," Travis said. "You can show me where you were when you heard the shots, and where you ran into Paige."

They drove back down the road to the public trailhead, then started hiking uphill. After about half a mile, the trail began to parallel the fence line for CNG's property. The black iron fence, eight feet tall and topped with curls of razor wire, was almost hidden in places by a thick growth of wild roses and scrub oak, but in other spots the undergrowth thinned enough to provide a glimpse through the bars of the fence.

"About this point is where I heard the shots," Rob said. "I thought they came from the other side of the fence. I picked up speed and I hadn't gone far when I saw Paige running down the trail toward me. I thought at first someone was pursuing her, but then I realized she was alone. She said two men had shot at her. Then my focus became getting her safely away."

"Did you stop by the entrance to the property before you went to the trailhead, the way we did just now?" Travis asked.

"Yes. The gates were locked and I didn't see anyone. No cars or anything."

"Let's see if we can figure out where Paige could have seen the shooters," Travis said.

They moved up the trail, which soon curved sharply, still following the fence line. Another hundred feet and they came to an opening in the wall of bushes and vines next to the trail. Broken branches and scuffs in the leaf litter told the tale of someone plunging into this opening—and exiting in a hurry.

Travis went first, with Rob close behind. Bending over, they had a clear view onto the resort property, but what they saw was unremarkable—a few stunted evergreens, oak brush with the last brown leaves of summer clinging to it, and some dried grasses. Travis took binoculars from his belt and scanned the area. "I don't see anything," he said.

They waited a moment, listening, but heard only the sound of their own breathing. The silence and the deserted—abandoned, really—property made Rob feel uneasy. "I don't think we're going to find anything here today," he said, keeping his voice low.

"No." They returned to the trail and started back toward the parking area. "I could try for a warrant to search the place," Travis said. "But I doubt a judge would grant the request."

"They were shooting at an unarmed woman," Rob said. "A woman who wasn't even on their property."

"That's what Paige said happened, but she wasn't hit and there weren't any witnesses."

Rob started to object, but Travis cut him off. "I know—it's not like her to make things up. I'm just telling you what CNG's lawyers are going to say."

"I heard the shots," Rob said.

"Right. People shoot guns all the time out here—at targets, at animals. It's elk season right now. Maybe they were hunting. It's not illegal to shoot off a gun."

Rob blew out a sigh of frustration. "So what do we do now?"

"We keep an eye on the place and look for a reason—any reason—to come back up here and take a closer look."

They fell silent, trudging down the trail. The sun was already disappearing behind the ridge, a chill descending in the fading light. Rob shoved his hands in the pockets of his jeans and reviewed the events of the morning in his head. Had he missed something—some clue that would help them figure out what was really going on? Had Paige's presence distracted him from noticing everything he should have noticed?

They reached the parking lot and Travis's SUV. The sheriff pulled out his keys and pressed the button to unlock the vehicle, but he froze in the act of reaching for the door handle, his gaze fixed on the door.

"What is it?" Rob, who had already opened the passenger door, asked.

"Take a look."

Rob walked around to the driver's side and stared at the thin gold chain affixed over the door handle with a piece of clear tape. A gold charm shaped like a bird dangled from the chain, stirred by a slight breeze. The sight of the delicate, feminine ornament so out of place sent a chill through him. "That looks like the necklace Paige described," he said. "The one she said she lost up here."

Chapter Four

Travis took out his phone and snapped several pictures of the necklace, then examined the ground around the vehicle. "This gravel is too hard-packed to leave prints," he said.

"We might get prints off the tape," Rob said.

Travis went to the back of the vehicle and opened it, then took out a small box. He put on gloves, then took out a paper evidence pouch and a thin-bladed knife. Carefully, he lifted the edge of the tape with the knife, then peeled it back. He transferred both tape and necklace to a plain white card, then slipped them in the pouch and labeled it. "I'll have a crime scene tech go over the car when we get back to the office," he said. "Though I doubt we're going to find much."

They both took another look around. Rob scanned the trees that surrounded the parking area. "Do you think they're watching us now?" he asked.

"The person or persons who put that necklace there?" Travis asked. He opened the door and slid into the driver's seat. "Maybe. Maybe they've been watching us the whole time."

"Why did they bother returning the necklace?" Rob

asked, as he buckled his seat belt and Travis started the SUV.

"Maybe a hiker came along behind us, found the necklace on the trail and figured it must belong to whoever was in this vehicle," Travis said. "Or they figured giving it to a cop was the right thing to do."

"And where is this hiker?" Rob scanned the empty trailhead. "Why didn't we see them? Where did they park?"

"They changed their minds about the hike?" Travis backed out of the small parking area.

"Or maybe the person or persons who left the necklace there was the same person or persons who shot at Paige," Rob said. "They left the necklace because they wanted us to know they were watching. That they could, in fact, have taken us out if they had been so inclined."

"Could be," Travis said.

They drove to the sheriff's office, where Deputy Dwight Prentice greeted them at the door. "Hello, Rob," Dwight said. "Are you here because of the report on Henry Hake?"

"What report is that?" Rob asked.

"It must have come in while we were gone," Travis said. "Because I haven't heard about it, either." He led the way into his office and settled behind his desk. "Tell us about this report."

"The medical examiner's office sent over an updated report on their findings in Henry Hake's death," Dwight said. He handed a printout to Travis, who scanned it, his face giving away nothing. He passed the papers to Rob.

"I thought the ME ruled Henry Hake probably died of a heart attack," Rob said.

"He did," Dwight said. "But one of his bright young

assistants got curious about some nasty-looking lesions on the body and did some more digging. This report is what he came up with."

Rob read quickly through it, only half listening as Dwight continued talking. His gaze shifted to the bottom section and the words *Conclusion: Death from Tularemia.*

"What is tularemia?" he asked.

"It's also called rabbit fever," Dwight said. "It's a naturally occurring bacteria that, if treated with antibiotics, is rarely fatal."

"And if untreated?" Travis asked.

"According to the Centers for Disease Control fact sheet attached to that report, a bite from an infected animal could cause skin ulcers, while inhaling the bacteria can lead to pneumonia or, in the most severe cases, typhoid-like symptoms," Dwight said.

"And the ME thinks that's what killed Henry Hake?" Travis looked skeptical. "Was he bitten by a rabbit or what?"

"Tularemia is one of the biological weapons the government experimented with in World War II," Dwight said. "It's one they were supposedly working on here in Rayford County. I remember reading about it." Recently, news about just such a secret government lab, located somewhere in the county, had come to light, causing a bit of a stir among history buffs.

Rob let out a low whistle.

"That government lab was supposedly located in an old mine somewhere near here," Travis said. "Could Henry Hake have picked it up in the soil while messing around looking for the lab?"

"Maybe," Dwight said. "But when I found his body, it

was hanging from the ceiling in that underground chamber on the resort property—Hake didn't do that himself."

"You found the body after the DEA determined that chamber didn't have anything to do with either the World War II experiments or any modern crime," Rob said. "And the ME ruled Hake died weeks ago—so someone brought his body to that location after we left, and several weeks after he died."

"Right," Dwight said. "So while it's possible Hake died in that underground chamber and someone hid his body for a while, then brought it back, I don't think it's likely. Why go to all that trouble?"

"How would the government have used tularemia as a weapon?" Travis asked.

"Apparently, the idea was to put the bacteria in an aerosol," Dwight said. "You could put it in the ventilation system of a building or simply spray it over a crowd. Not everyone would catch the disease, and of those that did, not everyone would die."

"You said antibiotics will kill it," Rob said. "So it doesn't sound like a very practical weapon today."

"Except that most people wouldn't realize they had been exposed, or that they were suffering from tularemia," Dwight said. "Anyone with a compromised immune system, or lung or heart disease, might die before anyone figured out what was wrong."

"Henry Hake had a bad heart," Travis said.

"Did whoever killed him know that?" Rob asked.

"More unanswered questions," Travis said. "Would this be enough for the DEA to go back into that underground bunker and do some testing?"

"Maybe." Rob sighed. "I'm not even supposed to be here, you know."

"Your aunt wanted to know what really happened to Hake," Travis said. "This might be your best chance to find out."

Rob glanced at the clock on the wall by the door. "It's after five in DC, where the decision would have to be made," he said. "I'll contact my boss in the morning and let him take it from there." That would give him a few more hours to come up with a better explanation for why he was in Rayford County right now. Maybe he could persuade his boss he had just come here to fly-fish.

"Let us know what he says." Travis glanced at the report once more. "I wonder what the market is for biological weapons."

"What made you think of that?" Dwight asked.

"Because so many times these things come down to money," Travis said.

"My guess is there are terrorist groups who would hand over a lot of cash to get their hands on a weapon that was easy to distribute, tough to detect and effective for mass destruction," Rob said.

"Is there a weapon like that?" Dwight asked. "Tularemia doesn't sound like it would be very effective."

"Then maybe the point of the lab is to develop something better," Travis said. "It's one angle."

"Hake had a lot of money tied up in that resort project," Dwight said. "CNG Development talks like they want to spend even more money up there."

"Yet we've had two murders there—three, if you count Hake," Travis said. "As well as two accidental deaths, three people kidnapped, and a number of unexplained discharges of firearms up there."

"Maybe we can get the county to declare the place a public nuisance," Dwight said.

"More likely, CNG will complain that local law enforcement isn't doing a good job of keeping the criminal element off their property," Travis said. He straightened. "I'll give CNG a call and see what they have to say about this latest discovery."

"Let me know what they say," Rob said.

"Don't worry," Travis said. "You're part of this now, whether you want to be or not."

PAIGE TOLD HERSELF she had to trust Parker, as she watched him drive away. He was a good kid. Or rather, a good man. She had to remind herself her little brother wasn't a child anymore, and she shouldn't treat him like one. Yes, he had made some mistakes, but he was too smart to make those mistakes again. She wanted to believe this.

She checked the clock as she passed through the kitchen on the way to her office. It was after three thirty. She had expected her new guest, Robert Allen, to check in before now. Then again, maybe he had gotten a late start from Denver, or decided to do other things before showing up at the B and B. She asked that guests notify her only if they planned to arrive after 9:00 p.m.

She switched on her computer and prepared to focus on balancing her books and updating her financial records—a task guaranteed to require all her attention. She was deep into the frustration of trying to make her numbers agree with the bank's when the doorbell rang. She started and glanced at the clock, surprised to see she had been working for almost an hour. She closed her laptop and hurried to the door, fixing a smile in place, prepared to play the gracious hostess.

A check of the security peephole wiped the smile from her face. She unlocked the door and swept it open.

"What do you think you're doing, following me around like this?" she demanded of a startled Rob Allerton.

He settled his features into his usual inscrutable expression. "I have a reservation," he said. "What are you doing here?"

"I own this place."

He glanced up at the neat white Victorian home, with its black shutters, and neatly mulched flower beds filled with lilacs and peonies fading into winter dormancy. "Nice," he said.

"You're Robert Allen?" she asked.

He had the grace to wince. "The assistant who made the reservation must have automatically used my cover name," he said. "Sorry about that."

He made a move to walk past her into the house, but she stepped forward to join him on the front porch and shut the door behind her. "You can't stay here," she said.

"Why not?"

"Parker lives here now."

"I'm not interested in your brother," he said.

"I don't want to upset him." Parker had enough to deal with without having to face over the breakfast table every morning the man who had arrested him.

"We're all adults here," Rob said. "I don't see why there should be a problem."

"It's a problem for me. You'll have to find somewhere else to stay."

"Eagle Mountain doesn't have that many choices for accommodations," he said. "I spent plenty of time at the only motel while I was part of DEA's investigation into that underground lab."

"The motel is very nice," she said.

"It's adequate, but everyone there knows I'm a DEA

agent. I prefer to keep this visit separate from that investigation. This is a personal visit and I'd like to keep to the appearance of a relaxing vacation as much as possible. When my assistant suggested a B and B I liked the idea."

Paige crossed her arms and scowled at him. She had the right to refuse service to anyone, but he could make a big stink if he wanted to. And turning away a paying customer at this slow time of year would be foolish, wouldn't it? But to have this man, who had almost ruined Parker's life, in her home—well, Rob had helped to almost ruin Parker's life, since she couldn't deny that Parker was the one who was mostly to blame. Still, it galled her to think of having Rob living here for the next week.

"What are you afraid of?" Rob asked. "If you're that worried, you can lock your door. Or should I lock mine?"

She wanted to slap the wolfish smile off his face, but before she could raise her hand, he grabbed her by the shoulders and shoved her to the ground. For the second time that day she found herself fighting him as he held her down. Then gunfire exploded very near her ear and tore into the door where she had been standing only seconds before.

Chapter Five

Paige's scream merged with the screech of tires and the roar of an engine as the black sedan raced down the street in front of the Bear's Den B and B. Rob, his weapon drawn, straightened and peered at the retreating car. There was no license plate, and the darkly tinted windows prevented him from seeing the occupants. Though there had been at least two people inside—the driver and the person who had fired the gun out the passenger window.

"What happened?" Paige asked, her voice shaky. She tried to sit up and this time he let her. He returned the gun to the holster at his hip, then reached down and pulled her to her feet.

"Was someone shooting at us?" she asked.

"Yes." He turned his attention from the street to look at her more closely. "Are you all right?" he asked.

"I'm okay." She rubbed her elbow. "Just a little banged up."

"Sorry if I was a little rough," he said. "I glimpsed the gun and had to move fast." He had acted on pure instinct, pushing her out of danger, shielding her with his own body.

"I'm okay," she said again. She straightened her

blouse. "Who was it? Was it the men from the resort property? The ones who shot at me before?"

Rob shook his head. "I don't know. I didn't get a good look at them. I saw their silhouettes and the gun." He pulled his phone from his pocket and dialed the sheriff's office—Travis's direct number.

Travis answered on the second ring. "Hello?"

"This is Rob Allerton. I'm at Paige Riddell's place. A black sedan, tinted windows, no plates, two men inside, just drove by and fired on us."

"Dwight is already on his way over," Travis said. "We had a report of gunfire in the area. Is anyone hurt?"

"No. Some damage to the front door." He surveyed the line of bullet holes across the bright red door, like a row of stitches. His roller bag sat inches from the door, but was unscathed.

"I think I need to sit down." Paige sank onto the bench beside the door, her head between her knees. Rob walked out to the street and studied the angle of the shot. He had parked his truck in the paved area between the B and B and the house to the left—which meant anyone driving by had a clear view of the front porch where he and Paige had been standing. The house was only about a hundred feet from the street, making for an easy target.

As he stood at the curb, a Rayford County Sheriff's Department SUV pulled up. Dwight rolled down the passenger window and leaned toward Rob. "I just heard from Travis. You and Paige okay?"

He glanced over his shoulder to where Paige sat, upright now, hands gripping the edge of the bench, staring at the floor between her feet. "She's a little shaken up," he said. "But she'll be okay."

"We've got a BOLO on the car you described," Dwight said. "Can you show me where the bullets hit?"

The two men walked up on the porch. "Hello, Paige," Dwight said. "You okay?"

She nodded.

"Did you get a look at the shooter?" Dwight asked.

"I never saw them. Rob pushed me out of the way before I even knew they were there."

Dwight nodded, then bent to examine the damaged door. He took some photos. "At least some of the bullets are embedded in the door," he said. "We'll get someone out here to collect them. Is there anything else you can tell me—about the car or the shooters?"

"I'm sorry," Paige said. "I can't think of anything."

"We'll do our best to patrol here more frequently," Dwight said. "But you might want to think about staying somewhere else for a while."

She stared at him. "I can't do that. I have guests. And Parker is here."

Dwight's eyes met Rob's. "It would be better if you went somewhere safer," Dwight repeated.

"How do you know I was even the target?" Paige asked, with more strength in her voice. "I imagine a DEA agent has made all kinds of enemies."

Rob looked at the door again. "Maybe so," he said. "But the shots were fired where you were standing."

Her face paled, but she set her jaw. "I'm not leaving my home and my business," she said.

"I can't force you," Dwight said.

"I'm staying here," Rob said. "I'll keep an eye on things."

"Let us know if you see anything suspicious." Dwight nodded to Paige, then left.

When they were alone again, Rob turned to Paige. "Where's Parker?" he asked.

"He's out."

"Out where?"

"None of your business."

He almost smiled. This was the Paige he was used to. "Do you know where he is?" he asked.

"He's an adult. I don't keep track of his every move."

Somehow he doubted this was a philosophy she had adopted willingly, having seen her mother-bear act in court. "Do you want me to call him?" he asked.

"No!"

"I thought maybe you would feel better with him here."

"No. There's no need to worry him."

"Did you tell him about what happened this morning? The other shooting?"

"No. He doesn't need to know."

"There's such a thing as being too independent, you know," Rob said.

She stood. "Come on. Let's get you checked in."

He could have pressed the issue, but what would be the point? Paige wasn't going to change on his say-so. He reclaimed his roller bag from beside the door and followed her inside.

The interior of the home was comfortably furnished with a mixture of antique and contemporary pieces. Art on the walls depicted local scenery. Rob saw none of the chintz and cutesiness he had feared when his admin had suggested a B and B for his stay. Instead, the decor was low-key and classy—like Paige herself.

She moved to a small desk in what must have been the home's front parlor or formal living room and unlocked an adjacent cabinet to reveal a computer. "What name is on the credit card you'll be using?" she asked, typing.

"Robert Allerton."

"Not Robert Allen?"

"As I said before, I'm not here on business." Not exactly. He had sworn his admin to secrecy. After he talked to his boss in the morning, he might be assigned to the case, but for now, he was on his own dime.

She scanned the card he handed her, then returned it, along with a set of old-fashioned keys on a brass fob. "The round one is for the front door," she said. "The other is for your room. You're in the Grizzly Suite. Turn left at the top of the stairs and go all the way to the end of the hallway. Breakfast is from seven to nine each morning."

He replaced the card in his wallet. "Dwight was right," he said. "You'd be safer if you moved to a location that was unknown to whoever is targeting you."

"I have a business to run and a life to live. I can't stop everything to go hide out in a cave somewhere until you or Dwight or whoever decides it's safe to come out. I'll be smart and take precautions, but I won't do what these men want."

"What do you think they want?" he asked.

She shut the cabinet door and locked it. "For me to keep quiet about what I saw. That has to be the reason they want me dead. They think they can frighten me into shutting up. But all they've done is make me more determined to find out what is going on up there."

She started to move from behind the desk, but Rob blocked her, one hand on her arm, near enough that when she inhaled sharply, the tips of her breasts brushed his sleeve. He fought the urge to pull her close and kiss the protest from her lips. Did she have any idea how maddening and enticing he found her? "Don't get any ideas about investigating this on your own," he said. "That could be dangerous."

"I'll be careful."

Careful might not be enough, but he wasn't going to get anywhere arguing with her about it. He moved aside and started to turn toward the stairs, but she put out a hand to stop him, then grabbed hold of the sleeve of his jacket. "Rob?"

He turned back, looking into her eyes, which were the color of storm clouds, fringed with thick brown lashes. Eyes that could make a man forget every angry word she had ever leveled at him. "Yes?"

She swallowed, color rising in her cheeks. "Thank you."

"What are you thanking me for?"

"For saving my life."

He could have dismissed this with a denial that he had done anything special. He had reacted on pure instinct, with no time to think about what he was doing or why. But he wouldn't let her off the hook that easily. "You know that old superstition," he said.

Two shallow lines formed between her eyebrows. "What old superstition?"

"When you save a person's life, then you're responsible for them."

She released her hold on him as if she had been scorched. "No man is responsible for me."

He smiled, a heated curve of his lips that had reduced more than one woman to breathlessness. "Have I ever told you I'm a very superstitious person? And I take my responsibilities very seriously." He leaned forward and kissed her cheek, feeling the heat of her skin and breathing in the herbal scent of her shampoo.

When he stepped back, he half expected her to slap him. Maybe he even deserved it, but that kiss had been worth it. Instead, she only tried to wound him with her gaze. Still smiling, he picked up his bag and headed for the stairs, taking them two at a time to the second floor. His stay at the Bear's Den was going to be very interesting, indeed.

Chapter Six

Paige lay awake for hours that night, reliving every moment of being shot at—the sound of the bullets, the fear that had threatened to choke her, the feel of Rob's weight on her, crushing and frightening and yet so reassuring. The man was maddening, one moment so tender and protective, the next knowing exactly what to say to make her angry. All that nonsense about him being responsible for her—and then he'd had the nerve to kiss her.

That the kiss hadn't been on the lips unnerved her even more. If he had insisted on kissing her mouth, she could have told herself he had practically assaulted her, and that he'd taken liberties to which he wasn't entitled. But that gentle brush of his lips against her cheek had been both tender and incredibly sensuous. She still trembled at the memory, at the intensity of her awareness of him—the scent of his aftershave, the soft cotton of his shirtsleeve, the incredible heat of his mouth.

She shouldn't have let him get away with it. She should have told him off then and there. But she couldn't find the words to do it. When he had left her, still smiling that *I'm-so-sexy* grin, she had had to bite her lip to keep from calling him back. In that moment, if he had tried to kiss her mouth, she would have pulled him to her willingly.

After that, it took a long time for her to drift into a restless sleep. She woke several hours later with a start and stared into the darkness, heart pounding. She held her breath and strained her ears to listen. Yes, that was definitely the sound of the back door opening. She turned her head to check the bedside clock. One thirty-two. She heard shuffling, then the sound of someone walking—no, tiptoeing—past her door.

She sat up and switched on the lamp. "Parker, is that you?" she called.

"Yes. Go back to sleep."

Instead, she got up and went to the bedroom door and opened it. Parker stood in the hallway, hair rumpled, shoulders slumped. Her first instinct was to demand to know where he had been, but she stifled the words. "You look tired," she said instead.

He shrugged. "I'm okay." He turned away. "Good night."

"Wait," she said. "There's something I need to tell you."

He stopped, but didn't look back at her. "What is it?"

"Rob Allerton is here," she said.

"Yeah. You already told me he's in town. So what?"

"No—he's here."

He did turn this time, and craned his neck, trying to see past her into her room. "Here?"

She flushed, even though the suggestion that Agent Rob Allerton would be in her bed was preposterous. "He's upstairs. In the Grizzly Suite. He has a reservation for a week."

"Okay."

She leaned forward, studying her brother more closely. He needed a shave, and he had the beginnings of dark circles under his eyes. Was he really just tired, or was something more going on? She pushed the thought away. She had to trust him. "You're okay with him being here?"

"I guess his money is as good as anybody else's. And it's not like I'll see him much, between work and school and stuff."

Stuff. What stuff? But she didn't ask. "It's probably a good idea if you stay out of his way as much as possible," she said.

"Don't worry. I will."

"He didn't make a reservation here because of you," she said. "He didn't even know I owned the place."

"Right." He smirked.

"He didn't," she protested.

"You can believe that if you want. I think Agent Allerton knew exactly what he was doing."

She resented everything his words—and that smirk—implied. "I actually asked him to leave, but there's another reason he needs to be here right now."

Parker leaned one shoulder against the wall, arms folded across his chest. "I'm really tired, sis. Can we make this quick?"

She wet her lips. He was probably going to find out sooner or later. Better she tell him rather than have him hear the gossip from someone else. "Someone took a shot at me while I was hiking up by Eagle Mountain Resort yesterday," she said.

He straightened. "What?"

"I saw two men on the resort property. One of them spotted me watching them and tried to shoot me. Later, a car—possibly with the same two men inside—drove by here and someone shot at me again. Rob pushed me out of the way. As it is, the front door is ruined and will have to be replaced."

"Sis! What have you done?"

"What have I done? I haven't done anything."

"You must have done something to tick off these guys enough to try to take you out."

"I didn't do anything," she said again. "But until the authorities can track down those men, I thought it wouldn't be a bad idea for Rob to stay here. He does have some experience with situations like this."

"You mean he's got a gun and he knows how to use it." Parker shook his head, as if trying to clear it, then looked at her more closely. "Are you sure you're okay?"

"I'm fine." A little shaky still, but she was determined to get past that. And her little brother's concern touched her. "I really think Rob scared them away yesterday," she said. "And now the sheriff's department and probably other law enforcement agencies are looking for them. I don't think they'll bother me again."

"I hope not." He ran one hand through his hair. "You say you were up by Eagle Mountain Resort the first time? This morning?"

"Yes. I was on the hiking trail that runs alongside the resort. You remember—we went up there right after you moved to town."

He nodded. "Why didn't you tell me about it this morning?"

"I didn't want to worry you. And I certainly didn't think they would track me down here."

"It's not hard to find anybody in a town this small," Parker said. "Maybe you should go away for a while, until this is all over."

"No!" The word came out louder than she intended. She lowered her voice. "I'll be careful, but I won't put my whole life on hold and hide."

"What were those guys doing up at the resort?" Parker asked.

"I don't know," she said. "I saw them carrying a big wooden box into a hole in the ground."

"That underground chamber where Gage and his girl-friend were trapped a couple months ago?" Parker asked.

"Maybe. I don't know. I'm going to try to find out."

"Don't go up there again," Parker said.

"If I do go, I won't go alone," she said.

"Get Rob to go with you. Or better yet, stay home."

"I don't want Rob to go with me. Maybe Gage can come."

"Rob wants to be your bodyguard, why not let him?" Parker yawned.

"Go to bed," Paige said. "And don't worry about me."

"I figure I probably owe you a little worrying." He patted her shoulder, then turned and shuffled down the hall to his room. Paige returned to her room and bed, but didn't go to sleep. She was going to end up back at the resort sooner or later, she knew. She wouldn't go alone, but she wouldn't sit here doing nothing and waiting for others to solve this mystery.

MAYA RENFRO WAS a petite dynamo whose shoulder-length black hair was streaked with blue. Even at seven thirty in the morning, she bounced into the Cake Walk Café with all the energy she displayed as coach of Eagle Mountain High's girls' basketball team. "Paige, it's so good to see you," she said. "And wow, doesn't this place look great? I haven't been here since they reopened. Gage told me a driver crashed into it this summer."

"Yes. The owner, Iris Desmet, decided as long as she was rebuilding, she would expand and add a coffee bar." She ushered her friend to a table. "How are you? And how is Casey?" Casey was Maya's five-year-old niece, who lived with Maya and Gage since her parents' murders that summer.

"She's great. Last week she asked if, when Gage and I get married, she can change her name, too, so we all match." Maya snatched a paper napkin from the dispenser on the table and dabbed at her eyes. "Sorry—I still get teary thinking about it."

"That's terrific," Paige said. "I guess she's really taken to Gage?"

"He's amazing," Maya said. "For a man who swore he was a confirmed bachelor, he's turning out to be a really great father. We don't want Casey to ever forget her real parents, but it's nice to think the three of us can be a new family together."

She pulled out a chair and sank into it. "Now you've heard all about me—what did you want to see me about so early in the morning?"

"I wanted to catch you before school." And before Rob was up, watching her and questioning her. Paige sat across from Maya. "I hate to bring up a painful subject, but I wanted to ask about the underground chamber up at Eagle Mountain Resort where you and Gage and Casey were held prisoner."

Maya's smile vanished and her shoulders slumped. "What about it?"

"Where was it on the property, exactly?"

"Paige, why would you want to know that?"

She shifted in her chair. "It's kind of a long story."

"Buy me a latte and I'll give you all the time you need."

Two vanilla soy lattes later, Paige had spilled the whole story of seeing the two men disappear into a trap-door in the forest floor with a mysterious crate, how they had later shot at her, and the drive-by shooting at her home.

"Wow!" Maya said, when the story concluded. "It definitely sounds like you stumbled onto something big. But I don't think the trapdoor you saw was over the chamber where Gage and I were."

"No?"

"No." Maya sipped her latte, then wiped foam from above her lips. "We weren't near the fence at all. I'm surprised Travis didn't tell you that already."

"I wanted to double-check." After all, Maya was the one who had been held prisoner in that chamber.

"What I don't get is why bother going through a trap-door when there was an exit right onto the resort's main street?" Maya asked.

"So, maybe there's another chamber?" Paige said.

"Maybe there are a bunch of them. There are a lot of mines in the mountains around here, and mine tunnels, right?"

"I guess so."

"Have you talked to Gage about any of this?" Maya asked.

"No. I thought it would be easier to talk to you. I mean, he can't really tell me anything because he's a cop."

"I might be a little prejudiced, but I think he's a good one," Maya said. "You should leave the investigating to him."

"I'm not investigating," Paige said. "I'm just curious. After all, those bullets were aimed at me. You can't blame me for wanting to know why. I wonder if I can get my hands on a map of the resort. Maybe the planning commission has something." She frowned. "Of course, they won't let me look at it."

"Why not?"

"The mayor, Larry Rowe, was head of the planning commission before he ran for mayor. He still has a grudge against me because my environmental group kept the project from going forward."

"You need to be careful," Maya said. "A lot of bad things have happened that are associated with the resort property. You couldn't pay me to go up there again."

"I understand why you feel that way," Paige said. "But if everyone avoids the property, it allows whoever is up there to get away with whatever they want. Whatever they were hiding in that space was something they didn't want me to see. I want to find out what it was and expose them."

"You need to let the sheriff's department do that."

"I will let them handle anything that turns out to be illegal," Paige said. "But that doesn't mean that, as an ordinary citizen, I can't ask questions and try to gather information. It's what I'm trained to do, as an activist."

"So who are you going to question about all of this?" Maya asked.

"I'll start with the new owners of the property, CNG Development."

"I'm sure Travis and Gage have already thought of that."

"I'm sure they have," Paige said. "But these corporate types won't tell the cops anything. They'll talk to me.

How do you think I got the scoop on Eagle Mountain Resort? I made phone calls and asked questions. There's nothing dangerous about that."

"It sounds safe enough." Maya pushed aside her empty cup. "As long as you don't ask the wrong person the wrong question."

"I'll be careful." Truth be told, she was excited about the prospect. Since they'd won the injunction against building Eagle Mountain Resort and the challenge over the gate blocking the Dakota Ridge Trail, life had felt a little stale. She looked forward to the challenge of finding out what was really happening on the former resort property. She would succeed where others had failed.

DEA SENIOR DETECTIVE Dale Foster was a busy man with no patience for time wasting, so when Rob placed his call to his supervisor the next morning, he got right to the point. "I'm here in Eagle Mountain," he said. "Sheriff Walker has requested the DEA reopen our investigation of that underground laboratory we looked into up here last month."

"What are you doing in Eagle Mountain?" Foster asked. "And why did the sheriff contact you instead of contacting our office?"

"I came to do some fly-fishing," Rob lied. "I ran into the sheriff yesterday and he relayed the request."

"Humph."

Rob's gut clenched. So much for thinking he would get away with that lame explanation.

"Why does Walker want us to reopen the investigation?" Foster asked. "You told me you didn't find anything. I trust you went over the location thoroughly."

"I did. But we were looking for any indication of illegal drug manufacturing. The sheriff suspects something else might have been going on down there."

"What?" Foster barked the word, an impatient man becoming more impatient.

"The week after we left, one of Walker's deputies found a dead man in the location," Rob said. "He had been missing about a month, and the medical examiner confirms he had been dead about that long, but someone had strung up his body in that old lab space underground. Originally, the ME was unable to determine the cause of death, but more recent tests indicate the man died from exposure to tularemia."

"What is tularemia?"

"Rabbit fever. But of more interest to us, it's something that the US government considered as a possible biological weapon in World War II. You remember in my report I mentioned that we were asked to rule out the lab's use during that time period."

"And you determined nothing in the lab was that old. So I repeat—what does this have to do with us?"

"Walker wants us to take another look, see if we can detect any tularemia in the space."

"Tell him to call the health department. That's not under our purview."

Rob had expected this answer. Like every government agency these days, the DEA was chronically underfunded and understaffed. "I'll tell him, sir."

"When are you coming back to work?" Foster asked.

"I have six days left on my vacation," Rob said.

"Humph." This time the sound was uttered with a little less ire behind it.

"Is there anything else you'd like me to tell Sheriff Walker?" Rob asked.

"Tell him I'm sorry we can't help him. And, Allerton?"

"Yes, sir?"

"Let the sheriff handle this. You stick to fish."

"Of course, sir."

They ended the conversation and Rob tucked his phone back into the pocket of his jeans. The only fish he wanted to catch right now were the two men who had fired those shots yesterday. If they led him to the real reason for Henry Hake's death, so much the better. But he'd be careful not to act in any official capacity.

He stepped out of the room, locking the door behind him. When he turned he was surprised to see Parker Riddell walking toward him. The young man looked healthier than he had the last time Rob had seen him— he had gained a few pounds and lost the sickly pallor Rob associated with addicts. "Hello, Parker," he said.

"Hey." He stopped in front of Rob, arms crossed over his chest, expression somber. "Paige told me what happened," he said. "With those guys shooting at her, up at the resort, and here in front of the house."

"I tried to persuade her to leave until this was resolved," Rob said. "She refused."

"Yeah, well, no surprise there. Look up *stubborn* in the dictionary and there's Paige's picture." He ran a hand through his close-cropped hair. "I need to ask you a favor."

"Oh?" Rob waited, wary. It wasn't as if he and this young man were on friendly terms.

"Look after her," Parker said. "I mean, I can't be here all the time, but she said you're on vacation, and you're here anyway, so maybe it wouldn't be a real hardship on you to stay close."

"Paige doesn't like me."

Parker didn't exactly smile, but his expression did lighten. "Oh, she likes you. She just doesn't want to admit it. Since that fiasco with her ex she likes to pretend she doesn't need a man in her life, but it's all bluff."

"What was the fiasco with her ex?" This was the first Rob had heard about an ex.

Parker frowned. "I don't know the whole story, but I guess he started out nice when they first married and ended up being a real jerk. I don't know if he actually hit her, or just threatened her, but they sure didn't end up on speaking terms, and ever since she's been kind of standoffish with men."

Rob supposed he could take comfort in knowing he wasn't being singled out for the cold shoulder. But the idea that a man—Paige's husband—had threatened her made him feel like finding the guy and making him regret he had ever come near her.

"I'm sorry to hear that," Rob said, his voice deceptively mild.

"Honestly, I think one of the reasons she's so hostile toward you—besides the trouble you and I had—is that she's attracted to you and fighting it," Parker said.

Was Paige attracted to him, or was Parker pouring it on thick to get him to stick around? "I'll keep an eye on her," he said. "As much as she'll let me."

"Thanks." Paige's brother shoved his hands in his pockets, apparently not ready to leave.

"Is there something else?" Rob asked.

Parker sighed. "Yeah. Last night, she talked about going back up to the resort and trying to find out what's going on. Don't let her go alone. I mean, I get that she wants to be independent, but she's not bulletproof."

"I won't let her go up there—alone or otherwise."

"Good. Well, I need to go. I have a class." He nodded and shuffled off.

Downstairs, the dining room off the kitchen was empty. A long cherry table held a single place setting, with a linen napkin, gold-trimmed china plate and polished flatware. A fruit cup in a crystal dish sat in the center of the plate, and a buffet against the wall held a silver coffee service and two covered chafing dishes.

As Rob stood surveying the scene, Paige came in from the kitchen carrying a bakery box. "Good morning," she said.

"This looks impressive," he said, indicating the table. "Am I your only guest?"

"I have an older couple staying a few nights. They were up early and are already off for a day of Jeeping on the backcountry trails." She began arranging muffins on a glass serving tray. "There's an egg casserole in the chafing dish," she said. "Help yourself."

He moved the fruit cup to one side, carried the plate to the buffet and selected a muffin from the tray. "You're up and about early."

"I like to get an early start."

"Do you have time to have coffee with me?" he asked, before she could retreat to the kitchen.

She hesitated, then sat in the chair across from him. "What are your plans for the day?" she asked, as he sat and tucked into his breakfast.

"That depends." He sipped the coffee, which was hot and strong, exactly the way he preferred it. "What are *your* plans?"

"Why are you asking?"

"Because I'm staying with you." He split the muffin—blueberry—and slid in a pat of butter.

"Rob, I—"

"Don't argue, Paige." He bit into the muffin and had to suppress a sigh. It practically melted in his mouth. He swallowed and picked up his fork. "Did you make all this? It's delicious."

"I picked them up at the Cake Walk Café earlier this morning," she said. "And don't change the subject. I don't need you to babysit me."

"We both know you'll be safer with someone to watch your back. You do what you need to do and try to forget I'm here." He savored the first bite of the egg-cheese-and-sausage casserole.

She snorted—an unladylike and at the same time endearing sound. Or maybe he was being influenced by the amazing breakfast.

She sipped her coffee, then set the cup down with a clink against the saucer. "I need to see about getting the door replaced, order some supplies and run some errands," she said.

"Consider me your chauffeur."

"I don't need—"

He set down his fork and looked her in the eye. "Maybe you don't, but I do. I need to know you're safe."

Her lips parted and her eyes widened. If the table hadn't been between them, he would have been tempted to lean across and kiss her, just to see what kind of reaction he would get. Had Parker been right when he had said she was attracted to him? Was the attraction strong enough for her to act on it?

"Why do you care?" she asked. "And don't give me that line about being responsible for me now."

He sat back, hiding his disappointment. No, she wasn't *that* attracted to him. "How about this for a reason?" he asked. "You may be our best chance of solving this case."

"How do you figure that?"

"We want to catch these guys and find out what they're up to. You're the only one who got a good look at them. They want you. If they do try to come after you again, we want to be ready."

"So you want to use me as bait?" Her voice rose on the last word, almost a squeak.

"No. I'm not going to let you wait for them out in the open. But if they do come back, I'm going to be here and I'm going to be ready to stop them."

She nodded, subdued. "All right."

She remained silent while he finished his breakfast, his attention focused on the food, though he was acutely aware of the woman across from him, close enough to brush his hand against. But she might as well have worn a sign around her neck that declared Don't Touch.

The doorbell rang and she jumped. "Are you expecting someone?" he asked.

"No." She stared toward the door, but didn't move. Deny it all she liked, she was clearly still upset by what had happened yesterday.

He pushed back his chair, wiped his mouth and dropped the napkin on his empty plate. "Let's go see who it is."

Chapter Seven

Rob had probably intended to lead the way to the front door, but Paige stepped in front of him. After all, this was her house. Whoever was there wanted to see her. She wasn't going to let what had happened yesterday keep her from answering her own door. He trailed behind her. The doorbell sounded again and her stomach fluttered as if she had swallowed live eels. She shoved her nervousness aside and focused instead on how angry it made her that two lowlifes she didn't even know had frightened her this way.

Relief flooded her when she looked through the security peephole and saw the calm face of the sheriff looking back at her. She unlocked the door and swung it open. "Have you found something?" she asked.

"We haven't found the men who shot at you," he said. He looked down at the splintered door. "Only the one burst of fire? They didn't try a second round of shots?"

"I already had Paige on the ground and returned fire." Rob stepped forward, one hand on Paige's shoulder. She should have resisted the gesture, but instead, she had to fight not to lean back into his strength. "They probably didn't want to risk sticking around," Rob said.

"I'm having the door replaced today," Paige said. "As soon as I file a claim with my insurance company."

"Adelaide can give you a case number if they need it," Travis said. "May I come in?"

"Of course." She stepped back and he moved past her. Rob shut and locked the door.

"Let's go in here," Travis said, leading the way into the dining room. He took an envelope from his pocket and emptied its contents onto the table.

"My necklace," she said, and scooped up the gold chain with the familiar bird charm.

"Is this the necklace you lost up by the resort?" Travis asked.

"Yes. Where did you find it?"

"Rob and I went up to the trail yesterday after we talked to you and took a look around," Travis said. "When we got back to my SUV, someone had taped this to the driver's-side door."

"They made sure we didn't miss it," Rob said.

"Another hiker must have found it and assumed it belonged to whoever was in your vehicle," she said. She examined the necklace. It was unharmed. "Or maybe they just wanted to turn it in to the police."

"We didn't see anyone else on the trail coming or going," Rob said. "We didn't pass any other cars or hear anyone, or see anyone on the other side of the fence at the resort. And there were no other cars in the parking area."

She looked from one man to the other. Their serious expressions were starting to worry her. "Someone must have been up there," she said. "Someone had to leave the necklace for you."

"We're thinking it was someone who didn't want us to

see them," Rob said. "Someone who wanted us to know they knew about you."

A shudder went through her at the words. "Why would they do that?" She tried to put on the necklace, fumbling with the clasp.

Rob stepped up behind her. "Let me." His fingers brushed the back of her neck as he fastened the necklace, sending heat radiating through her.

"I don't know what their motives might have been," Travis said. "Maybe it is as simple as them wanting the necklace returned to you. It's possible the person who put the necklace there didn't have anything to do with the shooting. Have you remembered anything else about the men you saw yesterday that can help us find them?"

Rob had finished hooking the necklace, but he remained standing behind her, one hand on her shoulder. She told herself she should move away from him, but couldn't make herself do it. "I'm sorry—no," she said. "Everything happened so fast."

"I've got a call in to CNG Development," Travis said. "We want permission to go up there and search. I'm waiting to hear back from them."

"I talked to my boss this morning," Rob said. "He says this really is out of our area of expertise. He suggested you contact the public health department. Maybe they can test for tularemia in that lab."

Travis nodded. "That's a good idea—if we can get permission to go back in."

Paige looked from one man to the other. "Tularemia? What the heck is that?"

"Rabbit fever," Rob said.

When he didn't offer anything more, she glared at him. "Why do you care about rabbit fever?"

"It's one of the agents the government was supposedly testing during World War II for use as a weapon," Travis said.

"And?" she asked.

"And I can't tell you anything else."

She frowned. It wasn't the answer she wanted, but about what she had expected. "Is there anything else you can tell me about this case? Any leads on the men who fired on me, or their vehicle?"

The sheriff shook his head. "We don't have anything yet, but we're going to keep looking." He turned to Rob. "Are you going to be around for a while?"

"I'm here all week, but not in an official capacity," Rob said.

"If I needed backup, could you help out?"

"Yes."

"Good. I'll keep it in mind."

"I want to go back up there," Paige said. "To the resort."

Both men looked at her as if she had sprouted an extra head. "That's a bad idea," Rob said.

"I agree," Travis said. "I'm considering closing the trail to public access until we get to the bottom of this."

"You can't close the trail unless you station someone at the trailhead to enforce the order," Paige said. "And you don't have the manpower to do that. Besides, it's not as if that many people go up there."

"You don't need to go up there," Travis said.

"I'll be fine," she said. "And I'll take my bodyguard." She looked at Rob.

"You can't go on CNG property without their permission," Travis said.

"I know. I'll stay on the public side of the fence. I just

want—I need—to take another look at the scene. Maybe being there again will trigger my memory of something that will help you find these men."

Travis gave her a hard look, but she met his gaze and didn't flinch. "All right," he said. "Then I guess that means we're all going. Together."

TRAVIS HAD A meeting he had to attend, so they agreed to meet up at the sheriff's department later that afternoon. Paige had spent her morning with Rob by her side, dealing with her insurance company and arranging to have the front door replaced. He had been quiet and unobtrusive, but there was no ignoring his presence—filling up the room. What was it about the man that he seemed to take up so much space, and use up more than his share of oxygen?

"Don't you have something else you need to be doing?" she asked.

"Not really."

"You didn't take a week's vacation to hang out with me."

"I can think of worse ways to spend my time." He sat back in his chair, regarding her with a hint of a smile, eyelids at half-mast. His expression should have come across as lazy and indolent, but instead conveyed a feline sensuality, as if he was feigning his lack of energy and at any moment might pounce. "You're almost pleasant when you aren't angry with me."

"You're making me nervous," she said.

"Interesting. You don't strike me as a woman who is easily unnerved."

She shuffled the papers on the table in front of her.

"I think having your life threatened twice in one day would upset anyone."

He sat up straight. His flirtatious mood had vanished. "You're right," he said. "I didn't mean to make light of what happened."

"I've been going over and over everything so much my head hurts." She pushed the papers—insurance forms and measurements for the new door—aside. "Let's talk about something else."

"Such as?"

"If we're going to be spending so much time together, we should get to know each other better. I really don't know much about you."

"All right," he said. "What would you like to know?"

"Have you ever been married?"

He blinked. He obviously hadn't been expecting that one. Why did it feel like such a victory to throw Mr. Cool off guard? "No," he said.

"Why not?"

He shrugged. "I never found the right woman."

"What a cliché. You can do better than that, can't you?" She leaned across the table toward him. "Are you afraid of making a commitment?"

"You're one to talk, Ms. Independent." He scooted his chair closer. "Though I understand you've been married before. What was he like?"

"How did you know that?" Had he been checking up on her?

"Parker mentioned it."

"Parker? When?"

"This morning, actually. He came to my room and asked me to look after you."

A storm of emotions swept over her—tenderness,

sadness, annoyance. "That really wasn't necessary," she said.

"Maybe not. It made me curious about your ex, though."

"My ex was not a nice person." She slid her chair back. "And that's all I'm going to say on the subject." Her marriage had been a bad time in her life, when a man she had made the mistake of trusting had used love as a weapon to break her. It had taken a long time for her to find her way back to herself after that. Like someone who had suffered a long, debilitating illness, she had had to build her strength slowly. She was determined to never again go back to that dark place.

Rob looked as if he wanted to argue, but he thought better of it. "Parker looked good," he said. "Healthy."

"He is. Good and healthy."

"He said he had a class this morning. What's he studying?"

"History. I told him there weren't many jobs in that field, but he's convinced he can make it work. And it's a subject he loves, so I'm not going to discourage him. Right now he's just taking the basics, with a couple of extra history courses thrown in. And he's working, as a delivery driver for Peggy's Pizza here in town. And he volunteers at the local history museum."

Rob nodded. "He's keeping busy. That's good."

"He is good. He's staying out of trouble."

"Has he made friends here in town? A girlfriend, maybe?"

Did Parker have a girlfriend? Why hadn't she wondered about that before? "I don't think so," she said. Though maybe that explained where he was disappearing to in his off hours. But if it was a girl, why hadn't he said so? Did he think she wouldn't approve?

Paige realized Rob had continued talking. "I'm sorry," she said. "I was thinking of something else. What did you say?"

"I asked if he planned to continue living here with you for a while."

"At least until he finishes school," she said. "Why shouldn't he? I like having him here."

"No reason," Rob said. "I just wondered. I wish him luck."

If he was so concerned about Parker's future, why had he been so dogged in sending him to jail? But that was an old argument that wasn't worth rehashing. "Why did you go into law enforcement?" she asked. "And why the DEA? Don't you get tired of arresting people and putting them in jail?"

His expression hardened. "The people I arrest need to be stopped and punished. Don't forget that I put away the people who make the drugs that ruin lives—the way Parker's life was almost ruined."

"All right. I'll concede that you probably do some good."

"So what is your problem?"

"Law enforcement sees the world in black-and-white. I see so many shades of gray."

"No, you don't," he countered. "You see the world in black-and-white, too, but your definition of black-and-white is different from mine, so that makes me wrong."

"That's not true!"

"I don't want to argue with you." He leaned toward her. "We can admit that the two of us are never going to agree on everything, but we don't have to be adversaries. People like me can sharpen your vision—and people like you can temper mine."

Where was the hard-nosed officer she had sparred with when Parker was awaiting trial and sentencing? It embarrassed her a little to remember some of the shouting matches they had had in the courthouse hallways back then. The man across from her now was smart and reasonable—and even compassionate. "I never thought of it that way before," she said. "But I guess you're right."

He sat back. "And I know how much you hate to admit that."

"I guess you're doing it already," she said. "Trying to sharpen my vision."

"And what do you see?"

She saw a man who was more nuanced than she had given him credit for. A man who tempted her to be far more vulnerable than she liked. Rob made her think about taking risks—an exhilarating feeling, but one she wasn't sure she would have the courage to act on. She stood. "Come on. It's almost time to meet Travis," she said.

She walked out of the room, aware of his gaze on her as she moved past him. It had all the force and heat of a physical caress.

ROB AND PAIGE met Travis and Gage at the sheriff's department and caravanned to the parking area for the Dakota Ridge Trail. "We can't trespass on CNG property," Travis said. "The company has referred me to their lawyers, but the legal team hasn't returned my calls."

"I checked this morning and the gate is still locked and there's no sign of anyone around the place," Gage said. "Of course, we have the authority to break the lock."

"Which I don't want to do if we don't have to," Travis said. "If no one is around, there's no point. Without a warrant, we can't search any of the buildings."

"So what's the plan?" Rob asked.

"Paige thinks retracing her steps that day might help her remember more about what happened," Travis said. "So that's what we'll do." He motioned for her to lead the way.

She shouldered the day pack she had brought and started up the trail, Rob close behind her. She walked quickly, with a sure stride, her head up, back straight. If she was nervous, she certainly didn't show it.

No one said anything for the first quarter mile of walking, until the trail began to parallel the former resort property's fence. Paige slowed, scanning the fence line, until she came to the break in the underbrush that Travis and Rob had investigated the day before. "I think about here was where I heard something and ducked to the side to look." She parted the low-growing branches of scrub oak with her hands and darted into the open space next to the fence. Rob and Travis followed, crowding in close around her. Gage stayed on the trail to keep watch.

For the second time in as many days, Rob looked through the fence to a stretch of vacant forest, at dry leaves carpeting the ground beneath the white trunks of aspens and the dark green branches of evergreens. Nothing disturbed the peacefulness of the scene, and the only sound was the soft whisper of the dry aspen leaves that still clung to the trees.

"What's that?" Travis whispered. He pointed at a spot to their right.

Rob turned his head and caught a glimpse of a figure in the distance, running away from them.

"Hey!" Travis called. "Come here!"

The figure wasn't completely visible through the trees, but Rob thought it slowed for a fraction of a second before running away even faster.

Travis grasped the iron bars of the fence. "Stop! Police!" But his shouts went unheeded.

"Let's go back," Paige said, already pushing aside the oak branches. "Whoever it was is gone."

"What's going on?" Gage asked, as they emerged onto the trail.

"We saw someone," Travis said. "Someone who ran when I ordered him to stop."

They hurried down the trail. Rob kept watch along the way for any sign of the fleeing man. It had been a man, he was sure, though not a big one—not someone who fitted the description Paige had given them. "Do you think the person we saw was either of the men who shot at you?" he asked, wanting to confirm his opinion.

"I don't know," she said. "I didn't get a good look. I don't even know that it was a man. Maybe it was a deer or elk or something."

"It was a man," Travis said. A slight man wearing dark clothes, not camouflage.

In the parking area, Travis stopped beside his SUV and scanned the small gravel lot. "Whoever that was must be parked up by the resort," he said.

"They could be behind CNG's gate," Gage said. "We wouldn't necessarily be able to see their car from the road."

"We'll go check."

Travis and Gage climbed into the SUV and left. Rob took Paige's arm. "Come on. Let's follow them," he said.

"We don't need to do that," she said. "Let's go back to town and wait there."

"They might need help," Rob said. He started the truck and followed Travis and Gage out onto the road.

The sheriff turned in at the entrance to CNG's property and stopped at the gate, his engine idling. He and Gage both climbed out of the SUV. Rob got out and followed them, though Paige remained in the truck. The three men looked through the bars of the gate, scanning the property, alert for the flash of sunlight on chrome or the metallic sheen of an automobile. "I don't see anything," Rob said after a moment.

"Me either." Travis studied the broken asphalt of the drive. "It's impossible to tell if anyone has driven over this recently." He studied the gate. "Though it doesn't look to me as if this chain and padlock have been moved in a while." He indicated the fine road dust sifted over the metal.

Gage looked around. "Maybe he parked somewhere near here and scaled the fence—or found a break and slipped through."

"How much farther does the road go?" Rob asked.

"Not far," Travis said. "It dead-ends in another fifty feet or so."

"Let's take a look," Gage said.

"Are we going back to town now?" Paige asked, when Rob returned to the car.

"In a minute. We just want to check the end of the road." He waited while Travis turned the SUV around, then followed him back down the drive. The sheriff had just started to turn onto the pavement when a dark-colored, older-model sedan came barreling toward them. Travis had to jerk the wheel sharply to the left to avoid being sideswiped.

Paige screamed and grabbed on to Rob, who had

stomped on the brakes, narrowly avoiding a collision into the rear of the SUV. Travis brought his vehicle around and lurched onto the road, in pursuit of the vehicle, which had already disappeared around a curve.

"Hold on!" Rob said, and shot after them.

"Did you see the license plate?" he asked, as they barreled down the road.

"I didn't see anything," Paige said. Her fingers dug into Rob's shoulder as they skidded around a sharp curve. "Slow down. You're going to get us killed."

"Sit back," Rob ordered.

She released her hold on him and did so, though Rob could hear her gasps and moans each time the truck skidded in gravel or rocketed over a rough spot in the pavement. They rounded yet another curve to find a straight stretch of empty road ahead. The SUV sped up even more, and Rob followed suit, but there was no sign of the sedan.

"I hope we haven't lost him," Rob said.

"He could be anywhere," Paige said. "On a side road or in a driveway—or halfway to Junction by now. And you don't even know if he had anything to do with what happened to me."

"It seems pretty suspicious if you run when a cop tells you to stop," Rob said.

"Not everyone trusts the police," she said.

Rob said nothing, but continued to follow the sheriff's SUV. By the time they reached Eagle Mountain, Travis had slowed to the speed limit. Rob's cell phone rang and he hit the button on the steering wheel to answer it.

"We lost him." Gage's voice filled the car. "Did either of you get a look at the plate?"

"No," Rob said.

"Paige?" Gage asked.

"No," she said.

"All right. You two can go on back to Paige's place. Travis and I are going to drive around a little more. Maybe we'll get lucky and spot him."

"Will do." He ended the call and drove to the Bear's Den, where he parked in the side lot.

Paige had her door open and was out of the car and headed up the walk before he could come around to her side. "Where are you going in such a hurry?" he asked, when he caught up with her in the entryway.

"I'm going to my room."

She started to turn away, but he took her arm and turned her to face him. Her skin was the color of paste and her lip trembled, as if she was fighting tears. "Hey," he said. "Are you okay?"

"I'm fine." But everything about her, from the haunted look in her eyes to the pinched sound of her voice, said that statement was a lie. Seeing that man up there and the subsequent chase had shaken her up more than he had imagined.

"It's going to be okay," he said.

He tried to pull her close, but she jerked free from his grasp. "I'm going to lie down," she said. She almost ran down the hall, and half a second later he heard a door slam.

Rob frowned after her, debating knocking on her door and demanding that she talk to him. But he had already learned that pushing Paige was never a good idea. Later, when she came out again, he would try to get her to open up about what had her so upset.

The back door opened and Parker came in. He started

when he saw Rob. "I, uh, didn't know you were still here," he said. He looked around. "Where's Paige?"

"In her room." Rob took a glass from the cabinet by the sink and filled it with water. "She's resting."

As if to prove him a liar, the door to Paige's room opened and she came down the hall to join them in the kitchen. She ignored Rob and walked straight to Parker, grabbed his arm and shook it. "What were you doing up at Eagle Mountain Resort this afternoon?" she demanded.

Chapter Eight

Paige was counting on Rob's presence to force Parker to tell the truth about what he had been up to this afternoon. Though she had caught only a fleeting glimpse of the figure running through the trees, the punched-in-the-gut feeling that glimpse had engendered had raised her worst fears. The sight of Parker's car speeding away from them had confirmed those fears.

She shook his arm again. "Don't lie to me," she said. "I saw you."

Parker's face had lost all color. He glanced at Rob, desperation in his eyes. Rob folded his arms across his chest and leaned back against the counter. "Yes, tell us what you were doing up there."

Parker slid his arms out of the straps of his backpack and let it fall to the floor with a thud. "I wasn't doing anything wrong," he said.

"You were trespassing," Rob said.

Parker jutted his chin out. "Are you going to turn me in for that?"

Paige wondered if she was the only one who recognized the fear behind her brother's defiant glare.

"That depends," Rob said.

Parker stared at the floor, the muscles of his jaw

clenching and unclenching. "I'm helping Professor Gibson with a research project," he said.

"Professor Gibson?" Paige searched her memory for the name. "The old man who helped Brenda get the grant for the history museum?"

"Yeah."

"Who's Professor Gibson?" Rob asked. "One of your instructors?"

"No, he's retired." Parker shoved his hands in the front pockets of his jeans. "But he's interested in the history of this area. He and I are trying to find the location of that World War II government research lab—the one that was developing biological and chemical weapons."

"We already determined the underground lab on the resort property isn't old enough to have been in use during the war," Rob said.

"That lab, sure," Parker said. "The professor thinks there's another one on that property."

"What makes him think that?" Paige asked.

"He's got all the declassified documents from the project, and letters and maps and stuff," Parker said. "He goes over them and finds out stuff, but he's eighty years old and it's hard for him to get up in the mountains and check stuff out. That's where I come in."

"So you were on the resort property, looking for this supposed lab?" Rob asked.

"Well, yeah," Parker said. "I told the professor about Paige seeing those two guys carrying a box into a hole in the ground, and he thought it was a good possibility. I didn't touch anything, I swear. I just walked around and looked."

"Did you find another underground chamber that could have been used as a lab?" Paige asked.

"No." His shoulders sagged again. "You came along before I could see much."

"How did you get in?" Rob asked. "The gate is chained shut."

"There's a place about two-thirds of the way along the fence line on the east side," Parker said. "Part of a big tree fell on the fence and took it down part of the way. All I had to do was shimmy up the trunk and walk right in on the fallen log."

"Why did you run from us?" Rob asked.

"Because I knew if Paige saw me, she'd have kittens," he said. "And trespassing is a violation of my parole."

Paige went ice-cold all over. She hadn't thought of that. "Promise me you won't turn him in," she said to Rob, clasping her hands together in a begging gesture. "Please." When it came to her brother, she had no shame.

He gave her a long look she found impossible to interpret. He turned back to Parker. "Did you see anyone else while you were up there?"

Parker shook his head. "Just you and Paige and the sheriff."

"Do you swear you don't know anything about the two men who fired those shots at Paige?" Rob asked.

"I swear!" Parker straightened, the color high in his cheeks. "They tried to kill my sister. If I knew anything at all, I swear I'd tell you. Why wouldn't I?"

Rob didn't answer this question. "Did you see any signs that anyone had been up there recently?" he asked. "Tire tracks or new excavation or equipment?"

"Nothing like that. But I wasn't really up there that long before y'all came around." He turned to Paige again. "You don't think the sheriff recognized my car, do you?"

"I don't think so," she said. "But Travis is really

smart. You should drive my car for a few days, until this settles down."

"What are you going to do?" Parker asked Rob.

"I won't say anything to anyone," he said. "For now." He didn't look at Paige when he spoke, which was probably just as well, because she had to fight to keep from throwing her arms around his neck in gratitude. She definitely didn't want him thinking she owed him anything for this particular favor—though maybe she did.

"Thank you," she said. Then she turned to Parker. "And you tell the professor you are not breaking any more laws in the name of research. You're not even going to jaywalk across the street on your way to the campus library."

"I'm not stupid," he said.

"Then why are you acting like you are?" Paige asked.

"You can settle that debate later," Rob said. He straightened and came to stand beside Paige, facing Parker. "What has the professor learned about this World War II project?" he asked.

"A lot, I guess," Parker said. "I mean, most of it is based on that old book he used to own—the one that was destroyed before Brenda could auction it to raise money for the museum."

Rob sent Paige a questioning look.

"It was a rare book that purported to be an insider's story about the government project here in Rayford County," she explained. "Brenda's late husband had borrowed it from Professor Gibson and it was apparently worth a lot of money to collectors. One of them paid a former sheriff's deputy to destroy the book—no one has been able to figure out why."

"Right," Parker said. "But the professor has the notes

Brenda took when she read the book, as well as government documents about the project that have been declassified."

"Do the documents say where the lab was located?" Rob asked.

"Not exactly," Parker said. "A lot of the documents are blacked out—all the names and stuff like that."

"Redacted," Paige said.

"What?" Parker frowned at her.

"It's called redacted, when they black out things in documents."

"Whatever. Anyway, the professor has been comparing topographical features described in a few reports with the terrain around here, and he's sure that the lab was on or near the Eagle Mountain Resort property."

"Why is he so interested in finding it?" Rob asked.

Parker stared at him. He didn't say "Duh!" but Paige was sure he was thinking it.

"Something like that would be a significant historical discovery," she said.

"Yeah!" Parker said. "And I'd be listed as one of the people who located it. I'd have an important research credit before I even graduated. It could really help me get a great job later on. Plus, it would really rock to be famous for something like that."

"What kind of things did they try to make in that lab, do you know?" Rob asked.

Parker made a face. "It was nasty stuff, that's for sure. I think the professor said they experimented with botulism and anthrax and something called Q fever."

"What about tularemia?" Rob asked.

"Yeah, I think that was on the list. Why?"

He shrugged. "Just curious."

Parker picked up his backpack and slung it over one shoulder. "Are we okay now?" he asked.

"For now," Rob said.

Parker nodded and shuffled out of the room. Paige waited until his door closed behind him, then turned to Rob. "What was all that about tularemia?"

"Didn't we already have this conversation?" he asked.

"You and Travis said you couldn't tell me anything, but it keeps coming up. Why is it so important?"

"I still can't tell you." He put a hand on her shoulder. "Trust me on this," he said. "If it had anything to do with you or with your brother, I would tell you."

"You'll keep quiet about him being at the resort today, won't you?" she asked. "I know it was a really bad decision on his part, but it wasn't criminal."

"I won't say anything," he said. "But you have to be prepared for Travis to figure it out. He's no dummy, and a good investigator."

"And he has a lot on his plate right now," she said. "I hope finding a random stranger he glimpsed for a few seconds is low on the list."

"Before we saw Parker, did you get anything out of today?" Rob asked. "Did the visit shake loose any new memories?"

"No."

"Do you think you'd recognize the two men if you saw them again?"

"I do."

"That's simple, then. All we have to do is find them."

ROB TOOK ADVANTAGE of Parker's presence at the B and B to check in with the sheriff. He was curious to know if

Travis had recognized Parker, and if he had heard anything from CNG Development.

Adelaide Kinkaid sat at her usual post behind her
desk in the lobby of the sheriff's department. When Rob
stepped through the door the normally stern expression
left her face, replaced by a smile that deepened the lines
around her eyes. "Good morning, Agent Allerton," she
said. "What can I do for you?"

"Good morning, Ms. Kinkaid," he said. "You're looking lovely this morning. That's a beautiful blouse you're
wearing." The blouse was a purple-and-turquoise paisley
print that wouldn't have been out of place at Woodstock.

Adelaide brushed her shoulder. "Oh, this old thing.
I've had it forever."

Rob had a sudden image of a much younger Adelaide, a flower child with a beaded headband, dancing
around at some outdoor concert in this very shirt. The
idea was disconcerting, to say the least. "Is the sheriff
in?" he asked.

"No. Lacy dragged him along with her to interview
caterers for the wedding. You know, when I got married,
my mother made a big bowl of punch and we served it
with little finger sandwiches and after-dinner mints and
called it good. But now brides want these big fancy din-
ners and dances that cost a small fortune." She leaned
toward him. "Have you ever been married, Agent Allerton?"

"No."

"One of those confirmed bachelors, aren't you?" She
pointed a pink-polished nail at him. "I know the type.
You think you're immune to love and then one day you
meet the right woman and bam!" She slammed her hand

down on her desk, making him jump. "You're down for the count."

She made falling in love sound like a wrestling match. "I don't know—" he began.

"I know what I'm talking about," she insisted. "Gage was that way—such a ladies' man until Maya came along."

"Is Gage in?" Rob asked.

"No. He had to go over to the other end of the county to deal with a traffic accident. Some fool ran off the road and took out a section of Herbert Kowalski's fence. Two of his llamas got loose and Gage is having to help round them up before they cause another accident. That could take a while. Llamas can be hard to handle."

"I wouldn't know." And he hoped he never would.

She fixed her smile on him again. "Is there anything I can help you with?"

Adelaide struck him as the type to keep up with local gossip. "Have you heard anything else about what's going on up at the old Eagle Mountain Resort property?" he asked. "Has CNG revealed their plans?"

"They won't return the sheriff's calls, I can tell you that," she said. "Though my neighbor, Sandra, has a brother-in-law who works for a concrete company in Junction, and she said someone she thinks was from CNG called about getting bids to pour some building foundations. Which is interesting, considering they haven't even gotten approval from the county to proceed with any building. And I'm pretty sure the injunction that Paige's group got is still in place, and it prohibits any development on the site."

"Maybe they think they can go ahead without county approval," Rob said.

Adelaide snorted. "They'd better not try it. People here

are keeping an eye on them, and if they make one wrong move, Paige and her bunch, especially, will be on them."

"They're that dogged, are they?"

"I don't always agree with her, mind you, but Paige Riddell knows how to get things done." She shook her head. "Of course, being pushy like that isn't the most attractive trait in a woman—which may explain why she's still single."

"Maybe she's choosy about who she dates," Rob said. "And I like a woman who isn't afraid to stand up for what she believes in."

"Well, I—" The phone rang, interrupting her. She held up one finger, to signal he should wait, and answered.

While Adelaide dealt with the caller, Rob wandered over to look at a series of photographs on the wall—Travis, Gage, Dwight and other officers at various community events. One photo showed Travis on horseback, leading a parade. In another, Gage was surrounded by a group of schoolchildren. Rob felt a stab of envy. DEA agents weren't normally part of a community like this. He believed what he was doing was important, but the public didn't always recognize that.

"Now, that was interesting." Adelaide had hung up the phone and looked pleased with herself. "Something you might want to know."

"Oh?" He returned to stand in front of her desk. "What is it?"

"That call was from my friend Shirley, over at the county offices. You'll never guess who is on the agenda to address the county commissioners at their meeting tonight."

He could see she wanted him to ask the question, so he did. "Who?"

"A representative from CNG Development. Apparently, he wants to present their plans for the old Eagle Mountain Resort property."

"That is interesting," Rob said. "Any idea what he's going to talk about?"

"No." She picked up her phone. "I've got to call Travis. He's definitely going to want to be there."

"Yes." Rob would make it a point to be there, too. And he was sure Paige wouldn't want to miss it.

PAIGE SURVEYED THE new front door with a critical eye. It was a darker shade of red than the old one, but she decided she liked the look. And at least she wouldn't have to explain bullet holes to her guests.

She went inside and closed and locked the door behind her. Parker was at the computer, typing away. "What are you doing?" she asked.

"While you were outside I took a call from a woman who wanted to book a room for next month," he said.

"You should have put her on hold and come and gotten me," Paige said.

"Why? I took care of it." He finished typing and looked up. "She wanted the Miner's Suite and it was available for those dates, so I took her credit card information and she's all set."

Paige came to look over his shoulder. Everything about the reservation looked right. "Thanks," she said. "How did you know what to do?" It wasn't as if she had ever shown him her system—though maybe she should have.

"It doesn't take a genius to figure out," he said.

"Even though you are smarter than the average bear."

She ruffled his hair, which he hated, but he only ducked out of the way.

"What are you doing, hanging around here this morning, anyway?" she asked. "Don't you have class?"

"Not this morning."

"You're not scheduled to do a shift at the museum?"

"I told Brenda I needed to take the day off."

He avoided her gaze, which immediately set off an internal alarm bell. "A day off for what?" she asked.

"I promised Rob I'd stick around this morning and look after you. He had to go to town to do some stuff, but he didn't want to leave you alone."

"So you're my designated babysitter?"

"Hey, I couldn't exactly tell the man no, could I? I owe him."

"I'll certainly talk to him about payback when he gets here."

"Paige, don't give him a hard time," Parker said. "He's only trying to protect you. And I would have stuck around anyway, even if he hadn't asked."

"I don't need a keeper."

"Maybe not, but until those creeps who shot at you are found, you don't need to be here alone, either."

She was sensible enough to admit he was right, but the idea chafed. She was about to tell him so when the doorbell rang.

A glance through the peephole showed an attractive, sandy-haired man in his midforties, wearing sharply creased khakis and a peach-colored polo shirt that showed off a good tan, broad shoulders and a trim waist. Paige opened the door. "May I help you?"

"Are you Paige Riddell?" He held out his hand. "I'm Bryce Reed, chief financial officer of CNG Development. We own the property up on Dakota Ridge that was formerly the proposed site for something called Eagle Mountain Resort. I understand you were instrumental in halting that development."

"Yes." She eyed him warily. He seemed friendly enough, but even the friendliest person could be bent on wholesale habitat destruction. "My organization is very serious about protecting the fragile environment at that elevation," she said.

"Which is exactly what I want to talk to you about," he said. "May I come in?"

She couldn't think of a good reason to tell him no. Parker was here with her—not that she couldn't look after herself—and she was curious to hear what Bryce Reed had to say. She held the door open wider.

"This is my brother, Parker. Parker, this is Mr. Reed, with CNG Development." The two shook hands. Then Parker stepped back and crossed his arms, tattoos and tough-guy scowl on display. Paige ignored him. "We can talk in here," she said, leading the way into the family room she used as a space for guests to hang out when they didn't want to be in their rooms.

She took a seat on a sofa and he settled into an armchair adjacent to her. Parker stood in the doorway, as if blocking Reed's escape. She scowled at her brother, hoping he would get the message that she wanted him to leave, but he ignored her and continued to glower at the CNG spokesman.

Reed either didn't notice or pretended not to. "I saw the plans Hake Development had drawn up for the property," he said. "A very ambitious project."

"A ridiculous project," Paige said. "There isn't enough water up there to support the kind of development he wanted to do, and keeping the roads clear and mitigating the avalanche danger would be a logistical nightmare. Not to mention the impact on wildlife and native trees and—"

Reed held up a hand. "You don't have to convince me, Ms. Riddell," he said. "I agree with all the points you've made. CNG has a very different use in mind for the property—one that will have much less impact."

She relaxed a little. She didn't get the impression he was trying to distract her with his charm or sell her a pack of lies. She had had enough experience with that type that she could spot them within seconds of meeting them for the first time. "I'm interested in finding out more about your plan," she said.

"I appreciate you hearing me out," he said. "What we have in mind is a small, exclusive high-altitude research facility. A few researchers and interns living on-site in the summer months in very low-profile, low-impact buildings. In the late fall we would close up the place and secure everything through the winter, and reopen when the roads are clear in late spring or early summer. No need to plow the road or worry about avalanches, no impact on elk calving season, very little traffic. We think we can use solar for much of our energy, and are looking into rainwater collection systems for our water needs, as well as compostable toilets and other green initiatives."

She let his words sink in. "It sounds almost too good to be true," she said after a moment.

He laughed—a hearty, friendly sound. "After dealing with Hake Development, I'm sure it does," he said. "I read your group's presentation of your objections against the resort development and you made some very good points. We're trying to keep them in mind as we plan this project."

"What do you want from me?" she asked.

"No wasting time with you, is there?" He smiled, fine lines popping out around his blue eyes. He really was a very attractive man. He didn't have Rob's movie-star looks, but there was something very appealing about him. Not that she trusted men in general, handsome or not. "Obviously, we'd like your support, if we can get it," he said. "I'm supposed to give a presentation about our plans to the town council this evening. I think your presence and approval of our project would carry a lot of weight with the local government."

"Now you're just trying to flatter me," she said.

"Maybe a little. But can you blame me? I think we've got a great project here—something that will make good use of the land and, incidentally, get rid of what I gather has been something of a blight on the local landscape. You've seen the property as it is now—abandoned foundations, crumbling streets, and I understand it has even attracted a criminal element. That isn't what CNG wants at all. We've already locked the gate and added additional fencing to try to keep out trespassers."

"You put a lock on a gate over the public hiking trail," she said. "I have a court order for the lock to be removed, but so far CNG has ignored it."

"This is the first I've heard about it," he said, frowning. "I wasn't aware there was a public hiking trail through the property. I'll certainly have to look into that."

"There's a public easement at one corner," she said. "The trail has been there since the late 1800s. You can't legally block it."

"I'm sure we can come to some compromise that ensures our property rights are respected as well as maintaining the public's access to the trail."

"You can either remove the gate or move the fence," Paige said. "Until you do, I can't speak out in support of this development."

She waited for his anger, but instead, he gave another smile, this one almost sheepish. "You drive a hard bargain, Ms. Riddell, but a fair one. I'll see that the gate is opened."

Paige stood, and he rose also. "I'll come to the county commissioners' meeting this evening," she said. "I'm looking forward to your presentation. And I appreciate your talking to me."

He took her hand, his grasp warm and firm. "Thanks for listening," he said.

She walked with him to the foyer, but before he could leave, the front door opened and Rob walked in. He stared at the two of them, who were still hand in hand. "Hello," he said.

Paige slipped her hand from Bryce's. "Bryce Reed, this is Rob Allerton," she said. "Rob is a guest here at the B and B. Mr. Reed is with CNG Development."

"Good to meet you." Bryce shook hands with Rob, who continued to eye him as if he suspected him of some crime.

"Are you the CNG representative who's giving the presentation to the county commissioners this evening?" he asked.

How had Rob learned that? Paige wondered. Maybe Travis had told him.

"I guess it's true what they say about word getting around fast in small towns," Bryce said. "Yes, I'm going to be talking about our plans for the property up on Dakota Ridge." He turned to Paige once more. "I'd really like to take you up to the property and show you around," he said. "I want you to see exactly what we have in mind. And I'm sure you could offer some good suggestions."

"The last time I was up there, someone tried to kill me," she said.

Maybe she had hoped to shock him a little bit with this bold statement. Clearly, she succeeded. He blinked at her, mouth half-open, eyes wide—as if he had been hit in the head with a heavy object. "Kill you? I hope you're exaggerating."

"She's not." Rob moved in closer. "Two men fired on her while she was on the hiking trail that runs alongside the fence bordering your property. Later, they came here to try to finish the job."

"Two men, you say?" He had regained some of his composure, but his affable manner of earlier was gone. "What did they look like?"

"They were big," Paige said. "They wore camouflage, almost like soldiers. But I didn't really get a good look at them."

"They drove a dark sedan and the weapon was an AR-15," Rob said.

"That is unacceptable," Bryce said. He took Paige's hand once more. "I'm so sorry you had to go through that. I had heard some criminal types had been taking advantage of what they probably saw as abandoned property. I promise you, that is going to stop now."

The fierceness of his tone—and the murderous look in his eyes—sent a shiver through her. She withdrew her hand from his. "That's good to hear."

"If you know anything about this, you need to tell the sheriff," Rob said.

"I think I know how to handle my business," Bryce said, his voice mild, but his eyes still frigid. He nodded to Paige. "I'll see you tonight."

Rob opened the door and closed it again after Bryce had exited. He locked it, then leaned back against it, arms crossed. "What was he doing here?" he asked.

"He invited me to attend his presentation tonight," she said. "And he wants my support—well, the support of Eagle Mountain environmentalists—for CNG's plans."

"He wanted to size you up," Parker said.

She turned to her brother, who leaned back against the desk, his pose strikingly similar to Rob's. "What do you mean by that?" she asked.

"He wanted to see what the opposition looked like," Parker said. "What he was up against."

"I think Parker's right," Rob said. "He may have asked you for your support, but he really wanted to gauge what kind of a fight you were likely to put up."

"Maybe so," Paige said. "But my take is that he was being smart and trying to recruit me to his side. And he made some convincing arguments for his project."

"I think he knows something about those men who shot at you," Rob said.

"You saw the look on his face when I told him about them," she said. "He was stunned—truly shocked."

"Maybe." Rob looked doubtful. "I think he bears watching."

"I agree," Paige said. "And I will be watching him. But I don't think he's dangerous."

Rob moved past her, pausing at her side to touch her

arm and look into her eyes. "Don't underestimate him," he said, in a low voice that sent a hot tremor through her. "And don't underestimate what I'll do to protect you."

Chapter Nine

Parker consulted the map the professor had given him, and compared it to the landscape around him. The map was dotted with the crossed-pickaxes symbol that indicated the site of old mines, several of which were within the dark line that represented the boundary around CNG Development's Dakota Ridge property. "There may be others that aren't marked on here," Professor Gibson had said when he gave Parker the map. "But these are a good place to start. Locate as many as you can and report back to me."

Yes, he had promised Paige he wouldn't come back up here, but that had been fear talking. Now that he had had time to think about it, he couldn't see what harm could come from him taking another look at the property. If CNG really was going to develop the place, he and the professor didn't have much time left to make their discovery. And with everyone focused on Bryce Reed's presentation to the county commissioners that evening, Parker had figured this was a good time to finish what he had intended to do before the sheriff had interrupted him the other day.

Paige would have had a fit if she knew he was back up here, of course, but the way Parker saw it, the property was unoccupied—practically abandoned. And he was engaged in important historical research, not petty vandalism. He doubted CNG or the local cops would see it that way, so he had been careful to park his car out of sight, and to come into the property through the break in the fence, where no one could see him from the road or the hiking trail.

Rob Allerton definitely wouldn't approve of what he was doing, though he had been cool about not turning Parker in to the sheriff when he'd recognized him here the other day. Parker hadn't expected that, and it made him like the cop in spite of himself.

He still couldn't decide how he felt having the DEA agent living in the same house. Paige could pretend all she wanted that Rob wasn't interested in her, but Parker knew he was right. Was that a good or a bad thing? She needed something to focus on besides Parker. He hadn't said anything to his sister yet, but he was thinking of moving to Boulder next year and enrolling in the University of Colorado. Professor Gibson had already said he would recommend Parker for admission, and even help him get a scholarship to study history.

The professor had been a surprise since Parker moved to Eagle Mountain. The old guy had really taken an interest in Parker. It was an odd friendship—a young ex-con and a staid old professor—but Gibson was supersharp, and the two had just hit it off. The research they were doing together fascinated Parker, and the professor had helped him to see a future for himself that didn't involve menial jobs and always running from the stigma of his past mistakes.

The professor had determined that the government's

secret World War II lab had been located in this area. He had unearthed accounts that mentioned a rocky ridge he thought was probably Dakota Ridge, and a nearby creek, the location of which matched up with the creek that ran along the back side of CNG's property. One letter the professor had found mentioned a view of Mount Wiley, which could be seen from where Parker was standing right now.

The problem was construction on the property had altered some of the natural terrain. Had the gully shown on the map been filled in or diverted to construct that street? Had the giant boulder indicated on the map been blasted into pieces to make room for the foundation of a house? It didn't help that Parker hadn't had much experience reading maps and orienteering, or that he had only about an hour and a half before it would be too dark to see much of anything. Where was a good GPS coordinate when you needed it?

He took a few steps toward a clearing ahead, thinking if he got out of the trees, maybe he could figure out where he was, but a loud noise startled him. Heart pounding, he hurried back into the thick undergrowth. The heavy *whump! whump! whump!* of a helicopter echoed off the rock face of the ridge behind him, growing so loud Parker wanted to cover his ears.

But he remained still, craning his neck and trying to see through the canopy of trees. He caught a glimpse of a dark shape, but that was all. Maybe just as well, since if he couldn't see the chopper through the thick undergrowth, then its occupants probably couldn't see him.

He didn't have to wait long to get a good view of the helicopter, though. A minute later, it set down in the clearing in front of him. Parker shrank farther into the underbrush as the rotors slowed, then stopped, and the roar of the engine faded. The door popped open and two men, dressed in military fatigues and carrying rifles, hopped to the ground. They scanned the area. Then a moment later, a man in a dark business suit exited the chopper. He had graying hair swept back from his forehead, and dark sunglasses perched on a crooked nose, with deep frown lines on either side of a thin-lipped mouth. He surveyed the area, then said something to the men with the guns that Parker couldn't hear.

The gunmen returned to the helicopter and unloaded a large wooden crate—about the size of a coffee table or a trunk. They set it on the ground next to the man in the suit. Stealthily, trying hard not to make a sound and scarcely daring to breathe, Parker took out his phone and began snapping photographs of the men, the box and the helicopter. He had taken half a dozen pictures when a branch cracked and a deer shot from the underbrush on the other side of the clearing.

Both men in fatigues raised their rifles and fired off a barrage of shots, peppering the deer with bullets, sending bark flying off the trunks of surrounding trees. Parker bit the inside of his cheek to keep from crying out. These guys were crazy! And he needed to get out of here as fast as he could.

The man in the suit didn't even flinch at the burst of gunfire. When the gunmen had lowered their weapons, he motioned to the crate and said something. They each took an end and headed off across the clearing, away from Parker. The man in the suit followed.

Parker waited until they were out of sight, then retraced his steps to the break in the fence, and from there to his car. His hands were still shaking as he fumbled the key into the ignition. What was going on up here?

And did he dare tell anyone about it?

WORD HAD OBVIOUSLY gotten around about that night's special guest speaker at the county commissioners' meeting, since latecomers ended up standing along the walls of the meeting room on the second floor of the Rayford County courthouse. Eagle Mountain *Examiner* reporter Tammy Patterson slid into one of the last empty seats, next to Paige, and gaped at the full house. "Most of the time Dean Eggbert and I are the only people in the audience at these things," she whispered, as she took out her tape recorder.

"Why does Dean attend?" Paige asked, picturing the short, round man whose balding head and ever-present white-shirt-with-red-suspenders combo always reminded her of the picture of Humpty Dumpty in her childhood storybook.

"His wife's book club meets at their place on Monday nights," Tammy said. "This gets him out of the house." She looked past Paige. "Hello, Agent Allerton. I heard you were back in town."

"Call me Rob," he said. "I'm here on vacation. Hoping to do some fishing."

"This meeting is called to order." The chief commissioner struck his gavel and the regular business of the commissioners proceeded, from the approval of the last meeting's minutes to authorization of funds to buy a new dump truck. Paige, who had endured her share of town meetings, struggled to keep her eyes open. Next to her, Rob sat slumped in his chair with his hands in his pockets and his chin on his chest. Paige was tempted to nudge him, to see if he was awake.

"And now, Bryce Reed with CNG Development has asked to address the commissioners."

A murmur rose from the crowd and audience members straightened in their seats as Reed, dressed as he had been that afternoon, in khaki trousers and a pastel golf shirt, strode to the microphone at the front of the room. He nodded and someone in the rear dimmed the lights, and an image appeared on the screen of a long, low building set against the familiar cliffs of Dakota Ridge.

"My company, CNG Development, wants to take a piece of land that has become an eyesore and a nuisance to this community and turn it into an important high-altitude research facility that will give back to your wonderful community rather than taking away from it," Reed said.

For the next ten minutes, he walked them through a series of before and after artist's renderings of the property, as well as bullet-pointed lists of the benefits of his proposed project—everything from green building practices to wildlife habitat protection.

"He's very persuasive," Paige whispered to Rob.

"Are you persuaded?" he asked.

"I'm reserving judgment," she said. "Companies often talk a good game, but they don't always follow through."

Reed finished his presentation and asked if anyone had questions. Seemingly everyone had a question, from Al Dawson's query about local jobs at the lab site—there would be a very small, very specialized staff, but there might be a few jobs for locals—to Merrily Rayford's concern over removing some of the dilapidated structures that were already in place on the property.

"No questions?" Rob leaned over to ask Paige.

"I'll have plenty—later. When I meet with Mr. Reed again."

Once more flashing a smile that attested to many thousand dollars of dental work, Bryce Reed closed the notebook he had brought to the podium with him. "If no one else has anything they'd like to ask—"

The door at the back of the room opened and Mayor Larry Rowe stepped in. Dressed for the office in dark slacks, white shirt and no tie, he smoothed back his graying hair and strode toward the podium. "Sorry I'm late," he muttered, as Bryce stepped aside to give the mayor access to the microphone.

"I should have known Larry wouldn't miss a chance to claim his share of the spotlight," Paige whispered to Rob.

"I just wanted to go on record as saying that the city of Eagle Mountain is one hundred percent behind CNG's proposal for their Dakota Ridge property," the mayor said. "We're pleased as can be that they're going to take something that has been a problem for the area and turn it into a facility we can all be proud of."

He looked out at the audience, as if daring anyone to contradict him.

"Thank you, Mr. Mayor," Bryce said. "I appreciate your support. And I hope in time to earn the support of many more of you."

Paige realized Bryce was looking right at her. She met his gaze with a cool look of her own.

"He thinks he's won you over," Rob said.

"As I said, I'm reserving judgment until after our meeting."

She braced herself for his argument that she shouldn't meet with Reed alone. She would let him rant for a while, then tell him she intended to take him with her. That should knock the wind from his sails. But before she had a chance to speak, a piercing siren sounded.

"That's the fire alarm." Travis, who had been seated behind them, stood. Half a dozen others in the room rose, as well. In a town with no paid fire department, the alarm was the quickest way to summon volunteers to their stations.

The room was emptying out fast when Tammy stood, her phone in her hand. "My editor just texted me," she said. "The fire is up on Dakota Ridge—at the old Eagle Mountain Resort property."

ROB STUDIED THE two bodies partially visible beneath the pile of charred timbers, illuminated by the white-hot glow of powerful LED work lights on stands on either side of the former building. The sharp scent of burning wood stung his nose, and he stood well back to avoid the rivulets of wet ash that trickled from the remains of the fire. "Any idea who they are?" he asked Travis.

"Reed says he's never seen them before—that no one was supposed to be up here." Travis glanced toward where Bryce Reed stood, talking to the assistant fire chief, Tom Reynolds.

"How did the fire start?" Rob asked. "Do we know yet?"

"Tom says he can't make an official assessment until after a formal investigation, but he's pretty sure it's arson," Travis said.

The building had been one of the few complete ones on the resort site. The eight-by-ten shed had been sided with weathered cedar and roofed with rusty metal, in an attempt to mimic an old mine shack. Rob and his team had searched the structure as part of their investigation into the underground laboratory, but found only land-scaping tools and a pile of real-estate signs. The structure sat by itself, surrounded by rocky ground and broken pavement, which had kept the blaze from spreading.

"Who called in the alarm, do you know?" Rob asked.

"Jim Trotter and his wife were driving home from dinner and saw the smoke," Travis said. "They live at the end of the road here." He turned to greet the assistant fire chief, a slim, redheaded man in yellow bunker gear. "Tom, this is Agent Rob Allerton, with the DEA."

Tom shook Rob's hand.

"I was just telling Rob that the Trotters called in the fire," Travis said.

Tom nodded. "It probably hadn't been burning very long at that point, but by the time we got here, there wasn't anything we could do except keep it from spreading to the forest."

"Was the gate closed when you arrived?" Rob asked.

"Oh yeah. We had to cut the chain. The roof was caving in by the time we got the trucks over to the structure."

"And you think it was deliberately set?" Rob asked.

"We could smell the diesel fuel as soon as we got out of the truck," Tom said. "And there hasn't been any lightning. There's no electricity to the structure, so that leaves out faulty wiring."

"Any chance it was a vagrant using the shack for shelter?" Travis asked. "Maybe they had a campfire that got out of hand."

"Anything's possible," Tom said. "We'll know more after my investigation."

"Any sign of a vehicle?" Travis asked.

"A vehicle?" Tom frowned.

"The two men who died in the fire had to get up here somehow," Travis said.

Tom looked around them, but Rob already knew there was no car or truck in sight, other than the fire and rescue vehicles and the sheriff's SUV. "I guess they could have walked in," Tom said.

"It's a long way to walk," Travis said. "And they'd have to have gear—backpacks, camping equipment, stuff like that."

"We may find what's left of it when we clear away the debris and move the bodies," Tom said. "We might even find identification on the bodies."

"What did Bryce Reed tell you?" Travis asked.

"That he didn't know anything," Tom said. "That no one was supposed to be up here. He thinks they must have climbed the fence and been squatting here and set fire to the building themselves."

"Why didn't they try to get out?" Rob asked.

"How do you know they didn't?" Travis asked.

"The way the bodies are lying." Rob gestured toward the burned-out building. "They're facing away from the door. Say an explosion caused the fire—a gas stove, or maybe they had a campfire and tried to get it going bigger by dumping some diesel on it, and the fumes ignited. It might have thrown them backward, away from the fire, but then I would think they would try to get out. Yet both of them are just lying there, next to each other."

"Maybe they were asleep," Travis said. "Or they had been drinking or doing drugs and passed out."

"Maybe," Rob said.

"Sheriff. There's something you need to see." One of

the firemen, his face and yellow bunker gear streaked with soot, trotted over to them.

Travis, Rob and the chief followed the firefighter over to a rock cairn about a hundred yards from the shack, across from the remains of what had once been a paved street. "Take a look at that," the firefighter said, and pointed behind the pillar. An AR-15 was propped against the rocks. "Funny place to leave a gun like that," he said.

"Unless you wanted to make sure it wasn't destroyed in the fire," Travis said. "And you wanted it to be found." He crouched down and examined it more closely, though without touching it. "We'll leave it until the crime scene team gets up here." He turned to look back at the black-ened ruins. The firefighter and the chief moved toward the fire truck parked closer to the now-open gate. "What do you think the chances are the two bodies in there be-long to the two men who shot at Paige?" Travis asked.

"I didn't get a good look at them," Rob said. "And to be honest, their own mothers wouldn't know them now."

"The gun is too obvious," Travis said. "As if someone left it there to find. I'm betting when we test it, we find out it's the same gun that fired the bullets we found in Paige's front door."

The rumble of an engine and the crackle of tires on gravel announced the arrival of the crime scene van, followed by a black SUV. Two men and one woman climbed out of the van and began donning Tyvek suits and booties. The SUV parked a short distance away, and Mayor Larry Rowe got out and walked over to join Travis and Rob.

"What are you doing here?" the mayor asked Rob.

"Agent Allerton is assisting us with the investiga-tion," Travis said.

The mayor's eyebrows rose, but he made no further comment to Rob. "What have they found out?" he asked Travis.

Rob wanted to tell the man the information was none of his business. Something about Rowe rubbed him the wrong way—though maybe that was only Paige's prejudice rubbing off on him. Clearly, she had little use for the mayor. Rob remained quiet and let Travis handle this.

"We're waiting on the investigation before we announce any results," Travis said.

A woman in white Tyvek coveralls walked over to them. "What have we got, Sheriff?" she asked.

Travis glanced at the mayor.

"You can talk in front of me," Larry said. "I know how to keep a confidence, and I think I'm entitled to be briefed about the situation."

Travis nodded, then summed up their findings for the woman—Darcy Collins, with the Colorado Bureau of Investigation. "We're going on the assumption this is arson, until we establish otherwise. If it is arson, then the two bodies could be murder victims."

She nodded. "We'll find any evidence there is to find."

Travis pointed to the cairn. "There's an AR-15 behind those rocks I want photographed and bagged for evidence," he said.

"Got it." She signaled to her team and they began setting small plastic flags on thin wire stakes to establish an entry and exit corridor. They strung crime scene tape, then began photographing the burned building and the surrounding area.

"It's pretty clear to me what happened here," the mayor said, when Darcy had left them.

"Oh?" Rob asked.

"The AR-15 belongs to the two dead guys," Larry said. "They were the ones who shot at Paige, up here and at her house. They were camping out in that shack and got careless with their fire."

"We don't know yet if this AR is the one that fired at Paige," Rob said.

"You can test it," Larry said. "I'm sure that will prove I'm right."

"Thank you for your input." Travis turned away.

"You'll let me know what you find," the mayor said.

Travis didn't answer. He and Rob walked over to Travis's SUV, where they stood in the shadowed darkness, watching the investigators move in and out of the glow of work lights.

Travis waited until the mayor had driven away before he spoke. "If the bodies belong to the shooter and his cohort, then we have the guilty parties and we don't need to look further," he said.

"Very convenient," Rob said. "Except we don't know why they tried to kill Paige, or what they were doing up here."

"She said she saw them carrying a big wooden crate into an underground chamber or hole or mine shaft or something like that," Travis said. "Maybe they were stashing stolen goods up here."

"Any burglaries in the area lately?" Rob asked.

"No. I can check surrounding areas. Maybe something will pop." He kicked at a rock, which rolled away down the small incline. "It's too neat. Too convenient."

"The mayor likes it."

"The mayor watches too much television."

"What does he do, your mayor?" Rob asked. "Or is that his full-time job?"

"He has a computer consulting company," Travis said. "They specialize in financial management firms."

"He's obviously a fan of CNG."

"He ran on a platform of bringing new businesses and jobs to the area," Travis said. "And he's the type who likes to have his name in the paper as often as possible. This is a hot story, so the mayor wants to make sure he's quoted."

"I've met the type," Rob said. He tried to stay far away from them. "Do you think Reed was telling the truth—that he didn't know the men or what they were doing?"

"I don't believe anyone I don't know well," Travis said.

"He came by the Bear's Den this afternoon to talk to Paige," Rob said. "He said he wanted to share his plans for the property with her and get her support."

"That sounds smart. Paige's group isn't that large, but they know how to make a lot of noise when they're unhappy about something."

"Are you saying they're troublemakers?" Rob asked.

"Not at all. They do a lot of good for the community, but they aren't subtle. They've made enemies."

"Reed asked Paige to come up here with him for a private tour. She told him the last time she was up here, someone tried to kill her. He seemed shocked to hear this. I don't think he was faking it."

"That's interesting."

"Something I thought was even more interesting—he told Paige that 'wasn't acceptable' and that he would put a stop to it."

"As if he had authority over the shooters?" Travis asked.

"Maybe. Or maybe he was just blowing smoke, trying to impress her with how powerful and in charge he was. Or maybe it was just a figure of speech. He could have meant he was going to make sure the property was secure and no one used it for criminal activity. CNG has held the position all along that they aren't responsible for anything that has happened while the property was essentially abandoned."

"I'm wondering if either of those two is the man we saw up here yesterday," Travis said.

"I don't think so," Rob said, keeping his tone casual. "I only got a glimpse, but the person we saw seemed smaller. Like a kid, even."

"What would a kid be doing up here?" Travis asked.

"Messing around. Seeing what he could find."

"He was old enough to drive," Travis said. "He almost ran us off the road. I'm going to have to talk to Paige again. I think she knows more than she's saying."

"Why do you think that?"

"Just a hunch. She was acting odd yesterday—evasive, even."

Rob started to defend Paige, then decided anything he said was going to make the sheriff more suspicious. Travis had a reputation as a shrewd and dogged investigator. Chances were, he was going to find out it was Parker who had fled from them when they were up here yesterday. Rob didn't know Travis well enough to predict how he would handle that information, but he hoped, for Paige's sake, that he would go easy on the young man.

A trio of firemen shifted the largest of the fallen timbers and the crime scene team moved in to get their first close look at the bodies. Rob didn't envy them the task. But they would want to establish the circumstances of the deaths, and secure any identification that was on the bodies before trying to move them.

"Sheriff!" Darcy raised her head and called to him.

Travis straightened and walked over to join her. Rob was too far away to overhear what she said, but he could see the scene clearly in the bright glow of the work lights. She gestured toward one of the bodies, then bent and rolled over the second one. Travis said something, then backed out of the building and returned to the SUV.

"What did she find?" Rob asked.

"Those two didn't die in the fire," Travis said.

"Why do you say that?"

"They were already dead. Both of them had been shot in the head."

Chapter Ten

Rob was eating breakfast in Paige's dining room the next morning when Travis called him. "I'm going to Bryce Reed's office this morning to talk to him," he said. "Want to come along?"

Rob pushed back his chair. "Let me check." He headed for the kitchen, but met Paige coming out. "What are you doing this morning?" he asked her, the phone tucked under his chin.

"Eagle Mountain environmentalists have a meeting at ten. Why?"

"I might need to be away for a couple of hours," he said.

"So go," she said. "I don't need a babysitter—certainly not now that those two men are dead. You said they were probably the ones who shot at me, right?"

"We don't know that for sure."

"I'll be fine." She set a bowl of fruit on the sideboard and turned back toward the kitchen. "Go."

Rob put the phone back to his ear. "Sure, I'll come with you. Should be interesting. Where are you meeting him?"

"CNG has an office here in town," Travis said. "Come by the sheriff's office and we'll go there together."

Travis was waiting, keys in hand, when Rob arrived. "Just to be clear, I'm not here in an official capacity," Rob reminded him as they walked to Travis's SUV.

"I know. But your law enforcement connection seemed to shake Reed a little yesterday," Travis said. "I want to take advantage of that. Besides, it's always good to have another perspective."

CNG Development's Eagle Mountain offices were located in a newer strip center on the edge of town. The front room contained an empty desk and three metal folding chairs—and nothing else. Rob would have expected a file cabinet or a plant, or even pictures on the wall. Apparently, CNG wasn't too concerned about impressing visitors.

"Hello?" Travis called when he and Rob entered.

Reed, in khaki slacks and another polo shirt—mint green this time—looked out from the doorway of the office's second room. "Sheriff!" he said. "Do you have any more news about last night's events?"

"I have some information for you," Travis said. "And some more questions." He indicated Rob. "I've asked Agent Allerton to sit in with us."

"Come sit down and we'll talk." He turned to Rob. "Agent Allerton. When I met you at Paige Riddell's yesterday afternoon, you didn't tell me you were a law enforcement officer."

Reed must have been stewing about that all night, Rob thought. "It wasn't relevant," he said.

"And now it is?" Reed asked. "What interest does the DEA have in CNG?"

"Agent Allerton is assisting us with our investigation," Travis said.

Reed looked as if he wanted to argue, but he merely

pressed his lips together and led them into a sparsely furnished office. He pulled up two folding chairs and took his place behind the cheap metal desk. He must have seen Travis's and Rob's skeptical looks at the budget accommodations. "We rented this space furnished, until we can construct a more permanent facility on the site," he said. He turned to Travis. "What have you found out about those two men?"

Travis took two photographs from the file folder he carried and handed them to Reed. "Identification taken from wallets found on the bodies identifies them as Joseph Welch and Dennis Petri," he said. "We'll be confirming that with medical and dental records as soon as we can obtain them."

Reed stared at the black-and-white mug shots. Travis handed Rob copies also. The photographs showed two men in their early thirties. Welch had thinning brown hair and Petri had close-cropped, curly black hair. Each faced the camera with a sullen look on his face, booking number across his chest.

"I've never seen either of them before," Reed said, and returned the photos to Travis.

"What were they doing on CNG property?" Travis asked.

"I already told you, I have no idea. They were trespassing."

"We searched the area and we haven't been able to locate a vehicle, or any personal belongings, like a backpack or camping equipment," Travis said. "How do you explain that?"

"I don't. That's up to you to investigate."

"Both men were shot in the head," Travis continued. "Do you have any idea who might have killed them?"

"Of course not." Reed managed to look indignant.

"Any theories about what might have happened?" Rob asked.

"No. It's not my job to come up with theories. These people were on CNG property illegally."

"What is it about that piece of property that attracts so many criminals?" Rob asked.

"I could turn that around and ask why this county has such a problem with illegal activity in general," Reed said.

Travis restored the photos to the folder and sat back in his chair. "Have you considered hiring a private security company to patrol the property?" he asked. "Cameras and some lighting might also help."

"We will be doing all of those things," Reed said.

"I'll be posting extra patrols in that area, also," Travis said.

Some of the stiffness went out of Reed's posture. "I appreciate that, Sheriff," he said. "But I know yours is a small department with limited staff. I would hate to take your deputies away from here in town, where they might be needed."

"Since most of the serious crime we've had lately has had some connection to that property or people involved with it, it makes sense to me to focus our efforts there," Travis said.

"From what little I know of the former owner, he was involved with some shady characters," Reed said. "The more I consider the situation, the more I believe those two men who died in the fire—and anyone else who might have been causing trouble up there before now—must be related to that. They haven't gotten the word yet that the property has new owners who have zero tolerance for anything untoward. That is going to change now, I assure you."

"I'm glad to hear it," Travis said.

"Hello? Bryce, are you here?"

Rob sat bolt upright at the sound of the familiar voice, and turned in time to see Paige in the doorway of Reed's office. Dressed casually, in a long denim skirt, boots and a long-sleeved red blouse, she still managed to convey an air of sophistication. "Oh!" She took a step back. "I didn't know you were with someone."

"Paige, come in!" Reed rose and greeted her heartily. "The sheriff and I were just finishing up."

"What are you doing here?" Rob asked, not caring if he sounded rude.

She scowled at him, but before she could answer, Reed said, "Paige and I have a lunch date."

Now her frown was for Reed. "We agreed to talk more about your plans for your research facility," she said.

"Over lunch." He came out from behind the desk. "Gentlemen, if you'll excuse me…"

"I was going to stop by and see you this afternoon," Travis said to Paige, standing also. "But if you have a minute, we can take care of my question now."

"Of course," she said.

Travis pulled out the mug shots of Welch and Petri. "Have you seen either of these men before?" he asked.

She studied the pictures for a long moment, then shook her head. "No. I don't think so."

"Could they have been the men who shot at you on the hiking trail the other day? Or who fired on you at your house that afternoon?" Travis asked.

She looked at the photos again. "I can't say these men weren't the ones who shot at me. But I can't say they are, either. I just didn't get a good enough look at them. I'm sorry."

Rob wasn't surprised at her answer. Despite her earlier assertion that she would recognize the men again, she had glimpsed them for only a few seconds, under tense circumstance. And looking at a two-dimensional mug shot was very different from seeing someone alive and standing nearby.

"That's all right." Travis put the photographs away.

"Are those the two men you found dead last night?" she asked Rob.

He looked to Travis. This wasn't his case, and he didn't know how much the sheriff wanted to reveal. Travis nodded. "We think so, yes."

"What about the gun you found last night?" Reed asked. "Can you connect it with the attacks on Paige?"

"We're waiting on ballistics tests," he said. "Interesting thing about that gun, though."

"Oh?" Paige and Reed spoke in chorus.

"There weren't any fingerprints on it," Travis said. "Whoever put it behind those rocks had wiped it clean."

PAIGE COULD FEEL Rob's eyes on her as she exited the office with Bryce Reed. Travis hadn't elaborated any more on the gun with no fingerprints, and Reed had hurried her out. But she couldn't get Travis's words out of her head. "What do you think it means, the gun being wiped off like that?" she asked as they walked toward their cars.

"My guess is the shooters wiped it every time they used it, in case someone found it." She had started toward her car, but Reed put a hand at her back and steered her toward his. "Come in my car," he said. "We'll have more time to talk."

She could have made an excuse about having to be somewhere else right after lunch, but it seemed both silly and paranoid. Reed had given her no reason not to trust him, and it was broad daylight, after all. Not to mention Rob and the sheriff were right behind them, she thought, glancing in the mirror as she slid into the passenger seat of the big SUV Reed drove.

"Would someone really do that?" she asked, as he started the vehicle. "Wipe down a gun every time he used it? And hide it in the rocks that way?"

"A guilty person might." Reed flashed her a smile. "But hey, I've never been a criminal, so I have no idea. What do you think about the Cake Walk for lunch?" he asked. "I know Eagle Mountain doesn't have that many choices, but I had breakfast there the other day and it was great. I figure the lunch will be good, too."

"The Cake Walk is fine," she said. "Did the fire last night do much damage to the property?"

"The truth is, there's not a lot up there to burn," he said. "Chances are we would have torn down that storage shed anyway." He glanced at her. "Not that I would be thanking those two for burning it down. We take trespassing very seriously and will prosecute anyone we catch up there who doesn't have proper authorization."

She shifted in her seat, thinking of Parker. She had half a mind to call Professor Gibson and read him the riot act for asking her brother to snoop around on CNG property. She would definitely warn Parker not to go near the place again.

Reed found a parking space in front of the café and they settled into a booth along one side of the cozy restaurant. Paige recognized most of the people in the room, and nodded to a few. No doubt the gossips would be busy speculating on why she was having lunch with the local face of CNG Development—especially since news about the fire and the discovery of two bodies up there would be all over town by now. It might be interesting to hear some of the local theories about that.

"You'll be happy to know I'm having the gate across the hiking trail removed today," Reed said, after they had placed their orders.

"I'm pleased to hear that," she said. Though the primary purpose of the EME meeting this morning had been to discuss their booth for an upcoming fall festival, several people had suggested making another try at cutting the lock off the gate blocking the trail. In the end, they had decided to wait until things had settled down on the resort site. No one wanted a repeat of what had happened to Paige.

"None of the people who use the trail are interested in trespassing on private property," Paige said. "We only want to hike a trail that's a favorite of many people around here. If you want to put a fence alongside the trail to protect your property, we have no problem with that, though most people who have public right-of-way across their land settle for posting No Trespassing signs that remind people to stay on the trail."

"We'll try the signs," Reed said. "The sheriff suggested hiring a security guard and installing cameras."

"That might not be a bad idea," Paige said.

The waitress delivered her salad and his sandwich. "I'd really like you to come up there with me," Reed said. "I want to take you around and show you where everything is going to be. I think you'll really like what we have in mind."

"I'd love to see it," she said. She was dying to know

his plans—and she had to admit she wanted to see the scene after last night.

"I can take you up there after lunch, if you have time," he said.

She hesitated. She didn't have any guests arriving this afternoon. "As long as we're back by five," she said. "And I need to call my brother and let him know not to expect me." Parker had proved he was capable of handling any reservations that came in.

"Great." Reed grinned, then took a big bite out of his sandwich.

When they were done eating, he took care of the bill while Paige went outside to make her call. "The Bear's Den Bed and Breakfast," Parker answered, sounding very professional.

"Parker, it's Paige. I called to let you know I'll be away the rest of the afternoon. Would you mind the phone while I'm gone? I'll be back before you have to leave for work."

"Where are you going?" he asked.

"Up to Eagle Mountain Resort. Bryce Reed is going to show me around."

"You can't go up there with him," Parker said. "You don't even know the guy."

"He's a perfectly respectable businessman." She glanced over her shoulder, relieved to see that Reed hadn't yet emerged from the café. "It's broad daylight. And I'm not an idiot. It'll be fine."

"What about those guys who shot at you?"

"The sheriff thinks they were the men who were found dead up there last night."

"I don't like it," Parker said.

"I don't like everything you do, either," she said. "But

we're both adults. I don't get to tell you what to do and you don't get to tell me what to do. Agreed?"

"I still don't have to like it," he said. "Just—be careful."

"I always am." She ended the call and turned to find Reed waiting behind her.

"Any trouble?" he asked.

"My brother is a little overprotective sometimes," she said. "It's sweet, really."

"I guess someone with his background knows a little too much about what the wrong kind of people will do," Reed said. He took her arm.

She stiffened. "What's that supposed to mean?" she asked. "What about Parker's background?"

"I didn't mean to offend," he said. "Someone told me he'd been in prison."

"Who told you?" she demanded.

"I don't remember—just something I heard around town. I apologize. I really didn't mean to offend you."

He looked genuinely contrite. She relaxed a little. "Parker made some foolish mistakes when he was younger, but he's working hard to get past that," she said. "I hate that some people will never let him forget his mistakes."

"Again, I'm sorry I brought it up." Reed held the door while she slid into the passenger seat, then closed it and walked around to the driver's side. "But as long as we're on the subject of the men in your life, what's your relationship to Agent Allerton?"

"He's a guest at my B and B," she said.

"I guess I read the signals wrong," Reed said. "He seemed a little overprotective of you, too."

"You must have misunderstood," she said. She was

already wishing she hadn't agreed to ride with him. She hadn't expected him to question her personal life this way.

"Sorry for the nosy questions," he said. "I've devoted the last few years to my career, so I'm a little rusty when it comes to interacting with attractive women."

And what was *that* supposed to mean? "Are you married?" she asked. If he was going to ask personal questions, she might as well, too.

"Divorced. No kids. I'm a boring workaholic, though I'd like to change that. A man gets to be my age, he starts to think about the mistakes he's made."

"You're not that old," she said.

He laughed. "Maybe not. But it feels that way sometimes." He sped up when they reached the road that started the climb toward Dakota Ridge. "This is beautiful country out here," he said. "A lot wilder and more rugged than where I'm from, back east, but definitely captivating."

"Most people who live here think it's pretty much paradise," she said.

He stopped at the gates to the resort property—she couldn't help but think of it that way, even though it would never be a resort. Maybe one day everyone would call it the research campus or something similar, but until then, it would be the resort. "The fire department destroyed the lock getting to the fire last night," he said. "We'll have to fix that." He pressed a remote device clipped to the visor and the gates swung open, smoothly and soundlessly. He drove the car over the cracking pavement and parked in front of the faded sign advertising the resort. "We're going to get people in here to take all of this out," he said, indicating the sign, the broken pavement and the foundations that had never been built on. "Come on. Let's take a walk and I'll show you around."

The air held the tang of smoke, and a short distance away Paige spotted the burned-out shed, yellow crime scene tape festooning the blackened ruins. Reed saw where she was looking and took her arm. "You don't need to concern yourself with that," he said.

She pulled away from him. "Of course I'm concerned," she said. "Two people died there—men who may have tried to kill me."

"You're right. I'm sorry." He jingled his keys in his pockets. "But there's nothing we can do about that now. Will you let me show you where we hope to put the new labs?"

She followed him away from the ruins, past a Quonset hut and more crumbling foundations to a cleared expanse near the top of the ridge that overlooked a valley filled with tall spruce and pine. "The building would have a low profile and really blend in with the environment," Reed said. "You shouldn't be able to see it from the road at all."

"Where would the people who work here live?" she asked. It was a beautiful setting. Peaceful, even, if you could ignore the scent of smoke that lingered in the air.

"Some would live in town," Reed said. "Although we would have a few houses here on the property—apartments, really, again with a low profile and very green."

"That's good." She was only half listening to him, her senses attuned to the woods around them. Not even a bird sang. It ought to have been the most peaceful setting in the world, yet she couldn't shake a sense of foreboding.

"Let me show you where we plan to build the apartments." He moved forward and a stick broke under his foot with a loud pop. Paige gasped.

"It's just a stick," Reed said. "Why are you so jumpy?"

"I guess what happened last time I was here affected me more than I realized," she said.

He moved to her side and put his arm around her. "Don't worry. I'll protect you. Here, look." He pulled back his jacket to reveal a gun tucked into an inside pocket.

She backed away. Knowing he was armed didn't make her feel safer, but there was no point saying so. Instead, she pushed down her fear and changed the subject. "Where is the underground chamber?" she asked.

He frowned. "You mean the one where the deputy and his girlfriend were held? It's over here." He led her back to the Quonset hut, through two empty rooms to one with a dirt floor and a metal grate in the roof open to the outside air. "We may use this for storage," he said. "It could be useful having a chamber like this that's fairly well insulated."

She suppressed a shudder and forced herself to look around.

"Did you know this is where they found Henry Hake's body?" Reed asked. "They said he died of tularemia. The sheriff suggested getting the health department up here to test, but it turns out tularemia is naturally occurring and even quite common in areas of the West, so testing wouldn't prove anything."

"I didn't know that." She followed him out of the building, relieved to be in the open air again. "What do you think happened to Henry?" she asked.

"I don't know," he said. "Though he was obviously hanging out with a criminal element. Didn't his former bodyguard murder some lawyer in town? And attack the sheriff's fiancée?"

"Yes." At the time, most people had thought Ian Barnes's murder of Andy Stenson had been an isolated incident, but now she wondered if that crime was somehow related to Henry Hake's death. She looked around them, getting her bearings. "Isn't there another underground chamber?" she asked.

"Another one? I don't think so."

"The day those men shot at me, I was looking through the fence. I watched them carry a crate to a trapdoor in the earth. They went down into the ground. But it wasn't here. It was farther that way." She pointed up the ridge.

Reed took her arm. "You must be turned around. This is the only underground space—and as you saw, it was empty. You know, the terrain here can be deceptive. Instead of going into the ground, maybe they just went downhill, behind some rocks or something."

She knew what she had seen, but there was no point arguing with him. "Maybe you're right." She pulled away from him again. "I'm ready to go now."

They walked silently back to where he had parked, Paige forcing herself not to hurry. As they neared the SUV, a pickup truck sped into the drive and stopped beside them. Rob got out. "Hello, Paige," he said. "Mr. Reed."

"What are you doing here?" Reed asked.

"Parker called and asked me to check on you," Rob told Paige. "He was concerned."

Paige wanted to be upset with him for thinking he needed to look after her—but all she felt was relief. "Thanks," she said. "But he had no cause to be worried."

"That's right." Reed put his arm around her again.

She could feel the gun in his jacket digging into her side. "Paige and I had a pleasant lunch, and now we're having a pleasant afternoon together."

Rob looked as if he wanted to take Reed's arm off at the elbow. "This doesn't strike me as the safest place to be, considering all that's happened up here lately," he said.

"You weren't invited here, Agent Allerton," Reed said. "You should leave now."

Paige had no desire for Rob to leave her alone with Reed again. For one thing, his insistence on continuing to touch her and hug her was giving her the creeps. She shrugged out of his grasp once more. "I need to get back to my business," she said. "Rob, could you give me a ride?" Before Reed could object, she turned her most dazzling smile on him. "Thank you so much for lunch, and for taking the time to show me your plans. I'm really pleased with what you're going to be doing with the property."

"I can take you back to town," Reed said. "I'm going there anyway."

"I don't want to keep you any longer," she said. "And Rob is going right to the B and B. Thank you again." Not waiting for a reply, she opened the passenger door of Rob's truck and climbed in.

He didn't hesitate, either, and left Reed standing alone while he climbed in the truck and backed out of the drive. He didn't say anything until they were on the road leading away from the resort property. "Are you okay?" he asked.

"Yes." She hugged her arms across her chest. "A little shaken up, maybe. I don't know what was getting to me more—remembering being shot at the other day, or the sight of all that crime scene tape around the ruins…or Bryce Reed's overly chummy manner. Did you know he was carrying a gun?"

"So am I," Rob said. "Does that freak you out?"

"No. You're a law enforcement officer. He's supposed to be a business executive."

"Maybe with everything that's happened up there, he thought he needed protection."

"Maybe. It still strikes me as odd." She shook herself, trying to dispel her dark mood. "I'm probably just being overly sensitive. There's probably nothing to worry about."

"Maybe not. But I don't trust Reed. I'm not convinced he's not part of whatever is going on up there."

She stared. "He was at the commissioners' meeting last night when those men were killed and that fire was set," she said. "And he was back east when the other crimes occurred."

"I'm not saying he pulled the trigger or lit the match," Rob said. "But I think he knows more than he's letting on." He glanced at her. "And it was very convenient to have those two out of the way, and that gun planted to link them to shooting you. A little too obvious, I think."

"I asked him about what I saw that day on the trail— the two men carrying a heavy crate and stowing it underground," she said.

"What did he say?"

"He said I must have gotten turned around. Or misunderstood what I saw."

"Maybe he really believes that," Rob said. "Or maybe he's a very practiced liar."

She fell silent, replaying everything Reed had said to her that afternoon. She couldn't point to anything in particular that rang untrue. But she couldn't shake the feeling that something was off, either.

Rob parked at the B and B. Paige checked the time on her phone—it was after five, so Parker would have left for his shift at Peggy's Pizza. She noticed Rob scanning the area around the house before he stepped out, and he followed her up the walk to the door, vigilant.

She unlocked the door and tucked her keys in her pocket. When the door was safely locked behind them, she turned to him. "I wanted to be angry with you for following me up to the resort," she said. "But I was so glad to see you."

He pulled her to him and she did what she had been wanting to do for days now, pressing her body against his and kissing him, hard. He responded in kind, his lips claiming hers in a kiss that left her dizzy, heart pounding, craving more. He caressed her waist, then slid one hand to her hip, the other one at the back of her neck, his thumb stroking the pulse at the side of her throat in a way that had her almost purring with pleasure.

She pressed him back against the wall and began fumbling with the buttons of his shirt. Her fingers brushed at the hair on his chest and he growled against her throat, sending a shiver of pleasure running through her. A button popped off the shirt and bounced on the floor at their feet, but she ignored it. He had pulled up the hem of her blouse and splayed his fingers across her ribs, tracing the underside of one breast. She moaned, eyes closed and forehead pressed against his chest.

"Any other guests here?" he mumbled into her hair.

"No. They checked out this morning."

"Good." He slid his hands beneath her thighs and

hoisted her up against him, then kissed her again. Her heart pounded so hard she imagined she could hear it.

Then she realized it wasn't her heart she was hearing—it was footsteps pounding up the walk outside. She broke the kiss and pushed at Rob. "Someone—"

But it was the only word she managed before the front window broke and flames leaped across the room.

Chapter Eleven

Rob grabbed Paige's hand and dragged her away from the spreading flames, toward the back door. He tugged his phone from his pocket as he moved and handed it to her. "Call 9-1-1," he said, and drew his gun.

Smoke was already filling the rooms, and he could hear the crackling sound of the fire spreading rapidly behind them. He eased open the back door and cautiously checked outside. No sign of anyone. Paige had reached the emergency operator and was reporting the fire, her voice surprisingly calm. He took her free hand in his and tugged her out of the house and around toward the front—in time to hear the screech of tires and catch a glimpse of a dark vehicle speeding away.

By the time they had made it into the front yard, the wail of sirens filled the air. He stared after the retreating car, swearing to himself, but a gasp from Paige made him turn around.

"My house!" she moaned, as flames leaped to the second story of the structure.

Rob pulled her close. "You're safe," he said. "Parker is safe. You can build another house."

She nodded, but he could tell she was fighting to hold back tears. She looked up at him. "What happened?"

"Someone threw a firebomb through your front window," he said. "A Molotov cocktail or something similar would be my best guess." The flames had spread so rapidly they must have been helped along by gasoline or some other fuel.

She shuddered. "Who hates me so much?"

He put away his gun so that he could wrap both arms around her. "I don't know," he said. "But I won't give up until I find out."

She fumbled at his chest, and he realized she was doing up the buttons on his shirt—the ones that were left, anyway. "You probably want to, um, straighten up before the firefighters get here," she suggested.

He took over buttoning the shirt and tucking it into his pants. "I'm sorry we were interrupted," he said.

But she didn't answer, her gaze fixed on the sheriff's department SUV pulling in across the street, followed by an Eagle Mountain Volunteer Fire Department pumper and ladder truck. The firefighters poured out of the vehicles and went to work right away. Rob and Paige walked out to meet Gage, who was just getting out of the SUV.

"What happened?" he asked. He scowled at the burning house. The flames were already licking at the roof.

"Someone threw something through the front window," Paige said. "In broad daylight."

A second SUV parked behind Gage's, and Travis climbed out. His fiancée, Lacy Milligan, got out of the passenger side. Lacy hurried to Paige and embraced her. "Travis and I were headed to his folks' place for dinner when the call came in," she said. "I'm so glad you're okay."

"Rob says this wasn't an accidental fire," Gage said,

as Travis joined the two men, a short distance away from the women.

"Paige and I were in the front hall when someone threw a firebomb through the front window," Rob said. "The flames spread immediately. We went out the back door and got to the front in time to see a car speeding away."

"You were in the front hall?" Travis asked. "Had you just come in, or were you going out?"

"We had been out and hadn't been home long." No point in mentioning they had been making out. They had been moments away from doing it up against the wall.

"Paige had lunch with Bryce Reed," Travis said.

"Right," Rob said. "And after that, he took her up to the Dakota Ridge property to show her around. Parker was worried about her and called me, so I drove up there to make sure she was all right. She elected to ride home with me."

"Why would she ride with you instead of coming back with Reed?" Gage asked.

"You'd have to ask her that."

"I'm wondering about the timing," Travis said. "Was someone watching the house, waiting for Paige to come home so they could throw that firebomb? Or did they even know she was home?"

"Reed would have had a good idea about how long it took to travel from his property to the B and B," Gage said.

"A firebomb doesn't seem like his style," Rob said. "And the car I got a glimpse of wasn't his. I'm betting if you question him, he'll have an alibi to prove he wasn't anywhere near Paige's place this afternoon."

A battered Toyota pulled in behind the sheriff's department vehicles and Parker got out. Leaving the driver's door open, he ran to them. "Paige! Peggy told me she heard there was a fire here? Are you okay? What happened?"

Paige hugged her brother. "I'm okay." She glanced over her shoulder at the fully engulfed house. "I'm sorry, but anything you had in there is gone. We didn't have time to save anything."

"I've got my laptop and most of my schoolbooks in the car," he said. "But what happened?" His arm still around Paige, he addressed this last question to Rob.

"Someone threw a firebomb in the front window," Rob said.

"Who?" Parker demanded.

"We don't know," Travis said.

"Do you have any ideas?" Gage asked. "Anybody mad at you for anything?"

"No!" Paige answered before her brother could speak. "Why would you think this has anything to do with Parker?"

"*Does* this have anything to do with you?" Travis asked, addressing Parker.

"No," he said.

"The B and B is my business," Paige said. "Whoever did this wanted to hurt me."

"Parker lives there," Gage said. "Even if he's not involved in anything illegal now, he might have friends from his past who think he betrayed them, or have some other reason to want to get back at him."

"No." Parker shook his head. "I don't even know anyone like that. I was a small-time addict and a petty thief." He looked to Rob. "You know my case. Tell them this doesn't have anything to do with me."

"He's right," Rob said. "I don't think this is connected to Parker."

Travis turned to Paige. "Then what have you done that has someone so upset?" he asked.

"I wish I knew," she said.

"What is your environmental group up to these days?" Gage asked. "Are you involved in any more lawsuits?"

"No," she said. "Nothing like that."

"None of this is Paige's fault," Lacy said. "It's the fault of whoever threw that firebomb."

"We're just trying to figure out what's going on," Travis said. "Knowing who might have a motive for wanting to harm her could help."

"I haven't done anything to anyone," she said. "I even agreed to support CNG Development's plans for the Dakota Ridge property."

"That must have made Bryce Reed happy," Rob said.

"It's not as if my support means anything," she said. "I imagine the county is thrilled to see the property put to good use. Right now it's an eyesore. The research lab CNG is proposing will at least bring in some tax money and maybe even a few jobs."

"What about your ex-husband?" Rob asked.

"What about him?" Her eyes met his, her expression defiant.

"You said he wasn't a very nice man. Would he try to hurt you this way?"

She shook her head. "I haven't talked to him in years. I was so grateful to get away from that marriage that I let him keep most of the money and property." She glanced at the burning house again. "I bought this place with money an aunt willed to me."

"You can rebuild," Lacy said. "Better than ever. You have a lot of friends here in town who will help."

Assistant fire chief Tom Reynolds crossed the lawn to join them. He removed his helmet and wiped sweat from his forehead. "I'm sorry, Paige, but we weren't able to save the house. It went up so fast, I have to think it had some help."

"Someone threw a firebomb through the front window," Rob said.

Tom nodded. "I'm sorry to hear that, but knowing that will help my investigation."

"Thank you for keeping the fire from spreading," Paige said. "I know my neighbors appreciate it."

"Second arson in twenty-four hours," Tom said. "Think we have a firebug in town, Sheriff?"

"I don't know," Travis said. "We'll be looking for any connection."

"The fire's under control," Tom said. "But we're going to be here for a while, until we're sure everything's cold. I'll give you a report when I have one from my investigator."

"Thanks, Tom," Travis said. He turned to Paige and Parker. "Do you two have somewhere to stay?" he asked.

"I can stay with Professor Gibson," Parker said. "He's already made the offer for me to stay at his place anytime, and it'll make it easier to work on our research project."

"Paige can stay with me at my parents' place," Lacy said.

"Rob was staying at the B and B, too," Paige said.

"Don't worry about me," Rob said. "I'll get a room at the motel." Their eyes met. He wanted to pull her close, to comfort her and tell her everything would be all right—but that didn't seem appropriate right now, with an audience.

She leaned forward and squeezed his hand. "Thank you for getting me out of there safely," she said. "I was in such shock, I'm not sure I could have moved."

"I'll be in touch," he said.

"I guess I'd better get back to work," Parker said. "Peggy let me come over here when we heard the news, but I don't want to leave her in the lurch."

"Go on," Paige said. "I'll be fine."

"She will be," Lacy said. "Do you have your car?"

"I left it at CNG's offices this afternoon," she said.

"We can walk over to Mom and Dad's and get my car," Lacy said. "Then I'll take you to get yours." She frowned. "That is, if you have your keys."

"My keys are in my pocket." Paige patted her skirt.

"I'll call my folks and let them know we're not going to make it to dinner," Travis said.

Paige cast a last look at Rob, then let Lacy lead her away. Parker drove off, and Gage left in his cruiser. Travis turned to Rob. "Any ideas?" he asked.

"I'm thinking Paige saw something—or someone thinks she saw something—up at the resort property the day she was shot at."

"The two men who shot her are probably dead," Travis said.

"They may have been the ones to fire at her, but maybe they were acting on the orders of someone else."

"Who?" Travis asked.

"I don't know. Maybe the same person who killed Henry Hake. I think it has something to do with that property, but I can't figure out what. I'm going to do a little deep digging of my own."

"Let us know what you find out," Travis said.

"I will." And then he was going to go after whoever was making Paige's life such hell, and make them wish they had never crossed her.

MR. AND MRS. MILLIGAN were happy to have Paige stay in their guest room. "Stay as long as you need," Jeanette Milligan said. "I'm so sorry about your home and business. I hope you'll be able to rebuild soon."

"As soon as possible," Paige said. Even so, she would lose months of business. She would probably have to find other work to pay her bills. She had money in savings, but she didn't want to exhaust that.

"Do you mind if I give you a little unsolicited advice?" Lacy asked, as she and Paige walked out to Lacy's car.

"Go ahead," Paige said.

"It's easy to get overwhelmed when something horrible happens," she said. "What has helped me is to focus on what is right in front of me at the moment—what I have to do in the next hour. You have a little control over that. Trying to think much further ahead than that can be too much."

"Is that how you survived when you were wrongfully convicted of killing your boss and sent to prison?" Paige asked. She still had a hard time imagining the sunny, stylish woman in front of her living in a women's prison.

"It is," Lacy said. "Now that I'm in a better place, I can afford to think about the future more, but back then, I stayed focused on the now. It helped."

"The future like your wedding to Travis." Paige welcomed the chance to change the subject. "How are the plans coming?"

"They're going great."

All the way to CNG's offices, the two women talked wedding gowns, wedding cakes and wedding decorations. Lacy's happiness was contagious, and life seemed less bleak by the time Paige stepped out in the parking lot of the strip center to claim her car.

The door of CNG's office opened and Bryce Reed stepped out, followed by Mayor Larry Rowe. "Hello, Paige," Reed said.

"Are we interrupting something?" Paige asked, addressing her question to the mayor.

"The mayor and I were discussing groundbreaking for the new research facility," Reed said. "We want to make it a real event, with a barbecue, balloons for the kids, maybe even some games."

"You don't have approval from the county yet, do you?" Paige asked.

"With the mayor behind us, and your support, we shouldn't have any problems," Reed said.

The mayor said nothing, merely glowered at the two women and moved past them toward his SUV. Apparently, Paige's support for his new pet project wasn't enough to make him forgive her for past sins.

When the mayor had driven away, Reed said, "I was wondering if you'd forgotten about your car. I thought it would be gone before I got here, since you left the Dakota Ridge property before I did. You know I would have been happy to give you a ride back here to your car. You didn't have to run off."

She wasn't going to defend herself to this man, who at the moment sounded more like a whiny little boy. "Someone firebombed my house this afternoon," she said. "Do you know anything about that?"

"What?"

"Someone set my house on fire," Paige said.

"Paige, that's horrible." He rushed forward to take her hand. If he was faking his shock and concern, he was doing an Emmy-worthy job of it. "Are you all right? Is the damage very bad?"

"It's gone—everything I own and my business with it." Her voice shook, and she fought hard to keep back tears—tears of both sorrow and rage. "Do you know why anyone would do something like that to me?"

He took a step back. "I'm really sorry to hear that," he said. "But why would I know anything about it?"

Was he really as innocent as he looked? "Nothing bad happened to me until that day I was hiking and looked over onto your property and saw those two men, and they saw me," she said. "Since then, it's been one horrible thing after another."

"I can see how the timing seems suspicious to you," he said. "But from what I know of you and your efforts with the Eagle Mountain environmentalists, I think it's not unreasonable to believe that you're a woman who has made enemies in her life. But I'm not one of them."

Lacy touched her arm. "Maybe we should leave," she said softly.

"Yes." Paige walked to her car. Lacy went with her.

"Maybe the best thing to do would be to avoid anyone from CNG until things cool off," Lacy said. "If they do have something to do with the threats against you, there's no sense making them angrier."

Paige nodded. "You're right. I shouldn't have taken my anger over all this out on Reed." She glanced toward the office, but the door was shut now, with no sign of Bryce Reed.

"It's understandable." Lacy rubbed her back. "When

we get back to the house, why don't you take a hot bath and try to relax? I'll find some clothes for you to change into."

Paige realized the clothes she was wearing smelled of smoke from the fire. A hot bath did sound relaxing, but she didn't want to go to Lacy's house—not yet. She pulled her keys from her pocket. "Is it all right with you if I come to the house later?" she asked. "I'd like to drive around for a while—do some thinking and clear my head."

"Of course," Lacy said. "You'll be careful, won't you?"

"I will. I promise." She got into the car and waited until Lacy had pulled out of the lot before she drove out behind her. When Lacy turned off toward her parents' home, Paige kept going, all the way to the motel out by the highway. She drove around the lot until she spotted Rob's truck; apparently, the fire hadn't spread to the parking area beside her house and reached his vehicle.

She studied the row of rooms facing the parking area, then slipped her cell phone from her pocket and dialed his number. "Can I come see you?" she asked when he answered.

"Of course," he said. "Where are you now?"

"I'm right outside."

She waited, and in a few seconds, the door to one of the rooms opened and he stood there, dressed only in jeans, the phone in one hand. She got out of the car and went to him. When he pulled her into his arms, and into the room, it felt exactly like coming home.

Chapter Twelve

Rob let Paige lead the way, letting her show him what she wanted—what she needed. If she wanted comfort, he would do his best to comfort her. But as she wrapped herself around him and her lips claimed his, he realized she was picking up where they had left off at the B and B—finally letting down her guard and giving in to the passion that had sizzled between them since he had moved in under her roof.

She broke off the kiss and leaned back a little in his arms, her gaze sweeping over him, assessing. "Nice," she said, the single word sending heat through him. She planted a kiss in the center of his chest, and smoothed her hands over his stomach, stopping at the snap of his jeans. His erection strained against the fly, and when she dragged her nails over it, he shuddered.

Her eyes met his. "I hope you have protection," she said.

"I do."

"Oh?" She looked amused. "Awfully sure of yourself, aren't you?"

He gripped her waist, pulling her tight against him. "Paige, that firebomb wasn't the only thing burning in your house and you know it." He slid his hands up to cradle her head. "I've wanted you from the first day I saw you, in the hallway at the courthouse."

She blinked. "I was terrible to you that day. I accused you of not knowing how to do your job."

"Yeah, and I didn't like that one bit. But if you could have seen yourself—so beautiful and fierce and doing everything you could to stand up for your brother. I had to admire that."

"So angry women turn you on?" She slid her hands around to cup his bottom.

"No. But you turn me on."

"That first day, sex was definitely not on my mind," she said. "But you've grown on me." She reached down and started to lower his zipper, but he stopped her, then began undoing the buttons of her blouse. He pushed the fabric off her shoulders and paused to admire the full breasts swelling above the lace of her bra before reaching around and unfastening this garment and tossing it aside also.

She gasped when his lips closed over her nipple, and squirmed against him in a way that made his vision momentarily blur. He grasped her hips, stilling her, and transferred his attention to her other breast. At the same time, he lowered the zipper of her skirt and pushed it and her underwear down, until they puddled around her ankles.

He began kissing his way down her body, her skin soft and warm beneath his lips. When he lowered himself and put his mouth over her sex, she cried out and dug her fingers into his shoulders. He closed his eyes and his senses homed in on the taste and scent of her, the feel of her hands on him and his own desire building within him. All he wanted and needed right now was to be here with her, to give her as much pleasure as he was able.

She squirmed against him, her breath coming in gasps. He looked up, transfixed by the passion playing across her face. Being able to make her forget, at least for this little while, her fear and loss made him feel ten feet tall and bulletproof. She was the most precious thing in the world to him in that moment, worth every bit of aggravation she had ever caused him.

She came with a cry of triumph, and he rose to catch her in his arms, gathering her up and carrying her across the room to the bed, where they fell together, entwined.

Paige reveled in the feel of Rob's body against hers— all warm muscle and masculine strength, his every touch both tender and insistent. They stripped each other of the last of their clothing, and then he fumbled in the plastic shopping bag on the floor beside the bed and came up with a condom packet. Watching him sheathe himself with it left her breathless and trembling, but instead of pushing her down on the bed and kneeling over her, he lay back against the pillows and beckoned to her.

"What do you want?" she asked, grinning.

"The question is, what do *you* want?" He pulled her up on top of him and looked into her eyes.

She felt stripped of more than clothing beneath that gaze. He made her want a lot of things she had told herself for years that she didn't really need—companionship, protection, even love.

She kissed him, long and hard, then positioned herself over him and let him fill both her body and her spirit. They moved together, led by instinct and pleasure. They kept their eyes open, watching each other, seeing passion and trust reflected back. Their movements grew faster and more intense, and she felt herself losing control. But instead of holding back, she gave herself up to the moment, and a second, deeper climax overwhelmed her, even as he found his release beneath her.

They clung together for a long time afterward, her head on his chest, his arms wrapped around her, his sex still inside her. Then, with a long sigh, he rolled them to their sides and slid out. He discarded the condom, then lay back down, pulling her to him once more. "I'm glad you came to find me," he said, stroking her hair. "I wanted to go after you when you left with Lacy."

"She took me to get my car. Then I told her I needed to drive around and think."

"And you drove here." His gaze held the unspoken question—*why?*

"You're the person I wanted to be with," she said. "To tell you the truth, that surprises me—and frustrates me a little, too. I've worked so hard to be independent, it's hard for me to lean on someone else."

"I'm not going to confine you, Paige," he said. "I meant it when I said I appreciated how strong you are. I don't want to change that. But even the strongest nation in the world needs allies. Let me be yours."

She rested her head on his shoulder again, in that warm hollow where she fitted so perfectly. "I'm happy to have you as my ally," she said.

His arm tightened around her. "Does it upset you to talk about what happened this afternoon?"

"I think it might help, actually," she said. "Talking, I mean. Or at least, having you listen."

"Did you run into any trouble when you went back to CNG's office?" he asked.

"Bryce Reed came out of his office when Lacy and I showed up to get my car. The mayor was with him."

"I got the impression the two were pretty cozy on this project," Rob said.

"Larry still isn't speaking to me," she said. "He's never going to forgive me for opposing the original development. Not that I'm losing sleep over it."

"What about Reed?" Rob asked. "What did he say?"

"It's not so much what he said as what I said." She winced, remembering. "I kind of went off on him. I accused him of knowing something about the fire, and about the men who shot at me. He denied it, of course, and I felt bad afterward."

Rob massaged her shoulder. "Don't be so quick to mistrust your instincts," he said. "I can't prove Reed had anything to do with what happened today, but I'm going to be watching him closely. Everything seems connected to that property on Dakota Ridge. CNG owns the land, so how could Reed not be aware of what is happening up there?"

"I think I'm going to let you worry about that, while I focus on rebuilding my business." *And my life*, she silently added. She kissed his neck and sniffed. "You smell like smoke."

He kissed the top of her head. "So do you," he said. "I was getting ready to take a shower when you showed up."

"A shower sounds good. Is it big enough for two?"

"For two people who really like each other."

"Then why don't we give it a try?"

"I like the way you think."

PAIGE LEFT ROB'S hotel room well after dark, after she had called Lacy and apologized for being absent so long.

Rob hadn't tried to persuade her to stay, sensing that she wanted a little space between them to think about what had happened. So they'd parted with a kiss and a promise to talk again the next day. He slept fitfully, the smell of her clinging to the sheets and disturbing his dreams. Paige Riddell was a complex woman who promised to complicate his life considerably. But he had been taking the easy road when it came to relationships for all his adult life. Maybe it was time he tried a different, more challenging path.

He rose early, in time to call his Denver office before his boss reported for work. As he had hoped, the admin, Stacy, answered the phone. "Are you calling to tell us you're cutting your vacation short and coming back to work early?" she asked. "Because we're swamped."

"No," he said. "I'm calling to ask if you can do me a little favor."

"I thought you were supposed to be fishing," she said.

"I am—just not always for trout."

"What do you want me to do?" There was no mistaking the suspicion in her tone.

"I want you to do a little background check on a guy named Bryce Reed. He's chief financial officer of an outfit called CNG Development."

"Is this related to a case you're working on?" she asked.

"Peripherally."

"Is that a fancy way of saying no?"

"I just want a little history on the guy, and to know if he has a record," Rob said.

"The boss won't like it."

"The boss doesn't have to know."

The silence on the other end of the line was so long,

he wondered if she had disconnected. But at last she said, "True. As long as you're on the right side of the law."

"I promise I'm one of the good guys. And I'll bring you a box of Godiva chocolates for your trouble."

She laughed. "I'm not too sure you are a good guy, but I'm not going to pass up good chocolate. I'll run this guy and let you know what I find."

"Thanks."

He ended the call and checked the time—8:45. Too early to call Paige, who had had a rough day yesterday. Too early to drive out to the CNG offices and watch Bryce Reed.

Someone knocked on his hotel room door, and his heart sped up. He hurried to check outside and felt a little foolish when he saw that his visitor wasn't Paige, but Parker. "How did you know this was my room?" he asked, after he had opened the door.

Parker shrugged. "I saw your truck and figured I'd knock on doors until I found you. It's not like the motel is that big."

"What can I do for you?" Rob asked.

"Can I come in?"

"Sure." He stepped aside and the young man moved past him. He sat in one of the two chairs at the small table in front of the window, and Rob sat across from him.

Parker was wearing the same black T-shirt he'd had on the day before, and the same jeans, though he had shaved and smelled of soap.

"Everything go okay with the professor last night?" Rob asked.

"Yeah. He's cool." He shifted in his chair and looked around the room—everywhere but at Rob.

"What can I do for you?" Rob asked again.

At last Parker's gaze met his. "I want to help find out who is doing all this stuff to Paige," he said.

"How can you help?" Rob asked.

"I don't know. But two people are better than one, right?" He ran his hand through his short hair. "I just don't want to stand around doing nothing while someone tries to hurt her again," he said.

"Any ideas who that someone might be?" Rob asked.

Parker frowned. "I was up on Dakota Ridge again the evening after that day you and Paige and the sheriff saw me." He held up his hand. "I know I promised I wouldn't trespass up there again, but this was important. If I was going to find that World War II lab, I had to do it before CNG broke ground on their new research facility. After that, the place will be crawling with construction crews."

"You were there the evening those two men were killed?" Rob asked. "And you're just now saying something?"

"I didn't see anyone killed," Parker said. "And I don't know anything about the fire, either. But I did see some strange stuff while I was up there. Maybe it doesn't have anything to do with Paige, but what if it does?"

Rob studied the younger man. Parker's shoulders were slumped, but his expression was that of a man refusing to accept defeat. "Why come to me instead of the sheriff?" he asked. "I don't have any official role in this case."

No fidgeting this time. "You heard the questions Sheriff Walker was asking me yesterday. He already thinks I might have something to do with all of this."

"I think the sheriff is trying to look at this from all angles and cover all the bases," Rob said. "He's being a good cop."

Parker's look of disdain said he didn't believe "good"

and "cop" should be used in the same sentence. "You didn't turn me in to him after you saw me up at Dakota Ridge that day," he said.

"Maybe I was just trying to impress your sister."

"I figured that was a given. But you wouldn't be the worst thing that ever happened to her."

Rob definitely hadn't expected that, and had to resist the urge to ask Parker to elaborate. But now wasn't the time. "What did you see up on Dakota Ridge?" he asked.

"A helicopter. One of those little ones, like a traffic copter or something. Only this one was very sleek and expensive looking. I heard it coming and ducked into some really deep undergrowth. I figured it was a medical chopper, or maybe military, and would fly over. Instead, it landed right there in the middle of what used to be a street. The door opened and these two guys in camo fatigues, with AR-15s, jumped out. Then a man in a business suit followed them."

Rob sat forward, alert and intrigued. "What did they do?"

"The guys with the guns unloaded a wooden crate from the helicopter, while the guy in the suit watched. There was a pilot, too, but he never got out."

Paige had mentioned seeing two men carrying a wooden crate that day on the hiking trail. "What did they do with the crate?" Rob asked.

Parker shook his head. "I don't know. About that time a deer wandered out of the woods. One of the guys with the guns whirled around and fired on it—just about cut it in half. Totally freaked me out. All I wanted to do was get out of there as fast as I could. I crept back in the woods, as quietly as I could. It was probably only five minutes, but it seemed like forever until I was over the fence, and maybe another fifteen before I got to where I had parked my car, in the woods about a quarter mile back toward town."

"What time was this?" Rob asked.

"It was early. The commissioners' meeting started at six thirty, and this was before then, but not too far ahead of time—maybe six o'clock."

"What time did you leave?"

"It was six forty when I got back to my car."

The fire had been called in at seven thirty. "The crate sounds like the one Paige saw," Rob said. "Similar, at least. Did you recognize any of the men?"

"No. But I have pictures." He took his phone from his pocket, swiped through a few screens, then turned it toward Rob. "I was back in the woods a ways, and I was so nervous I was shaking, but maybe if you blow them up or work some magic in a photo lab…"

Rob stared at the blurry photograph of two men in fatigues and one in a suit, standing by a helicopter. Their faces were too indistinct to make out.

"There's more, if you want to flip through," Parker said.

The next image was a closer shot of the man in the suit. The third picture was zoomed in even closer. Though still not distinct, the photograph did make one thing clear.

"This isn't Bryce Reed," Rob said. And he didn't think the men in fatigues were either of the ones who had been killed and left to burn in the shack.

"No," Parker agreed. "I never saw this guy before in my life."

Chapter Thirteen

Paige spent much of the next day canceling reservations, helping people find new accommodations, dealing with the insurance company and transferring money from savings to pay her ongoing bills. Later, she would need to go shopping, to replace at least a few of her necessities, and she would need to start hunting for a place to live.

She hung up the phone after yet another call and stared out the window of the guest bedroom where she was working. Lacy and her parents were warm and gracious hosts, who lent her clothes and toiletries, and didn't ask questions about where she had been until late the night before, but Paige couldn't stay here long-term. She wasn't comfortable being an unexpected guest, and though the Milligans weren't at all intrusive, she valued her privacy.

She resisted the urge to call Rob. He was probably working, and the last thing she wanted was for him to think that one night of incredible sex had turned her clingy. She had decidedly mixed feelings about getting involved with the lawman. On one hand, he had been a rock at a time when everything else in her world was unsteady. He was a lot smarter—and a lot more compassionate—than she had given him credit for. He liked—

or at least he said he liked—her independence. And yes, the sex had been pretty incredible.

But he wasn't going to stay in Eagle Mountain, and she had no intention of changing her life for the sake of a man ever again. And who was to say all these warm feelings between them hadn't been generated by her current crises situation? When life settled down again, they might turn out to hate each other. Better to not let herself get too emotionally invested until she knew for sure.

She closed the notebook she had been using to keep track of all her tasks and went downstairs. She needed to get out and clear her head, so she took a walk downtown, and ended up at the Eagle Mountain History Museum.

Brenda Stenson looked up from behind the front counter when she entered. "Paige!" Brenda came out to envelop her in a hug. "I heard about your B and B. How horrible for you."

"Yeah, well, I figured I'd see if you had any advice for me when it came to rebuilding." Brenda's own house had been destroyed by an arsonist earlier in the summer. That man had been caught, but what were the odds of two women being the victims of intentional fires in such a short period of time, in such a small town?

"I can tell you plenty of things not to do," Brenda said.

"Such as?"

"Such as don't decide to build something completely different from the original house and expect the insurance company to just hand over the check," she said. "I had to threaten to take my insurer to court, and jump through dozens of hoops, before they finally agreed I could build a triplex in place of my original single-family home."

"I drove by the site the other day and it looks as if things are coming along nicely," Paige said.

"They are—finally. And I have a waiting list of potential renters."

"I guess this means you won't be moving back into one of the units?" Paige asked.

"Dwight and I prefer his cabin on the ranch."

"I'm happy for you." Paige was telling the truth. Brenda had suffered through a lot since her husband, Andy, had been murdered, and she deserved all the happiness she had found with Deputy Dwight Prentice. But Paige wasn't in the same situation as Brenda. "Too bad your rental units aren't already finished," she said. "I'm going to need some place to live until my house can be rebuilt. From everything I heard this morning, it could be a year or more before I'm ready to open for business."

"Oh, Paige, I'm so sorry." Brenda leaned over and squeezed her hand. "What will you do in the meantime?"

"I'll have to find a job. Not a lot of those around, either."

"Maybe you could find another house to run as a B and B," Brenda said.

"I thought of that. But I'd never be able to swing the loan, not when I still have a mortgage on the Bear's Den." Those payments would have to continue to be made while the house was being rebuilt. "I've got a business degree and experience running my own business," she said. "I'll find something."

"When you're ready, I can put you in touch with my contractor," Brenda said. "And if you have any questions about permitting or zoning, I feel like I'm becoming a local expert on those topics."

"Thanks," Paige said. "That's not the only reason I

stopped by this afternoon. I wanted to ask you about Professor Gibson."

"Oh?" Brenda looked surprised. "What about him?"

"Parker is staying with him until I can find a place for both of us," she said. "And they're working together on some kind of project involving that secret World War II laboratory that was supposedly located in the county."

"That's right," Brenda said. "You can blame me for getting the two of them together. I heard the professor was interested in digging into the history of the lab and I knew Parker would be the perfect person to help him. From what Parker tells me, they've really hit it off."

"I guess so," Paige said. "I just worry about Parker getting into trouble, trespassing on private land or poking his nose where he shouldn't while trying to find this lab. And wasn't the government working on some really dangerous stuff there? What if he finds it and is exposed to some horrible disease?"

"I wonder if that's what happened to Henry Hake," Brenda said.

"I heard a rumor he died of tularemia," Paige said.

Brenda nodded. "The rumor is true. And the professor tells me tularemia is one of the things the government was working on in that lab."

"But the underground space where they found Henry Hake wasn't the World War II lab," Paige said.

"No, it wasn't." Brenda shrugged. "Maybe it's just a weird coincidence. Do you want me to put a bug in the professor's ear about making sure Parker plays it safe? He and I have gotten to be pretty good friends since he took an interest in the museum."

"I'd appreciate it," Paige said. "But make sure he

doesn't know it came from me. Parker already thinks I meddle in his life too much."

The bell on the door rang as a couple with two elementary school–age girls entered. Paige excused herself and went back outside. Her phone rang as she was crossing the street—a number she didn't recognize. When she answered, she was surprised to hear Bryce Reed's voice.

"Paige. I'm glad I caught you," he said. "How are you doing?"

"I'm coping." The best answer she could think of, considering all that had happened.

"I'm calling to invite you to a press conference at our Dakota Ridge property tomorrow morning," he said. "We're going to officially unveil our plans for the site and I'd love to have you there."

So he hadn't really been calling to see how she was doing. She couldn't decide whether to be annoyed at his lack of concern or relieved. "So the county commissioners have approved your plans?" she asked.

"Oh, they will," he said. "We've heard only good things from that quarter. This is to get the public excited about what we're going to be doing. Will you be there?"

"I'll try to make it," she said. "What time?"

"Ten o'clock. I'll save a place for you."

He disconnected before she could tell him she wasn't going to be CNG's pet environmentalist, but decided that was her bad mood talking. She would go to the press conference tomorrow, if only for a chance to have another look at the property.

PAIGE WAS WAITING on the front porch when Rob arrived to pick her up for dinner that evening. As he made his way up the walk, he felt a little like a teenager, picking up his date from her parents' house. The full-skirted, flowered dress she wore added to the retro feel of the moment. He took a chance and kissed her cheek in greeting. "How are you doing?" he asked.

"All right." She smoothed the skirt of the dress. "Lacy loaned me this. It's a little frillier than I usually go for."

"It looks good on you," he said. He glanced toward the door. "Should we go inside and say hello?"

"Lacy and her folks are having dinner at Travis's family ranch. They asked me to come, too, but I think they were relieved when I told them I had other plans. They've been great about respecting my privacy."

Maybe that was because Paige was the type of woman who gave off very clear warnings for others not to get too close. Which made him feel especially privileged that she had let down her guard with him. "Where would you like to go for dinner?" he asked.

"Would you mind if we stayed here?" she asked. "I can't go anywhere in town without people stopping me to say how sorry they are about the fire, and wanting to know exactly what happened. I appreciate their concern, but it's wearing me out, not to mention the strain of reliving everything over and over again."

"Staying in sounds good." He followed her into the house, and through to a sunny breakfast room.

"Mrs. Milligan was happy to let me use her kitchen." The table was set for two, with salads and bread already in place, and a bottle of wine chilling in a silver tub. He sat where she directed and a feeling of contentment washed over him—surprising, since he had never considered himself the domestic sort.

While they ate, she talked about her day—the telephone conversations with her guests and the insurance company, and her visit with Brenda. "Do you think Henry Hake could have stumbled upon that old lab and contracted tularemia that way?" she asked.

"It's possible, I suppose," Rob said. "Though no one has found anything to indicate that. Apparently, tularemia lives in the soil in a lot of areas—so it might have been something as simple as digging a hole and breathing in particles of dirt, and being particularly vulnerable because of his heart condition."

"It probably is something like that," she said. She refilled their wineglasses. "Oh, I almost forgot—Bryce Reed called me this afternoon and invited me to a press conference he's giving up at Dakota Ridge tomorrow, to publicly unveil CNG's plans for the research facility."

"Still trying to get your support for the project?" Rob asked.

"I suppose. I want to go to the press conference, if only to get another look at the property."

"I'll go with you. I'd like to have another look at it, too," he added, before she could protest that she didn't need a bodyguard.

"I did some digging into Bryce Reed's background today," he said.

"Oh?" Paige laid down her fork and gave him her full attention. "What did you find out?"

"He's been chief financial officer for CNG for nine months, in charge of special projects. Apparently this research lab is a special project. Before that, he worked for a couple of oil companies, a financial management firm and a manufacturing conglomerate. Pretty run-of-the-mill corporate stuff."

"So nothing juicy?" Paige picked up her fork again and resumed eating the lasagna she had prepared.

"Not in his business life. His personal life is a little more interesting."

Her mouth full, she nodded that he should continue.

"He's been married three times, divorced three times. Five children, none of whom live with him."

"None of that makes him a bad person," Paige said. "I'm divorced."

"I never said it did. No, the interesting part is how he spends his time outside of work. He's been a member of several organizations the FBI classifies as fringe groups."

Paige wrinkled her nose. "What does that mean? I imagine more than a few people here in town consider Eagle Mountain environmentalists to be a fringe group."

"In this case, these are extremist groups that have advocated for things like white supremacy and limiting voting in elections to those with a certain income level."

"Is he a member of any of those groups now?" she asked.

"No. And he's never been convicted of a crime."

"So maybe those earlier affiliations were mistakes of his youth and he's a more moderate thinker now." She pushed her plate away and sipped her wine. "Lots of people make mistakes when they're young. They shouldn't have to pay for them the rest of their lives."

Rob was sure she was thinking of Parker. "Your brother came to see me this morning," he said.

She straightened. "He didn't come to see me. I haven't even talked to him since yesterday."

"He volunteered to help in any way he could to find out who has been harassing you."

Her expression softened. "And he accuses me of worrying too much about him. What did you tell him?"

"I don't know that there's much he can do—not now, at least." He decided not to mention Parker's story about the helicopter and the men with guns. She was worried enough without that burden. "I'm not even sure where to focus our efforts. I can't figure out if CNG is legit or not—they're deliberately calling attention to themselves with this new high-altitude research facility, when they could have pretended they weren't going to do anything at all with the land, and probably gotten away with whatever they wanted for a long time. So maybe they really have nothing to do with any criminal activity and someone has simply been using land they thought was vacant. Something else interesting I found out about them."

"What's that?"

"Your mayor, Larry Rowe, is a stockholder in CNG."

"You're kidding." She paused, thinking. "That's a conflict of interest, isn't it?"

"It could be. Especially if he received the stock recently, in exchange for his support for the Dakota Ridge project. I haven't had time to dig into that yet."

"I always suspected Larry was for sale to the highest bidder," Paige said.

"Reed is the man I'm most interested in," Rob said. "I asked my admin to do some more digging."

"I think we should get to the site early tomorrow," Paige said. "I want to hike up the trail and see if he kept his promise to take down the gate over the trail."

"And if he hasn't?"

"If he hasn't, I might have to raise the question at his press conference."

"That won't make him happy."

"I'm not interested in making him happy," she said. "I'm interested in making things right."

That was the Paige Rob knew best—the crusader, ready to wage battle and defeat injustice. She ignored her vulnerability by being strong. How could he get past the toughness she wore like body armor and prove she had no need for shields with him?

Chapter Fourteen

Paige couldn't have asked for a better day for a hike when she and Rob set out on the Dakota Ridge Trail the next morning before CNG's press conference. The autumn air was so crisp it practically crackled, and the gold of aspen leaves carpeted the trails and shone bright against a Colorado blue sky. Eyes closed, she breathed in deeply of the pine-scented air, her muscles unknotting as some of her tension eased.

"It's better than a tranquilizer, isn't it?" Rob asked. He had pulled a day pack from the back seat of her car and shrugged into it. Dressed in hiking boots, jeans and a flannel shirt worn open over a black T, he didn't look like a cop today—if you ignored the pistol under that shirt, which she intended to do.

"I need the outdoors like some people need coffee," she said. She wore her own pack over a cropped denim jacket, skinny jeans and a muted gold turtleneck. "And this is one of my favorite places—which is why I was so upset when the gate was installed over the trail." She led the way up the red dirt path.

Rob fell into step beside her. "I did a lot more of this kind of thing before I moved to Denver," he said. "I used to hike in the Alleghenies almost every weekend when I lived in West Virginia."

"Why did you stop?" she asked. "It's not like Denver doesn't have hiking trails."

He shrugged. "I got busy at work. I didn't have anyone to go with. Really, I think I just got lazy. You've reminded me of what I've been missing." His eyes met hers and she wondered if he meant he had been missing more than hiking.

She looked away and he continued, "I'm still hoping to get in some fishing before I leave town."

She didn't look at him. "And when will that be?"

"The fishing? I don't know. It depends on the case."

"I meant, when will you be leaving town?"

"That depends on the case, too."

Right. But he *would* be leaving. She needed to remember that.

He took her hand in his. "I'm not going yet," he said. "Maybe I'll take you with me fishing."

Her breath had stopped at the words *maybe I'll take you with me*, and then she scolded herself for being so foolish. Since when had she wanted a man to take her anywhere? To his bed, maybe. Out to dinner occasionally. She appreciated a man who took her into his confidence, though she could admit she didn't readily return the favor. No, she didn't want Rob to take her anywhere. She didn't know what she wanted from him, really, and the idea frustrated her. She was never this indecisive about anything. Could she blame the stress she was under, with the threats on her life and the destruction of her home and livelihood?

Beside her, Rob tensed, one hand reaching for the gun beneath his shirt, the other at her back. "What is it?" she asked, fear tightening her throat and making the words come out strained.

"I thought I heard someone over there." He nodded toward the fence that marked the boundary of CNG's property.

They stood still, listening. After a long moment, Paige shook her head. "I didn't hear anything. It was probably just a bird or a deer or something."

"You're right." He took his hand from the gun, but kept his palm against her back. "As beautiful as it is up here, it spooks me."

"Me, too. And that makes me even angrier. Whoever fired those shots took away my peace of mind in the wilderness."

"The way to regain that peace is to fight back," he said.

"Yes. And that's exactly what I intend to do." She quickened her pace as they passed the place where the shots had been fired, but she couldn't resist the urge to look in that direction. There was nothing to see but an opening in the trees and part of the fence.

Rob put a hand on her back again. He didn't say anything, but he didn't have to. The warm, firm weight of his touch told her he had faith in her to fight through this—and that he would be fighting with her. "I should have brought the bolt cutters and hacksaw with me," she said, her tone teasing. "Would you have to arrest me if I cut off the lock?"

"I don't know," he said. "I might have to place you in my personal custody."

"You might have to handcuff me to keep me from escaping."

"I might have to," he said. "And do a thorough search to make sure you aren't carrying any weapons."

The slope they were climbing had little to do with her heavy breathing now. She hoped the press conference was short. She would suggest they go back to Rob's hotel room and try out some of his ideas.

He must have had the same idea, because he began to walk faster, and she hurried to keep up. They topped a rise and she could see the gate—and the section of trail where the gate wasn't supposed to be. The heavy iron structure was still in place, blocking the way, with heavy barbed wire preventing anyone from getting around it.

She stopped and swore.

"When did Reed say he was going to remove it?" Rob asked.

"Right away, I thought," she said. "Just wait until I see him. I'm going to give him a piece of my mind about this. And I'll make sure every reporter at this press conference hears. If he expects my support for this project, then he needs to keep his promises. He can't restrict public access to a historic trail. This hiking trail has been in use for over a hundred years. The easement transfers with the title and all his money and power can't make it go away. When I finish with him—"

She stopped, aware of Rob's calm gaze on her. He looked as if he was trying very hard not to smile. "What?" she demanded. "What's so funny?"

He shook his head. "Nothing's funny. I just love how you're so passionate."

Warmth spread through her body as she remembered how he had brought out another kind of passion in her— one she had kept in check for too many years. Had he deliberately chosen that word to distract her? "At least you didn't tell me I'm cute when I'm angry," she said.

"No, not cute," he said. "Beautiful, and more than a little intimidating—but not 'cute.'"

He shuddered, and she couldn't help but laugh. She took his hand. "Come on. Let's get over to the press conference."

On the way back down the trail, she stopped again at the opening where she had looked in and seen the two men with the crate. "While I'm holding Reed's feet to the fire," she said, "I'm going to ask him to walk back here with me and look for that opening where the two men I saw stowed the crate. He says he has nothing to hide—let him prove it."

"He's not going to know what hit him," Rob said.

"By the time I'm done," she said. "I have a feeling Bryce Reed is going to wish he hadn't invited me today."

They returned to the car and, after she unlocked it, stashed their packs in the back once more. Instead of then going to the passenger door, however, Rob took a slow walk around the vehicle, studying it carefully.

"What are you doing?" she asked.

"Making sure no one's tampered with it while we were gone." His eyes met hers over the top of the car, and his grave expression sent a shiver down her spine. "Just being careful."

"Do you see anything?" she asked.

He opened the passenger door. "No. I think we're fine."

Her heart sped up when she turned the key in the ignition, movie scenes of exploding cars replaying in her brain. But the engine turned over smoothly and she backed out of the parking space without incident.

The gates to the resort compound were open. The first thing she noticed was that the fading sign advertising the resort had been replaced with a new placard that proclaimed this was the Future Home of Dakota Ridge Research and Development, a project of CNG Development.

The second thing she noticed was that hers was the only car in sight. "Where is everybody?" she asked. She checked the time. Nine forty-five. "The press conference is supposed to start at ten. I would think at least some people would be here by now. Reed, at least, should be here."

"Let's take a look around," Rob said. "But do me a favor and drive back out and park on the shoulder of the road."

"Why?" she asked, even as she turned the car around.

"If someone comes along and closes that gate, you don't want to be stuck in here."

She stared at him. "Do you always think in terms of worst-case scenarios?"

"It's part of my training."

She parked on the shoulder, facing toward town, and they both got out and walked back up to CNG's property, and through the open gates. Their footsteps sounded overly loud on the gravel, and louder still as they crunched over a carpet of dried leaves that had settled in a low spot where the asphalt had worn away from what had once been the main street of the resort.

She zipped up her jacket and fought off a chill. "Maybe I got the time wrong," she said. "Maybe it's supposed to be at noon instead of ten. Though I could have sworn Reed said ten."

"The gate's open," Rob said. "Someone's been up here."

"Then where are they now?" She stopped and scanned the empty streets and abandoned buildings. Empty landscapes usually didn't upset her. Deserted forests and vacant mountaintops usually made her feel surrounded by peace. But this ghost town, where people had tried and failed to make their mark, creeped her out right down to her toes.

Rob took her arm, breaking the eerie spell. "Come on," he said. "Let's go find out where everyone is."

"THIS PRESS CONFERENCE will be the perfect opportunity for us to visit CNG's Dakota Ridge property with no worries about trespassing." Professor Gibson wore an excited expression that made him look years younger than the eightysomething he would admit to. "As much as I appreciate you doing the legwork so far, I'm determined to see the place for myself."

"I doubt they're going to let people wander anywhere they please," Parker said. "And maybe they're only going to let in people they've invited. Paige said Bryce Reed from CNG called to invite her."

"My guess is there will be a lot of people there," the professor said. "You can't keep something like this quiet in a small town. Everyone in the county who can make the time will be there to see what's so special it has to be protected with a big iron gate and razor wire. They won't be able to keep track of all of us. Besides, I intend to question this CNG executive—Reed—to try to determine how much he knows about local history. It could be his bunch has already located the secret lab and is keeping the find to themselves."

"If they're doing that, they won't tell you about it," Parker said.

"You might be surprised how persuasive I can be in my 'teacher' guise," Gibson said. "Most people are con-

ditioned from a young age to obey that voice of authority. It's a very hard habit to break."

Parker wasn't buying it, but he kept quiet about it.
The professor did have an uncanny way of getting things
done. "Paige said the press conference is at ten," he said.
"What time do you want to leave?"

"I want to get there a few minutes early," Gibson
said. "I can introduce myself to Mr. Reed and talk to
him while you have a look around. You still have the
map I gave you?"

"Yes, sir." Parker grinned. He might have guessed the
old man intended for him to do his dirty work. Which
was fine by Parker. Working with the professor was way
more exciting than delivering pizza or writing English
papers.

"We'll take my car." Gibson handed Parker the keys
to the late-model Nissan. "You drive. And park on the
road—not on the property itself. I would rather walk
than get caught in the press of people leaving."

"Okay." Parking on the road was better if they needed
to make a quick getaway, too.

"I've uncovered some new material on how Russia
tested tularemia as a weapon of mass destruction in some
very remote populations on the steppes," Gibson said.
"Fascinating stuff."

For the rest of the drive out of town and up toward
Dakota Ridge, the professor retold the tales of Russian
experimentation, which were both fascinating and hor-
rifying.

"The US didn't do anything like that, did they?"
Parker asked.

"Not that I have been able to determine," Gibson said.
"Of course, the work they were doing in Rayford County

lasted less than a decade. I think by the end, they had determined that tularemia wasn't as effective a method of infecting a large number of people as things like anthrax or Q fever."

"Not with the antibiotics we have today, right?" Parker asked.

"Antibiotics don't do any good if you don't administer them," Gibson said. "In remote areas, or on particularly vulnerable populations, I imagine it would still be quite harmful."

They fell silent for the rest of the drive, Parker remembering the last time he had been up here—the day he had watched a helicopter land and a mysterious tall man in a suit and two men in camo emerge. He hadn't told the professor about that yet. Partly because he didn't want to upset the old man, and partly because he worried Gibson would call off the search for the lab just when they were so close to finding it.

"I had expected more traffic coming up here," Gibson said, as they passed the turnout for the hiking trail and climbed toward the entrance to CNG's property. "Park anywhere in here." He motioned to the side of the road.

Parker swung the car around so that it faced back toward town, and parked on the shoulder. He got out and waited while the professor unfolded himself from the seat and stood. Then he locked the vehicle and pocketed the keys. He figured he would be driving back, so he might as well keep them.

They walked up the road a short distance and turned in at the entrance to the property. The professor stopped first, staring at the big iron gate, which was pulled over the drive and locked with a large padlock. Parker stared at the lock, then shifted his eyes to a piece of paper affixed to the gate with duct tape.

The professor moved toward the paper, and Parker followed. The note, written on what looked like a plain 8½-by-11-inch piece of copy paper, was neatly typed, and read, "Today's press conference has been canceled. It will be rescheduled for a later date. We apologize for the inconvenience."

That was it—no explanation and no signature. The professor pushed back the sleeve of his jacket and checked his watch—a big, old-fashioned nickel-colored one with an expandable metal band. "It is almost exactly ten o'clock," he said.

"There must have been other people who didn't get word about the cancellation," Parker said. "Where are they?"

"I don't know." The professor tugged at the gate. It didn't move. He looked at the fence on either side, which had wicked curls of razor wire along the top. *Prison wire*, Parker thought, then pushed the thought aside.

"Did you say there's another way in?" the professor asked.

"There is, but you have to climb a tree. It's pretty rough going."

Gibson took Parker's arm. "Show me. And don't look at me as if I've lost what mind I have left. I was quite the athlete in my day. I think I can handle a tree. And I didn't come this far not to get a look at this place."

Chapter Fifteen

"I feel like an extra in some B-grade horror movie," Rob said, as he and Paige made their way down the deserted streets. He stared hard at the few remaining buildings. "I keep expecting a badly made-up zombie to lurch out at us."

"You're not helping," she said, and took his arm. "Maybe we should leave. Obviously, no one is here."

"Someone is here," Rob said.

"What makes you say that?"

He shrugged. "It's like when you're in a room in the dark—you can tell someone else is there because the air is different."

She looked at him as if he had grown an extra head. "I have no idea what you're talking about."

"Maybe it's a cop thing."

"Or maybe you're paranoid."

"Maybe that, too."

She inhaled slowly and straightened her shoulders. "If someone else is here, that means they're watching us," she said. "So I really think we should leave."

"We'll leave in a little bit," he said. "But something is going on here, and I'd like to find out what."

She nodded. "Yeah. I would, too. But I'd like to do it without getting shot at this time."

"Me, too." He took her arm and pulled her closer. "We'll just look around a little more. If we don't find anything, we'll leave. Why don't we try to find that entrance you saw to that underground chamber?"

This idea apparently intrigued her enough to set aside her fear. "It's nearer the fence," she said. "Do you remember where I showed you?"

"I think so." He led the way across a crumbling foundation, rusting rebar jutting up from the concrete, weeds sprouting in cracks. They both jumped when a chipmunk darted in front of them.

Paige gave a nervous laugh. "Maybe that was a zombie squirrel," she said.

"Can't be," Rob said. "He wasn't badly dressed."

They relaxed a little after that. Moving into the woods, out of the open, helped, he thought. He didn't feel so exposed in the shelter of the trees. They moved slowly, studying the ground for any sign of a trapdoor or grate, or any access to an underground chamber.

"I know I didn't imagine those two men disappearing into the ground with that crate," Paige said, frustration tightening her voice. "I'm sure it was right around here. I can see the fence where I was standing." She gestured toward the iron bars, and the small opening in the trees on the other side.

"They would have hidden it well," Rob said. "Let's keep looking."

He moved forward a few more steps, scanning the ground. Behind him, Paige let out a cry. "Rob. Come here!"

When he joined her, she was kneeling in the dirt and

leaves, tugging at what he thought at first was a tree root. "I think this is the handle to the trapdoor," she said. "I remember now one of the men lifted a door out of the way before he climbed down into the hole."

Rob dropped to his knees beside her and together they raked back dirt and leaves to reveal a square piece of rusty steel, with a metal handle attached. He stood and helped Paige to her feet, then took hold of the handle and tugged. "Uh." He let out a grunt. "It's heavy."

"Let me help." She wedged her fingers next to his and together they hauled back on the door. With a groan of metal on metal, it shifted, and they managed to drag it aside.

They leaned over and stared down into a black opening. Cool air hit Rob in the face, bringing the scents of damp earth and rusting metal. He pulled his phone from his pocket and switched on the flashlight app, then shone the beam into the opening, illuminating an iron-runged ladder affixed to wooden timbers sunk into the earth. But the darkness beyond quickly swallowed up the light.

"I think it might be an old mine shaft," he said.

"Just down in the ground like this?" she asked. "Don't they usually have some kind of structure over them?"

"Maybe there was one, but it was torn down," he said. "Or the main entrance is somewhere else and this is just a side tunnel someone decided to access. The ladder looks new." He leaned over, trying to see into the darkness. "I wonder what's down there."

Paige took a step back. "I'm not going to go check."

"No." He pocketed the phone again. "Maybe we can get a warrant and come out here with a team." Someone had gone to a lot of trouble to conceal this place, and he wanted to know why. And he wanted to find out what those two men had been hiding down there that had been so important they had tried more than once to kill Paige. "I'd like—"

But he never finished his sentence, as the rapid tattoo of gunfire echoed off the ridge. Men's voices shouted, and branches popped and the ground rumbled with the pounding of running feet.

"We have to get out of here before they see us," Paige said.

But it was already too late for that. A man in forest camo emerged from the woods and raised a rifle to his shoulder. Rob shoved Paige hard toward the opening in the ground. "Get down there," he said.

He was prepared to force her out of the range of gunfire if he had to, but she didn't argue, merely descended the ladder. Rob dropped in after her, as bullets struck the dirt near his head. At the last minute, he reached up and, strengthened by fear and dire need, dragged the trapdoor back into place.

"What do we do now?" Paige's voice trembled as it came to him in the utter darkness.

Rob switched on his flashlight again to illuminate a narrow tunnel lined with rock and timbers. He took Paige's cold hand in his. "Now we run."

THE PROFESSOR NAVIGATED the fallen tree with more agility than Parker would have expected. The old man seemed energized by this adventure, striding through the woods ahead of Parker, looking around with interest. "Do you have the map?" he asked, when they were several hundred yards into the property.

"Right here." Parker took the map the professor had drawn and unfolded it.

Gibson studied the drawing, one hand rubbing his chin. "I think we're about here," he said, pointing to a spot on the map. "So we want to walk this direction." He indicated a large circle on the map. "I think the lab we're looking for is somewhere within this perimeter."

"That's a pretty big area," Parker said. Judging by the scale of the map, the circle took in half a dozen acres or more.

"Then we'd better get busy." The professor pocketed the map. "We have a lot of ground to cover."

They started walking again, but hadn't gone far when a volley of gunfire froze them in their tracks. "We'd better get out of here," Parker said, and turned to leave.

The professor grabbed his arm. "We need to see what—or who—they're shooting at."

Parker gaped at him. "Why do we need to see that? And what makes you think they won't decide to start shooting at us?"

"Come on." The old man pulled on his arm, a lot harder than Parker would have thought possible. "We won't let them see us. But we need to find out what's going on so we can report it to the sheriff."

Reluctantly, Parker let the professor lead him in the direction of the shots. After all, he couldn't run off and abandon the old guy. And despite his heart beating so hard his chest hurt, he had to admit he was curious.

They crept through the trees, keeping to the deepest shadows and moving as soundlessly as possible. They both froze when a man in forest camo ran past, cradling a rifle to his chest. He was only about five feet from them, but he never saw them, so intent was he on his destination somewhere ahead.

They stood frozen for several minutes, Parker scarcely

daring to breathe. The professor's fingers dug into his arm, but Parker didn't flinch. "We need to leave," he whispered, trying again.

"Not yet," Gibson said, and started forward, in the direction the man with the gun had run.

Parker wanted to tell the old fool that while he might have lived a full life and not care if he lost it now, Parker had a lot of good years left, and he wanted to enjoy them all. But then he remembered the professor's tales of growing up in the Great Depression and fighting in Korea, and knew the man wasn't foolhardy; he was just a lot tougher than Parker would ever be. And Parker couldn't let him walk into whatever trouble was up ahead alone. So he tried to straighten his shoulders and not think about getting killed, and walked on.

The gunshots grew louder and more frequent. The two of them reached the edge of a clearing and Parker had to bite his lip to keep from crying out. Ahead of them, Paige and Rob crouched on the ground as half a dozen men with guns ran toward them. Parker closed his eyes, not wanting to see his sister cut to pieces by bullets. Then he opened them again, unable to abandon her to her fate.

"We have to do something!" he whispered to the professor.

Gibson remained silent, though his grip on Parker tightened, as if he feared the younger man might charge into the clearing.

As they stared, Paige and Rob disappeared. Or rather, they dropped out of sight, apparently into a hole in the ground. Rob pulled some kind of trapdoor after them.

Parker's eyes met the professor's, who had pulled out his cell phone and was taking photographs—though his hand shook so badly, Parker wondered how in-focus those pictures would be. He took the phone and snapped a few more shots of the scene, amazed that his own hand was so steady. Then he passed the phone back to the professor, who pushed it into his pocket and motioned that they should head back the way they had come.

Parker glanced over his shoulder at the men with guns standing around the now-closed trapdoor. He hoped he and the professor could get help in time. Or that hole in the ground might as well be Paige's grave.

Chapter Sixteen

Paige followed Rob down the long, dark corridor. Or rather, she followed the glow of his cell phone, which reflected dirt walls braced with rocks and timbers slick with moisture. The floor they ran on was wet, too, so they occasionally slipped and caught themselves by grabbing hold of the wall. "Where are we going?" she said to Rob's back.

He stopped, one hand braced on a timber, and looked back at her. "I don't know," he said. "But the farther away we get from that trapdoor, the better."

"They know where we are," she said. "They don't have to hurry." Whoever "they" were.

He raised his hand. "Listen."

She held her breath and focused on detecting any sound. Was that the scrape of metal on metal as they opened the trapdoor—or merely her own ragged breathing?

Rob frowned. "They're not coming in after us," he said.

"Like I said, they don't have to hurry. Maybe they're waiting for more men to show up, with more guns." She shuddered, picturing the figures in military fatigues who had run out of the woods, guns blazing. The shock had been like stumbling onto a battlefield in the middle of an otherwise peaceful setting.

"Why wouldn't they come after us?" Rob asked. "They saw us climb down here."

Times like this, she wished her imagination wasn't quite so vivid. Maybe their pursuers hadn't followed them down here because they were going to flood the tunnel with gas and asphyxiate them. Maybe they'd throw explosives in after them. Maybe they intended to just seal them off and let them starve to death down here. She didn't say any of this—saying the words out loud would make them too real.

She swallowed hard, forcing back panic. "Why do you think they didn't come after us?" she asked.

He looked up and down the corridor. "I think there's another entrance," he said. "Maybe one that's easier to access." His eyes met hers, difficult to read in the dim light. "But they'll have someone—probably a couple of people—watching the trapdoor, to make sure we don't get out that way."

Paige felt light-headed and weak in the knees. She steadied herself with one hand on the clammy stone wall. "You mean we're trapped down here?"

"Maybe not," he said. "Maybe there's another way out."

"A way they don't know about?" That didn't seem likely.

He touched her arm. "Let's keep moving."

She looked around at the narrow, dark passage and tried not to think about the tons of rock over their heads, or the creepy crawlies that might lurk in the darkness. "What are we going to do?" she asked.

"Come on. Let's go."

They started forward again, walking instead of running this time. "Do you think Bryce Reed is behind all this?" Paige asked. Maybe she shouldn't talk, and instead try to move as silently as possible, but what was the point? Their pursuers knew they were down here, and so far this narrow tunnel was the only place they could be. And talking—thinking out loud about what had happened and giving her mind something to focus on besides their dire circumstances—helped her stay calm. "Was the press conference just a ploy to get me up here?"

"He has to know at least some of what's going on," Rob said. "I've never believed CNG wasn't involved somehow. But why try to lure you up here? Most likely you would have seen no one was here, turned around and gone home. I was the one who suggested staying to look around."

"And I went along with you—willingly. I'm not going to play the guilt game."

He looked at her so long without saying anything that she began to feel uneasy. "What?" she asked. "Why are you looking at me like that?"

"You're incredible, did you know that?"

You're incredible, too. But she bit back the words. They sounded so sappy, and not nearly adequate to convey all she was feeling right now. She had started out hating this man, because of what she thought he had done to her brother, and for what she thought he represented. He knew how she felt, and yet he had come through for her at every turn. "Incredible" didn't begin to express what she was feeling, and part of her—she could admit this, if only to herself—part of her was waiting for him to fail her. For him to show another, uglier side, the way her ex-husband had. The way most people had.

"Come on," she said. "I want to hurry and get out of here."

They had traveled perhaps another hundred yards when the tunnel began to widen slightly, until they were able to walk side by side. Light glowed up ahead. "Is that an exit?" she asked, and began to walk faster.

He took her arm, forcing her to slow down. "Careful," he said, and drew his gun from its holster.

She moved in behind him and let him go first. They hadn't gone much farther before she realized the light they were seeing wasn't from outside the tunnel, but the glow of electric lights. They came to an intersection. The main tunnel continued straight into darkness, while a shorter side turning led to the source of the illumination—a room whose door stood open.

"Wait here," Rob whispered, motioning for her to stand in the main tunnel, just out of sight.

She wanted to protest, to insist that she go with him. But what could she do if they ran into trouble? She didn't have a weapon. At least if she stayed here she could try to go for help if he ran into trouble. She pressed her back against the rough stone of the tunnel wall and waited, counting the seconds. "One Mississippi, two Mississippi…"

She was at fifty Mississippi when Rob called to her. "It's all right. Come look at this."

Still uneasy, she walked down the short hallway and stood in the open doorway, and gasped when she saw the concrete-floored, brightly lit chamber. Rob stood in the middle of the high-ceilinged room, next to a stainless-steel counter lined with lab equipment. Paige recognized a microscope, Bunsen burner, racks of test tubes, beakers and various glass flasks. Several crates were stacked against the wall, like the one she had seen being carried down here. There were many more items she couldn't identify, all of which looked technical and complicated. "It's a laboratory," she said.

"Yes," Rob said. He picked up a flask half filled with a dark liquid and squinted at it. "And unlike the last one we found, this one is clearly in operation." He set the flask down.

She joined him in front of the workbench. "This doesn't look like World War II–era equipment," she said. "What are they doing down here? And who is doing it? Reed didn't strike me as the scientific type."

"I don't know who." Rob looked around them. "As for what, I think it might be related to that World War II operation. Maybe this is the location of that original lab and whoever is behind this decided to update it for their own purposes."

"What purposes?" she asked.

"Henry Hake died of tularemia," he said. "That's one of the diseases the government was supposedly experimenting with back then. What if someone decided to continue that research? Maybe Henry stumbled on it and contracted the disease accidentally—or maybe he was deliberately given it."

She shuddered and wrapped her arms around herself. "Maybe we shouldn't be here," she said. "What if we've already been exposed to something horrible?"

"I don't think there's too much chance of that," he said. "They have to keep the contaminants contained, or no one could work down here." He gestured toward a locked refrigeration unit that hummed in the corner. "Anything dangerous is probably in there."

He pulled out his phone and began taking pictures

of the room. Too bad there was no cell service here. He could call for help.

Paige shook her head. No sense dwelling on what they couldn't do. She needed to focus on what they could do. "If you're right about the purpose of this lab, then it would explain a lot," she said. "The secrecy, and the armed guards."

"The willingness to kill people to keep the operation secret," he said.

"Do you think CNG's plans to build a high-altitude research facility is a cover for this underground operation?" she asked.

"It would be a good one," he said. "It would explain any orders for lab equipment, and any traffic in and out of the property."

"Where are the people who work here now?" Paige asked.

"My guess is Reed sent them away until after the press conference. After that, anyone seeing something like a person in a lab coat would think they were part of the new facility. Reed could even explain away the armed guards as necessary because of the sensitive nature of scientific research."

"The mayor is certainly going to be surprised when he learns his pet project is a big lie," she said. "That won't go well for his career. Is it wrong of me to be a little happy about that, at least?"

Rob reached out and pulled her close. "Remind me to never get on your bad side," he said.

"You've already been on my bad side," she said. She rested one hand on his chest, over the reassuring, strong beat of his heart. "Or have you forgotten already?"

He moved her hand to his lips and kissed her fingers.

"I loved that you were so fierce. And you were attracted to me even back then, though you wouldn't admit it."

She pulled her hand away and tried to muster a look of outrage, though she was afraid the most she could manage was amusement. "Just like a man—imagining that every woman he meets is falling all over herself for him."

"But you're not just any woman." He kissed her cheek.

She wanted to turn her head and capture his mouth with her own, to lean into this moment and let desire and affection obliterate the fear and worry. But that wouldn't be smart, and it wouldn't help get them to safety. So instead, she pulled away from him.

"Come on," she said. "Let's go find a way out of here."

PARKER DROVE WITH his foot to the floor, the engine in the Nissan screaming in protest. Professor Gibson gripped the dash and spoke through gritted teeth. "You're not going to help your sister if we crash before we get to town. If you slow down, I could call for help."

"There's no phone service up here. And we won't crash," Parker said over the screech of brakes, as the car fishtailed around a hairpin curve. Now wasn't the time for caution. Paige and Rob didn't stand a chance if those thugs with guns caught up with them.

The professor's only answer was a sharp intake of breath as the rear wheels of the car skidded on gravel. Five minutes later, they shot out onto the pavement of the highway that led into town. The needle on the speedometer edged up to ninety. Parker wouldn't have believed the little econobox could go that fast. As they entered the town of Eagle Mountain, a cruiser parked on the side of the road hit its lights and siren and swung in a U-turn to follow them. Parker ignored the cop and kept going, skidding to a stop in front of the sheriff's department. He left the engine running and was out of the car before the professor had unfastened the seat belt.

"Parker Riddell, what the—?" The rest of Deputy Dwight Prentice's shouted question was cut off when the door to the sheriff's department closed behind Parker.

Adelaide Kinkaid looked up from behind her desk in the lobby, then stood as Parker trotted past. "Young man, where do you think you're going?"

"I need to see the sheriff," Parker called over his shoulder.

Sheriff Travis Walker stood in the doorway of his office. "Parker? What's going on?"

"Paige and Rob are in big trouble up on Dakota Ridge."

The professor and Dwight had caught up with him, Gibson looking much paler and older than he had up on the ridge. Dwight had him by the arm and led him to a chair in front of Travis's desk. "I clocked him doing ninety as he came into town," Dwight said. "He's lucky a dog or a kid didn't run out in front of him."

"You have to get as many officers as you can up to Dakota Ridge now, before it's too late," Parker said. They had already wasted too much time.

"Calm down and tell me what's going on," Travis said. He sat behind his desk, clearly not in a hurry to go anywhere.

"We might already be too late!" Parker's voice broke on the words, and he closed his eyes, fighting for control.

Travis turned to the older man. "Professor Gibson, what happened?"

"Bryce Reed invited Paige to a press conference up at CNG's Dakota Ridge property," he said. "Agent Allerton insisted on accompanying her. Parker and I decided to go, as well."

"Why did you and Parker decide to attend the press conference?" Travis asked.

"What does that matter?" Parker asked. "The point is, when we got there, there was no press conference. There wasn't anyone there. The place looked deserted."

"We decided to take the opportunity to look around." The professor took up the story again. "As you may know, I have an interest in the World War II–era laboratory that operated somewhere in the county. My research indicated that the lab was probably in an old mine on the property now owned by CNG Development. I wanted to see if my hypothesis was correct."

"Except we heard gunshots, and then a bunch of men wearing camo came running out of the woods," Parker said. "Then we saw Paige and Rob. The men with guns were shooting at them." He swallowed, still unable to believe what he had seen.

Travis looked at the professor again. "He's telling the truth," Gibson said. "Paige and Rob managed to escape by descending into a hole in the ground, and pulled a trapdoor over them." He leaned forward, hands gripping the arms of the chair. "In thinking it over, I believe they may have found an entrance into the mine where that historic lab is probably located. I'm almost sure of it."

"What happened then?" Travis asked.

"What happened is that we got out of there and came to get you," Parker said. "You've got to do something."

Travis nodded. "How many men with guns did you see?" he asked.

"A dozen," Parker said.

"There were six," the professor said. His eyes met

Parker's. "It seemed like more, with all the shooting, but I took the time to count. There were six."

"We'll need reinforcements," Travis said. He picked up the phone.

"Who are you calling?" Parker asked.

"We'll need to get the SWAT team from Junction here."

"We don't have time for that," Parker protested.

"We can't go in without a plan and enough personnel to overwhelm them," he said. "If you want us to save your sister, we need a little time to prepare."

"We don't have time," Parker said again, though with less fervor. "They could already be dead."

"I hope not," Travis said. "But going in unprepared won't save them."

"Parker." The professor's voice, strong and steady, cut through some of his panic.

He looked at his mentor. "What?"

"Remember that Paige is with Agent Allerton," Professor Gibson said. "He's a trained law enforcement officer, and he's armed. And I believe he will do everything in his power to protect her."

Parker nodded. He wanted to believe that. He couldn't afford not to believe it. "What do we do now?" he asked.

The professor motioned to the chair beside him. "We wait. And we pray."

BEYOND THE LABORATORY, half a dozen smaller tunnels branched off from the main corridor. Paige and Rob shone the light of Rob's phone down some of these. Most of them led nowhere, either blocked by piles of debris and collapsed timbers, or simply unfinished, as if the original miners who had excavated here had found nothing worth further exploration.

"How far have we walked?" Paige asked after a while. Her feet ached from navigating the uneven, rocky tunnel, and the damp chill underground had settled in, so that she shivered every time they stopped to rest or check out a detour.

"A couple of miles, I think," Rob said. "I understand some of these old mines extend for miles."

"I can't believe no one has come after us yet," she said. "Are they going to try to starve us out?"

Rob didn't answer. Instead, he illuminated yet another niche carved out of the rock, this one starting about five feet above the level of the main tunnel. "They didn't get very far with this one," he said. "Or maybe it was supposed to hold some kind of equipment?"

"Unless it leads to a way out of here, I don't care," she said. "Did you hear what I asked? Why hasn't anyone come after us?"

"I heard you, but I don't have an answer." He must be as tired and scared and cold as she was, but he didn't show it. Though maybe what she had mistaken for calm was merely grim determination.

"I wish we'd thought to bring our backpacks from the car," she said. "Then at least we'd have water and food and a warm jacket." The pack she carried hiking was equipped with all kinds of emergency supplies.

"And if I'd brought my submachine gun maybe we could blast our way out of here."

"Do you have a submachine gun?" she asked.

"No. But as long as we're wishing for things, that's what I'd wish for." Rob took her arm and they started forward again, but had gone only a few feet before he yanked her against him, hard. She would have cried out, but he clamped his hand over her mouth. "Listen!" he hissed, so close to her ear she felt the warmth of his breath.

She listened, and heard a sound she thought at first was rain drumming on a metal roof. Her knees turned to jelly as she realized she was hearing the sound of running feet on stone—running toward them.

"This way." Rob yanked her back the way they had come. When they reached the niche in the side of the tunnel, he boosted her up into it, then crawled up beside her, then switched off his phone, plunging them into darkness.

She clung to him, dizzy with fear and disoriented, afraid if she moved she'd go sliding out of the narrow space. She could fall, and never stop falling into the bottomless blackness.

Rob gripped her just as tightly with one hand. She imagined his other hand held his gun. She wondered how many of their attackers he could kill before he was dead himself. Or maybe they would both be dead before he could fire a single shot. She hoped the end was quick, and then in the same breath, rage rose up at the very idea. She was too young to die! And how cruel that she might do so just when she had found a man she could love again.

She hadn't seen that one coming—falling in love with Rob Allerton, of all men. But here in the darkness, with his arm around her and their lives in danger, all the fears and worries that had kept her from love before seemed beyond petty. Here was a man who respected—even admired—her independence, who laughed at what he called her fierceness and who made her feel more alive than anyone she had ever been with. How cruel to find all that only to lose it.

Faint light glowed in the corridor now, and the sound of tramping feet was much louder—louder even than her pounding heart, which hammered painfully in her chest. Surely they would hear it and discover them in their hiding place.

The light grew brighter, the tramping feet louder. These people weren't even trying for stealth, they were so certain that they would find their prey. "Spread out!" one man commanded. "Search all the corridors. They won't have gone far."

She closed her eyes and rested her head on Rob's shoulder. She didn't feel fierce now—only numb and almost paralyzed with weariness. The running men grew closer, closer, the echoes of boots hitting the hard stone floor bouncing off the walls and filling up the narrow space with sound. She clenched her teeth, dug her fingers into Rob's arm and waited for the end.

Time stopped, and she didn't know how long she waited like that, until Rob shook her shoulder. "They're gone," he whispered.

She opened her eyes to darkness again, and silence. She resisted the urge to shake her head and try to unclog her ears. "They didn't see us?" she whispered.

"They didn't see us." He caressed her cheek, then kissed her, his lips strong and tasting so sweet. She returned the embrace, all the love and fear and despair that warred within her distilled into that desperate, drowning kiss. She wanted to throw her arms around him, to climb into his lap and press her body to his, but their narrow hiding place prevented that. She had to settle for the connection of that kiss, tongues twined and lips melding, a communication that went beyond words.

When they broke the kiss she was left breathless, and it was a moment before she could speak. "Maybe this really isn't the time for this," she said.

"Maybe not." He traced her lips with one finger. "But I can think of worse ways to spend my time."

"Rob, I—"

"Shhh." He pressed his finger to her lips. "We'll talk later. Right now we have to go, before they come back."

He climbed down from the niche, then helped her down, and they hurried away, in the opposite direction from where the armed men had headed. Rob kept the phone off, so they had to navigate in the darkness, but it wasn't as difficult as she would have thought. The tunnel was straight and the walls close enough that she could place a hand on either side to guide her way.

When Rob stopped abruptly, she stumbled into his back. "What is it?" she whispered.

"Another side tunnel." He switched on the cell phone and shone the light to their left, then swore under his breath.

Paige bit back a scream and stared at the body of Bryce Reed, slumped against the wall, his throat cut like an awful red grin.

Chapter Seventeen

Rob switched off the light, but he had seen enough to know that Bryce Reed hadn't been dead very long. The blood that spilled over the front of his shirt still shone wetly, and rigor hadn't yet stiffened the body.

"Does this mean Reed didn't know about what was going on, after all?" Paige asked. "He must have stumbled on the operation, the way we did, and they killed him."

"Maybe," Rob said. "Or maybe he was working with them, but had outlived his usefulness to them."

"When those men don't find us, they'll come back this way to search again," she said.

"Yes." They couldn't afford to stay here. "We know there has to be another entrance, since they came that way," he said.

"They'll have someone guarding it," she said.

"But probably only one or two people," he said. "They can't have had that big of a force. The two men you saw that first day on the trail are dead—probably killed because they had attracted too much attention to the operation. Reed is dead. That leaves whoever is in charge—the man in the suit—and half a dozen guards."

"What man in a suit?" she asked. "I never saw a man in a suit."

"Parker saw him. He was up here one day and a helicopter landed. A man in a suit and two guards in fatigues got out and unloaded a crate, like the one you described."

"He never said anything to me about that."

"He didn't want to worry you."

"But he told you. And you're a cop. He doesn't want to have anything to do with cops."

"Neither did you. I guess people can change their minds." Rob had once thought she was an overly protective, cop-hating crusader who viewed him as the devil incarnate. Now she was the dearest person in the world to him. He took her arm. "It doesn't matter now. We need to get to the entrance before they come back. Once we're there, we'll figure out how to get past whatever guards they've established."

"You make it sound so simple," she said, as they started down the tunnel once more. "I wish I had your confidence."

It was more bravado than confidence, but he'd rather go out charging into daylight than cowering in the darkness.

They moved quickly now, more confident with navigating by feel and instinct. The floor had a steady upward incline, a good indication that they were moving toward the surface.

"Do you feel that?" Paige asked. "It's cooler air. I think we're getting close."

"Not far now," he agreed.

Another fifty yards and he could discern the outline of the timbers that shored up the tunnel. "The light must be coming from the entrance," Rob said. He halted and put a hand out to stop her. "Wait here," he said. "I'm going to check things out."

For once, Paige didn't argue, though she squeezed his hand and held on, so that he had to pull away from her. He drew his gun and moved stealthily forward, ears attuned to any sound. Soon he could make out the entrance, or adit, a wooden structure that jutted out from the rock face of the ridge, heavy beams supporting a metal roof. An exit gate made of thick iron bars stood open.

Rob moved forward, staying close to the wall, as much in shadow as possible. He couldn't hear any voices, or people moving about, but he wouldn't risk his life—and he especially wouldn't risk Paige's—on the chance that their pursuers had been careless enough to leave the entrance unguarded. Most likely, one or two people were out there, their guns trained on the adit, waiting for anyone to emerge.

He moved all the way into the adit, stopping when he bumped up against a stack of crates that lined the wooden wall. The lid was partially off one of the boxes. Rob stared down at sticks of dynamite with long fuses attached. Other boxes contained metal construction fasteners and nails. A few lengths of metal pipe lay alongside. Sacks of concrete mix lined the opposite wall. It looked like someone planned to expand the operation, perhaps by opening up some of the sealed-off tunnels, or blasting new ones. They had better know what they were doing, or they could bring the whole place down.

Bring the whole place down. This thought echoing in his head, Rob snatched up a handful of dynamite sticks and retraced his steps to Paige. "Hold these," he said, shoving them at her.

"What?" She stared at the objects in her hands. "Is this dynamite? As in explosives?"

"Yes. And we're going to use it to get out of here."

"How?"

He took the dynamite sticks from her and began arranging them at the base of one wall of the tunnel. "I'm going to set up an explosion to collapse the tunnel here. That will keep the men we saw earlier from traveling back this way. Any guards out front will probably come in to investigate—or they'll head to the other entrance to help their coworkers."

"Or they'll stay put and wait for us to come out," she said.

"That's a possibility, too, but I'm betting on them running in to investigate, in which case I'll be ready to pick them off." He finished arranging the dynamite and stepped back.

"What makes you think you won't bring a ton of rock down on us?" she asked.

"Because you're going to be waiting up at the entrance. And I'm going to be standing as far away as possible when the explosion occurs."

"How are you going to light the fuses?" she asked. "We don't have any matches."

"No, but I have this." He drew his gun. "A bullet striking the dynamite will set it off."

She looked doubtful. "And you know this how?"

"Let's just say my friends and I experimented during a kegger when we were young and stupid."

She laughed—nervous, desperate laughter. "It's a crazy, dangerous idea."

"It is," he agreed. "But I can't think of a better one. Can you?"

"No."

"All right." He took another step back. "You go up to the entrance. There are a lot of boxes and stuff piled against the wall. If you crouch down behind them, anyone running past shouldn't see you. After the explosion, I'll wait here to catch whoever comes in to investigate."

"Okay…" She started to move away, then came back and grabbed his shoulders and pulled him down for a fierce kiss. "I love you," she said. "Remember that."

"I love you, too," he said, but she was already gone, hurrying up the tunnel. He hoped that wouldn't be the last time he would see her. Though he had laid out the plan for her as if it was a sure thing, there were plenty of variables he couldn't account for. If things didn't go their way, they might both be dead in a very short time.

PARKER STOOD IN the parking lot for the hiking trail, hands shoved into the pockets of his jeans, staring down the road as if he could somehow see through the trees to what was going on at the abandoned resort. Almost two hours had passed since he had seen those men go after Paige and Rob. She might very well be dead by now.

"The sheriff is doing everything he can." The professor joined him at the edge of the lot. On the other side of the gravel space, Sheriff Walker and his deputies milled about with half a dozen men and women in black pants and shirts, body armor and helmets.

"What are they waiting on?" Parker asked. "Why are they wasting time standing around?"

A sheriff's department SUV pulled into the lot and Gage climbed out. "I've been trying to locate Bryce Reed," he said. "He's not at his office. He's not answering his phone. None of the news outlets knew anything about a press conference."

"He made it up, to get Paige up here," Parker said. "If something has happened to her and he's still alive—"

"Don't say anything rash." The professor gripped Parker's shoulder. "Wait and see what happens."

All he had been doing was waiting. This was worse than being in prison. At least then he had had an idea of when the waiting would end. And he had known that he deserved to be there, to pay for the crimes he had committed. Paige had never hurt anyone. She didn't deserve to die this way.

The sound of tires on pavement made them all turn, to see a black SUV make a screeching turn into the lot. It came close to hitting some of the SWAT members, who jumped back and glared at the new arrival. The driver's-side door opened and a tall man with a crooked nose and heavy jowls stepped out, his expression thunderous.

"You don't have any business here, Larry," Travis said, walking toward him.

"Who is that?" Parker asked the professor.

"That's the mayor of Eagle Mountain, Larry Rowe," he said.

"What is going on here?" Rowe demanded. "Why are all you people here? What's happened?"

"This isn't your concern, Larry," Travis said. "You need to leave."

Parker stared at the mayor, who looked like a boxer. Where had he seen him before, very recently?

"I won't leave," Rowe said. He turned to one of the SWAT team members. "Is this some kind of training exercise? Do you have CNG's permission to be here?"

"We're not on CNG property," Travis said.

"You're adjacent to it," Rowe said. "What you do here could affect them."

"Go home, Mayor," Travis said. "As I said, this doesn't concern you."

"I won't leave until you answer my questions." Rowe folded his arms across his barrel chest. "Just because you have a gun and a badge doesn't mean you can throw your weight around."

Parker moved closer, to get a better look at the mayor. "You're the man I saw here that day," he said. "The man who was in the helicopter."

The mayor glared at him. "Who are you?"

Parker ignored him and turned to Travis. "He was here, on CNG's property," he said. "He landed in a helicopter, with two men in camo, with guns. Like the men who were after Paige and Rob." Was the sheriff believing any of this? He had such a stone face, Parker couldn't tell.

"I don't know what he's talking about," the mayor said. He glared at Parker. "What were you doing on CNG property? That's trespassing. Sheriff, you need to arrest this man for trespassing."

The sheriff stared at Parker, as if he was considering doing just that. Parker took a step back. He had made a mistake, saying anything.

The leader of the SWAT team joined them. In the black clothes with all the extra elbow, knee and shoulder pads, and the heavy helmet, he looked like something out of a cyborg movie. "We're ready to go," he said.

Travis turned to Parker. "You stay here," he said. "We'll radio when it's safe for you to join us."

Parker nodded. "All right."

A car door slammed and they turned in time to see

the mayor, tires squealing, speeding out of the parking area. "Want me to go after him?" Gage asked.

"What was that about a helicopter?" Travis asked.

Parker shook his head. "I'll tell you later. Go help Paige."

Travis turned to the others. "All right," he said. "Let's go."

PAIGE CROUCHED BEHIND the crates piled at the entrance to the mine, trying not to think about the sticks of dynamite she had seen lying in the top box like rows of Christmas crackers, but so much more deadly. She watched the entrance, while her ears strained to hear what was going on behind her, back with Rob.

He had promised to stand well away when he fired into the pile of dynamite, but what if something went wrong? What if some fault in the rock made it come down on his head? What if the explosion brought down only part of the wall and the gunmen were able to get through?

What if? What if? She had to stop thinking about all these questions that couldn't be answered and focus instead on what she could control. When the explosion happened, men were likely to come running through that entrance and she had to be ready.

She thought she was prepared for the explosion, but when it came, the shock threw her forward against the crates, and a wave of dust rolled through the tunnel and over her. Her ears rang from the concussion of the blast, so that she was only dimly aware of a deep rumble and a sound like cracking earth. Then all fell silent, so silent she wondered if she had gone deaf.

The light shifted and she looked up to see the silhouette of a man in the mine entrance, broad shouldered and holding a rifle. She ducked down lower behind the boxes, praying he couldn't see her in the haze of dust.

Then he began running, boots pounding hard against the stone as he raced past her. A few seconds more and a single shot pierced the silence. She held her breath, waiting for more, but all was still. She wanted to call out to Rob, to make sure he was safe and alive, but she knew she couldn't. She didn't know who might be listening.

So she kept silent and waited, as seconds and minutes dragged by. She had no idea how much time had passed when a shadow fell over her and she looked up to see a second man in the doorway. This man was shorter than the first, and not as burly, but he, too, carried an automatic rifle. He took a step toward her, and then another. "Jake?" he called.

Jake didn't answer. The second man shifted his rifle so that it pointed forward, his hand near the trigger guard. Would he see Rob before Rob saw him? Would he kill him?

Without moving, Paige scanned the area around her, searching for a weapon. She needed to stop this guy before he got to Rob. He took another step toward her, and another, moving faster now, his rifle at the ready. When he was even with her hiding place, Paige lunged, grabbing on to his calf just below the knee and yanking with all her might.

He went down like a tree felled in the forest. Before he hit the floor, she stood and brought a length of metal pipe down on his head as hard as she could. When the pipe made contact with his skull it sounded like a melon splitting open, and she dropped the pipe in shock. The man moaned, then didn't make another sound.

Paige hurried down the tunnel and met Rob running toward her. "What happened?" he asked, grabbing hold of her.

"Another man came in and I was afraid he was going to kill you, so I hit him with a pipe. I think I might have killed him."

"Let's get out of here," he said, and pulled her toward the entrance.

They had to step around the man she had hit. He lay very still in a pool of blood. "Don't look," Rob said, and tugged her past him.

After spending so much time in the dark tunnel, Paige found the light outside blinding. She and Rob both put up hands to shield their eyes. She expected to see yet another man there with a gun, but there was no one, and she sagged against Rob with relief. "We did it," she said, the words barely audible. "We did it."

"Let's get out of here," he repeated.

"Oh, I don't think you're going anywhere."

They turned at the words and Paige gasped as she recognized the man who had said them. "Larry?"

"Throw down your weapon, Agent Allerton," Mayor Larry Rowe said.

"Larry, what are you doing here?" Paige asked. And with a gun. Larry had always struck her as the quintessential corporate type, comfortable only behind a desk or in a boardroom. Seeing him here, threatening them, threw her off balance.

"You're the man in charge of this operation, aren't you?" Rob asked.

"The gun, Agent Allerton."

Rob tossed the gun into the dirt. Larry kicked it aside, sending it skittering into the underbrush, well out of reach.

"I don't understand," Paige said. "What are you doing here? That laboratory we saw—are you really making biological weapons down there?"

"So many questions," Larry said.

"Why not give me the answers?" Paige said. "You're going to kill me anyway." The longer she could keep him talking, the longer they would stay alive. And the longer she and Rob might have to see some way out of this dilemma.

"You always did think you were the cleverest person in the room, didn't you?" Larry's mouth twisted into a sneer. "No one dares cross Paige Riddell, because she has all the answers. And yet you had no idea what was going on up here, right under your nose."

"You found the World War II lab and decided to resume the research that was done here," Rob said. "Some foreign organizations will pay a great deal of money for what you could produce there."

"Very good, Agent Allerton," Larry said.

"Did you kill Henry Hake?" Paige asked.

"Henry was happy to lease the land to us after you stalled his plans for his resort," Larry said. "So you could say that you're the one who set all this in motion."

"Why did you kill him?" she asked.

"He discovered what we were doing and objected, so we had no choice but to eliminate him."

"Henry's bodyguard, Ian Barnes, worked for you," Rob said. "Henry told everyone Barnes came to him from one of his business partners—that was you. Barnes murdered Henry's lawyer, Andy Stenson."

"Stenson was the first to figure out what we were doing here, so I asked Ian to get rid of him." He shrugged, as if ordering a murder was no big deal.

"Were Wade Tomlinson and Brock Ryan working for you, too?" Paige asked. "The men who murdered Angela and Greg Hood and kidnapped Deputy Gage Walker and his girlfriend?"

"Tomlinson and Ryan were two of my best allies," Larry said. "But they balked at killing that kid, so they had to go, too."

"Those two men whose bodies we found in that burned-out shed—did they work for you, too?"

"Oh yes." He frowned. "I thought they'd take care of you and you'd be out of my way for good, but no such luck. After that, they weren't any use to me."

"So pretty much everyone who helped you ended up dead," Rob said.

"Not everyone," Larry said. "My brother, Garrett, played the part of a billionaire who wanted to buy that mining book from Brenda Stenson. I didn't want someone else to get their hands on it and figure out where the original laboratory was." He chuckled. "He was the 'top secret agent' who fooled Eddie Carstairs, too. That was a role he really liked." Eddie had threatened Brenda Stenson and destroyed the book about the secret World War II laboratory.

"Where is your brother now?" Paige asked.

"In Connecticut, believe it or not. Acting. I told him I'd pay him a lot more money than some two-bit dinner theater, but he wasn't interested. Go figure."

"Why did you kill Bryce Reed?" Rob asked.

"He was getting nervous about the project," Larry

said. "So few people have the courage of their convictions these days."

"But—" she began.

"Enough!" He jabbed the gun in their direction. "Back into the mine."

Paige darted her eyes to Rob's, hoping to see that he had a plan. But the only emotion she could read on his face was the same desperation she felt.

"Quit stalling!" Larry barked.

She lurched forward, stumbling on a rock near the mine entrance, and fell hard, the rough grit scraping her palms. "Get up!" Larry shouted, and fired into the ground near her head.

Rage filled her. How dare he shoot at her while she was down? She closed her fingers around a handful of grit and rose up on her knees. Larry bent toward her and she hurled the grit into his face. The gun went off again, the bullet thudding into the dirt near her feet.

Rob jumped on Larry's back and forced him to the ground, then struck a savage blow to his hand, sending the gun flying. He was kneeling on Larry's back, forcing his face into the dirt, when half a dozen figures in black pants and bulletproof vests and helmets jogged toward them.

"No!" Paige cried, and lunged toward the discarded gun. She hadn't come this far to go down without a fight.

"Paige, it's all right." One of the men raised the visor of his helmet and she recognized Travis. "Put the gun down," he said gently.

She let the weapon fall and sank to her knees. One of the other officers moved forward and secured the mayor, while another helped Rob to stand.

Rob walked over to her, pulled her to her feet and put his arm around her. "Let's get out of here," he said.

She laid her head on his shoulder. "That's the best idea I've heard all day."

Chapter Eighteen

All Paige wanted was to take a shower, have a good stiff drink, eat a steak and collapse, but first she and Rob had to reassure Parker and Professor Gibson that they really were okay. Then they had to repeat the reassurances for Lacy and Brenda and Adelaide and pretty much everyone else in town.

Then they had to tell their story to the sheriff, and tell it again for their official statement. Repeating the details made the events of the last six hours seem even more surreal. It was like recounting a movie, or a horrible dream. Those things hadn't really happened to her, had they? But she had the bruises and scrapes to prove it, and memories that would haunt her for a long time to come.

"We've contacted the authorities in Connecticut," Travis said. "They'll arrest Garrett Rowe for the part he played in all this and we'll extradite him here."

"I'm amazed that Larry persuaded so many people to work with him," Paige said. "I never thought he was particularly charismatic."

"For some people, money substitutes for personality," Rob said.

"What was in the crate you saw them carrying, that first day when you were on the trail?" Travis asked.

"I have no idea," she said. That was one question she hadn't gotten around to asking Larry.

"My guess is it was lab equipment," Rob said. "It will take weeks—maybe months—to collect and analyze everything in that lab. It's also possible one or more of the crates Paige and Parker saw contained lab cultures or samples of bacteria or germs they wanted to experiment with."

"What are you going to tell your aunt about Henry?" Paige asked Rob, remembering what had brought him back to Eagle Mountain.

"I'll tell her the truth—that he was doing business with some bad people and they killed him. That's all she wanted, to know what really happened."

"It's so sad," Paige said. "What does Larry say about all of this?"

"He isn't talking," Travis said. "But with your testimony and Rob's, and the evidence from the site, I don't think we'll have any problem putting him away for a long time."

"What about the armed guards who tried to kill us?" Paige asked.

"We found one of them dead near the mine entrance, and another one with a pretty severe concussion, but he'll live," Travis said. "We arrested four others as they emerged from the trapdoor at the other end of the mine."

"I can't believe so many people died because of this," Paige said. "Andy Stenson, Brock Ryan and Wade Tomlinson, the Hoods, Henry Hake, Bryce Reed—even those two men who tried to kill me were killed because they drew too much attention to the place."

"There were millions, probably billions, of dollars at

stake," Rob said. "That's how much some foreign powers would be willing to pay for biological weapons."

"But weapons like that are illegal," Paige said. "I mean, they're against the Geneva convention."

"Some people don't care."

That idea was too depressing to consider.

"I know you're both exhausted," Travis said. "You can go for now, but we'll have more questions for you later, and you'll probably eventually have to testify in court."

Outside, Parker and the professor waited for them. Parker wrapped Paige in a hug that squeezed the breath out of her. "Don't scare me like that again," he said, his voice husky.

She pulled away and studied him. He had dark circles under his eyes and needed a shave. When had the little boy she had loved for so long grown into such a man? "Thanks for calling in the cavalry," she said.

"I understand you told the sheriff about seeing Larry Rowe in that helicopter that landed on CNG property," Rob said.

"Yeah. He said if I agreed to testify about that, he'd overlook the parole violation for trespassing."

"Excuse me." The professor moved closer. "I understand now isn't a good time, but when you've had a chance to rest, I'd appreciate hearing more about the lab you found. Do you really think it's the space used by the government during World War II?"

"It could be," Rob said. "Larry as much as confirmed it. I think finding it gave him the idea to work on developing biological weapons in the first place."

"Then I definitely want to hear more about it. At your convenience."

"Right now I just want a shower and a drink." Paige looked down at her dirty jeans and scraped hands.

"Sure thing," Parker said. "Where do you want me to take you?"

"I'll take care of her." Rob put his arm around her.

Parker took a step back. "I guess you're in good hands, then." Parker looked at Rob. "But if you do anything to hurt her, you'll have me to answer to."

Rob nodded, his expression solemn. "Understood."

When Parker and the professor were gone, Paige looked up at Rob. "Don't worry about him," she said. "If you do anything to hurt me, you'll have *me* to answer to."

"I'm definitely more frightened of you. But you don't have to worry. I won't hurt you. Ever."

"I believe you." She smiled up at him. "Let's go back to your motel."

They didn't speak even after they were inside Rob's room. He merely drew the drapes and she began to strip off her clothes in the dim light from the bedside lamp. Rob did the same, until they stood facing each other, naked. He smoothed a hand along her shoulder, and his fingers trembled. "If anything had happened to you..." he began.

"Shhh." She silenced him with a kiss. "We're both okay," she said, her lips almost touching his. "We're going to be okay."

He nodded and tried to pull her close, but instead, she took his hand and led him into the bathroom. She turned on the shower, jets all the way up and water steaming hot. Then she stepped in and beckoned for him to follow.

She thought of all the ways water could cleanse, from removing dirt from laundry to the soul cleansing of baptism. As they took turns soaping each other's bodies, she felt the strain and fear of the past days wash away, replaced by an exultant joy that they were here now, alive and able to enjoy each other this way.

The water was still warm when Rob tossed aside the soapy washrag and pulled her closer, full against his naked body, her breasts pressed against the firm wall of his chest, her hips just under his. Salty tears mingled with the shower spray as his lips claimed hers, and when he bent his knees and slid into her she stood on tiptoe to accept him, reveling in the sensation of being united with him, yet so fully herself.

They emerged from the shower replete and renewed and ravenous. The motel didn't offer room service, but Rob ordered a large pizza and promised extra if the delivery driver—not Parker—would stop at the liquor store and purchase a bottle of wine. They ate at the table by the window, sipping wine and feeding each other pizza, half-dressed and unable to stop looking at each other.

They made love again in the bed, burrowed under warm covers, alternately giggling with delight and moaning at the depth of their need. When Paige fell asleep in Rob's arms, she didn't dream of anything.

She woke with gray light showing through the gap in the curtains, and stretched like a cat, more relaxed than she could remember being in years. She rolled over onto her side to watch Rob sleeping. He lay on his back, his hair mussed, the dark shadow of beard along his jaw. She knew how intimidating he could look, how insistent he could be on doing the right, legal thing, upholding the commitment he had made as a law enforcement officer. Where once she had bristled at his unwillingness to see gray instead of black-and-white, now she drew comfort from his steadfastness.

Her chest hurt when she thought of how close she had come to losing him. Loving someone this way was so wonderful and so terrifying.

He looked up at her, his brown eyes clear and calm. "How long have you been watching me?" he asked.

"A while." She smiled.

"What does that smile mean? What are you thinking?"

"I'm thinking that I've lost just about everything, and I'm happier than I've ever been."

He reached for her hand and pulled it to his chest. "Marry me," he said.

She tried to pull her hand away, but he held it fast. "This is your romantic proposal?" she asked. "Naked and in bed?"

"I thought you weren't a traditionalist. Do you want me to get down on my knee? I will."

She wrinkled her nose. "What if I say no?"

"I'll keep asking. Are you going to say no?"

She wanted to laugh—he looked so worried. "No. Yes. I don't know."

He shoved himself into a sitting position, forcing her to sit up also, or risk a pain in her neck from trying to look up at him. "You faced down an armed killer yesterday and defeated him with your bare hands," he said. "After that, how can you be afraid of anything?"

"When you put it like that—yes."

"Yes, what?"

"Yes, I'll marry you."

He crushed her to him and kissed her until she was dizzy. Gently, she pushed away from him. "Where will we live?" she asked.

"Where do you want to live?"

"I don't know. Eagle Mountain feels like home, but your work is in Denver. And maybe a change would be good for me."

"I have a feeling I'm going to be here in Eagle Mountain for a while yet."

"Oh?"

"Somebody has to inventory that lab. That's going to take a while, and I already have experience on the property, so I think there's a good chance I'll get the job."

"So we can live here," she said.

"For a while. And then decide what we want to do. After all, we have the rest of our lives to be together."

"Yes, and I hope that's a very, very long time." She settled against him, her head on his shoulder.

"I hope so, too." He wrapped his arm around her.

"One thing's for sure," she said.

"What's that?"

"I'll never have to worry about being bored with you."

"Not every woman would see that as an advantage," he said.

"As you've pointed out before, I'm not every woman."

"Thank God for that."

"Shut up and kiss me."

"Yes, ma'am." And he did.

* * * * *

WYOMING COWBOY JUSTICE

NICOLE HELM

For all the Heroes readers who took a chance on a new Heroes author last year. Thank you.

Chapter One

Laurel Delaney surveyed the dead body in front of her with as much detachment as she could manage.

"Know him?" the deputy who'd first answered the call asked apologetically.

"We're distantly related. But who am I not related to in these parts?" Laurel managed a grim smile. Jason Delaney. Her third cousin or something. Dead in a cattle field from a gunshot wound to the chest, presumably.

"Rancher called it in."

Laurel nodded as she studied the body. It was only her second murder since she'd been hired by the county sheriff's department six years ago, and only her first murder in the detective bureau.

And yes, she was related to the victim. Unfortunately, she wasn't exaggerating about the number of Bent County residents she was related to. She'd known Jason in passing at best. A family reunion or funeral here or there, but that was all. He didn't live in Bent, his parents—second cousins, she thought, to her parents—weren't part of the main offshoot of Delaneys who ran Bent.

"We do have a lead," Deputy Hart offered.

"What's that?" Laurel asked, surveying the cattle field around them. This ranch, like pretty much everything in Bent County, Wyoming, was in the middle of nowhere. No highway traffic ran nearby, no businesses in the surrounding areas. Just fields and mountains in the distance. Pretty and isolated, and not the spot one would expect to find a murder victim.

"The rancher says Clint Danvers broke down in front of his place last night. Asked to use his phone. He's the only one who was around. Aside from the cows, of course."

Laurel frowned at Hart. "Clint Danvers is a teenager."

"One we've arrested more times than I can count."

"Had to be a Carson," she muttered, because no matter that Clint wasn't technically a Carson, his mother was the mother of a Carson as well. Which meant the Carson clan would count him as theirs, which would mean trouble with a Delaney investigating.

Laurel herself didn't care about the Delaney-Carson feud that so many people in town loved to bring up time and again, Carsons most especially. Her father could intone about the generations of "bad element" that had been bred into the Carsons, her brother who still lived in Bent could sneer his nose at every Carson who walked into his bank, her sister could snidely comment every time one of them bought something from the Delaney General Store. The street could divide itself—Delaney establishments on one side, Carson on the other.

Laurel didn't care—it was all silliness and history as far as she was concerned. She was after the truth, not a way to make some century-old feud worse.

A vehicle approached and Laurel shaded her eyes against the early-morning sun.

"Coroner," Hart said.

Laurel waved at the coroner, Gracie Delaney, her first cousin, because yes, relations all over the dang place.

Gracie stepped through the tape and barbed wire fence easily, and then surveyed the body. "Name?"

"Jason Delaney."

Gracie's eyebrows furrowed. "Is it bad I have no idea how we're related to him?"

Laurel sighed. "If it is, we're in the same boat." It was a very strange thing to work the death of someone you were related to, but didn't know. Laurel figured she was supposed to feel some kind of sympathy, and she did, but not in any different way than she did on any other death she worked.

"All right. I'll take my pictures, then I'll get in touch with next of kin," Gracie said.

Hart and Gracie discussed details while Laurel studied the area around the body. There wasn't much to go on, and until cows learned how to talk, she had zero possible witnesses.

Except Clint Danvers.

She didn't mind arresting a Carson every now and again no matter what hubbub it raised about the feud nonsense, but murder was going to cause a lot more than a hubbub. Especially the murder of a Delaney.

She processed the crime scene with Hart and Gracie. Even though Hart had taken pictures when he'd first arrived, Laurel took a few more. They canvased the scene again, finding not one shred of evidence to go on.

Which meant Clint was her only hope, and what a complicated hope that was.

Gracie loaded up the body with Hart's help, and Laurel tossed her gear back into her car. "I'm going to go question Clint. You on until three?"

Hart nodded. "Let me know what I can do."

Laurel waved a goodbye and got into her car. She didn't have to look up Clint's residence as Bent was small and intimate, and secrets weren't much of ones for long. He lived with his mother in a falling-down house on the outskirts of Bent.

When Chasity Haskins-Carson-Danvers and so on answered the door, freshly lit cigarette hanging out of her mouth, Laurel knew this wasn't going to go well.

"Mrs. Danvers."

Chasity blew the smoke right in Laurel's face. "Ms. Pig," she returned conversationally.

"I'm looking for Clint."

"You people always are."

"It's incredibly important I'm able to talk to Clint, and soon. This is far more serious than drugs or speeding, and I'm only looking to help."

"Delaneys are never looking to help," the older woman replied. She shrugged negligently. "He's not here. Haven't seen him for two or three days."

Laurel managed a thin-lipped smile. It could be a lie, but it could also be the truth. That was the problem with most of the Carsons. You just never knew when they were being honest and helpful, or a pack of liars trying to make a Delaney's life difficult. Because to them the feud wasn't history, it was a living, breathing entity to wrap their lives around.

Laurel thanked Mrs. Danvers anyway and then sighed as she got back in her unmarked car. Most unfortunately, she knew exactly who would know where Clint was. And he was the absolute last man she wanted to speak to.

Grady Carson. Clint's older half brother and something like the de facto leader of the Carson clan. Much like the men in her family, Grady Carson put far too much stock in a *feud* for this being the twenty-first century.

A feud over land and cattle and things that had happened over a hundred years ago. Laurel didn't understand why people clung to it, but that didn't mean she actively *liked* any of the Carsons. Not when they routinely tried to make it hard for her to do her job.

Which was the second problem with Grady. He ran Rightful Claim, which she pulled up across the street from.

She glared at the offensive sign outside the bar—a neon centaur-like creature, half horse, half very busty woman, a blinking sack of gold hanging off her saddle. Aside from the neon signs, it looked like every saloon in every Western movie or TV show she'd ever seen. Wood siding and a walk in front of it, a ramshackle overhang, hand-painted signs with the mileage, and arrows to the nearest cities, all hundreds of miles away.

Laurel refused to call it a saloon. It was a bar. Seedy. It would be mostly empty on a Tuesday afternoon, but come evening it would be full of people she'd probably arrested. And Carsons everywhere.

Grady wasn't going to hand over Clint's whereabouts, Laurel knew that, but she had to try to convince him she only wanted to help. Grady was a lot of things—a tattooed, snarling, no-respect-for-authority hooligan—but much like the Delaneys, the Carsons were all about family.

Mentally steeling herself for what would likely amount to a verbal sparring match, Laurel took her first step toward the stupid swinging doors Grady claimed were original to the saloon. Laurel maintained that he bought it off the internet from some lame Hollywood set. Mainly because he got furious when she did.

She blew out a breath and tried to blow out her frustration with it. Yes, Grady had always rubbed her completely the wrong way, and yes, that meant sometimes she couldn't keep her cool and sniped right back at him. But she could handle this. She had a case to investigate.

Laurel nudged the swinging saloon doors and slid through the opening, making as little disturbance as possible. The less time Grady had to prepare for her arrival, the more chance she had of getting some sensible words in before he started doing that…thing.

"I see you finally found the balls to step inside, princess."

Laurel gritted her teeth and turned to the sound of

Grady's low, easy voice. Doing that…thing already. The thing where he said obnoxious stuff, called her princess, or worse—deputy princess—and some tiny foreign part of her did that other thing she refused to name or acknowledge.

Her eyes had to adjust from sunlight to the dim bar interior, but when they did, she almost wished they hadn't.

He was standing on a chair, hammering a nail into the rough-hewn wood planks that made up the walls of the main area. Lining the doorway were pictures of the place over the years—a dingy black-and-white photograph of the bar in the 1800s, a bright pop of boisterous color from the time a famous singer had visited in the sixties, and photos documenting all Grady had done inside to somehow make it look less like a dive bar in a small town and more like a mix between old and new.

Much like the man himself. Laurel always had the sneaking suspicion Grady and the Carson cousins he routinely hung around with could straddle the lines of centuries quite easily. Sure, he was dressed in modern-day jeans and a simple black T-shirt that she had no doubt was sized with the express purpose of showing off the muscles of his arms and shoulders along with the lick of tattoos that spiraled out from the cuff and toward his elbow.

But he, and all the Carsons she had pulled over or served a warrant on more times than she could count on two hands and two feet, wore old battered cowboy hats like they were just dreaming of a day they could rob a stagecoach and escape to a brothel.

She wouldn't put it past Grady to *have* a brothel, but for the time being the worst thing he did in Rightful Claim was sell moonshine without a license.

Something she'd reported him on. Twice.

"Gonna stand there and watch me work all day? Want to slap my wrist over some made-up infraction?"

"It's funny you call this work, Carson. You don't have a single patron in here." She glared at the picture he rested on the nail he'd just pounded into the wall. It was a cross-stitched, nearly naked woman. Cross-stitched. Oh, she *hated* this place.

"There are no patrons because I don't officially open until three. But there's nothing like a Delaney coming into *my* place of business and criticizing *my* work ethic when your family has—"

"Please spare me the trip down family feud lane. I have business to discuss with you. It's important."

"*You* have business to discuss with *me*?" He got off the chair, just an easy step down with those long, powerful legs of his. Not that she noticed long or powerful, even when he was roaring his way down Main Street on that stupid, *stupid* motorcycle of his.

"I'm going to need a drink to go with this interesting turn of events," he drawled.

"You're going to drink before three in the afternoon on a day you're working?"

He walked past her, way closer than he needed to, and that wolfish smile was way too bright, way too feral. How could anyone call him attractive? He was downright…downright…*wild, uncivilized, lawless.*

All terrible things. Or so she told herself as often

as she could manage to make her brain function when he was smirking at her.

"That's exactly what I'm going to do, princess."

"Deputy. This is official." She followed him toward the long, worn bar. Again, Grady claimed it was original, and it looked it. Scarred and nicked, though waxed enough that it shone. She couldn't imagine how anyone balanced a glass of anything on the uneven wood, or why they'd want to.

"All right, deputy princess—"

She was trying very hard not to let her irritation show, but the little growl that escaped her mouth whether she wanted it to or not gave her away.

The bastard laughed.

Low, rumbly. She could feel that rumble vibrate through her limbs even though there was this ancient big slab of a bar between them. *Hate, hate, hate.*

"Gonna report me again?"

She schooled her features in what she hoped was a semblance of professionalism. "Not this afternoon, though if I see you serve the moonshine when I know you don't have a license for it, I will contact the proper authorities."

"If that's your idea of pillow talk—"

"I know, all those multisyllable words, too hard for you to comprehend," she snapped, irritated with herself, as always, for letting him get to her. "But this is about your brother. And murder." His eyes went as hard as his expression, which gave her a little burst of satisfaction. *Not so tough now, are you?* "Care to shut up and listen?"

GRADY HAD ALWAYS had a little too much fun riling up the Delaneys, Laurel in particular. She got so pinched-looking, and when he really got her going, the hints of gold in her dark eyes switched to flame. And unlike the rest of the Delaneys, Laurel gave as good as she got.

But her words erased any good humor riling her up had created. Murder and Clint. Damn. Clint might be his half brother without an ounce of Carson blood in him, but he was still family. Which meant he was under Grady's protection.

Grady jerked his chin toward the back of the bar. Though the regulars knew not to swing through the old saloon doors until three on the dot or later, he didn't want anyone accidentally overhearing this conversation.

"I'm sorry, I don't speak caveman. Is that little chin jerk supposed to mean something?"

He flicked a glance down her tall, slender frame. He could see her weapon outlined under the shapeless polo shirt she wore. The mannish khakis were slightly better than the polo because they at least gave the impression of her having an ass. A shame of an outfit, all in all.

"Let me ask you this," he said, leaning his elbows on the freshly waxed surface of the bar. He'd spent most of a lifetime learning how to appear completely unaffected when affected was exactly what he was, and this was no different. "Is this visit personal or professional?" he asked, making sure to drawl the word *personal* and infuse it with plenty of added meaning.

"Professional," she all but spat. "Like I said earlier. Trust me when I say I will never set foot through those pointless swinging doors for anything other than strictly professional business."

"Aw, sweetheart, don't lay down a challenge you won't be able to win."

"I see that even when it comes to your brother, you can't take anything important seriously. How about this? The murder victim is Jason Delaney. The only person around at the time of the murder was Clint Danvers."

Grady swore.

"I need to question your brother before news of this murder and that *he was a witness* spreads through town like wildfire. All we need is for one person to see a Delaney's been murdered, and know Clint is technically a Carson and a witness, and we have a whole feud situation on our hands. Are you going to help me or not?" she said evenly, the only show of temper at this point in her eyes, where he could all but picture the flecks of gold bursting into flame one by one.

He didn't trust a Delaney in the least, but Laurel Delaney wasn't quite like the rest. She hated the feud, and he almost believed she might be more interested in the truth than crucifying Clint without evidence. The rest of the town would be a different matter. This would result in the kind of uproar that could only cause problems for *everyone*.

Clint was in trouble, and Bent was in trouble, and the thing that kept the Carsons and Delaneys in this town, most of them hating and blaming each other for good or for bad, was that something about Bent had been poured into their blood at birth.

Something about the buildings that had stood the test of time in the shadow of distant, rolling mountains, far away from any kind of typical civilization. Something about the way history was imprinted into their fingerprints and their names, even if some people chose to ignore it.

Bent was like an organ in the body of those who stayed, and no matter what side of the feud you were on, Bent was the common good. Usually no one could agree on what that meant.

This wouldn't be any different. Laurel would want to solve the problem with warrants and investigations and all sorts of time-consuming bull. He and his cousins could have it sorted out with a few well-timed threats, maybe some fists, probably within the week.

So, he smiled at Laurel, as genially as he could manage for a man who wasn't used to being genial at all. "Have to pass, princess. Guess you and your gun will have to do all the heavy lifting."

Her eyes narrowed. "Sometimes I can't decide if you think I'm stupid or if that's just you. This is real life, Grady, not the Wild West—especially your lame version of it. If you want to arrest a murderer, you have to conduct an investigation. If you want to save your brother from the possibility of not just being a suspect, but being convicted, you need to work with the police. This isn't about Delaney versus Carson. It's about right and wrong. Truth and justice."

"Guess we'll find out."

She shook her head. "Don't come crying to me when Clint is locked up."

"Don't let the doors slap that pretty little ass of yours on the way out. You might end up enjoying it."

"You know, I don't get to say this enough in a day. Screw you, Grady." She flipped him off as she sauntered out of the saloon. The doors didn't hit her on the way out, but that didn't stop him from watching her disappear.

He waited until she was completely gone, then watched the clock tick by another few minutes. Casually, he pulled out his phone, then gave one last glance at the doors that had gone completely still. As if he didn't have a care in the world, he sent off a text to his cousins.

We need a meeting.

Ty was the first to respond. Mine, cow, or woman?

Grady's mouth quirked at the code they'd developed as teens. *Mine* was property, because the Carsons had managed to eke out some of their own, even with the Delaney name stamped all over this town since the first Delaney bastards had screwed the first Carsons out of their rightful claim to land and gold. Because of that nasty start of things in Bent, the Carsons didn't let anybody mess with what was rightfully theirs.

Cow meant family, because the Carsons and the Delaneys of old had gone to great and sometimes disastrous lengths to protect their livestock around the turn of the twentieth century, and these days, going to great lengths to protect family was still a number one priority for the Carsons.

And *woman*…

Grady stared at where Laurel had gone. Well, she was a woman, and she was a pain. A cop. A Delaney.

Yeah, he had a woman problem, but it was one that he was going to ignore, and it would go away. So, he typed Cow into his phone before grabbing his keys and heading out the back.

Chapter Two

Laurel wasn't big on breaking rules or protocol, but considering she was currently investigating a murder, and Grady likely knew where the only potential witness/suspect was, following him was necessary.

It was, however, difficult to follow someone surreptitiously in Bent. There weren't any cars to hide behind, and the roads that crisscrossed in and out of town were surrounded by long, wide stretches of plains, the mountains a hazy promise in the distance.

Still, when Grady's motorcycle roared out of town toward the west, quickly followed by another motorcycle, Laurel was pretty sure she knew where the motorcycle parade of doom was headed. Which made her job a hell of a lot easier.

She gave them a few minutes, then drove out of Bent in the direction of the Carson Ranch. Though Grady didn't live there full-time, everyone knew he routinely bunked out at the ranch Noah Carson ran.

Much like the Delaneys tended to congregate around their own ranch on the exact opposite side of town. As if the two ranches were facing off, Bent their no-man's-land in between.

Laurel sighed. This whole thing was going to make that no-man's-land erupt into a chaos they hadn't seen for decades, if she didn't get some information out of Clint, and soon. She'd been stupid to think Grady had half a brain and would grant her access.

But she wasn't stupid enough to give up, and she was too darn stubborn to let Bent get dragged into another foolish war. It might not be the Wild West anymore, but people—many of whom were far too armed for their own good—getting riled up and fighting was never a good thing.

Especially when she had a murder to solve.

Laurel parked her car at the curve in the road, the last place she couldn't be seen. She'd have to hike up the rest of the way and do her best to stay behind underbrush and land swells and whatever she could find. Hopefully the Carson clan would be too busy planning how to hide away Clint to look out the windows and see her.

She pocketed her keys, checked her weapon and set out into the brisk fall afternoon. She remembered to turn the sound on her cell and radio off as she walked, keeping her eyes on where the Carson spread would eventually come into view.

When it did, she paused. She might be the practical, methodical sort, but she never failed to take a moment or two to appreciate where she lived. The sky was a breathtaking blue, puffy white clouds drifting by on the early fall breeze. The grass and brush were a mix of browns and gold. Surrounded by the all-inspiring glory of the majestic peaks of the Wind River mountains and the rolling red hills was a cluster of buildings sitting in the middle of a broad golden field.

The Carson Ranch wasn't much like its Delaney counterpart. It was populated with sturdy, mostly Carson-built buildings. They'd preserved most of the original ranch house, making improvements and expanding only when necessary. Like the saloon, it was a bit like stepping back in time with a modern layer over top.

The Delaney Ranch, on the other hand, was sleek, modern and gleaming, thanks to Laurel's father. The only building on the entire spread that predated her father was the one Laurel used as home right now. A tiny cabin that had supposedly been her ancestor's original homestead, though modernized with plumbing and electricity and whatnot.

It would fit in well enough on the Carsons' land. Laurel frowned at that uncomfortable thought. Nothing about her or her life would fit in with this group of ne'er-do-wells.

She edged along the fence line, trying to stay out of sight from any windows. Two motorcycles were parked in front of the main house, and Laurel had to wonder if they'd come here because Clint was here, or if they'd chosen the place to have some kind of pseudo-planning meeting.

Laurel knew one thing: Grady wasn't as nonchalant as he'd pretended. She'd never known him to bow out of the bar this close to opening before.

Maybe Clint *was* here. She could go to the house,

demand to see him and show the three Carson cousins she wasn't scared of them—not Grady and his swagger, not Noah and his quiet stoicism, and not Ty, who'd recently returned after having served years as an army ranger. They might be big, strong men, but she was a law enforcement agent, and she'd faced bigger, badder men than them.

It would set a good precedent to stare them down, to demand access or answers. The Carsons seemed to think they were above the law, especially if it was a Delaney trying to enforce it, and she didn't have to let that stand.

But she didn't see another intact vehicle anywhere, just a handful of rusting, tire-less old cars and trucks. If Clint was here, he'd either gotten here on foot or hidden his vehicle.

There were a ton of outbuildings. While the Carson boys sat inside and planned whatever they were planning, maybe she could find a clue in one of those.

She quickened her pace, making it into the stables first. There were four horses in stalls, huffing happily, and a surprising amount of tidiness inside for the lack of it out. She made her way to the empty stall toward the back. It could fit a motorcycle or—

"Hands up," a husky feminine voice commanded.

Laurel whirled at the sound, hand on the butt of her weapon, and then scowled. "Vanessa, do not point a gun at me."

"Got a warrant?" Vanessa Carson asked, holding an old-looking rifle pointed directly in Laurel's direction.

"Is that a musket?" Laurel asked incredulously, then

shook her head. "Regardless, stop pointing it at me. That's an official order."

With a hefty sigh, Grady's sister lowered her rifle. Laurel felt the same thing she always felt when she looked at her former best friend. Regret, and a pang for a childhood before things had been poisoned by some stupid feud.

"Why are you sneaking around our stables?" Vanessa demanded.

"Official reasons."

Vanessa smirked and pulled her phone out of her pocket. She held it up to her ear. "Hey, Grady. I'm out in the stables. We've got an uninvited visitor."

Laurel threw her hands in the air, frustrated beyond belief. "When will you all realize I am *trying* to help you. Help Bent." It was all she'd ever wanted to do. Help Bent. Even people who hated her because of her last name knew *that* was true.

"Helping Bent usually translates to helping the Delaneys when it comes to your people, Laurel. Why should this be any different?"

Laurel had a million arguments for that. Even though she'd beat her head against that concrete wall time and time again, she had no compunction about doing it again now. But she saw something out of the corner of her eye.

Something that looked suspiciously like a skinny teenager running for the mountains.

Laurel didn't hesitate, didn't concern herself with Vanessa's *musket*, of all things, and most definitely didn't worry about the impending arrival of Grady.

She pushed past Vanessa and ran after the quickly disappearing figure. She ignored Vanessa's shouts and put all her concentration into running as fast as she could.

"Clint Danvers, stop right there," she yelled, gaining absolutely no ground on the kid, but not losing any, either. "Bent County Sheriff's Department, I am ordering you to stop!" She could threaten to shoot, of course, but that would cause more problems than it'd ever solve.

Clint darted behind a barn at the west edge of the property, and Laurel swore, because he could go a couple different directions hidden behind that barn and she wouldn't be able to see which one he chose.

Her lungs were burning, but she pushed her body as fast as it would go, cutting the corner around the barn close. Close enough she ran right into a hard wall of something that knocked her back and onto her butt.

She would have popped right back up, ignoring her throbbing nose and butt, but the hard object she'd run into was Grady himself. And now he was standing there, giving no indication he'd let her pass.

She glared up at him and his imposing arms folded over his chest. "I detest you," she said furiously, even knowing she should tamp down her temper and be a professional.

His all-too-full lips curved into one of those wolfish smiles. "My life is a success, then."

"He's getting away, and if you think that's going to go over well for him, you're sorely mistaken."

Grady jerked his chin toward the house. "Ty's after him on his bike. We'll have him rounded up in a few."

"Oh," Laurel managed to say, blinking. That was not what she'd expected out of Grady. At all. She figured he'd purposefully stepped in her way so Clint could escape.

"But I'm not going to let you talk to him, princess." He held out his hand as if he was going to help her up.

She pushed herself to her feet. "*Let* me?" she muttered. As if he could *let* her do anything in her official capacity.

"But I am going to clean you up. I think you might have broken your nose."

She touched her fingers to her nose, surprised to find a sticky substance there. She'd been so angry, she hadn't even realized her nose was bleeding. "I could arrest you for assaulting an officer."

"Babe, you ran right into me. That's not assault. It's not watching where you're going."

She didn't screech or growl or pound her fists into his chest like she wanted to. No, she took a deep breath in and then out.

She had a job to do, and Grady Carson could break her nose, threaten her sanity, but he could not stand in her way.

GRADY DIDN'T LIKE the uncomfortable hitch in his chest at the sight of Laurel's face all bloody. It was her own damn fault she'd crashed into him. He'd heard her coming, of course, but he hadn't known she'd turn the corner at the same exact time he had.

At full speed.

She was entirely to blame, but somehow he felt

guilty as he walked her back to the main house. "We'll clean you up, then you can be on your way."

"I'm just going to come back with a search warrant. Clint is the only potential witness in a *murder*, Grady. I can't stop going after him until he answers some questions."

He hated that she was using that reasonable, even-keeled cop tone with him when there was a trickle of blood slowly dripping down her chin.

"Ain't none of my business what you got to do, Deputy," he said as lazily as he could manage, even though he didn't feel lazy at all.

His teenage half brother was a dope, plain and simple. Grady didn't think Clint had actually killed anyone, but he had a bad feeling based on Clint's running away that Clint knew *something*. Considering Clint's mom had kicked Clint out of the house just last week and had lectured Grady on getting him sorted out, Grady could only feel pissed and more of that unwelcome guilt.

He hated feeling guilty. So, when Ty pulled up on his bike, alone, Grady cursed. "Where the hell is he?"

"I don't know, man. Disappeared."

"That's impossible."

Ty shrugged. "Noah took one of the horses to go search the trees. What the hell happened to her?" Ty asked, gesturing toward Laurel.

"Your cousin broke my nose," the infuriating woman stated.

Ty's eyebrows winged up.

"I did not break her nose. She ran into me at full speed and broke her own damn nose."

"Want me to go open the saloon for you?" Ty asked.

Grady nodded and fished his keys out of his pocket. He tossed them at Ty. "I'll be there soon."

"You don't have to do this," Laurel said as Ty rode off. "My nose isn't really broken. It's just bleeding. I can clean myself up in my car."

"How do you know it's not broken?"

She shrugged. She was a tall woman, but narrow. Narrow shoulders, narrow hips. Her hair always pulled back in a bouncy brown ponytail. Her face always devoid of makeup. Her body always covered up. The complete opposite of his type.

Which was why he'd never quite understood why his gaze tended to linger on her when they happened to be in the same vicinity, or why he got such a kick out of pissing her the hell off, and always had, since she'd been a girl hanging around his sister back before Vanessa had decided Delaneys were evil incarnate.

But one thing he did know and always had known— no matter how fragile Laurel Delaney could look on the outside, she was as tough as nails when it came down to it.

"I've had my nose broken before," she retorted. "I know what it feels like."

"You?"

"Yes, me." She glared at him, all piss and vinegar and a special brand of spitfire unique to her. "Methhead head-butted me once."

"A meth-head head-butted you and your father let you stay in police work?"

"You don't know what I did to the meth-head in return."

Hell. Bloodthirsty was such a turn-on, even on a Delaney. Maybe especially on one. "Come inside so we can wash you up before you slink back to wherever you hid your car."

"I did not hide my car."

Grady raised an eyebrow at her and she returned his look with an arch one of her own.

"I parked it down the hill so I could have a nice, head-clearing walk." She smiled sweetly.

"Sure." Grady pushed the front door open and led her into the kitchen. "Sit." He pointed to a barstool situated under the kitchen counter.

He grabbed a washcloth and ran it under some warm water before walking around to her.

"I can clean it myself," she said, holding her hand out for the cloth.

Instead he did what he knew would piss her off. He gripped her chin and held her head still as he used the washcloth to wipe away the blood.

She sat there regally, not sniping at him or pushing him away, and he had to fight back a smile over the fact she had changed tactics with him.

He wiped the blood from her nose and where it had dripped down her chin. She was fair-skinned and her nose was faintly freckled. While most Delaneys reveled in the finer things, the more genteel side of life, and her elegant face sure fit all that, Laurel had never been one for elegance and pretty things.

"You sure it's not broken?" he asked, and he was close enough that the hair hanging around her face stirred.

"I'm sure." She stared at him with those golden-brown eyes and there wasn't an ounce of animosity hiding there. He couldn't help that his gaze dropped to her unpainted mouth.

Laurel had always been easy to resist, not because he'd never found her attractive, but because it only ever took him opening his mouth to rile her up enough to have her walk away. But she wasn't bristling like she usually did, and he figured that was all kinds of dangerous.

"I'm not out to get you," she said as sincerely as she'd ever said anything to him.

Her sincerity was good enough to break this particular spell. "You'll have to pardon my lack of belief, considering how many times your father has tried to get Rightful Claim shut down." He stepped away and tossed the cloth in the sink. He crossed his arms across his chest and frowned intimidatingly down at her.

"That doesn't have anything to do with me. Should I blame you for everything your father's ever done? Because I hear it's quite a list."

He wouldn't admit she had a fair point.

"Work with me, Grady," she implored, speaking to him for once like he was a person instead of a Carson. "For your brother's sake. For Bent's sake. Put everything that came before behind us for the sake of *this* case and this case alone. If Clint is innocent, I don't want to be the one who puts him away for murder. I don't want a real murderer to get away with something because of feud crap."

"Haven't you ever heard the old saying that those who fail to learn from history are doomed to repeat it?"

"Well, I don't think there's any chance of me falling in love with you and dying in some army-led Native American massacre, or you and all the Carsons going off to war and eradicating an entire generation. So we might just make it. Did I cover all the idiotic Delaney-Carson fairy tales?"

His mouth curved. "I don't know, the illegitimate Carson who married a Delaney as payback always struck my fancy."

"That poor woman died in childbirth."

"And thus the waters between Carson and Delaney never commingled."

"You're terrible."

"Don't you forget it, princess."

The door squeaked open and Noah entered, slapping his cowboy hat against his thigh so that dust puffed up. "Must have had some help. That boy isn't anywhere out there."

"I need a list of friends, places he might have gone, that sort of thing," Laurel said in her demanding cop way that got Grady's back up like few other things.

But she'd implored him to help, and while helping a Delaney was the first and biggest thing on his *Don't Ever Do* list, this was about Clint. It was about Bent. Much as he might enjoy the feud tales and riling up the Delaneys, he didn't actually want any trouble in town. Trouble wasn't good for business, and as much as he would never admit to anyone, a little too hard on his heart.

He loved the town like he loved his brother. He loved his saloon like he loved the graves of every Carson before him. He might not have sworn to protect this place like Laurel had, but he had the sneaking suspicion they both wanted the same thing.

Damn it all.

"Your best bets are Pauline Hugh or Fred Gaskill," Grady offered.

Laurel hopped off the barstool. "Hugh, Gaskill. Got it. And if he comes back here, call me. Or bring him to me. I only need to question him. The longer he runs, the worse this looks. Please let him know that."

Grady nodded and Noah did, too, and then Laurel was striding out of the house.

"So, we're working with a Delaney," Noah said as if he didn't quite believe it.

"That Delaney and *that* Delaney only. And only until we get a handle on what Clint's involvement is and how much we need to protect him."

Noah made one of his many noncommittal sounds that Grady usually found funny, but he wasn't much in a mood to find anything funny today. "What's that grunt supposed to mean?"

"Oh, nothing. You just seemed awfully cozy with Deputy Delaney there."

"At least I wasn't blushing in front of her."

Noah bristled. "I was not blushing."

"Just don't get any hooking up ideas of your own." Which was the wrong thing to say. It was beyond irritating, since he always knew the right thing to say, or when to keep his mouth shut. Grady never gave too much away.

Noah's rare smile spread across his face. "You staking a claim, cousin?"

"No, I am not. We just have to be careful how we play this. I'm going to work now. Go shovel some manure or something."

"Oh, there's plenty right here to shovel up," Noah replied.

Grady flipped him off and headed out of the house. He took a second to stand on the porch and look at the blazing sun in the distance, the rolling red hills, the rocky outcroppings of this beautiful Wyoming world.

He definitely wasn't watching Laurel Delaney stride down the long gravel driveway, a woman on a mission.

A mission he was more than a little irritated to find he shared.

Chapter Three

Laurel fumbled with her phone to turn off the beeping alarm. She wanted desperately to hit Snooze, but there was too much to do.

She hadn't gotten home until well after midnight, after tracking down all the names the Carsons had given her yesterday. She'd questioned both teens, but neither one had been able to give her the faintest hint on Clint's whereabouts.

She yawned and stretched out in bed. Oh, she didn't believe any of the shifty teenagers, but she couldn't force them to tell her anything. Which meant today would be another long day of investigating. Even if she got ahold of Clint to question him, she wasn't hopeful she'd get anything out of him.

She didn't have time to find Clint *and* investigate a murder that would be common knowledge in Bent and the surrounding areas by now.

Murder. Who had *murdered* Jason Delaney?

She forced herself out of bed and walked from her small room to the tiny kitchen. It was a cold morning, but it would have to be a quick one. Coffee, shower, get on the road. No time to build a fire and enjoy the cozy fall silence.

She frowned at the odd sound interrupting said silence as she clicked her coffee maker on. Something like a rumble.

Or a motorcycle.

"Hell," she muttered. She could not argue with Grady before she had coffee. Before she even had time to get dressed. She looked down at the flannel pajamas. It could be worse—she could be wearing the ones with bacon and eggs on them, or more revealing ones.

But she wasn't wearing a bra and she very nearly blushed at the idea of being bra-less in the same room as Grady.

She jumped at the pounding on her door, which was silly when she knew it had been coming. But she hadn't expected it to all but shake her little cabin.

Well, no time to fix the pajama situation. Worse, no time to fix the no-coffee situation. So she put her best frown in place and opened the door. "What do you—" But she stopped talking because it wasn't just Grady.

Grady shoved Clint through the door before following, and for a few seconds Laurel could only stand there and stare. Grady had brought her the only potential witness and the main suspect all rolled up into one. He'd brought a Carson into Delaney territory.

Grady scowled at—she assumed—the naked shock on her face. "The sooner you question him, the sooner you can clear him. You said you know he didn't do it, after all."

"I didn't say that," Laurel returned, shaking herself out of her shock and going for a notebook and a pen.

"What do you mean you didn't say that? Never mind, Clint. Let's go."

Laurel stepped in front of him, holding out a hand to stop him. Somehow that hand landed on his chest. Because even though it was something like thirty degrees outside considering the sun was just beginning to rise, he only had a leather jacket on, unzipped, so that her hand came into contact with the soft material of his T-shirt, covering the very not-soft expanse of his very broad chest.

She jerked her hand away and focused on her notebook. "Calm down," she said, hoping *she* sounded calm. "I said I don't *think* he did it. I'm only out for the truth, and if the truth is Clint's nose is clean, I'll make sure my investigation reflects that." She lifted her chin and met his blazing blue gaze.

She'd never seen Grady this riled up before. He was more of the "annoy the crap out of people till they took a swing at him, then gleefully beat them to a pulp" type.

Which was why it didn't surprise her in the least when he relaxed his shoulders and his gaze swept down her chest. "Nice jammies."

She sidestepped him and gestured Clint to a seat at her small kitchen table. "Sit, Clint. I have a few simple questions for you. Now, right now, we don't know what happened, so I need you to be honest and forthcoming, because the more we know, the quicker we can get to the bottom of this."

Clint sat in the chair, slumping in it, looking everywhere but at her or Grady. "Sure. Whatever," he muttered.

Laurel opened up to a clean page in her notebook and quickly jotted down Clint's name, the date and time. She left out Grady's presence, and she didn't have time to wonder about why. "Now, Mr. Jennings said you came to his door around ten asking to make a phone call. Is that true?"

Clint shrugged again, fidgeting and sighing heavily. "Guess so."

"And why did you go to Mr. Jennings's door?"

"Crap car broke down not far from that rancher's house. I walked up, asked to use his phone since mine was dead, and then my girl came and picked me up." He pulled at a thread on the cuff of his jacket. "I wasn't anywhere near that field."

"How did you know the dead body was in the field?" Grady growled before Laurel could voice the same question.

Clint opened his mouth, but no sound came out. Laurel had to close her eyes. The idiot kid couldn't even lie? Hell, she'd come up with one if Grady's furious blue gaze was on her like that.

"You promised me you were telling the truth," Grady said, leaning over the table and getting in Clint's face. "So help me God, Clint, you do not lie to me and get away with it."

"Gentlemen," Laurel said in her best peacemaking tone, smiling encouragingly at Clint and then Grady. "Let's take a calming breath."

She was pretty sure Grady's calming breath included picturing breaking her neck, but he stood stock-still, fury and frustration radiating off him.

If she hadn't grown up in this town, if she hadn't fascinatedly watched against her will, her whole life, how the Carson clan worked, she might have been concerned.

But where the Delaneys were all cold silences and sharp words, the Carsons exploded. They acted, and it was oftentimes too much and foolish, but Laurel had never doubted it came from the same place her family's way of dealing came from.

Love. Family.

Grady was pissed and frustrated—not just because Clint was lying to him, but at the fact Clint was clearly in trouble and Grady couldn't fix it.

"Let's start from the beginning, Clint," Laurel said evenly and calmly. "With the truth this time."

"Why are you making me talk to a Delaney?" Clint demanded of Grady. "She's going to railroad me no matter what I say."

Grady's entire face looked hard as marble, and the way he had his impressive arms crossed over his chest, well, Laurel didn't think she'd mess with him the way Clint seemed to be doing.

Clint sighed heavily, slouching even further in the chair. "Okay, yeah, I saw the body."

"You…" Grady was clearly working very, very hard not to come unglued.

Laurel held up a hand, hoping it kept him quiet

rather than riling him further. "And you didn't call the police because?"

"Because me plus a dead body was only going to make me a suspect. I'm not stupid. I know how you cops work. Maybe you got something on Grady or are getting naked with him, but you got nothing on me."

Laurel hated that a blush infused her cheeks. Naked with Grady? Ha. Ha ha ha. What a laugh. But somehow she couldn't stop thinking about how she didn't have a bra on under her pajamas.

Laurel managed to clear her throat and look condescendingly at Clint. "Would you like me to arrest you? Because I can."

Clint began to bluster, but Laurel continued on in her even tone, because she would not be upset by a couple Carsons in her cabin. "Or you can truthfully answer my questions and allow me to investigate this. And, if you had nothing to do with it, this questioning will be all there is to it."

"I stood up for you with your mom, kid. You screw that up, you're out of chances, and you know it."

Clint stared at the table, but clearly, whatever Grady was talking about got through to him. "The story's all true. I just broke down on the other side of the ranch. I was walking up to the door to see if I could make a call when I heard a shot. I thought it was…" He shook his head. "Well, anyway, it was dark. I didn't see anything. But I heard the shot, a thump like a guy fell over, and footsteps running away."

Laurel scribbled it all down, her heartbeat kicking

up. This was something. A lead, no matter how tiny, and that was important. "That's all you heard?"

"Think so."

"Thinking isn't good enough," Grady sneered.

"All right. That's enough out of you." Laurel stood and began pushing Grady into her bedroom. "You are officially uninvited to this questioning. You just stay in here until I'm done."

She pushed him and pushed him until he was far enough in her room she could close the door. Which she did. On his mutinous face.

GRADY STARED AT the rough-hewn wood of the door and tried very hard to resist the urge to punch it.

What did Clint think he was doing? Noah had found Clint holed up in the stables early this morning and they'd all surrounded him and demanded to hear what he knew. To make a plan. To protect their kin.

In *that* moment Clint had said he hadn't seen anything, that he was the innocentest of bystanders. That was the only reason Grady had decided to throw Clint on his motorcycle and drive him to Laurel's place.

If Grady had known the kid had *seen* it? Witnessed the murder go down and walked away? He would have called any lawyer he could afford.

Instead… Grady swore angrily, pacing Laurel's tiny bedroom. His idiot brother had just made everything ten times worse and *in* the house of a Delaney. How the hell was Grady going to get Clint out of this one?

He took a deep breath. He had to curb his temper,

because getting angry wouldn't help Clint. He needed a cool head and a plan.

He took stock of the room around him. Neat. Tidy. The bed was unmade, but considering Laurel was still in her pajamas, maybe she hadn't had a chance. Deputy Delaney did not seem like the type to leave a mess lying around.

She had a tiny bed, all in all. Bigger than a twin, he supposed, but not by much. Which was when he knew the best way to find a sense of inner calm in order to formulate a plan. It was not to go out there and bang his head against a hardheaded moron teenager, but to irritate the hell out of Laurel Delaney while she beat *her* head against Clint's teenage woe-is-me.

Grady settled himself in the middle of Laurel's bed. Comfortable, he'd give her that. The sheets were nice, and the pillows firm and plump and a lot better than the ones he had back at his apartment above the saloon or his bedroom at the ranch.

He grinned to himself, imagining asking her about where she got her pillows. Her eyes would do the fire thing, and she'd probably fist her hands on those slim hips.

Hips that had been settled in this bed this morning. In those ridiculous flannel pajamas. Except, he didn't think she was wearing a bra under said pajamas, and he wouldn't mind seeing what Laurel looked like a little unwrapped.

As it was, he could smell her. Something floral and feminine and so unlike her usual asexual appearance he was a little tempted to get his nose in there and take a good sniff.

Which was insane and more than a little perplexing. He didn't care what a woman smelled like. Vanilla. Citrus. Nothing at all. It was all the same to him as long as they were warm, willing and up for anything.

Laurel Delaney would not be up for anything.

Yeah, couldn't let himself go down *that* particular road. At least, not unless he was making her blush while he did it.

The door opened. Laurel stood with her notebook and pen in hand, her mouth opening to say something that was no doubt important.

Then she saw him and fury flickered across her features like a thunderstorm sweeping through the valley. "Get out of my bed, Grady."

"You know, a woman has never ordered me *out* of her bed before," he returned conversationally, crossing his ankles.

"There's a first time for everything. Your brother's answers are sufficient for now, but he needs to stay in town in case I have more questions, and it's very possible he'll still be considered a suspect if I can't find something more concrete. But I don't have enough on him to apply for warrants, so I suggest you do your darnedest to get through to him."

"Will do, Deputy."

"Now, if you aren't out of my bed and my room in ten seconds, so I can get dressed, I will get my weapon and shoot."

Grady folded his arms behind his head and flashed a grin at her. "Go ahead and get dressed. I don't mind."

She made a squeal of outrage, or maybe she was actually having an aneurysm. "You have got to be the most infuriating man alive."

"Part of my charm."

"I'll claim immunity."

"Oh, don't tempt me to test that when I'm in your bed, princess."

"Ten, nine, eight…" She began to count, looking at the ceiling, which he'd count as a bit of a victory, because if she wasn't glaring at him maybe she was at least having a few inappropriate thoughts about him in her bed.

He would have been more than happy to let that countdown run out, see what she did. Would she really pull her gun on him? He doubted it. But whatever fun he was about to have was completely ruined when he heard his motorcycle engine start.

Without him anywhere near it.

Grady swore and hopped off the bed so fast the bed screeched against the hard floorboards. He ran past Laurel and out the door of her pretty little cabin and yelled after Clint's retreating form.

"That little punk will rue the day he touched my bike."

"Rue the day, huh?"

Grady whipped around to glare at Laurel, who was leaning against her open doorway, looking more than a little smug.

"No one, and I mean no one, touches *my* bike."

"It appears he already did."

Clint had indeed, and he would soon find out what it meant to cross Grady Carson, half brother or no half brother.

"I'll get dressed and drive you into town. Just wait for a few minutes," Laurel said, pushing off the doorway and stepping inside. Grady took a few steps toward the doorway, but Laurel lifted an eyebrow.

"Out here," she added. And for the second time this morning, she slammed a door in his face.

Chapter Four

Laurel hummed to herself as she poured her coffee into her thermos. Turned out watching Grady get the crap end of the annoyance stick was quite the morning pick-me-up.

Plus, now she had a lead. It wasn't much of one, all in all, but Clint hadn't heard any yelling. Just murmured voices, which Laurel could safely assume meant Jason knew his murderer. Knew him and agreed to meet him in a field in the middle of nowhere.

Which meant Jason had been more than likely into something shady. So, her investigation needed to start focusing on her deceased distant relative.

It was a relief, in some ways, that it might be personal or even professional rather than random. Random was harder to solve. Random was more dangerous.

But Jason had known who killed him, there was a trail to follow, and she'd do her job to follow it.

With renewed purpose, and the image of Grady nearly losing his crap firmly in mind, Laurel slipped on her coat, hefted her bag and grabbed her thermos before heading outside.

She frowned a little when Grady was nowhere to be seen. Had he decided to walk back into town? No skin off her nose and all that, but quite the long walk in the cold when he didn't have to.

She walked to her car parked on the side of the cabin, and that was when she saw him.

He stood with his back to her, clearly surveying the sprawl of Delaney buildings—houses, barns, stables. Shiny, glossy testaments to the wealth and success of the Delaney clan.

It shouldn't make her uncomfortable. Her family had worked long and hard for their success, *and* they'd always upheld the law while they did it. She was born of sheriffs and bankers and good, upstanding people. She *knew* that.

But no matter how traitorous the thought, she'd always been a little jealous of the Carsons. Not their wildness by any means, but the way they treated their history. They didn't just know the dates and the people, they lived it. Embodied it. A Carson today was not much different than a Carson one hundred years ago, she was sure.

Laurel had always felt a little disconnect at her father's edicts of bigger, better and more when they had so much to be proud of just in who they were.

"Tell me something, princess," Grady said, his voice something like soft. Which might have bothered her, or affected her, if she thought it was sincere. As it was, she figured he was just trying to lower her guard.

"What's that?"

He turned slowly, those blue eyes of his direct.

Sometimes she wondered if she couldn't just see the past through them.

Get a hold of yourself, idiot.

"You don't believe in the feud," he said in that rusty scrape of a voice that might have made women weaker than her shiver. "So, what do you believe in?"

She didn't need to think about it, or even look away. "Bent."

He sighed heavily, his gaze traveling to the mountains in the distance. "I was afraid that's what you'd say," he muttered. "I suppose we don't agree about the way people go about it, but I feel the same. As long as Clint's a suspect, Bent's at risk."

"I agree."

"So, I'm going to help you."

Laurel frowned. "I don't need your help, Grady. This is my job."

"And if everything Clint says is true, that relative of yours was in some shady business that got him killed."

Laurel's frown deepened. She hated that he'd put that together, even if it was easy enough. Grady had good instincts, and she didn't want to have to compliment him on them. Or anything.

"And, baby, you don't know a thing about shady. But I do."

"What are you going to do? Eavesdrop at the bar? Beat a few answers out of people? This is a police investigation."

"I can be subtle."

She barked out a laugh. "You're as subtle as a Mack truck. One that nearly broke my nose."

Grady quirked one of those smiles that, if she wasn't careful, could make her believe there was some softness in this man. But that was utter insanity. Grady was and always had been the opposite of subtle or soft.

"I can listen. I can put out a few feelers. I can do it all without anyone raising an eyebrow. It's the beauty of owning a saloon."

"Bar," Laurel muttered. But she didn't get the rise out of Grady she expected.

"This is my brother we're talking about, Laurel."

Her first name. Not *princess*, not Delaney. Just her first name.

"Okay," she said carefully, because even though she knew she shouldn't let it get to her, it did. If the positions were reversed, if one of her siblings were in trouble... Well, she'd probably break a few laws. Who was she to think Grady couldn't uphold a few to save his brother? And Bent. "But you'd have to promise me, really, honestly promise, that we do this *my* way. If there's a murderer out there, I have to be able to build a case on him. One with evidence, and no questions as to the validity of that evidence. Or a *murderer* gets away." She refused to entertain that thought, but Grady had to.

His jaw tightened, but he didn't smile or joke or do anything except nod. Then hold out his hand.

"You have my word."

Laurel could not have predicted this turn of events in a million years. Working with a Carson... It was insane, and risky, but maybe if the town saw a Carson and a Delaney working together for the truth, they'd be able to find something of the same.

She took his outstretched hand and shook, firmly. "So. We're in this together," she said, because she couldn't quite believe it.

"Only until my brother is cleared and to save Bent from another wave of feud crap."

"I thought you believed in the feud wholeheartedly."

"I believe in enemies. I believe in history. I believe in Delaneys mostly being so high on their horses they don't see anything."

Laurel tried to tug her hand away, but Grady held it in his, his large hand grasping hers tightly.

"I believe violence is *sometimes* the answer. Just like I can believe in the feud, the importance of that history, and think not *all* Delaneys are scum of the earth." His mouth curved into that dangerous thing. Dangerous and feral and so completely the opposite of arousing.

She wished.

"But mostly, Deputy Delaney," he said, holding firm on her hand and even tugging her closer. Close enough she could feel his breath mingle with hers, close enough she could see that the vibrant blue of his eyes matched the blue of the fall sky above them.

"I believe in Bent. And I believe you do, too. So, we'll do this your way until we have the murderer behind bars."

"And after that?"

"After that, I'll go back to doing things my way, princess." The curve of his mouth morphed into a full-blown grin. "So try not to fall in love with me."

"Such a hardship," she muttered, and when she gave one last tug of her hand and he didn't let go, she let her temper take over a little bit. She moved quick and clean and managed to land an elbow to his stomach that had his grasp loosening enough for her to free herself.

"Next time you hold on to me like that, you'll let me go the first time I pull away, or that elbow to the gut will be a knee to the balls."

Grady made a considering noise. "I like that you plan on there being a next time I hold on to you like that. Desperate for another touch?"

"I don't know how you'll hear anything shady going on in that bar of yours over the infernal buzz of your outrageous ego."

"I think I'll manage."

And the irritating part was, she was quite positive he would.

GRADY HAD CONSIDERED, for a moment or two, hauling her over his shoulder as payment for the elbow to the gut. Maybe he'd even slap that pretty ass of hers for good measure. It was a fantasy with some merit, but it would have to stay a fantasy.

He'd heard enough bedtime stories about a one-hundred-dred-and-fifty-year-old feud to know that Carsons and Delaneys getting mixed up in each other's asses was never, ever a good thing.

Besides, he needed to focus on Clint, which meant figuring out this case. A lot faster than the police would. He got that Laurel had some of the same concerns he did, and he got and respected the fact she knew what she was doing.

But he didn't have time for bureaucratic red tape, or

following all leads. *His* goal wasn't so much the truth as it was making sure his brother didn't get wrapped up in this. Laurel could do her police work, focus on her job, and Grady could focus on Clint.

It made them something like the perfect team. Which made it something like amusing to follow her to her car and get in as a passenger. She tossed her bag in the back, and got into the driver's seat as he stretched out in the passenger's.

"Can't say I've ever sat in the front seat of a cop car before."

"And I've never been pushed into the back of one. Such different lives we've led," she returned dryly, turning the keys in the ignition.

She drove away from the Delaney spread, a monstrosity of glitter and shine, the antithesis of what it should be in Grady's estimation. You built a name for yourself, you ought to give some nod to the past platforms you built yourself on. But the Delaneys liked it slick and *new.* And if he was being honest, at least part of the appeal for the Carsons was finding joy in the old and patched-together.

"You guys really hire *all* your ranch work out?" Grady asked, more because he knew it would make her stiffen than because he didn't know.

"Dylan helps some. Cam might when he comes home. Being a navy SEAL keeps him busy."

Grady made a humming noise he knew would irritate her. "Seems a bit of a misnomer to call it the Delaney ranch, then."

"If you insist," she replied, and though she clearly

tried to use cop tone on him, some of her snap crackled through.

Grady grinned. Laurel always gave a hell of a snap. "Where exactly are you planning on letting me out?"

"Rightful Claim," she replied matter-of-factly as she maneuvered her neat, sparkling car down the winding road back toward the town's heart.

"So, you're going to drive through town, for all and sundry to see, and then drop me off at my bar to do the walk of shame?"

Her head whipped to his for a brief second before she returned her concentration to the road. "No one will think that."

"Baby, *everyone* will think that. What better story is there in Bent? Number one: a Carson murdered a Delaney. Number two: a Carson defiled a Delaney. Hell, we could create our very own Civil War."

"That isn't funny."

"It wasn't a joke." Though he couldn't blame her exactly for thinking he took this lightly. He wasn't a man prone to giving away his deeper emotions. Especially to the Delaneys, but he was also no idiot. Once the whisper of murder made it through town and who the suspect was, added to any whisper of him and Laurel spending time together—no matter how ludicrous— things would really get going.

Any romance rumors now would only fan the fire, and make him and Laurel's life harder while they were trying to clear Clint.

Laurel sighed heavily. "So, where do you want me to drop you off?"

"Go out of town to the north, circle around back, and there's a small, gravel access road back of Carson property we can sneak through."

"I should not have to sneak. Or waste half my morning sneaking."

"Lotta things we shouldn't have to do in this life, princess, but we do them anyway."

Her lips firmed, but she posed no other arguments. Her dark hair was pulled back in a ponytail, as it usually was, her jaw clenched tight, also usual. But something about seeing her in her pajamas, lying in her bed—it was like seeing a slightly different, softer side to Laurel Delaney.

He clearly needed more coffee. He didn't needle her the rest of the way. Well, he fiddled with the buttons on her fancy police car dash, even in this unmarked car, before she slapped at him, but other than that he was on his best behavior.

He couldn't imagine Clint had ridden Grady's motorcycle anywhere else but the Carson ranch, because if the kid had, well… Grady wouldn't consider it on account of a bad temper and an insane dislike to people touching his few prized possessions. His bike chief among them.

Morning broke like a glorious blast, rays of sunshine reflecting the gold of everything. Fall in Bent could make the snobbiest of city folk smile. As for Grady, it was always a reminder his soul belonged here. Those roots that bound him to this land and that sky weren't shackles but gifts.

He glanced at Laurel. She did everything efficiently.

The turn of the wheel, the checking both ways before making a turn. Always so serious and conscientious. He supposed that was the fascination. He'd never known anyone quite like her, even in the passel of uppity, glossy Delaneys that ran Bent, or tried to.

"Turn here," Grady instructed, gesturing toward a barely visible turn off the highway. Laurel nodded and drove her car through a canopy of green and gold, leaves and pine, until they reached the gate.

"You can walk from here," she said primly.

Something about her prim always made him grin. "A polite woman drops her man off at the door."

"Consider me impolite and you very much not my man."

Grady pushed the car door open and stepped out. "I'll put a few feelers out tonight at Rightful Claim, let you know what I come up with."

She nodded, all business. "I'm going over to the mining company to talk to Jason's boss and any co-workers he might have been friendly with. I'll let you know if I've got a specific lead I want you to listen for."

"Look at that, Deputy, we're acting like partners already."

She rolled her eyes. "We'll be lucky if we don't kill each other."

The grin that had never fully evaporated spread across his face. "Funny, killing each other isn't what I'm worried about."

Her eyebrows drew together, all adorable, innocent confusion. Oh, to be as sweet and rule-abiding as his deputy princess.

"You just think on that, and we'll be in touch." He closed the door and started walking toward the old homestead. The wind was cold, but he didn't mind. It was a good kind of cold. A thinking cold. And he needed to get his head in the thinking game. The keeping-Clint-out-of-trouble game.

When Laurel's car didn't immediately turn around and drive away, he chuckled. He kept walking, but he waited for what he knew would come. Because deputy princess didn't know when to quit.

He supposed that was fair. Neither did he.

"I will never sleep with you, Grady Carson," she shouted through her open driver's side window.

He just raised a hand in salute. He didn't think of "never" so much as a challenge as he considered it a curse. And there were already plenty of Carson and Delaney curses in the air.

Chapter Five

Evergreen Mining existed about thirty miles outside of Bent, and straddled Bent and Freemont counties with its sprawling compound in the middle of just about nowhere. Little boxlike things dotted the landscape as Laurel explained who she was and showed her badge to the security entrance.

Laurel didn't know much about the company. No one in her immediate family or group of friends worked this far outside of Bent. She did remember the mine here getting in trouble a few years back for some safety regulations, but she hardly expected her accountant victim to have been involved in any of that.

At best, she'd find a link to someone who might have wanted Jason dead. At worst, it was a dead end and she'd have to start prodding Jason's family. She sighed. She almost wished she knew that line of the family better, but as the son of her father's second cousins, they were so far removed she barely even heard gossip about Jason.

Laurel was led to the office of Jason's boss by a secretary. The secretary knocked on a door and then pushed it open, stepping inside and gesturing Laurel to follow. "Mr. Adams, the police are here to ask you a few questions."

"Yes. Of course." A well-dressed middle-aged man stood from behind a desk and held out his hand. "I'd be happy to assist you in whatever way I can, miss."

"Deputy Delaney," Laurel said, shaking his hand in return.

The man shook her hand, looking at her quizzically. "You're related to Jason?"

Laurel forced herself to smile. "Yes, though distantly."

"Ah. Well, have a seat. I'd be happy to answer any questions you may have. I do have an appointment with my foreman in twenty minutes that I can't miss." He smiled apologetically. "Regulations and all that."

"Of course. I mainly just need a list of anyone Jason had routine contact with, and if you know of anyone he might have had a disagreement with or dislike of."

"Well, our administrative staff is somewhat isolated out here, Miss Delaney."

Laurel bit back the need to correct him. *Deputy, not Miss, jerk.* "Did he have a secretary or an assistant?"

"No. Jason was a satellite accountant, meaning he kept track of our accounting at this plant alone. He would have answered to the head accountant in our main office in Nebraska."

Laurel continued to ask him questions, and Mr. Adams continued to give vague, unhelpful answers for twenty full minutes. Finally, Mr. Adams stood. "I have my meeting. Is there anything else—"

"I'd like access to Jason's things. Did he have an office?"

Mr. Adams frowned but quickly smoothed it out. "Follow me, miss."

Laurel scowled at Mr. Adams's back, but followed him back out into the hallway and down a few doors. Mr. Adams pulled out a key ring and unlocked the door.

"Feel free to look around as much as you'd like. If you need to take anything, I'm afraid I'll have to approve it. Jason did have access to some sensitive documents."

"I'm sure copies can be made of anything that might aid me in my investigation." Laurel smiled brightly at him.

Mr. Adams smiled thinly. "Of course. If you can't find me, my secretary should be at her desk. She can also summon anyone else you may need to talk to. If you'll excuse me."

Laurel nodded and stepped into the office. It was small and cramped, and messy. She sighed. It was hard to find clues when you didn't know what you were looking for. Long, frustrating hours of sifting through crap. Her least favorite part of the job.

But it was part of her job, so she got to work. She didn't know how long she filtered through the papers on Jason's desk before she finally found something of potential interest. A scrap of paper in a file with the name Jennings scribbled on it.

Considering Jason had been found by a Mr. Jennings, that seemed incredibly pertinent. A quick scan of all the papers in the file gave Laurel no clue as to why, but with some closer reading, she might be able to find something.

The door swung open and a man entered, stopping short. He was youngish. Maybe midtwenties, dressed like he didn't belong in the administrative building. Jeans, a heavy-duty jacket and heavy work boots.

"Who are you?" he demanded. "Where's Jason?"

Interesting. She supposed the appropriate thing would be to tell this man what had happened to Jason, but she wanted a little information first. Especially since Mr. Adams considered Jason so isolated.

"Hello. I'm sorry, who are you?"

The man frowned. "Jason get fired or something?"

"Actually..."

"You know what, never mind," the man mumbled and rushed out the door.

Very, very curious. Laurel clutched the file and hurried after him, trying to make her strides look relaxed.

He passed the secretary, busting out the door with a hard push.

Laurel stepped up to the secretary's desk. "Who was that man?"

The secretary didn't even look up. "Hank Gaskill."

Gaskill. Why did that sound familiar? Laurel pushed the file toward the woman, getting out her notebook and writing down the name. "Can I get copies of everything in this file?"

The secretary took the file and frowned. "This was in Jason's office?"

Laurel raised an eyebrow as she placed the notebook back in her pocket. "Yes."

"It shouldn't have been. This is Mr. Adams's file, and it doesn't have anything to do with accounting or finances."

A lead. A *real* lead, then. "Then I definitely need copies."

The secretary nodded and turned to a copy machine behind her.

"Does Hank Gaskill come to visit Mr. Delaney often?" Laurel asked.

The secretary shrugged. "Lately they've gone to lunch together. Childhood friends, from what I could tell."

Yet, Hank hadn't heard that Jason had been murdered. Interesting. "Thank you." Laurel got her card out of her pocket and handed it to the secretary. "If you or Mr. Adams or anyone thinks of anything else, please be sure to call me."

The secretary handed over the copies and took Laurel's card. "I will. Jason was so young. Such a tragedy."

Laurel nodded and slipped the papers under her arm, heading back out to her car. *Gaskill. Gaskill.* Why was that familiar?

She walked to her car, turning over the events of yesterday in her mind, and that's when it dawned on her.

Fred Gaskill. Clint's friend she'd questioned yesterday.

Oh, damn that kid and his lies.

GRADY WAS IN a piss-poor mood as he opened Rightful Claim. He'd spent too much of his morning searching for Clint. The teen had, sensibly, left Grady's bike at the ranch, but had disappeared after that.

Grady had a saloon to run and things to do, and his half brother was putting a dent in both.

"I take it you don't have any ideas on how to bring him to heel," Ty asked, pulling chairs down off the tables. Since Ty had basically just gotten back to Bent after a stint as an army ranger, he was going to be working at the bar until he decided what he wanted to do next.

"I'm washing my hands of that kid," Grady muttered, putting cash in the register for the evening.

"Yeah, you're so good at washing your hands of people."

Grady only grunted. So, maybe giving up on people wasn't exactly his strong suit. But that was because he always did some good. If Clint didn't want some of that good, well, fine. Grady would let him off the proverbial hook.

Soon as he got Clint cleared of murder.

The saloon doors swung open and Laurel stepped into the dim light of the bar. She was dressed exactly as she had been this morning, except her weapon was strapped to her hip.

The fact his spirits lightened enough he could feel a weight lift in his chest was kind of worrying, but he'd wrap that up in sarcasm and irritating the crap out of her.

"She deigns to walk through our doors, Grady. To what do we owe the unwanted nonpleasure?"

Something about Ty giving her a hard time bothered him in a way he did not care for at all. "Watch the bar," Grady ordered gruffly.

He ignored the shock on Ty's face and jerked his head toward the back. "Follow me," he said to Laurel.

She pressed her lips together, but didn't argue. So, instead of leading her to one of the back rooms or the kitchen or anything that might have been easy and safe, he led her upstairs to his apartment.

Her pressed-lips look had morphed into a full-blown scowl as he opened the door and gestured her inside.

"Do we really need to talk up here?"

"Private," Grady returned cheerfully. He entered the apartment and turned to give her an impatient look.

She huffed out a breath but stepped inside. She wrinkled her nose. "Your bedroom isn't even separate from your kitchen?"

"But the bathroom is separate, which is probably far more important." He nodded toward the bed that took up a considerable amount of space in his kitchen/living/bedroom area. "You want to lie down on my bed? Tit for tat and all that?"

"Gaskill," she said firmly, though he didn't miss the way her eyes drifted to his messy, unmade bed. "Fred Gaskill is friends with Clint, and claimed he didn't know anything about Clint's whereabouts."

"Yeah."

"Do you know anything about Hank Gaskill?"

"Fred's older brother. Works at the…mine." Which was where Laurel had been headed today.

"Friends with Jason. He popped into his office today while I was looking through Jason's things. Skittered off like he was afraid." Laurel frowned, a line digging into her forehead. "But he didn't seem to know Jason was dead."

"What does it mean?" What did it mean that one of Clint's friends had a brother who was friendly with a dead man? It could mean nothing in a small, rural county. A coincidence. But Grady wasn't sure he believed in those with a murder having gone down.

"I don't know. I've got some more digging to do, but—"

"What kind of digging?"

"Police digging. Does Hank ever come in here?"

Grady didn't care for the brush-off, but he didn't press it. Yet. "A handful of the mining guys do occasionally. Not much else in the way of a place to hang out and get a drink for those who live on this side of things."

"I need you to call me if they ever come in. Day or night. On duty or off. You call me."

"What? So you can oh so subtly eavesdrop?"

"Maybe."

Grady snorted. "Princess, everyone knows you don't come into Rightful Claim, and this is time number two in a week. Make it a third, especially during working hours, the whole town might implode with the implications of a Delaney in a Carson establishment."

"Carsons bank at Delaney Bank and shop at Delaney General all the time."

"It ain't the same, and you know that."

Laurel blew out an irritated breath. "Regardless. You call me. Something is off with everything I witnessed today. Hank coming into Jason's office, then files on his desk that shouldn't have been. I can't tell if the boss is just a patronizing, sexist douche or an actual criminal."

"Maybe even both."

She frowned. "He called me *miss*."

"So, if I really want to piss you off I should call you Miss Deputy Princess."

She rolled her eyes and made a move for the door, but Grady blocked it.

"Out of my way."

"What's the plan, Delaney?"

"The plan is for me to continue investigating per my job. If you see Hank *or* Fred Gaskill in your bar, or doing anything fishy, you call me."

"And that's it? My kid brother might be on the hook for murder and I'm just supposed to play lookout?"

Some of that pissed-off hard edge softened. "What else is there to do, Grady? I have due process to follow. You can't go with me to search Jason's place, and I can't hand over evidence. Both of our hands are tied."

"I really prefer to do the tying," he joked even though he didn't feel like joking in the least.

Laurel's gaze slid to the bed again before she seemed to shake herself out of it. "Regardless. I need you to sit tight and watch. I need you to have some patience."

Grady ran his palms over his beard. Hands-tied patience. When had he ever not balked at that? But no matter how many times he'd acted against all he'd been told to do, when he *acted* he did so knowing he was right.

The worst part of all this was knowing Laurel was right. He was no cop. He had no authority to arrest or try a murderer, and an eye for an eye wasn't going to work.

"You get really quiet when you know I'm right," she offered with a smirk.

The hands-tied frustration bubbling through him and that self-satisfied smirk of hers right next to his bed was the kind of terrible concoction that led to bad decisions.

Still, holding himself back in one arena meant holding himself back in another wasn't a possibility. So, he stepped forward, and when she lifted her chin to meet his gaze rather than step back, he grinned.

"Do I, now?" he asked quietly, reaching out and taking one of those flyaway strands of her hair between his fingers.

She kept that haughty expression on her face, but he watched her elegant throat move as she swallowed.

"You don't believe in the feud, but do you believe in the curse?"

"What curse?" she asked, clearly attempting nonchalance. But she didn't meet his gaze when she asked.

"The one that says if a Carson and a Delaney even look at each other with so much of an ounce of kindness, or *other* nice things, the whole world goes to hell. Just like my favorite illegitimate Carson and his Delaney bride who died, and the Delaney girl who would've married the Carson boy if not for World War II, and then there's your sis—"

That dark, irritated look returned. "There's no curse. I'm being nice to you, aren't I?"

He twisted her soft strand of hair in his fingers. "Could be nicer."

Her eyebrows furrowed, but she didn't pull away and he'd be damned if her gaze didn't drop to his mouth. But when she looked back into his eyes, there was something he didn't want to notice, even if he did.

A note of vulnerability to invulnerable Laurel Delaney. "What game are you playing, Grady? Because I'm not playing one."

"No games. Just…" He leaned a little closer. "Chemistry. Admit it. Does it hurt so very much to admit it?"

Laurel stared at him for a few humming seconds. Seconds he thought she might have actually considered *chemistry.*

But then she shook her head. "You're not funny." She stepped around him, her hair sliding out of his fingers.

There were ways to stop her, sarcastic things to drawl her way, but he couldn't get over the fact she didn't seem so much irritated by him as something else. Something a lot softer.

Grady didn't poke at soft. He might be his father in a lot of ways, but not that one. "Listen." He turned to face her, frowning at the fact she already had the door open and was striding out of it. "I'll give you a call if anyone from the mine shows up."

She paused in his doorway and straightened her shoulders, but she didn't turn around. "Great. Thanks."

Then she was gone, and he was left in the same piss-poor mood he'd been in before she'd arrived.

Chapter Six

"This isn't going to work."

"Not with that attitude," Jen said to Laurel, all too cheerfully. "This was your idea. Don't start pooh-poohing it after all the work I've put in."

Laurel sat in her sister's tiny bathroom, second-guessing her plan. And then third-guessing it. Until the number got too high to count.

"I watched too many detective shows as a kid. It's infected my brain and this is a terrible idea," Laurel said dejectedly.

"No, the terrible idea is trusting Grady Carson."

"Don't start."

Jen handed Laurel a small mirror and Laurel studied her reflection. The wig didn't look ridiculous, and though she *felt* silly, Laurel knew that on the surface she looked like any normal twentysomething.

The problem was she'd *never* been a normal twentysomething. Her life since she could remember revolved around becoming and then being a cop. No parties, little dating. She didn't go to bars or flirt with guys. Ever.

Plus, she didn't think she'd be able to recreate any of

the things Jen had done to make her look different. She was terrible with makeup, felt uncomfortable in decent-fitting clothes and didn't know if she could jab the wig pins into her scalp with as much glee as Jen had done.

"People are starting to talk, Laurel. Murder is murder even without the feud. Add the Delaneys and Carsons, and my store is a veritable gossip station."

"People have too much time on their hands, then. The murder has nothing to do with the feud."

"Then why are you suddenly being seen all over the place with the Carsons?"

It was stupid to be caught off guard by that. Laurel knew how this town worked. The Delaneys didn't go into Rightful Claim, ever, let alone twice in one week. And loud, disruptive Carson motorcycles did not make their way up to the Delaney Ranch. She'd been so focused on the case and clearing Clint, she'd been sloppy with anticipating how the town would react.

Or maybe that's Grady's influence. Just the thought of Grady filled her with… Well, it was irritation, but something in addition to that annoyance Grady normally evoked. And she was all too afraid it was familiar. A tingle. A shutting down of her rational brain. That same stupid thing that used to sizzle through her when she'd been a teenager hanging out with his sister and would catch a glimpse of him.

"Laurel. What's going on? Really. I know you can't share all the police stuff, but you can share the *you* stuff."

Her stuff? There was no *her* stuff. There was her

job and her duty to this town and that was her entire life. She was proud of that. She *was*.

But something about Grady's obnoxious comment about chemistry had dug inside of her and stirred up all the lonely she so often ignored.

Like some sort of horrible cosmic sign, her phone vibrated with an incoming text message. Jen snuck a quick glance at the sender's name, which read *GC*, and frowned.

"Yes, I'm going to ask who GC is, and yes, it better not be Grady Carson."

"Jen."

"I thought you grew out of this."

"Grew out of what?"

"Oh, like it wasn't obvious when we were in high school that you mooned over the guy?"

"Pot. Kettle," Laurel said, pointing to Jen and then to herself. "Ty Carson is back in town, by the way."

Jen's entire body stiffened. Yeah, Laurel might be stupid and a little bit weak in the head when it came to Grady, but her sister had no moral high ground to stand on. Laurel had only ever *looked*. She was pretty sure her sister had done more than that with Grady's cousin back in the day.

Ignoring her sister's waves of disapproval, Laurel brought the message up on her screen.

Gaskill here. On alert. Do. Not. Come. Here. Will report back.

"Well. Time to put my plan into motion," she said, taking one last glimpse at herself in the mirror. Anyone who knew her and looked right at her might figure out who she was, but if she stayed in the shadows, kept a low profile, she could sit next to Hank Gaskill and listen to everything he had to say.

Maybe it would be pointless, but maybe it wouldn't. She had to try. She'd sent Hart over to search Jason's place while she'd been at the mine, but he hadn't come up with anything. She'd take another look herself tomorrow, but for now she had to work on the people involved. The leads she *did* have.

"I should go with you."

"I believe the point of the disguise is, you know, Delaneys not going into Rightful Claim."

"Someone should go with you. I don't like you going there by yourself."

"It's police business, Jen. It's hardly dangerous. I'm just going to listen for some information that I may or may not even find. If someone is with me, it ruins the whole point."

"You're going to Grady's bar. That's not *all* police business."

"I don't know why you suddenly think I can't control myself, but I can. Besides, looking at Grady and Grady looking back are two very separate things." Which was probably not the way to convince her sister she didn't have a thing for Grady.

"You don't honestly think Grady Carson has never looked back at you."

Laurel turned her attention from her reflection in

the mirror to her sister. After all, she and Jen looked a lot alike. Jen's hair was a shade lighter, and her eyes had hints of hazel. They were only about ten months apart, and they'd always been close.

But Jen had always been into the whole girlie thing. Understanding how to put on makeup and dressing to attract attention. Laurel had never been comfortable with that. She was more interested in police procedure and appearing tough and untouchable. She'd always wanted to be a cop, and a female cop *had* to be a little untouchable.

So, it didn't matter if her mind on occasion wandered to Grady, and touching him. It was all…fantasy. And irrelevant to her current situation at hand. "This conversation is ridiculous. I'm going to go do my job. Beginning and end of story."

"Fine. But I want regular text updates and I want to know when you're home. In fact, I'd feel even better if you come back here when you're done and assure me it was all police work and nothing dangerous."

Laurel stood and stepped out of the bathroom, adjusting the bra holster that wasn't comfortable, but the only way to conceal her gun effectively. At least in the jeans Jen had loaned her, because all of Jen's dresses were far, far, far too short for Laurel's taste.

"I'll text you when I get home."

"I don't like that you're wearing that gun. That means you think something bad is going to happen."

Laurel took a deep breath. "No, it means I'm on duty. You know who you sound like right now."

Jen wrinkled her nose. "Much as I hate sounding

like Dad, it *is* a terrible feeling to know you're going off into danger."

"You're not usually this silly about my work stuff. What's going on?"

Jen crossed her arms over her chest. "Nothing is going on except you're not usually walking the line between Delaney and Carson while investigating a murder. A murder of someone we're related to, I might add."

"It's my job, Jen. I do it well." She picked up the purse Jen had laid out for her to match the outfit. A little clutch that made no sense to Laurel. "What do you do with this thing? There's no strap. How am I supposed to attach it to myself?"

Jen rolled her eyes. "You carry it. It's cute. Not everything has to be functional."

"In my world it does." But she was playing a part. A part her sister had helped her get ready for. She turned to Jen and pulled her into a hug. "Thank you for helping me. You know I appreciate it."

"You owe me. Stay away from Grady Carson. Please just listen to me on that. Even if you take out all the feud nonsense, the Carsons are not meant for us. Period. I don't want you getting hurt by that moron."

"You ever going to tell me what happened between you and Ty?"

"Nothing happened between me and Ty. Ty Carson does not exist as far as I'm concerned. You should go. Policewoman business awaits."

Laurel rolled her eyes. She'd always been close with her siblings, but none of them had ever poked much at each other's romantic lives. It was considered a separate, no-go zone. Laurel wasn't sure why things were that way, but she supposed it was small-town complications. Everyone else poked into everyone else's business enough, why add to it?

Besides, Jen's worry was irrational, and Laurel shouldn't keep defending herself. It was pointless. She was not going to get *involved* with Grady Carson. No matter how much chemistry they had or how much he wanted her to admit it.

She had bigger things to worry about than chemistry. Carsons. Delaneys. Bent and feuds. She had a murder to solve.

And solve it she would.

GRADY WAS LOATH to admit that running a bar and trying to eavesdrop on someone was at cross-purposes. Any time he got remotely close to Hank's table and was able to overhear something of the conversation, someone called his name or clapped him on the back and asked him a question. Men made loud, raucous jokes in his direction and women offered smiles and innuendo and whatever.

It was something he usually enjoyed, the banter and flirting. The noise, the conversations. But today it only served to piss him off.

If he couldn't get any of the information Laurel needed, he'd have to admit he failed. That galled for too many reasons to count.

He was not a guy who had to prove himself to people. He was what he was, and anyone who didn't like it could go to hell. The only person who had ever challenged that had been his dear old deadbeat dad.

And Laurel Delaney.

If he didn't get the information she needed, *she* would, and it seemed like adding insult to injury to fail at this, as well as know that she inevitably wouldn't.

The saloon doors swung open and Grady glanced up at the latest patron as he always did. There were a few people who tried to stir up fights in his bar, and he liked to cut them off at the pass.

But this customer was a woman. She looked vaguely familiar, but he couldn't quite place her. Dark eyes scanned the bar, moving past him rather quickly.

He frowned. She wasn't a regular or a known troublemaker, or he would have been able to place her. She didn't look like any Bent resident he knew. Something prickled through him, though, some kind of omen, as if he *should* be paying attention.

He shook his head. He was being some kind of paranoid, hyperalert idiot because he'd let Laurel's crap get into his head, and that just wasn't acceptable.

He focused back in on his target. If he could go clean off the table next to Hank, he might be able to hear *something* before someone bothered him again.

But just as he pulled the rag out of his back pocket, the woman who'd just entered slid into a chair at the table he'd been about to pretend to clean.

"It's not clean," he said gruffly.

"I don't mind," she replied airily.

Something about that voice… Grady glanced over at her but she studiously ignored his gaze. What was going on here? He thought about asking her if he knew her, but he was a little afraid she was some unhappy ex-lover. He didn't have time for that, and she didn't seem interested in rehashing anything.

"Get you something to drink?"

"A Coke, please," she said, her head turned so far away from him he could only see curly blond waves of hair and the peekaboo of an ear.

"Be right back."

She nodded, tucking her hair behind her ear. Which was when he saw it. The little wink of a silver star earring. Which Grady supposed could be a coincidence. Maybe tiny silver star earrings were all the rage and young women everywhere were wearing them.

But the woman's behavior, her voice, those familiar eyes darting all over his bar... He reached out and grabbed her wrist. When she jerked her gaze toward him, all flashes of gold fury, he very nearly dropped his jaw.

"What do you think you're doing?" he demanded. He was more than a little angry she'd fooled him for as long as she had with that ridiculous blond wig and clothes that actually fit her all-too-enticing body.

"Nothing," she hissed. "Now, if you would get me my Coke."

He gave her hand a tug. "Come over to the bar so I can get a tab started for you."

She held firm in her seat, staring him down with those dark, expressive eyes. "That won't be necessary," she said, over-enunciating each word.

She nodded her head toward Hank's table as if to

tell Grady to stop in case someone in the group might overhear. Maybe he should. But he'd told her not to come in here. He'd told her he could handle it.

But he *wasn't* handling it. Even if her disguise didn't do much, if she sat here and sipped a Coke she had a far better chance of hearing something than he did. No one would recognize her if she calmly sat there. No one would believe Laurel Delaney was in Rightful Claim in a blond wig with an actual hint of cleavage showing.

Damn it.

He released her wrist. "One Coke coming right up," he muttered. Because he was *not* his father, and could back off even when he was irrationally pissed.

"Who's that chick?" Ty asked as Grady moved behind the bar and grabbed a glass.

Grady was an excellent liar in most situations, but he always hesitated at lying to family—especially Ty, Noah and Vanessa.

But this was important and bigger than him. "Some out-of-towner. She said she came in looking for a little Wild West charm."

"Is that a euphemism?" Ty asked with a grin.

Grady filled the glass with Coke and tried not to scowl. "Guess we'll find out," he muttered and headed back for Laurel and her stupid disguise.

Everything about the situation grated. The fact his hands were tied. The fact she was the one sitting there in a blond wig. So, he did what he always did when she irritated him.

"You make a hot blonde."

She glared at him. "Did you know that at a restaurant or bar, you don't have to tip the proprietor?"

"Says who?"

"The law," she returned, giving him a haughty look before glancing over at Hank's table.

He should let her be. Let her eavesdrop. Let her do her *job*, but he slid into the seat opposite her instead. When she didn't object or even send him a nasty glare, he decided he'd do her a favor in return by not asking her how she came upon a wig and clothes that actually fit.

She grabbed the sparkly purse that looked about as much like Laurel as the curly blond hair. Everything about her right now was the opposite of Laurel, and it was a little annoying to find he rather preferred her to be *her*.

She scribbled something on a piece of paper and casually slid it over the surface of the table toward him.

He flipped over the paper and read the question in her neatly printed letters. *Who are the others at the table?*

He wanted to make a quip about her needing his help, and he doubted the table of three men next to them would notice, but he could be subtle. He wrote down the names of the men Hank was sitting with and returned the paper to her.

She read the names quickly, then slipped the paper into her sparkly handbag. She daintily sipped her Coke and studiously ignored him.

"Most female strangers who come into my bar flirt with me." He flashed a grin.

She rolled her eyes so far back in her head it must've hurt.

"Of course, you don't strike me as the type of person who knows how to flirt."

She curled her lip at him, as he'd hoped, but she didn't snipe back. Merely straightened in her chair.

Grady couldn't help the fact his gaze drifted to the hint of cleavage, and the whole outfit, really. Laurel Delaney actually had a body under there, and he couldn't even be surprised because the baggy clothes and fierce appearance no doubt served her in her job. And, unfortunately for her, in a small town you didn't get to be someone else once you clocked out of your job. Laurel Delaney *always* had to be Deputy Delaney, or risk a lot of things.

Why did he have to *understand* this infernal woman?

The table next to them laughed uproariously, but as Grady glanced over just like Laurel did, he imagined she saw the same thing.

The two men at the table with Hank were laughing, but Hank wasn't. He was staring down the bottom of his drink. Abruptly, he pushed out of his chair. "Going to grab a smoke," he grumbled to his jovial companions.

Hank wasn't even three steps toward the door before Laurel was picking up her purse. Luckily Grady was paying enough attention he could grab her hand before she got up. "Don't you think about it."

She glared at his hand on hers. "Don't *you* even think about telling me what to do."

"What do you think you're going to do after you follow him?" He leaned forward so that no one could hear them, though no one was paying any attention. "Ask for a cigarette? Smoke one? You?"

She jerked her hand out of his grasp. "If that's what it takes. Don't follow me or I will be forced to arrest you for getting in the way of a criminal investigation."

"I don't think that's legal, princess."

"I don't think I care. Stay here."

He could've grabbed her again. He could do a lot of things. But the fact he needed to get through his thick skull was that Laurel was a *cop*. She was investigating an actual murder case, and he didn't have any claim to sit here and tell her what to do.

If she wanted to be stupid and go have a smoke with Hank, as if that would get her any information, well, that was her prerogative.

She stood and walked out the same way Hank had. Grady scowled as he watched her go, her hips swaying mesmerizingly in the tight denim.

Which was *really* unfair, all things considered.

He'd give her ten minutes. Tops. And then he was going after her.

Chapter Seven

Laurel pushed through the swinging door and walked out of Rightful Claim with her heart beating a little too hard in her chest.

It had rattled her that Grady had seen through her disguise so quickly. But she'd grown up with Grady. She'd only met Hank Gaskill once in passing. Granted, it had been this morning, but why would he expect the blonde in a bar to be the brunette in Jason's office he'd talked to for five seconds?

She inhaled and exhaled, slowly walking toward where he leaned against the corner of the building, lighting a cigarette. He took a long drag and Laurel steeled herself to approach him.

"I don't suppose I could borrow a cigarette?" she asked, making her voice a little breathless and then berating herself for it. Over-the-top was suspicious.

"How can you borrow a cigarette? Plan on giving it back once you smoked it?"

Laurel couldn't tell if his response was snarky or flirty. That was always the trouble. While she could read murderous intentions or abusive husbands or drug addicts, she really wasn't very good at reading the opposite sex's reaction to her. There were always too many mixed messages and ulterior motives and it just didn't make any sense.

But she was on a job, playing a part. She wasn't Laurel Delaney. She was someone else entirely. So, she smiled as sweetly as she knew how. "Truth be told, I'd just like a puff of one. I quit a few years ago and I have just had the worst day."

"Well, this is the bad day corner," Hank replied and held his lit cigarette toward her.

Luckily, Laurel had seen enough bad movies to know you didn't take a deep inhale of a cigarette when she'd never smoked a day in her life. She put her mouth to the cigarette for a second and then pulled it away, pretending to sigh heavily as if it was a great relief.

"Thanks," she offered, offering the cigarette back to Hank.

He shook his head, tapping another cigarette out of the package he held. "Keep it. Had a rough day myself."

Laurel smiled understandingly. "They must really be going around, huh?"

"Yeah." His gaze moved down her body and back up, a kind of subtle checkout she probably wouldn't have caught if she wasn't looking for clues for a murder case.

"What's your sob story?" he asked.

"Just your average 'lost my job, boyfriend kicked me out' type thing. You?" she asked, sounding awfully casual if she did say so herself.

He shrugged and stared off into the dark, taking a deep drag of his cigarette before he replied. "Friend died."

"That's awful. Was he sick?"

Hank shook his head, and no matter how badly Laurel wanted to press, she knew that would only look weird coming from a stranger.

He looked her up and down again. "Why'd your boyfriend kick you out?"

"Oh." Laurel worked up her best sheepish smile. She was playing a very strange game here, but if it got her *any* information, did it matter? The important thing was if Hank thought she was available and interested he might tell her more about what he knew of his dead friend.

She had no other leads and a town whispering about murder and Delaneys and Carsons, so, sometimes the end justified the means.

"I may have kissed another guy," she said quietly, conspiratorially. "We'd been together a few years, and it just got boring, you know?"

Hank's mouth curved a little bit. "Wouldn't know. I must get bored before a few weeks is up."

Laurel laughed right along with him.

"You want to go back inside? I'll buy you a drink."

"Your friend died. I feel like *I* should buy *you* a drink."

Hank smiled. "Okay. I'll let you."

Grady wouldn't like that, Laurel knew. He'd think she was being stupid or something. But she couldn't care what Grady would like. She couldn't care what kind of lines she was tiptoeing on either side of right now.

If she had a drink with Hank, he might say *something* that could be a lead. Sometimes strangers were the best people to confide in. It wasn't as though he was the murderer. This morning he clearly hadn't known Jason was dead. But that didn't mean he might not know how or why.

Hank finished off his cigarette and flicked it into the street. Trying to hide how little she'd smoked, Laurel slipped hers into the ashtray canister on top of a trash can.

"Hank," he offered, holding out his hand to shake.

Laurel smiled and ordered herself not to panic at how many lies she was weaving. "Sarah," she offered, shaking his hand in return.

"You're not from Bent."

"No. Fremont. Well, that's where I lived with my boyfriend, but now I need a place to crash. So, I came to Bent to stay with my cousin for a bit."

"Oh, yeah? Maybe I know her. What's her name?"

Laurel fiddled with her clutch, trying to look like she was doing something purposeful while she tried to come up with the best lie. "Dylan Delaney." She figured using her brother's name was better than using that of any of her female relatives. And she couldn't use a Carson name. God knew they'd never back her up.

"Don't you know the Delaneys aren't supposed to be in Carson bars?" Hank asked with a grin.

Laurel smiled as flirtatiously as she could possibly manage. "I've never been very good at doing what I'm supposed to do." What a laugh.

"Well, then let's head inside and let you buy me a drink."

Laurel nodded and tucked a strand of hair behind her ear and turned toward the door.

Which burst open—and hit her square in the face.

GRADY SLAMMED HIS palms against the outward-swinging door, but instead of a satisfying, loud swing there was only a thump followed by a squeak.

It was not possible that he'd…

Gingerly, he pushed the out door again, this time meeting with no resistance, but when he stepped onto the well-lit boardwalk in front of his saloon, blonde Laurel was standing there holding her nose.

Again. For the second time in as many days.

Dark eyes met his, flashing all-too-enticing gold fury. "What is wrong with you?" she demanded.

"Me? I wasn't the one standing on the other side of the *out* door, sweetheart. That's why we have big signs that say *Out* and *In*, so people don't get knocked into unless they're drunk or stupid." No matter how acidic his voice was, his chest pinched painfully. Which was beyond stupid. She'd been the idiot standing on the wrong side of the wrong door.

Hank handed Laurel a bandanna from his back pocket, which she put to her bleeding nose.

"I think you owe her a drink on the house, man," Hank said, a little too cheerfully.

Grady raised one eyebrow at Hank and didn't move another inch of his body. Just stared down the little prick. "You think so?"

Hank wilted and looked away. Coward.

"Come with me and we'll get you cleaned up," Grady ordered Laurel.

"No, thank you," she replied, biting off each word.

"You should let him clean you up, Sarah. Get some ice and we'll get our free drinks. Okay?" Hank patted Laurel on the shoulder, seeming a little too jovial for the situation.

"Shall we… *Sarah*?" Grady offered, gesturing at the door. Specifically the *In* side of the door.

She tried to smile. He could tell she really, really tried. And if she didn't have a handkerchief pressed to her nose, he might have found it all funny. As it was, he took her arm far too gently for his own liking and pulled her inside and through the loud, crowded bar.

He motioned Hank toward Ty. "Ty, get this man two drinks on the house." Ty nodded and Hank walked up to the bar while Grady propelled Laurel toward the back. When he started leading her toward the stairs up to his apartment, she jerked out of his grasp.

"I'm not going to that stupid apartment of yours and you are not ruining this for me." She pulled the handkerchief away from her nose. He didn't think it was quite as bad as the last one, but there was a slight smudge of blood underneath.

She looked at the bandanna and shook her head. "How. How is it possible? Twice in one week you smash me in the nose."

"Might I remind you that in the first instance, *you* ran into me. And in the second instance, I was going out the *out* side of the swinging doors. That's why they have the signs on them. You don't stand next to the out one, because people push *out* of them."

She closed her eyes, standing still as she breathed in, and then out. In and then out. Clearly trying to calm herself. When she reopened her eyes, all of that fury had been smoothed out of her features. "Grady, why were you coming out at all?"

"Guess I just wanted to witness how far you were willing to go for a little information. Call it curiosity."

"You are..." She shook her head. "I cannot work with you. I don't know why I ever thought that would actually be beneficial. Stay out of my way. Stay out of this case."

"You can't be serious."

"I can't include you in this if this is how you're going to act. I need you to listen to me. I need to trust that I can do something without you swaggering in and breaking my nose."

"It isn't broken." And he was behaving like a...like a contentious, surly teenager. "Stay here," he grumbled before stalking back to the kitchen. He grabbed one of the ice packs they kept in the freezer for bar fight injuries.

When he returned, he held it out to her. She took it, and placed it on the bridge of her nose with a wince.

He hated what he knew had to come next. Hated it beyond measure, but he hadn't gotten through life without having to do a few things he hated. He had a strict moral code for himself, no matter how a Delaney might sneer her nose at it. It didn't allow acting like a punk.

"I'm sorry."

She blinked at him, and he wanted to rip that idiotic wig off her. "What did you say?"

"I said, I'm sorry," he repeated, shoving his hands into his pockets. He wasn't going to *explain* that he'd charged out of the saloon and pushed that door far harder than he'd needed to, but he would apologize for causing some harm.

"For what part?"

"The nose part."

"Is that all you're apologizing for?" she asked coolly.

"You're right that's all. We're in this together, and I wasn't about to let you get dragged off in the dark by some—"

"We aren't in this together. This is not an equal partners thing. I am the detective. You're an informant at best. I need you to act like one instead of the over-the-top, makes-trouble Starsky to my Hutch."

"I'm sorry... Did you just make a Starsky and Hutch reference? What thirty-year-old makes a Starsky and Hutch reference?"

She all but growled in frustration. "I'm going back to Hank. You are not going to interrupt me. You are not... Is it me?" she demanded.

"Is what you?"

"That people think I can't hack it at my job. All of a sudden I have a *real* case and people are worried about me and think I can't handle myself. That I need help or protection or whatever. So, based on you and my sister's actions today I'm wondering, is it me? What kind of vibe am I putting off that makes you think I am incapable of handling myself?"

She flung her arms up in the air, clearly exasperated and pissed and maybe even a little hurt, and why could he *see* all that in the set of her mouth and the lines in her forehead? As if he knew what she was feeling just by looking at her. As if he'd spent a lifetime memorizing every emotion that flitted across her face.

Bull.

"Speaking from your sister's standpoint, she cares about you. I think if she were in some sort of dangerous situation, no matter how well-equipped she might be, you would worry about her, too. And express that worry. I believe that's called family love and devotion."

"Okay. Fine. Maybe you're even right. What's your excuse? Don't you think a woman can hack it?"

"Vanessa is my sister. Believe me, I know what women can hack."

"Then what? Why is it that you can't stand down and let me do my job? I'm a Delaney? You think I'm soft? You—"

"Maybe I don't like watching you smile and flirt with a stranger." Which shut her up. And was the only reason he said it. Not because it was true.

Her eyebrows drew together and he didn't know how a woman who was clearly intelligent and yes, fantastic at her job, could be so completely dense.

"Why would that bother you?" she asked as if there was no reasonable answer.

"Maybe, on occasion, I'd like it if you smiled at me." Which in fairness to Laurel wasn't a *reasonable* answer.

"That doesn't make any sense," she persisted.

"Why not?" he demanded, leaning closer. Closer and closer, making her eyes widen and the air between them crackle with electricity. It was an electricity he'd avoided his entire adult life out of duty, out of a healthy belief in the history of Carsons and Delaneys and Bent and destruction.

But Laurel stood there staring at him, her eyes a shade of dark, unfathomable brown, and no matter that she had that wig on, and makeup making her lips redder and her eyes smokier, she was so wholly *Laurel*.

"You're a Carson," she said on a whisper.

He stared at her for something like a full minute, and then he laughed. Because Ms. Doesn't Believe In The Feud thought he couldn't want her to smile at him. All because of his last name and hers.

He supposed he had two choices here in this little back room, empty since everyone working was up front at the bar. He could let her go back to Hank, find out whatever information she'd hoped to find, and wash his hands of messing with her or her investigation.

Or, he could do what he should have done fifteen years ago when he'd caught Laurel Delaney snooping around his room after a sleepover with his sister.

She dropped the ice pack from her nose, clearly still confused, and clearly ready to get back to cop mode.

"Grady, I—"

But he couldn't stand it. He cupped his hand around her neck and pulled her mouth to his.

Chapter Eight

Grady Carson was kissing her.

On the mouth.

She was sure there was something she was supposed to do about that, but her brain was all crackling static while her body…took it. She absorbed the feel of those full lips on hers, the warmth of his rough hand on the back of her neck, holding her still and there as his mouth took hers like they'd been doing this for centuries. Like everything about this kiss was right exactly as it should be.

She knew, somewhere, that was all wrong, and yet sensation seemed to mute that knowledge. Sweep it away into some strange, distant part of her. So distant it didn't seem weird to lean against him, to open her mouth to him, to press her palm against the hard, hot wall of his chest.

When he broke the kiss, slowly, so slowly, easing her body away from his, she had to tell herself to breathe, to open her eyes, to *think*. But all she saw was the vibrant blue of Grady's gaze, and the only thoughts she could manage were in gibberish.

She tried to inhale but it was shaky, the exhale unsteady. Everything felt jittery and unstable, and somehow she was still leaning toward Grady, only his arms keeping her upright.

She shook her head, trying to find sense or reason or some grasp of what was happening. She managed to rock back on her heels, holding herself upright so Grady's arms fell away.

He didn't say anything. He didn't move. If it weren't for that intense, heady gaze of his, she might have thought he was wholly unaffected. She wasn't sure he was *affected*, but he wasn't exactly...

Well, she didn't know. *He'd* kissed *her*. She didn't know why. She didn't know why she'd kissed him back. She didn't *know*, and that was her least favorite feeling in the world.

"I... I don't know what that was." She wasn't even sure she knew her name.

Laurel Delaney. Delaney. Deputy Laurel Delaney, and if you recall, you have a murder to solve, not a Carson to kiss.

Kiss. Grady had kissed her. Kissed her with his mouth. His tongue. She could only stare at him because surely, surely no matter how...*wow*...that kiss was, he'd lost his mind.

His mouth curved in that infuriating way, except now she knew what that felt like against *her* mouth and she couldn't muster irritation because she was just... jelly. Boneless, spineless, thoughtless jelly.

"In my world they call it a kiss."

In her world it was something far more primitive

than a kiss. Kisses were nice. Affectionate. Not a wild, all-encompassing thing.

"Go on back to your informant, smile some information out of him, and then…" He tilted his head, studying her with something in his expression she couldn't read. It was like humor, but not mean. He wasn't making fun of her, like she might have expected, but she certainly didn't know what he felt, or what he saw when he looked at her.

"Then what?" she asked, feeling entranced no matter how much she told herself to come back to reality.

"We can finish this discussion."

"I thought it was a kiss."

"Oh, princess. It was both."

Before she could make any sense out of *that*, he turned and walked away, disappearing into the main room of the bar while she stood in this little back area by herself.

By herself. Which was good. She could jam her brain back into gear by herself. She could think and plan and somehow compartmentalize, because she was here not to get even more confused about Grady. She was here to get information from Hank.

Hank, who was out there drinking a free drink and waiting for her. Hank, who certainly hadn't killed Jason, but might know *something*. Or have some clue whether he knew it or not.

Her job was her life. Had been since she'd joined the police academy. When she'd made time for any kind of…man-woman thing, it had been a relationship. Not a surprise kiss in the back of a bar from a man she wasn't even sure she *liked*.

It was all so complicated and confusing, and the point of being a cop was that it wasn't those things. There was right and wrong, legal and illegal, and the blurring of lines was only ever to find justice or the truth.

Which was what she needed to focus on. Grady had left, was clearly just messing with her or something. Which might make sense if he'd laughed or teased her for kissing him back, but he'd only told her to do her job and come back later to talk.

Talk.

Did he really mean talk?

She could not be worried about that. She placed the ice pack to the bridge of her nose, willing the icy jolt to get her to focus. On Hank, murder and her job. With a stern nod to herself, she walked back into the noisy, crowded bar, repeating four very important words over and over in her head.

Don't look at Grady. Don't look at Grady.

She focused on Hank, who was now sitting on a barstool, two empty glasses in front of him as he watched the TV above the bar intently.

Laurel approached, keeping her gaze steady on Hank and Hank alone. There was a phone placed on the seat next to him.

Laurel swallowed and picked it up. "Saving this seat for me?" she asked in her best throaty tone.

Hank glanced over at her and smiled. "'Course.

You're my free drink ticket." He winked as if it was a joke, but Laurel had to admit she wasn't so sure it was.

Which was fine. Drinking a little too much might convince Hank to tell her what he might know. Something Jason was into. Someone who was bothering him.

She placed his phone on the bar and slid into the seat. Hank waved at Ty down at the other end of the bar, and Ty made no bones about ignoring him.

Hank spared her a glance. "Don't worry. He owes you a drink. I'll get you one."

"No, it's—"

But Hank was already off his chair, striding down the bar to where Ty was serving.

Hank's phone vibrated and Laurel glanced at the screen. A text window popped up, and since Hank was occupied trying to scam himself into another free drink, Laurel nudged the phone so she could read the text.

There was no sender's name, only a number. The message read, Eagle Creek Park. 7. Bring folder.

Laurel frowned. Eagle Creek Park was an isolated state park that barely functioned as a park anymore. She didn't even think they had full-time staff. It was an odd place to meet anyone, unless you were teenagers hoping to get drunk or high. Which certainly didn't require any folders.

Hank returned, grumbling. "Said I had to wait my turn." He slid back into the seat, his hand going over his phone. "Maybe you should try..." He trailed off as he read his text.

"Everything okay?" Laurel asked.

Hank scratched a hand through his hair, then took one of the empty glasses and brought it to his mouth, trying to shake the last drops onto his tongue. His hand shook.

"What's wrong?" she asked, hoping it sounded like worry and compassion and not a cop demand.

"Nothing. Just gotta run. Hey, give me your number so I can hit you up sometime."

"Oh, sure, you want me to type it in?" she asked innocently, holding out her hand.

"Nah, just tell it to me." He sat, fingers poised on his phone screen, but Laurel didn't miss the way his eyes darted around the room.

It was almost ten o'clock, so he couldn't be rushing to meet the guy. Unless seven meant something else besides time. But what else could it mean? Eagle Creek Park was the location, and its address wasn't seven.

She rattled off a fake number. Much as she'd like to use this particular fake flirting to her advantage, she didn't want to push it too far. Especially when she might have to interrogate him as herself.

"Hope I see you around."

"Hope so," she offered cheerfully even though she wanted to stomp her feet and demand he tell her the answers. Instead she let him walk away.

But she had *something* to go on. Eagle Creek Park. Either seven tomorrow morning or seven tomorrow night. She'd be there both times and get to the bottom of this one way or another.

GRADY WATCHED HANK slink out of the bar. Based on the frustrated expression on Laurel's face, she hadn't gotten what she'd wanted out of him.

Grady shouldn't be happy about that. But, regardless, he had a few questions of his own. He slipped out the back, grabbing a half-full bag of trash as a prop, and pushed out into the parking lot. The Dumpster was right there, and he made a big show out of tossing the bag into the bin.

Hank approached a beat-up old truck and Grady cleared his throat. "Hey, Gaskill, right?"

Hank looked over at him suspiciously, so Grady did his best not to look intimidating. He probably failed in the dim light of a bar parking lot, a big man with a gruff voice.

"Fred Gaskill your kid brother?" Grady asked when Hank didn't respond.

"Yeah. What of it?"

"Clint Danvers. *My* kid brother. Who didn't get mixed up in trouble until good old Freddy came along." Which was a bald-faced lie, but might lead him somewhere at least. There were too many connections going on here, connections that led to his dumb brother.

Hank scoffed. "First of all, bull. Second of all, it ain't Freddy, and it ain't Clint, it's that chick that's got 'em wrapped around her pinky finger."

Which was certainly news to Grady. "Which one?"

"Lizzie Adams. She's got four kids in Fred's class following her around town, doing her bidding like she's some kind of TV mob boss. Those idiots are hard up enough to think she's going to put out if they do what she wants. Whatever trouble Clint's got, I guarantee you it started with her."

Lizzie Adams. Grady committed that name to memory. "Well, thanks for the tip, man."

Hank shrugged. "I've been telling Fred to stay out of her orbit for weeks, but he's seventeen. Imagine Clint is the same."

"More than," Grady grumbled.

Hank got in his truck and Grady offered a wave before heading back inside. Lizzie Adams. He didn't think a bunch of teenagers were really involved with murder, but something wasn't right.

He walked back into the bar, stopping at the sounds of crashing coming from the little kitchen. He peeked in to find Vanessa slamming things around with seemingly no purpose.

"Everything okay?"

She glared at him over her shoulder. "Fan-freaking-tastic. What's a Delaney doing in our bar? In a wig?"

"Don't worry about it."

Vanessa fisted her hands on her hips and glared at him, but he wasn't about to be intimidated by his little sister. "Hey, you used to invite her into our house. Consider this payback."

"I was a kid."

"And today I happen to be a grown man." He flashed her a grin that had her reaching for something to throw at him, so Grady picked up the pace and hightailed it into the main area of the bar.

Scanning the people sitting at the barstools, he was gratified to find Laurel still sitting there, typing things into her phone. Notes, no doubt. But she hadn't scurried off to do that. Her target had left, and she was still here. In his bar.

He wondered how long she'd stay. If she would share her information with him. If he should share his information with her. Or if all she wanted was to finish their discussion from earlier.

He grinned to himself, and as if that was some kind of beacon, Laurel glanced up and looked over at him.

She didn't grin back. She scowled. But when he nodded to the back room she slid off her stool and headed toward him. He didn't mind Laurel Delaney walking toward him at all, even in a blond wig.

"I need to talk to you. About the case."

His grin didn't falter. "That all?"

"Yes."

He made a considering noise to rile her up. "Upstairs is the only private place around here."

She rolled her eyes. "Fine."

He stepped through the opening into the back and headed for the stairs, but Vanessa stormed out of the kitchen.

"What are you doing?" Vanessa demanded. When Grady opened his mouth to tell her to mind her own business, she wagged a finger. "Not you." She moved the finger to point at Laurel. "You."

Laurel leveled her with a cool look, and didn't even pretend to be blonde Sarah. "Police business. That's all I care about, remember?" And with that she sailed past Grady and up the stairs.

Grady glanced at his sister with an eyebrows-raised

questioning look, but Vanessa only huffed and stalked into the bar to start her shift.

Women.

He took the stairs, slowly, because he kind of liked the idea of Laurel waiting for him. She was tapping her foot when he reached the top.

"Can we move this along? I have things to do."

"At your command, princess," he said, pulling his keys out of his pocket and unlocking the door to his apartment. He dramatically gestured her inside.

Once he closed the door, she didn't hesitate to start in on cop mode.

"I need some information out of Clint, and I don't think he's going to give it to me."

"I don't think he's going to give it to me, either."

"What about another family member? Vanessa, maybe?"

"Because she's known for her reason and charm? Pretty sure you were just on the brunt edge of that. What happened between you two?"

"A question only your sister can answer. I have no idea."

"Dad was pretty hard on her about being friends with you."

"Yeah, so was mine."

"He ever hit you?"

Laurel stilled, but she didn't wilt. "No. He didn't." She blew out a breath. "I am not here to drudge up ancient history. Or Delaney-Carson nonsense. I saw a text Hank got that I can only assume is important or linked, and I need to know what Clint knows about Eagle Creek Park."

"You mean the place all the high school kids go to get high?"

"Yes. Exactly."

"I could probably get someone to ask him that without him bristling. Why do you need to know?"

"Because."

Grady crossed his arms over his chest and frowned down at her. "Try again."

"It's confidential."

"Fine, then I won't tell you what Hank told me out there in the parking lot."

"Hank didn't tell you anything."

Grady raised an eyebrow. "You calling me a liar? I believe back in the day that ended up with shoot-outs in the streets and a lot of Delaneys on the wrong side of a standoff."

"Tell me, and *then* I'll show you the text."

"Promise?"

She wrinkled her nose, clearly balking, but eventually she pushed out a breath. "Fine, I promise."

"Hank said his brother and Clint and a couple of the other idiot boys they hang out with are all gone over this girl, and she's the cause of any trouble they get into. Girl named Lizzie Adams."

"Adams? The man in charge of the mine is named Adams. These kids are connected somehow."

"I agree."

Laurel started moving toward the door, but Grady grabbed her arm. "Hey, you have to show me the text."

"I have to go, Grady. I have to look into this. Make sure Lizzie Adams is—"

"You promised, princess," he said, not letting her arm go no matter how she jerked it. "Now, spill."

She grunted in frustration, but she pulled her phone out of her pocket with her free hand. "Let me go now."

He did so, but stayed alert, because he wouldn't put it past her to make a dash for it. And if she did, he'd have no compunction about throwing her over his shoulder. He'd enjoy it.

She held the phone out to him and he read the notes she'd typed.

"This is what his text said, verbatim. And this is the number."

"Eagle Creek Park. 7. Bring folder."

"So, I need to be at Eagle Creek Park at seven, and if he's not there in the morning, I'll go at night. But if Clint can get me some information—"

"What if it's not a time?"

"Huh?"

"What if seven isn't a time? It could be a…hike marker, a cabin—it could be a campsite. Hank wasn't just meandering out of here after a few drinks. If he didn't have somewhere to be, he'd be trying to get into your pants." Because it was damn weird Hank had hightailed it out of here.

"I have to go."

"Like hell."

"Grady, this is police bus—"

"Then call backup because I'll be damned if I'm letting you go to an isolated park all by yourself. I don't care if it's me or some cop crony of yours, but there's gonna be somebody."

"I don't have time for this. He's got a good ten-minute head start on me, and Hank could be going into danger. Another isolated place like we found Jason? I'll call for backup on my way." She jerked the door open, but he followed.

"Fine, but I'm at your side until that backup shows up."

"Grady," she growled, already jogging down the stairs.

But he jogged right after her. "Sorry, princess, you don't have time to argue."

Chapter Nine

Laurel didn't have time to argue, and while she had half a mind to pull out her gun and use it on Grady to keep him put, she knew where night shift zones were, and she knew she could get to Eagle Creek Park long before any of the deputies on duty.

It *wasn't* smart to go alone, but it was hardly smart to go with a civilian. Especially this one.

But what choice did she have? She couldn't help thinking Hank was in danger, and she couldn't ignore that and wait for backup.

So, she got into her car, and let Grady get into the passenger seat no matter how much she shouldn't.

"Don't say or do *anything*," she instructed. She pulled her radio out from the glove compartment and switched it on. She relayed the information, what there was of it. A mysterious location in a big park, no idea of who was involved or if it was even criminal. It could be some romantic assignation. With folders.

She focused on the road, ignoring Grady's large presence in her passenger seat.

"You gonna take off the wig?"

She cursed under her breath and started digging for the pins keeping the wig in place. Every time she found one she plucked it out and tossed it over her shoulder. When Grady's fingertips skimmed her ear, she nearly jerked off the road.

"Easy," he murmured, far too close as she sped down the highway out of Bent. "Just going to help."

Somehow she focused on the road as Grady finished pulling all the pins out of her hair. Admittedly, her heart was beating too hard against her chest, but she could chalk that up to adrenaline and worry about Hank over the feel of Grady's fingers in her hair.

That man kissed you!

She could not even begin to think about that right now. Once it felt loose enough, she tugged off the wig and threw it in the back.

"Stick with brunette, princess."

"I'll keep it under advisement," she muttered, flipping on her brights as they approached the park.

She squinted, surveying the side of the road. She knew the sign for the park had long ago been knocked over and not put back up, so the entrance was hard to find in the dark if you weren't looking for it. When she reached the entrance, she switched the lights back to normal. It would be hard to sneak up on anyone in a car, with the lights, the sound of an engine and the tires on the road, but she and Grady couldn't exactly hike the whole park, either.

"Do you know your way around?"

"I know the campsites are in the back. You take that left there," he said, tapping the windshield in the direction of a small gravel one-way street. "Campsites are numbered one through however many there are, if I'm remembering right. Road goes up, then around a cul-de-sac, so seven should be on our right as we drive up there."

Laurel nodded and navigated the turn onto the narrow road. She scanned the dark for the sign of a vehicle, a person, or anything that might lead them to believe someone was out here.

"How much space between campsites?" Laurel asked as her headlights flashed against a crooked sign that read *Campgrounds closed.*

"Not much, so if we're only going to seven, we could stop here and walk. Can't imagine it taking more than ten minutes. We could surprise them. Well, assuming they haven't already heard the car."

Laurel nodded. It would be at least another twenty before backup could get to the park. She radioed out the plan to the officer en route, then brought the car to a stop in campsite one. She backed in, in case they needed to get out of here quick, before grabbing her flashlight and utility belt, and fishing the gun out of the bra holster.

She ignored Grady's raised eyebrows as he watched her, and got out of the car. She snapped everything into place except the flashlight, clicking it on as Grady quietly closed the passenger door and met her at the hood of the car.

"You should stay in the car," she said, knowing she was wasting her breath.

He huffed out a laugh. "Lead the way, Deputy."

She sighed heavily. "Stay behind me. Don't make any noise. If you try to be a hero, I'll shoot you myself."

"Sure you will."

It was so incredibly annoying he knew her threats didn't hold any weight. But they didn't have time for bickering. She started walking up the gravel drive, training her flashlight on the ground and the signs alternatively, keeping her ears tuned to the sounds around them.

Wind whistled through the trees and against the grasses. Animals scurried through both. The dark took on a life of its own, a moving, unpredictable thing. Laurel kept her hand on her gun, and her flashlight at the ready.

As they reached the sign for campsite number five, she flicked off the light. Grady didn't say anything, and she gave them a few moments to adjust to the dark. It was a clear, cold night, but even the vibrant glow of the stars and moon above didn't make the dark any less daunting.

Laurel began to inch forward, keeping one foot on the gravel and one foot on the grass to make sure she was following the path of the road. When a hand grabbed her shoulder, she nearly screamed, but she bit it back in time, reminding herself *Grady* was behind her.

"Listen," he whispered into her ear. He was suddenly close enough she could feel his body heat, the slight movement of his breath against her hair, but she had more important things to focus on.

Listening.

It took a few moments, but finally she heard it. It

sounded like the wind at first, but the more she listened, the more she picked up the cadence of speech in whispers.

She reached up and moved Grady's hand from her right shoulder to her left, then placed her own left hand over it. She patted it, trying to make a nonverbal sign for him to keep it there as they inched forward.

She needed to be close enough to hear what the whispers were, and she needed to know where Grady was. So, she stepped forward, and Grady followed, his tight, warm grip on her shoulder.

She pulled out her gun, wanting it at the ready in case whoever they came upon was armed as well. She hated that she wasn't wearing her vest, but she also hated Grady unprotected behind her and the fact Hank was in danger, no matter if he'd gotten himself in it.

The whispers got louder, but still Laurel couldn't make out the words, and couldn't tell how close they were getting. With the open spaces and sparse clusters of trees, sound bounced everywhere.

Still she inched forward, forcing herself to breathe evenly, to focus on her mission. Keep Hank safe. Keep Grady safe. Then, find out what was going on.

There was a quick shout, and then the unmistakable sound of a gunshot.

Grady's hand clamped on her shoulder, but Laurel jerked out of his grasp and ran toward the shot.

WAS SHE CRAZY? Grady understood Laurel was a cop and all, but what woman went running toward a gunshot?

Then again, what unarmed, civilian man ran after a

woman running after a gunshot? Apparently him. So maybe he had to question his own sanity.

When he caught up with her, she was crouching over a body. The flashlight was on a bloody spot on the guy's shirt.

Hank.

"Hank, can you hear me? Can you focus?"

Hank just groaned as Laurel pulled her cop radio to her mouth, relaying the need for an ambulance ASAP, while her flashlight moved back and forth across the ground, clearly looking for clues as to where the shooter had gone.

She shoved the radio into its slot on her utility belt as she stood, then tossed Grady the flashlight and her phone. "Call 911 and have them walk you through keeping pressure on the wound."

"What are you going to do?" he demanded, and maybe he should have cared more about the fact Hank was moaning on the ground below him with a gunshot wound, but he was a little more concerned about Laurel ending up this way.

"I'm going to find the man who did this." He opened his mouth to tell her something to the effect of *over his dead body* when sirens sounded in the distance.

"It won't be the ambulance, but it will be the cops. Call 911. Look after Hank. Let the police handle this."

And she meant *her*, which was against every impulse inside of him. Unfortunately, so was leaving a man bleeding profusely from a gunshot.

Laurel had taken off, already murmuring into the radio that she needed the park secured. She'd left him the flashlight and it was all he could do not to grab it and rush after her. But Hank moaned, clearly trying to say something and unable to do so.

Grady cursed and used Laurel's phone to dial 911. How she had service out here he'd never begin to know, but as the 911 dispatcher answered, he explained his emergency and was given instructions on how to deal with the wound.

Hank groaned and thrashed as Grady applied pressure to the wad of fabric that had once been Hank's jacket. He placed the flashlight on the ground, beam pointed toward the wound, so he'd have both hands to work with.

"Didn't get it," Hank rasped, squinting at Grady as if he didn't see him. But he was talking, so he saw something.

"Didn't get what?"

Hank's hand thrashed around, his breathing becoming more labored even as Grady pressed on the wound. The ambulance needed to hurry.

"Pocket," Hank rasped, pointing to his left side.

Keeping the pressure as even as he could manage while also reaching across Hank's body, Grady grimaced and shoved his hand into the other man's pocket.

And pulled out a crumpled piece of paper.

"He didn't get it," Hank managed, his breathing getting shallower, his movements less erratic.

Grady frowned, trying to uncrumple the paper with one hand and read it in the beam of the flashlight. It was handwritten notes on a piece of graph paper. A list of dates, and next to each one a note. Most of it was nonsense to Grady. Names he didn't know, words he'd never seen before. But there was one line, dated two weeks ago, that was written in all caps.

CLEANUP WILL NOT MEET EPA STANDARDS.

Which meant nothing to Grady, and he doubted it would make sense to Laurel, either. But he figured out that whatever Hank, Jason and the man going around shooting people were involved in, it was centered at the mine.

It also meant whatever was going down at the mine was a big enough deal to kill, or try to kill, two men over. Blatantly. Without too much worry about being caught or repercussions if someone did put it all together.

And Laurel was out there in the dark.

If he hadn't been thinking about Laurel, about how many men she had out there with her now that the sirens had stopped and clearly the other cops were searching as well, he might have missed it.

A slight shuffle of leaves, the unmistakable sound of someone stepping on a twig or a branch or something. Then the eerie silence that followed.

Grady didn't move. No doubt if it were Laurel or any of the officers, they would announce themselves. Especially knowing they had a shooting victim.

It could be an animal, but animals typically didn't pause after they'd made a loud noise.

Grady didn't make any sudden movements. Whoever was out there had too good a vantage point, and hadn't shot yet. Which didn't mean he wouldn't, but it certainly meant he was considering not shooting him, too.

So, slowly, almost imperceptibly, Grady began to turn his head to look over his shoulder.

"Don't move," a faraway-sounding voice rasped.

"All right," Grady replied, keeping his head exactly where it was, inflicting his tone with as much ease as he could manage.

"Who are you?" the man growled in an undistinguishable voice that didn't stay still. Grady couldn't tell if the man was pacing or just moving around.

"You think I'm going to tell a strange man in the woods who I am?" Laurel wouldn't approve of this particular method of dealing with a man and, presumably, a gun, but Grady had known his fair share of desperate men. He could handle this one.

He hoped.

The ambulance had to get here soon, and if it didn't, the officers would have to circle back. So, maybe at worst he ended up with a bullet to the gut like Hank and lived to tell the tale.

Worst-case scenario is probably bullet to the head, genius.

Grady pushed that thought away and focused on the task at hand. "Just trying to help a guy out here. I don't want any trouble."

The man made some scoffing sound and Grady tried to focus on his surroundings. Was there anything he could use as a weapon? Did Hank have anything on him that could be grabbed and used as a weapon before the guy shot him?

He just needed the thug to come closer so Grady could knock him down. He had no doubts he could win in a fair fight, no matter how big the guy was, but this man had a gun, and Grady had nothing.

"Step away from Hank."

Grady looked down at Hank's form illuminated by the flashlight beam. He'd gone still, but his breathing continued, labored as it was. Grady wasn't sure the man could survive if he lost any more blood.

And you're not going to survive with a bullet to the brain.

But he'd never been very good at backing down to bullies. "Why don't you just let my friend here—"

"What's in your hand?" the man demanded, and he'd either forgotten to use his raspy voice or just didn't care.

Grady looked at the paper. The last thing he wanted to do was give the evidence up, but if he could remember the date, and the exact verbiage of the all caps message, plus some of the names...

Suddenly the paper was torn from his grasp, which gave Grady the chance he needed. He immediately kicked out, making contact with the man's shin. The man howled in pain, but unfortunately he didn't go down.

Which meant Grady had to take the pressure off Hank's wound. It would be precious time and probably precious amounts of blood, but they were both going to end up dead if Grady didn't fight.

So in a stealth move, Grady got his feet underneath him in a crouching position. As the attacker raised his arm, moonlight glinting off the gun in his hand, Grady lunged.

He rammed into the attacker, which sent them both sprawling, and Grady hoped the clattering sound mixed with crunching leaves was the gun falling out of his attacker's grasp.

Suddenly, over the sound of their grunts, Grady heard sirens, loud and clear. He looked up to see the flashing red, which was stupid, because it gave his attacker just enough time to land a blow that had his world going black.

Chapter Ten

Laurel swore and then swore again. She'd scoured the back of the park as much as she could manage with no artificial light, but there was no sign of the shooter. The only men she'd run into were the two officers she'd called in for backup.

"He could be anywhere. We just don't have the manpower for this kind of search," Deputy Clarion said disgustedly.

He was right, but that didn't ease Laurel's irritation or anger. Having someone *else* shot while you were investigating a murder wasn't exactly the thing stellar detective careers were made of. Especially when she had no suspects, no clues. Only forest and darkness and questions.

This was all her fault. She did everything in her power to push away the crushing sense of failure, but it rooted deep. She'd missed clues and hadn't thought things through, and another man was hurt because of her and could very well end up dying.

"We need to head back and make sure he hasn't

doubled back," Laurel ordered, a little sharper than necessary, but she felt sharp and pissed.

She'd left Grady behind unarmed, and it was more than possible a man with a gun had outsmarted them, circled back, and was going to do his best to finish off the job of killing Hank. Because they were dealing with someone who was desperate enough to murder one man, and attempt to murder another. She didn't think he'd stop to consider the moral implications of murdering Grady as well.

She swore and increased her pace. "Keep your eyes peeled, but our focus right now is getting back to the victim," Laurel called over her shoulder, breaking into a jog. "If our suspect gets away, we're just going to have to chalk it up to a loss, but if our victim is finished off, or a civilian is, that's on us."

Her, really. She'd been the idiot to let Grady strongarm her into bringing him here, and then she'd been the fool who'd left him to fend off anything that came his way with a dying man and no weapon. She'd left him defenseless.

The idea of Grady being defenseless was *almost* laughable. Grady was big and strong and inherently capable of handling himself, but he wasn't Superman. He couldn't fight off a bullet.

She heard the two other deputies huffing behind her so she walked faster. Through the trees and dangerous open areas, back to the campsites where she'd left Hank and Grady. Moonlight lit her way, and as she got closer, the flashing lights of the ambulance helped lead her exactly where she needed to be.

The fact the ambulance was there eased some of the worry clogging her chest. It had made it to the correct location, which meant Hank had a chance and Grady hadn't been hurt. Surely they'd gotten to Hank and Grady before anything had happened.

The suspect had probably made a run for it without a second thought to look back. He probably figured Hank was as good as dead and had gotten what he was after.

And yet somehow Laurel didn't feel any better. She got close enough to see Hank's body strapped to a stretcher and being lifted into the ambulance, but no Grady.

She swallowed down the panic. He was around here somewhere. Had to be. "Where's the other man?" she demanded of the paramedic as he closed the doors.

"What other man?"

"There was a man here guarding Hank, the victim."

The paramedic raised his eyebrows. "I didn't see anyone, and I've got to transport this man. He's lost far too much blood and is unresponsive."

"Wait. There was another man. There was an-other—"

"I have to go, Deputy, if you want this man to—"

They both stopped arguing when a loud groan came from somewhere nearby, along with the rustling of leaves.

Laurel immediately moved toward the sound and she was gratified the paramedic didn't take off.

"Grady?"

The response was a string of truly filthy curses.

"Give me your light," Laurel demanded of the paramedic. He handed her a flashlight and she flicked it on, moving the beam of light up toward the groaning and cursing.

"Grady." He was sprawled out in a shallow gully. As she moved closer, he rolled onto his side, clearly tried to sit up and failed. "Don't move," she ordered, scurrying down the little swell of earth and kneeling at his side. "Oh, my God. Are you shot?"

"I don't know," he grumbled. "Am I?"

"Grady." She tried to run her fingers over his chest, but the paramedic was pushing her out of the way.

"Where does it hurt, sir?"

"Probably the bleeding wound in my head," Grady snapped back, and though he had some fire to his responses, even in the weird illumination provided by the ambulance lights and flashlights, Laurel knew he looked pale.

"Simon, we have to go," the other paramedic yelled from the ambulance. "This guy isn't going to hold on much longer."

"Got another one, Pete. Blunt force trauma to the head. Lost consciousness. Bring out the other stretcher."

Pete swore, but moved quickly and efficiently.

"I don't need a stretcher." Grady pushed at the paramedic, and nothing made Laurel's blood run colder than the fact he didn't even budge the paramedic. Big, strong Grady Carson's push was ineffective at best.

She swallowed at the fear trying to lump itself in her throat. "Let them put you on the stretcher, Carson." She turned to the other officers she'd almost forgotten about. "You two, canvas the area. Anything you can find, you bag up. Got it?"

"Piece of paper," Grady mumbled as the two paramedics worked to move him.

"What?"

"Hank had a piece of paper. Something important. It's all a little fuzzy." He lifted a hand, but dropped it.

"A piece of paper. Okay, I'll look for one."

"What did that guy hit me with? I knocked his gun away."

He'd knocked the shooter's gun away, dear God. The paramedics started hefting him to the ambulance, and Laurel had to order herself to focus. Not on Grady, not on how badly he might be hurt, but on figuring out who did this.

"We're looking for a gun, something that could have been used as a blunt force trauma weapon and a piece of paper," she announced to the two deputies searching the area.

The ambulance revved its way out of the campsite parking space and Laurel had to force herself not to look at it. Grady was in good hands.

And hurt. Because of you.

She wasn't sure she'd ever been so close to crying on the job, but she ruthlessly blinked back the tears. "Anything you even question for a second, bag it. We need a clue."

She moved her beam to the gully Grady had been lying in. She didn't see anything outright, but it was covered in leaves. She reached into the part of her utility belt she kept rubber gloves in and pulled one on.

She began to sift through the leaves, looking for anything at all that wasn't natural debris. Anything that could have been used to hit Grady over the head.

She found the tiniest scrap of paper, white and dry, which meant it couldn't have been here long. She squinted at the words, but there weren't enough to make any sense out of it. Still, she placed it in her evidence bag.

Then her hand ran into something hard. She pulled it out of the pile of leaves and studied it. A shoe. A nice shoe at that. Men's. Big enough. With a sole hard and sharp enough to do some damage.

Laurel slipped that into the bag. She probably couldn't get an identity with a shoe, but it was certainly *something*.

"I found a gun," one of the deputies said a few yards south of her.

Laurel nodded. A scrap of paper, a shoe and a gun. It wasn't much.

But it was something.

GRADY HATED HOSPITALS. They were so white and every noise was so mechanical. He'd watched a few too many people die in hospital rooms. He'd been with all of his grandparents, holding hands or murmuring prayers, because his grandparents had raised him right in the shadow of everything else.

Then there was the time Dad had died. Grady trying to shield Vanessa, being pushed away as monitors went crazy and nurses jumped into action. And somehow feeling sad when all was said and done, even though his father had never been anything more than a mean SOB.

Grady blew out a breath and glared at the door. They'd stitched him up and talked over his head about concussions and being watched overnight, and he was about ready to lose his usually impenetrable cool.

They were going to release him soon, or he was going to fight his way out. One way or the other. He just had to figure out whom to call. Noah or Vanessa or Ty. Hell, he should call Clint and demand some payment for what a mess he was in because of the kid.

But the only person he wanted to call was Laurel, and that was messed up.

When the door opened, Grady was ready to go after whatever poor soul dared darken his door without discharge papers.

"Mr. Carson," a young, timid thing asked, hovering there as though she were afraid of him. "There's a police officer here who wants to speak with you, and I couldn't find—"

"Is it a woman?"

"Um, well, yes."

"Send her in, then."

"Oh. Right. Well."

"Now," Grady growled, sending the girl scurrying out the door. A few seconds later, Laurel appeared. She was still wearing what she'd been wearing in his bar earlier, sans wig. She'd tamed her hair back, though, in one of those serviceable braids she tended to favor. And she looked serviceable and a little bit formidable on top of it.

Hell, he wanted to get her into bed.

"Why are you torturing that poor candy striper or whatever it is she is?" Laurel asked, and he noted she hovered close to that door opening even as her gaze scanned his bandage.

"Because no one will let me out of this hellhole."

Her mouth flattened and she jammed her hands into her pockets. "Well, I need to take your statement."

"You came all this way to take my statement, princess?"

"Yes. Is your head a little clearer now, or should I wait until morning?"

"My head is just fine," Grady said, willing the snap out of his tone and failing. "Everything about me is just fine." To prove it, he slid off the hospital bed and into a standing position.

"Sit back down right this instant," Laurel demanded, crossing the room as if she was going to push him into bed herself.

"You ain't in charge of me, Deputy," Grady returned, folding his arms across his chest and fighting back the dizziness that had taken over him. "The doctor is working on my discharge papers, so I can stand just fine." He glared down at her, but that scowl she'd been using seemed to fall away as she took in the bandage on his temple.

She looked…defeated. Sad. Guilty.

Hell.

"I just need to get your statement," she said quietly. "We don't need to argue."

"But arguing is what we do best."

Laurel shook her head faintly, and that weird cloak of sadness didn't leave her. "Did you get a look at the attacker?" she asked, pulling her ever-present notebook out of her pocket, along with a pen. "Any identifying marks or facial features that might distinguish them from other people? A height, weight or build."

It galled that he didn't have any answers, but he couldn't exactly make any up, so he had to be honest. "No. It was dark and I couldn't see anything except for the fact he had a gun. Did you guys find it?"

She swallowed and gave a sharp nod, her dark eyes soft and something else. Something he couldn't recognize no matter how many other emotions on her he could.

"Yes," she said, her voice rough. "We found it. Ideally it's traceable and this is over, but…"

"The murderers of the world don't usually use traceable guns."

"No, they do not. We also recovered a shoe, which was the weapon that…" Her eyes darted to his bandage again. "Did you have to get stitches?"

"Yeah. Ten. Must've been some shoe."

"It was sharp. Hard-soled." She inhaled shakily and he didn't understand what this was. Just guilt over someone hurting him? He wasn't sure he understood why she should feel that way. Which made it hard to know if he wanted to comfort her or tease her.

"I'm so sorry," she said, all earnestness and Laurel. Just Laurel, this bastion of right and fighting wrong.

Which answered that question for him. He didn't

want to tease her when she was all soft. "For what?" he demanded a little bit too brusquely.

"I shouldn't have left you there. I shouldn't have taken you there at all, but I really shouldn't have left you with a hurt man completely unarmed. I should have known or predicted he'd double back and… He could've killed you, Grady. So easily. He could have killed you both, and I wouldn't have been able to do anything about it. And that… It was shoddy police work and I'm sorry that you got caught in the middle."

"See, I just thought it was one of those instances where you did your best but bad things happen because life is unpredictable," Grady returned gruffly, because he didn't want her guilt or her apologies. Not when he'd forced her hand, and not when… Well, she had done her best. He was no idiot.

"I should've known better," Laurel said firmly.

"How?"

"Because as a police officer you're trained to deal with these things. You are trained—"

"You're trained to know exactly where a murder suspect might go in the dark? In an isolated, enormous park that no one has been to in years and therefore has no brush cleaned up, no identifying markers, no nothing?"

"I am trying to give you an apology," she said through gritted teeth.

"I don't want your apology. I was the one who made it impossible for you to go without me, and I'm sure glad I did. Because the fact I could stay with Hank made it certain *you* didn't both end up dead."

"It would've been in the line of duty. It would have been my job. It's not your job. You shouldn't have been there, and you shouldn't have gotten hurt, and it's my fault that you did."

"How long you going to self-flagellate, because I'm out until you're done."

Laurel threw her arms up in the air. "You are insufferable. And ridiculous. I'm trying to be nice and… and…be a good person, and you're throwing it back in my face!"

Even though his head was starting to throb, Grady couldn't help smiling. Maybe it was sick, but he sure liked seeing her irritated more than he liked seeing her…contrite or upset or whatever that was.

"I need your statement," she snapped, hitting her pen against the notebook, eyes flashing angry gold. "Tell me everything that happened once I left."

To placate her, he did just that. He went through calling 911, and trying to stop Hank's bleeding. He remembered the paper, but then things started to get a little gray. Not quite linear. There was something about a paper. Hank had a paper?

"You can't remember?" Laurel asked gently and he scowled at her.

"I remember. Some things. Bits and pieces, but I can't seem to put it all back together in the right order."

"I think that's a fairly common concussion symptom."

"It's not a serious concussion."

"But it is *a* concussion. And ten stitches."

"And not your fault. I probably would have gotten

knocked around a lot worse if I hadn't been thinking about you." Which was not an admission he needed to make, except he was tired. Exhausted. His head hurt, and he didn't... He didn't want her guilt or her cop crap. He just wanted her.

"What do you mean you were thinking about me?"

"I was worried about where you had gone, and what might be happening to *you*, and I was listening for you. I heard a twig break and shuffling of leaves and then I knew someone was there. Which gave me time to prepare and fight back." But he couldn't remember much of the fight.

"You don't have to worry about me," she said, shoving her notebook and pen into her pocket. "I'm the cop."

"You're not invincible because of a badge," he snapped, wanting to shake some sense into her.

"No, but—"

"Just shut up," he bit out, because if she spent any more time talking about her line of duty, he was going to end up kissing her until they both forgot their last names.

Which was the number one thing he wanted, and not just because of this night. He couldn't remember a time he hadn't wanted a piece of Laurel Delaney, and the events of this night made him tired of pretending.

"I found a scrap of the paper you mentioned," Laurel said, using that cool cop tone that seriously tested his self-control. "It doesn't make any sense to me. But I took a picture of it." She took her phone out of her back pocket and handed it to him.

He looked down at the screen. It really was just a scrap. Two dates listed, then not even two full words after. He knew he'd looked at this. He'd looked at this paper and...

"It's okay if you don't remember," Laurel said gently. "It'll come to you. In the meantime, we have a shoe, a gun and the first real evidence-related lead we've had this whole investigation. And, unless either comes back as being Clint's, which I find very hard to believe, your brother is off the hook. Which means so are you."

Off the hook. Because Clint would be proven innocent. It didn't make him feel any better. In fact, it pissed him right off. "Like hell I am."

Chapter Eleven

Laurel didn't think Grady would ever make any sense to her. He should be relieved. He should be skipping out of the hospital room. Free.

But he was fuming. *Fuming*.

"Clint isn't a part of it," she repeated. Maybe the concussion was making it hard for him to think straight or understand everything properly. "Which means I don't need your help anymore. At least, there's no reason for you to help me. Your brother is in the clear. Probably."

"You really don't think I have a reason to still be involved in this?" Grady asked incredulously.

"Well—"

"Someone hit me over the head with a shoe and gave me a concussion. It could have been a lot worse, too. So, I am going to be a part of bringing him down."

"Grady," she began, doing her best to find a reasonable tone.

"Do not argue with me, princess. I am in this now. No one knocks me out and gets away with it. I've got a little revenge to enact."

"My job isn't about revenge. It's about justice, so you wanting revenge can't—"

"Consider my revenge justice. Now—"

A knock sounded at the door and an older woman in nurse's scrubs stepped in. "I have your discharge papers, Mr. Carson." She smiled pleasantly at Laurel. "And good, you have someone who can drive you home."

Laurel opened her mouth to argue. She should not be driving him home. He needed to call one of his cousins, or his sister or even Clint. Anyone who was not her.

She needed some distance from Grady. No matter if he had revenge *or* justice on the brain. She had let herself be compromised by all his irritating goading and charming smiles and that kiss, and she had done things she knew went against protocol.

Laurel *never* went against protocol.

But Grady flashed the nurse a charming smile. "Yes, I got myself a ride home. Now let's get me out of here."

"We just have to go over some paperwork, I'll need a signature, then you'll be free." Again the nurse turned to Laurel. "Will you be staying with Mr. Carson overnight?" she asked innocently.

Grady grinned. "Yeah, I think she owes me that."

Again Laurel opened her mouth to protest, but there was no point in arguing in front of the nurse. There was no point in arguing, period. Grady would get her to do what he wanted. He always seemed to.

So, she would get him home to the Carson Ranch. The other Carsons would kick her out so fast her head would spin, and the fact that idea disappointed her was reason enough to go through it. She needed a Grady-ectomy and stat.

"Here is a list of symptoms you may have for the next few weeks," the nurse said, handing Grady one of the sheets of papers she'd brought in. "You should avoid driving for at least twenty-four hours and tonight, if you're sleeping, you should be woken up every two hours to make sure you're responsive. All of these papers have information on how to deal with a concussion and when to call us, but mostly the main concern is if you're unresponsive or your symptoms get significantly worse." She went through the medications Grady could take and rattled off more instructions before letting him sign his release form.

"You are free to leave whenever you're ready," the nurse said cheerfully. "Take care of Mr. Carson," she added to Laurel before striding out of the room.

"Come on, driver. I'm ready to go home."

"I'm going to take you to the ranch and drop you off with your family," Laurel said firmly. No matter that looking at the bandage on his head made her want to touch his face. Press her cheek to his chest and listen to his heartbeat.

Maybe *she* had been hit over the head.

"You'll drive me to Rightful Claim and take good care of me all through the night," Grady returned, that sharp, wolfish smile on his face as he gathered his belongings.

What was wrong with her that she *wanted* that, and so much more? And, worst of all, she always kind of had, but she'd learned to keep her distance, to force her focus elsewhere. But Grady Carson had always been that thing she couldn't want or have, and so she'd turned it off.

But it was impossible to turn off when he was *here* all the time, when he'd kissed her, when he was saying 'take good care of me all through the night' with that glint in his eye.

She wanted to be him for a second. To say outrageous things and not give a crap. She wanted to be *free* of all the rules and protocols she'd placed on herself. "I'm pretty sure she said no vigorous activity," she retorted.

Grady barked out a laugh and she hated the part of herself that was warmed by that. Encouraged. The part of her that wanted to fuss over him and, yes, have a little vigorous activity. It was a lot more than a concussion standing in her way of all that.

"That makes me wonder all kind of things about you, Laurel."

"I'll drive you to Rightful Claim, but I'm not your nurse. Someone from your family should come stay with you." Because she did not trust herself. A sad, pathetic fact.

"Someone from my family isn't the reason I have a concussion."

She knew he was trying to use her guilt against her. She knew she absolutely shouldn't let him. A good cop knew they weren't at fault for something that went wrong. It was the fault of the bad guys. Murderers and rapists and burglars—they were at fault when bad things happened.

But knowing something and feeling something were two very different things—hence her current predicament. She walked down the squeaky hospital corridor and toward the exit, warring with herself. With knowing and feeling.

She knew better than this and yet some part of her wanted to take care of Grady. She wanted to talk over the details of the case with him, and she wanted to be there when he remembered what he would inevitably remember. Something about that paper.

Grady slung his arm across her shoulder, casual as you please. "Don't think so hard, princess. You're giving me a headache."

"I think the concussion gave you a headache."

"Nah, it's you."

They stepped into the cold chill of late-night autumn. Or, more accurately, way-too-early morning. She led him to her car and felt a sudden wave of exhaustion roll over her. This had been the longest night and it felt as though nothing concrete or impactful had been accomplished.

You have evidence. You are making progress.

She was, but it was the knowing versus feeling thing again. She didn't *feel* progress. She couldn't seem to feel anything that wasn't futility, despair or frustration.

She glanced at Grady sitting in the passenger seat of her car. He had his eyes closed, and the white bandage stuck out against the tan skin and dark beard of his face.

It really wasn't fair he was so handsome, and that he was here, the living incarnation of her current life crisis. He was so many things she couldn't want, and yet did. Why couldn't her emotions ever follow the reason she was so desperate to live by?

"We going to sit here all night?" he asked, eyes still closed, voice a rumble in the quiet of the car.

"I'm not going to sleep with you," she said firmly, because if she put it out there, in real, spoken words maybe she could be sure.

"You've said that a few times now. I can only assume that means you think about sleeping with me an awful lot." He turned his head to face her, eyes open and far too blue, and he grinned.

But Laurel didn't have it in her to grin back. There was this out-of-control thing inside of her she didn't know how to rein back in, and she didn't know what to *do*—when knowing what to do was all she'd ever done.

"For the record," Grady drawled. "I don't think I have it in me tonight. But I never say never."

Laurel turned on the car and pulled out of the parking spot. "I didn't say never," she grumbled.

GRADY FELT NAUSEOUS and his head was pounding and if he had any energy at all, he would be tracking down the person who'd done this to him and bashing his head in.

He pulled his keys out of his pocket and unlocked the back doors of Rightful Claim, Laurel hovering behind him. Her presence was the only thing that kept him from actually punching something. Because somehow just her being there felt comforting.

He'd never thought to look for *comforting* in a person he spent time with before, but Laurel gave him all sorts of interest in the feeling. Especially considering his body felt like hell and working up any other interest probably wasn't happening.

Grady stepped inside and Laurel followed. He locked the door behind her and walked toward the stairs to his apartment. He paused at the bottom of them. Stairs he undoubtedly ran up and down a thousand times a day suddenly seemed daunting. Too much.

"They should've kept you overnight," Laurel observed in a brisk tone.

He scowled in her direction. "I'm fine."

"You're struggling," she said firmly.

"Then why don't you help me up the stairs and take good care of me?" he asked, trying to flash a cocky grin her way and failing mostly. All he could seem to do right now was grimace.

She rolled her eyes, but she stepped closer to him so that they were side by side. With a huff of irritated breath she cinched her arm around his waist.

"Come on. Let's go."

He looked down at her incredulously. She really thought she was going to help him up the stairs? "You're a slip of a thing."

She made a scoffing noise. "I only seem like a slip to you because you're ginormous."

"Ginormous, huh?"

He noted the faint blush that crept across her cheeks and wished he had the wherewithal to lean down and capture her mouth with his.

"I'm sturdy enough," she continued, gauging the

stairs in front of them. "Probably kick your ass in the PT test."

"No. Definitely not."

She began to take steps with him, and he didn't lean on her so much as let her presence be a guide in keeping his dizziness at bay.

"We can test that theory sometime, but not today."

Grady grumbled irritably and let her help him up the rest of the stairs. It was just that all of his limbs felt heavy. His body, his head, everything felt stonelike and sluggish.

"I cannot fully express the unfairness of being rendered this weak by a shoe."

She patted his back sympathetically. "It was a very hard shoe."

"Don't placate me." They reached his apartment door and he unlocked it before pushing it open and stepping inside. It was good to be back in his own place. In his own air.

"Go lie down."

"Yes, ma'am. I find your bossy so hot."

She muttered something under her breath and went over to his little kitchenette. She started looking through his cabinets, muttering all the while. Grady toed off his boots and sprawled out on the bed. The covers were all tangled at the end of the mattress and it seemed like far too much work to pull them up.

"Don't you have any tea?" Laurel asked, rummaging through his stuff.

"Yes, Laurel, I keep *tea* on hand. Do I seem like a *tea* guy to you?"

"Don't you have anything warm and comforting?"

He patted the bed next to him. "I have you."

He thought he saw her mouth curve a fraction and he'd mark that down as a success.

"You know you're impossible, right?" she asked, fisting her hands on her hips and doing her best to glare at him.

"You would not be the first person to tell me that. I believe that was the lullaby my mother used to sing me to sleep with."

"You should call Vanessa. She'd be in a much better position to take care of you."

"Vanessa? My sister Vanessa? She couldn't take care of a pet rock."

"Fine. Noah? Ty? They're your family." She had that soft, earnest look about her and he much preferred the almost smile he'd earned a few seconds ago.

"Right. Which means I don't get nearly as much enjoyment out of pissing them off."

"I'm not pissed off."

"No, you're guilty. Which pisses *me* off. Come sit next to me."

"I am not sitting on the bed with you."

"Can't control yourself around me, princess?"

"Grady."

"I want you to show me the picture again. I want you to go through everything that happened, and if you go through it, maybe it'll jog my fuzzy memory and I can put these pieces back together."

"I think you should sleep. I have to wake you up in

two hours and see if you're responsive. Then we can go through all that."

"Then you're staying?" he asked.

"If you're not going to call anyone else, what choice do I have? I don't have any of their numbers. I could wrestle your phone from you, but I have a feeling that wouldn't end up the way I'd like it to."

Grady chuckled. "No, baby, wrestling would not end the way you want it to."

"Get some sleep."

"I need to work through this or I'm never going to fall asleep." And he wasn't even just trying to get her into his bed. It was eating at him, all those murky pieces he couldn't remember.

She sighed heavily and shook her head as though she couldn't believe what she was about to do. Then she walked over to the bed. Gingerly and hesitantly she rested her butt on the very edge opposite him. She handed over her phone. "Here's the picture of the scrap we found."

"If I start scrolling through your pictures am I going to find something interesting?"

"In your dreams."

"Yes, interesting images of you have appeared in many of my dreams."

"Grady," she scolded exasperatedly.

"Okay. So we got there, and we heard the gunshot. We found Hank, and then you took off."

"First you argued with me, and then I took off," Laurel corrected, sliding just a little bit more into the bed so she could stretch out her legs and rest her back against the headboard.

"Semantics," Grady replied. "I called 911. They told me to put pressure on the bullet wound. He was losing a lot of blood. I remember all that clearly." Grady looked down at his hands. For a moment he could almost see Hank's blood on them, but they'd washed that off at the hospital.

"How is Hank?" he asked, surprised at how rusty he sounded.

"He lost a lot of blood. He's still alive, but it's fairly critical. Out of surgery. They'll call me if anything changes or when he wakes up," Laurel said gently.

He'd never much appreciated gentle. Gentle tended to get trampled in this life, but Laurel's gentle was somehow steel, too, and it washed over him like a soothing balm.

"He said something to me. He said 'he didn't get it.' Then he gestured to his pocket and I pulled out a piece of paper. I read it over and tried to remember what it said. Something important."

Grady stared at the picture of the scrap of paper on Laurel's phone. He knew there was something he was supposed to remember, and it was just somewhere in the gray, frayed edges of his mind.

"You can't beat yourself up about it. I think the more you focus on trying to remember, the harder it's going to be *to* remember."

"I have an excellent memory and never forget anything. I could probably name every person who's ever walked through the doors of my bar."

"Saloon," she corrected for him, and when he glanced at her there was a hint of a smile.

He didn't have words for how badly he wanted to kiss that smile. "I'd probably remember more if you scooted a little closer."

"Grady, you have to understand that I have already put my investigation in danger because of you."

"Excuse me?"

"I don't mean that as a blame on you. It's a blame on me. For whatever reason, I have a hard time..." She looked away, clearly embarrassed and irritated with herself. "I have a hard time saying no to you. I should have put my foot down and not brought you with me."

"So you could have been shot?"

"If I'd waited with the deputies..."

"Hank could be dead. The what-ifs work both ways. Good and bad. What if-ing it is pointless, and I think you know that. You haven't compromised your investigation. Not because of me, and not because of you. Your investigation is fine. Things just aren't going easily."

"Maybe I'm used to things going easily."

"Thankfully for you, I'm not. I'll teach you."

"The thing is, Grady... Maybe there is this weird pull between us. Attraction or chemistry or, I don't know, DNA. Carsons and Delaneys forever attracted to each other like magnets only to ruin everything. But we are night and day. Opposites in every way except the one that has us working together. I am serious and permanent and all the things you avoid like the plague."

"Maybe I'm not serious about everything, but I'm

serious about plenty. My family. This town. And that's permanent. I'm not all one-night stands and parties or whatever it is you think of me."

"Then what are you?" she asked, looking at him with earnest brown eyes. So earnest and pretty and, yeah, everything that wasn't usually *him*.

She was right. They should be oil and water but their Carson and Delaney roots somehow acted like soap, mixing them all together.

"Probably no good for you, princess deputy."

"It's not about being good or bad for—"

He reached over and curled his fingers around her upper arm. He was tempted to give her a good jerk, till she was sprawled out on top of him, but his body wasn't up for it. "Come over here."

"Grady—"

"Now, Laurel."

No one was more shocked than him when she obeyed.

Chapter Twelve

Laurel knew she was losing her mind, but it felt so good. Because letting Grady pull her toward him, until she was practically sprawled across half of him, felt like a relief. It cleared all the arguments in her head and released nearly all of the tension in her body.

"How often do you think you've called me by my actual name?" she asked.

"Haven't exactly kept track." He curled his finger into a strand of her hair, wrapping it around and around. "Still not going to sleep with me?"

She sighed, glancing up at the bandage on his head. "Nope."

He grinned. "Because of doctor's orders?"

She could lie. She could go back to her usual circuitous denials, but he was warm and comfortable to lean against. She didn't feel much like lying or denying or focusing. So, she told the truth. "Yes, that is why."

He pulled on the finger he'd wrapped some of her hair around, drawing her face closer to his. "Doctor's orders don't last forever."

"Maybe I don't want them to."

His eyebrows went up and she couldn't ignore the fact she got a thrill out of shocking him. Except, the thrill was immediately followed by exhaustion. "I am so tired, Grady, and I have so many things to do." So many things and all she wanted to do was rest her cheek on Grady's chest and sleep.

For a second, just one little second, she gave in to the impulse.

"Set the alarm on your phone, princess, and we'll take ourselves a little rest."

"Like this?" she asked incredulously.

Before she could explain to him that she wasn't about to take a nap curled up on top of him when he was suffering from a concussion and they weren't even…whatever it was they weren't, he'd shifted lower on the bed and they were both prone.

She was on her side, all but curled against him, her head resting on his shoulder. His arm was around her, strong and protective. She should get up. Roll away. She wasn't going to sleep with—actual sleep—with Grady. It was wholly incongruous to him and what they were or weren't and yet her eyelids were already drooping. Where it usually took her a good hour to shut up her brain and fall asleep, she already felt relaxed. Safe.

The next thing she knew her phone was jerking her out of sleep. At first she thought it was her alarm, but as she pawed on the mattress to find it, she saw the name of the hospital flashing on her screen.

She hit Accept as fast as she could, somehow all tangled up with Grady in the dark. "H-hello?" she answered breathlessly, trying to roll away from him and being caught in a hard, uncompromising grasp.

"Deputy Delaney?"

"This is her."

"Hank Gaskill is awake and doing well enough to receive very brief visits, if your questioning is absolutely necessary."

"It is. It is. I'll be there soon." She clicked End, already scooting toward the empty side of the bed so she could slide off without any physical contact with Grady. "Hank's awake. I have to go."

"We were asleep for an hour," Grady said. "You can't keep going at this pace."

She pulled on her jacket, patting herself down to make sure she had everything. "I have to. Now, can you please, *please*, call someone?"

He sighed heavily but he held up his phone. "Ty should be around."

"Promise me you'll call him, and make sure he follows the doctor's instructions. A promise, Grady. Your word."

"You think my word means anything?"

She studied his face, all sharp edges and challenge, and yet she knew what she'd always known about Grady Carson. He might be wild, he might be antagonistic and frustrating and not necessarily law-abiding, but he was not a man who went back on his word. "Yeah, I think a promise from you means something."

Something on his face altered into an expression she couldn't read and wasn't sure she'd ever seen on him, at least not directed at her. "This case won't stand in our way forever, Laurel."

She met his gaze, and she knew he was right in the same way she knew Carsons and Delaneys would never get along, and never leave Bent. Even with an hour's sleep under her belt, she didn't have the energy to argue. "I know it won't. But I still have a job to do. Call Ty. I'll…check on you later."

He smiled, back to slick charm and self-satisfied humor. "I'll be waiting."

She couldn't let that mean anything. She had a job to do and a case to focus on, and Grady… Well, everything all jumbled up with him would have to wait. No matter how nice it had been to simply lie next to someone and feel safe and comfortable.

She drove back to the hospital, pushing away the exhaustion that dogged her. She'd grab a cup of coffee, then question Hank, then… She'd have to grab a few hours. The sun was just hinting at the horizon, ready to start a new day.

And you're still no closer to an answer.

So far. So far. That wasn't final.

She parked at the hospital lot and made her way up to Hank's floor. After a lot of asking around, she found his doctor.

"I don't know how lucid he'll be, and he shouldn't be agitated. So this needs to be quick and low-key. In a few days, he should be recovered enough to handle more."

Laurel nodded at the doctor before following her into the room. Hank was connected to all sorts of machines and monitors. His eyes fluttered open.

"Mr. Gaskill, this is Deputy Delaney. Do you feel well enough to answer some questions?"

"Yeah," Hank rasped. "Yeah. Did you find who did this?"

"I'm afraid not," Laurel said. "Is there anything you can tell me that would help me identify and apprehend the man who shot you?"

"I don't know who it was. It could have been someone I know. It could have been a stranger. It could have been a hit man for all I know. It was dark. Everything so dark."

Laurel eyed all the beeping machines nervously. "It's okay, Hank. You've been seriously shot. I'm going to do everything in my power to find out by who. You don't have to have all the answers."

He stilled a little. "I don't have any proof, but Adams has something to do with it. Jason was sure of it."

"Do you know why Jason met with whoever killed him?"

Hank closed his eyes, and Laurel knew she was running out of time. This was too much for a man who'd been shot a handful of hours ago.

"He was going to blackmail the higher-up. There's someone higher up who knows, and Jason wanted to get paid to be quiet. He was going to pay me, too."

"What higher-up?"

Something beeped shrilly and the doctor moved, nudging Laurel out of the way. "Deputy, you'll need to leave. I'll alert you when he's up to a more thorough questioning."

Higher-ups and blackmail, and none of it made any

sense. But she had her next step. Not sleep like she'd hoped, but Mr. Adams.

"A SHOE?"

Grady glared at Ty, who was sprawled out on a recliner in the corner. "It was hard, everything was dark, and I was a little busy knocking a gun out of his hand."

"Would have been more badass to have gotten a concussion from a gun over a shoe."

Grady scowled. "I'll keep that in mind next time I'm accosted while trying to save a man's life."

"See that you do," his cousin replied good-naturedly. "Hurt?"

"Fading," Grady lied. His head was still pounding, and every once in a while he felt sick to his stomach, but it was getting better. Maybe.

He glanced at his phone again. No updates from Laurel. It had been a little less than an hour. Plenty of time to get there and question Hank.

"A watched phone never rings from an inappropriate wannabe hookup."

Grady looked up from his phone with a doleful expression. "I'm not allowed to have an interest in this case?"

"Well, considering you said it looks like Clint is in the clear, yeah, you shouldn't. The dead Delaney wasn't anybody to you."

"That how you felt in the army? Dead guy. Not my problem."

Ty's expression went blank, and Grady regretted bringing it up. His cousin was an army ranger, had done some dangerous, amazing things in his time serving this country, and no matter how pissy Grady was, he didn't have a right to poke at that.

"Listen—"

But Ty held up his hand as his eyebrows drew together. An odd swishing sound went through the apartment, then the squeak of one of his stairs. He didn't hear footsteps, but the stairs outside didn't squeak without someone standing on them.

Grady flung the covers off his legs, but again Ty's hand stopped him. Ty moved out of the chair, cat-like and silent. When he reached the door, he picked something up off the ground. A piece of paper. His quizzical frown went furious.

He tossed it on the bed. "Be right back," he whispered.

"What the—" But Ty was already gone. Grady picked up the paper and felt as though he'd been transported into some kind of movie. Little magazine letters had been cut out and pasted onto the paper.

Watch your step and your back.

He was out of bed before he'd made it to the last word, but by the time he pulled on his boots, Ty was back.

"Gone," Ty muttered in disgust. "Someone must have been waiting. Though I didn't hear a car, which I would have." Ty shook his head. "I imagine this is about Delaney's case and not some wronged ex-lover."

"I imagine," Grady returned.

Ty sighed heavily. "Call your little deputy, Grady. If this is about the case, she needs to know."

Part of him wanted to leave her out of it. He could handle whatever coward thought he could intimidate a Carson, but it *did* have to do with the case, undoubtedly, which meant there might be a clue.

He grabbed his phone and pulled up Laurel's number. When she answered, she sounded exhausted and pissed.

"Grady—"

"I received a little message under my door about ten minutes ago."

"A message?"

"I'm afraid you're going to need to come check it out."

"Is this a joke? Because—"

Grady held out the phone to Ty. "Would you tell her?"

Ty rolled his eyes but took the outstretched phone. "Delaney? Ty. Stop being difficult and come do your job, huh?"

It was Grady's turn to roll *his* eyes. "Charming as ever," he noted, grabbing the phone back. "Laur—" But the call had ended.

"Does it always have to be antagonism?" Grady demanded of Ty.

"To a Delaney? Yeah, I'm pretty sure that's how it works."

"It doesn't have to work that way. Did it ever occur to you that the people who fed us all that feud garbage weren't exactly good people?"

Ty's eyes widened. "You slept with her."

"No, I haven't," Grady returned, irritable and edgy.

"But I am thirty-three years old and playing cops and robbers is getting old. My dad was a miserable SOB. My mom wasn't much better. Blaming the Delaneys for everything wrong in their lives never got them anywhere but more miserable."

"Sometimes the Delaneys *are* the source of a person's misery, and before you start reading into *that*, let me just say that if you're letting some woman convince you everything our entire family, and lives, and town are built on is crap, then maybe you need to get a hold of yourself."

"Maybe I don't want my life to be built on a feud that's older than my saloon."

"Then you aren't the Grady Carson I know, and I'm not sure one I want to."

Grady clenched and unclenched his jaw, enough unspent fury pumping through him he wouldn't mind a little bit of a fight. Except he had a concussion and he *was* tired. Tired of fighting and feuds and things that only existed because they always had.

He still believed in Bent and history, but he wasn't a boy playing at a man anymore, and he wasn't going to let history or this town dictate how he lived his life.

"Guess you can go, then."

"Guess I will," Ty replied, grabbing his coat and striding out the door.

Grady gave in to the impulse to slam his hand against the wall, and immediately regretted the way it jarred his head.

When Laurel finally made it back, she didn't knock

or even pause. She barged right into his apartment. She looked around, frowning.

"Where's Ty?"

"Left."

She fisted her hands on her hips. "He was supposed to take care of you."

"Yeah, well, he was being an ass. So I booted him. Now, are you here to do police work or what?" He handed her the paper.

She read, her expression going flat and hard, and Grady wasn't surprised to see some mean-edged cop on her, or the fact it turned him on. But she also had dark circles under her eyes and her usually creamy complexion was near gray.

"You're going to crash, princess."

"Sooner or later," she agreed, frowning at the paper. "I don't like this."

"Can't say I care for it, either."

"You can't be alone. Not until we figure this out."

He offered her a smile. "You going to play body-guard?"

"I have an investigation to run."

"I can help."

"I'm going to take you to the Carson Ranch. There's enough of you to keep an eye on things."

"On a big spread like ours? I'm not taking this to the ranch and potentially endangering my family. You want me not alone, you're up. Since you're already involved."

He could tell she wanted to argue, but in the end, she nodded. "Unfortunately, you're right."

"Well, now, those are words I never thought I'd hear from you. 'Unfortunately' notwithstanding."

"But there are conditions."

"Of course there are."

"You go where I go, not the other way around. You listen to me. You *obey* me. Because this isn't a joke, and it isn't a game. I have a ticking time bomb of an investigation, more and more people in danger by the second. You're going to have to swallow your Wyoming-sized pride and do what I tell you to do."

Grady gave her a grand mock salute, but she didn't even crack a smile.

"I don't want anything to happen to you," she said in that earnest way that made him feel something close to *vulnerable*. Which was crap.

"Get it through your head that the same goes, okay?"

She sighed. "Well, let's get going, then."

"Where are we off to?"

"We have to question a possible suspect."

"Please tell me it's not my brother. Or any Carson."

Laurel quirked a tiny smile at that. "It's your lucky day. This suspect is as Carson-free as you can get."

"So, he's a Delaney?"

"Worse. An outsider."

Chapter Thirteen

It wasn't easy to pretend the warning letter to Grady didn't rattle her, but she knew she needed to present the tough cop facade right now. Not just because Grady was now under her protection, no matter how laughable that seemed, but also because she had to face Mr. Adams in a professional, smart way that hopefully led to a confession or more of a lead.

It was hard to believe the pudgy, middle-aged manager of an unassuming mine could be a cold-blooded killer, strong enough to hit Grady so hard with a *shoe* it gave him a concussion, and agile enough to slip through darkened woods and out again without getting caught.

But she couldn't rule it out, either.

The town of Clearwater was quite a bit larger than Bent. Many of the nonlocal mine workers lived here, so there was a sprawling residential area. Since the town had sprung out of meeting the needs of those workers, everything was more modern than Bent. Fast food, a Walmart, even stoplights.

"How much you want to bet this guy lives in the nicest house in town?" Grady asked, clearly not impressed.

"Well, he is the mine manager."

Grady made a rude noise. "You think this guy is the one who knocked me out?"

"No," Laurel said firmly, turning onto the street Mr. Adams lived on. "But he's involved. Now, we need to go over a few procedure ground rules."

"Of course we do."

Laurel ignored the sarcasm. "You can't go in with me."

"I thought I was under your protection, Deputy," Grady returned, all mock innocence.

"It's tricky and it's complicated, but I can't have you shooting off at the mouth. It will call into question my investigation and if there is a trial, and Mr. Adams is accused of some wrongdoing, your presence and interference will be noted and used to undermine everything. I can't risk it."

Grady was silent as she pulled to a stop in front of the Adams residence. She turned to him, surprised when he hadn't mounted an argument, but also not convinced he would listen to her. When did he ever listen to her?

"Stay put. For the sake of making a murderer, and possibly his accomplice, *pay*."

"What about a little creative use of the truth?"

Laurel frowned, but he had said truth, and Grady might be all manner of wild, rule-breaking things, but he tended to dwell in the truth of it all. "I'm listening."

"We'll say I'm looking for Clint, since we know he's

been hanging out with Lizzie. He's not here, I say fine. Then you can question Mr. Adams in a separate room and I can quietly and patiently wait."

"You can't snoop."

Grady grinned. "I can't snoop and tell you about it, but I can snoop for my own peace of mind." He put a hand to his heart. "My brother could be missing."

"And is more likely at the Carson Ranch sleeping off teenage idiocy."

"More than likely, but you never know. Might as well give it a shot."

Laurel blew out a breath. She didn't know if it was genius or stupid and that was always the problem with Grady. He obscured both with those sinful smiles and mischievous glances.

"It's like having a partnership with mayhem," Laurel muttered, pushing out of the car.

"I'll take that as a compliment *and* agreement."

They walked up the well-kept path to the door side by side. Laurel reached out and pushed the doorbell as Grady surveyed the yard and house.

"I was right about the nicest house in town," Grady mumbled as Mr. Adams slowly pulled the door open.

His eyebrows were furrowed and he was clearly surprised and concerned to see her. "Uh, Deputy. I'm sorry, I don't recall your name…"

"Deputy Delaney. Mr. Adams, do you have a few moments to answer some questions for me?"

Mr. Adams looked nervously from Laurel to Grady's bandage and back to Laurel. "Erm, I suppose. Is…is something the matter?"

"We hope not. I have a few more questions about the Jason Delaney murder case, and Mr. Carson here is looking for his missing brother, who was last seen with your daughter."

Mr. Adams blinked at that. "I don't know anyone named Carson."

"His last name is Danvers. Clint Danvers," Grady supplied, and Laurel was quite impressed with how concerned brother he sounded.

"Oh, Clint. Yes, he and Lizzie have been working on a school project together."

Laurel did her best not to snort. She'd have almost felt bad for the guy for being so clueless if it wasn't for the fact he might be linked to murder.

"I haven't seen him in a while, and I have to say I'm starting to get awfully worried. I don't suppose Lizzie is around so I could ask her if she knows where he is."

Mr. Adams blinked in surprise and clearly balked at the request, so Laurel fixed her kindest smile on her face.

"If you'd feel more comfortable with a woman asking her, I can do it."

"Why don't I go get her and we'll... We'll all discuss it together." Mr. Adams smiled thinly. "She's in her room."

"Do you mind if I come with? I have some—" she glanced at Grady, then back at Mr. Adams "—confidential questions I'd like to ask you."

"Oh. Oh. Well, I suppose."

Laurel followed Mr. Adams from the entryway toward a staircase. She glanced back at Grady, who was whistling as he wandered the large entryway. She wanted to roll her eyes, but instead she focused on Mr. Adams.

She had to consider her words carefully. Hank's not-quite-clear answers didn't give her specifics to go on, so she had to fill in some blanks and hope she was right. "Were you aware Jason Delaney had evidence something criminal was going on at the mine, and was threatening to blackmail a higher-level official within the company?"

Mr. Adams stopped in his tracks. He looked genuinely surprised, but his next question left Laurel more than a little suspicious.

"How do you know that?"

She smiled apologetically. "I'm not at liberty to say."

"I… I had no idea." Mr. Adams resumed his pace up the stairs, but Laurel noted he'd gone pale.

"There's some concern you could be involved, Mr. Adams."

Again he paused, this time at the top of the stairs. He licked his lips, looking around nervously. "Involved… I… I didn't know… I…" He cleared his throat. "You've caught me quite by surprise."

"Clearly." Though Laurel didn't know if it was the right kind of surprise. "Please understand, I have to do my due diligence, and I hope if you know anything at all, you'll pass it along to the police. It's always so much worse on someone when they try to hide the truth."

He was all but sweating now, swallowing nearly convulsively as he reached out for a doorknob.

"This is Lizzie's room," he said, his hand shaking, his voice weak. When he tried to turn the knob, he frowned. "Locked. How odd." He knocked on the door. "Lizzie. Are you awake? I'm afraid I need you to come talk to some people for me." He chuckled weakly and looked at Laurel. "Teenagers do love their sleeping in."

"Mr. Adams. If you don't answer my questions in a forthright manner, I will be forced to investigate you further. Not just for whatever criminal activity is happening at the mine, but the murder of Jason Delaney, as well as attempted murder of an unnamed victim and the attack on another man. Do you understand?"

Mr. Adams nodded, jiggling the doorknob desperately. "Of course, Deputy. I don't know a thing about any of those things. I swear."

That Laurel didn't believe for a second, but the door swung open and a young, blonde teen answered, flushed and nervous-looking. "Hi, Daddy." She gulped. "Who's this?"

"The police, sweetheart. They're looking for your school friend Clint."

Lizzie's eyes widened at Laurel. "Clint?" she squeaked. "Uh, why?"

Laurel noted a boy's boot was partly visible, as though someone had attempted to shove it under the bed, along with a pair of men's jeans crumpled on one side of the room. Laurel decided to go for a little creative truth herself.

"His brother's been injured and—"

A rustling sounded and Clint tumbled out of the closet. "Grady's been hurt?" he demanded.

Mr. Adams made an outraged, choking sound.

"Grab your pants and head downstairs," Laurel said, stepping between the fuming Mr. Adams and the half-dressed teen. "I suggest you hurry."

Clint scrambled to gather his clothes and darted out the door while Laurel stood in front of Mr. Adams. When he made a move for the boy, Laurel put her hand out.

"Let's all calm down now."

"You little slut!" Mr. Adams shouted.

The poor girl began to cry and Laurel wasn't exactly gentle pulling Mr. Adams out of the room. "I suggest you calm yourself."

But he pushed her away, heading for the stairs Clint had just run down. "I want him arrested! This instant!"

"Your daughter is eighteen. There's nothing arrest-worthy happening here. Now, if you would stop—"

Clint skidded to a stop in front of Grady.

"What are you doing here?" they asked each other in unison.

"You're not that hurt," Clint said, frowning at Grady's bandage.

"But apparently you're that dumb," Grady muttered in return, glancing up at the furious Mr. Adams.

Clint quickly shoved his legs into his jeans, then his feet into the boots he'd been carrying. "I gotta go."

Laurel took the moment of surprise and confusion to move past Mr. Adams on the staircase. "Let him go," she mouthed to Grady, nodding at Clint.

Grady moved out of the way of Clint's escape, but

he stepped side by side with Laurel to block Mr. Adams from him as Clint slipped out the door.

"He… He defiled my daughter!" Mr. Adams shouted, pointing at Clint's retreating form, his face growing redder and redder.

Grady raised an eyebrow. "Seriously?"

"Mr. Adams," Laurel said as calmly as she could manage. "Your daughter is eighteen. And upset by your behavior. You should calm yourself and have a civil conversation with her."

Mr. Adams poked his finger wildly at her "I don't need *you* telling me how to handle my daughter."

"Clearly," Laurel replied sarcastically before she could bite back the response. She forced herself to retrieve a card from her pocket. "If you have any further information you'd like to divulge on the mine, Jason Delaney, et cetera, please give me a call."

Mr. Adams stared at the card, but seemed to regather his wits and took it. "I assure you, I know nothing about any of that."

Laurel nodded. "I hope my investigation reflects that, for your sake." Laurel turned for the door, ushering Grady out.

"That asshole is lying," Grady said flatly.

"Through his teeth," Laurel agreed, pulling her phone out of her pocket. "I need search warrants ASAP."

"How long is that going to take?"

A question she didn't want to answer. "Long enough for him to tip off whoever's got a hold on him."

"What about the girl? You think she might know something?"

"Maybe. Maybe." Laurel slid into her car and waited for Grady to get in the passenger side. "We'll go to the station so I can apply for the search warrant. Then... Why don't you call Clint? See if he can get Lizzie to come over for dinner at the Carson Ranch."

"Dinner?" Grady asked.

"Get her there under the guise of meeting Clint's family. Get her away from her father and in a neutral, safe space, and she might feel comfortable enough to talk. Maybe she doesn't know anything, but if she does I doubt she's going to tell me under her father's roof, and I don't want to drag a young girl into the police station if I don't have to."

"And that's legal?"

Laurel shrugged. "Depends on what she says. If I have to go the straight and narrow route with the search warrant, I can get a little creative in the questioning department."

"My, my, my, Deputy Delaney, you are full of surprises."

"Don't you forget it."

GRADY HAD SPENT more than his fair share of minutes trying to rile Laurel up, but watching her reaction to the judge denying her search warrant application was like nothing he'd ever seen.

She swore admirably. She fumed. She ranted as she drove from the sheriff's department all the way to the Carson Ranch.

"I don't think I've ever been more turned on," he offered once she took a breath.

"Oh, shut up," she returned, wholly unamused. Which, admittedly, served to amuse *him* more.

"Still no word from Clint?" she asked irritably.

"Not since he picked Lizzie up. They should beat us here, though."

She shook her head. "Something doesn't feel right. Something is off. I'm *missing* something."

"Then we'll find it."

She took a deep breath and let it out, straightening her shoulders as she drove up the bumpy, curving drive to the main house.

He liked that he'd calmed her some, and wished he could feel it inside of himself, but mostly he felt the same way she did. Something didn't feel right, and he didn't know what.

"You have to deal with this every case?"

"Deal with what?"

"That dogged not knowing what is going on?"

"Not every case, but some. A lot of not knowing is part of the job."

"Your job blows."

Her mouth curved. "It's not such a bad thing, putting it all together, knowing you can."

"Well, if you know you can, you can. So, you should stop ranting."

"I thought it turned you on."

Grady chuckled, but it died when they reached the house. "He's not here."

"He could have parked in one of the outbuildings, couldn't he?"

"Could have, but wouldn't." Clint wasn't that thorough. Grady shaded his eyes against the setting sun and looked around the property before turning his attention back to Laurel. "We should head back into town. Retrace what would have been his steps. They might have stopped somewhere to make out or something, but..."

"But maybe not. Is Ty in town?" she asked, already reversing the car and heading back the way they'd come. "We could split up our search and meet in the middle."

"Good thinking." Grady sent a quick message off to Ty as Laurel sped down the drive they'd just ambled up. Her gaze was shrewd on the road, hands grasped tight on the steering wheel, and it was an odd thing to not be in charge and not have it grate.

But his little brother might be in trouble and there wasn't a lot of room for any other emotions above fear.

"Keep your eyes peeled and tell me if you see anything," Laurel said. But as they drove, all he saw was road and the expanse of a Wyoming landscape.

"He's dead to me," Grady muttered, pissed off beyond belief the way fear gripped him. But he'd been attacked and threatened, a man had been killed, and now his brother was nowhere.

"Keep trying his cell," Laurel instructed calmly.

Anyone else's calmness in this situation would have only served to stoke his irritation higher, but something about Laurel's no-nonsense approach and the clear seriousness she took this with soothed rather than rattled.

"Let's stop at the gas station, see if anyone noticed anything. Ty should be catching up with us soon."

"Okay."

Laurel pulled into the gas station's parking lot and pushed her door open, but she glanced at him before she stepped out. She reached over, squeezed his forearm. "We'll find him. We will."

He took in those serious brown eyes and the determined set of her jaw and he nodded, some of that panic settling into something a lot more peaceful.

He stepped out with her and heard his name shouted. Clint burst from the front door of the station, blood dripping down his face. "Grady!"

Grady grabbed his brother, trying to figure out why he had blood all over him. He opened his mouth to demand answers, but Clint was already talking.

"Someone grabbed her. Just…grabbed her." He turned to Laurel, all heavy breathing and fear and desperation. "You gotta find her."

"Did you call the police?" Laurel asked composedly, though her whole body had tensed next to his.

"You are the police!"

Laurel didn't respond to that, but immediately began speaking in low tones into her radio.

"What was she wearing?" Laurel asked.

"Uh. Jeans. A T-shirt. Pink, I think. Pinkish. She had my jacket on. Leather jacket."

"What can you tell me about the car?" Laurel asked gently.

Clint swallowed, tears clearly swimming in his eyes. "Black. Slick." Clint rattled off a few possible makes and models. "The plate wasn't Wyoming. It was yellow, I think. Yellowish or something close."

Laurel relayed the information into her radio as Ty roared into the gas station, screeching to a halt on his motorcycle in front of them. "What's going on?"

"We need to get him to a hospital," Grady said roughly.

"No way, man. I have to find her."

"That gash is nasty. You need stitches. Did you lose consciousness?"

"No, I'm fine. They just knocked me down and I hit my head. He was gone by the time I got back up."

"Did Lizzie know the man who took her?" Laurel interjected.

"No! He had a ski mask thing on. I was gassing up and he just got out of his car and pushed me down and grabbed her. It took me a minute to get up and he shoved her in the car and left."

"He knocked you out."

"Whatever, man," Clint replied, pushing Grady's concerned hand away. "We have to find her. We have to."

"We've got a lot to go on. Write anything else you can think of down, okay? Ty, you take him to the hospital. I'll send an officer to watch and take Clint's statement."

"And what are we doing?" Grady asked.

"This time, we're getting consent to search Adams's house without having to wait around for a search warrant." She stopped midstep toward the car and then turned to him. "I mean, you don't have to come with me. I've given Lizzie's name and description to county, and I've sent the closest officer to the hospital to question Clint. You'd be safe there, if you want to be with Clint. I'd under—"

"I'll be safe with you, too. Let's go."

Chapter Fourteen

Laurel knocked on Mr. Adams's door for the second time in two days. When Mr. Adams opened the door, his face was red, his thinning hair wild. "Did you find her? Is she—"

"Mr. Adams, I need consent to search your house. We're looking for any clues that might help us find Lizzie."

"My...consent." The man choked on something like a sob, but Laurel couldn't let that sway her. "My daughter is missing."

"Yes, and the Bent County Sheriff's Department is doing everything in their power to find her. Including this. If you give us consent, Deputy Hart and I will search the entire house." Laurel nodded at Hart, who was standing behind her. "We'll take anything that might aid us in finding her whereabouts."

"I..." Mr. Adams raked his shaking hands through his hair. "All right. You can search the house."

"Sign this, please." Laurel nodded to Hart, who held out the consent form. With shaking hands, Mr. Adams signed it.

"If you'd leave the door open while we search, and find somewhere out of the way to be." She glanced back at Grady, whom she'd instructed to stay in the car.

He, of course, wasn't *in* the car, but leaning against it, looking somehow lazy and lethal at the same time, the stitches on his head adding to the dangerous vibe. She sighed heavily. She didn't like leaving him out there, but there weren't a lot of choices right now.

"I... You..." Mr. Adams made another choking sound, but he finally got out of the way of the door.

"Upstairs. First door on your left," Laurel directed Hart.

Laurel herself headed through the lower level of the house while Mr. Adams trailed after her, sputtering ineffectively. What she wanted to find was some kind of home office or place where he'd have things related to work. "I don't suppose you have any information as to who might have taken your daughter, or why."

"Miss Delaney, I don't know who's responsible," Mr. Adams rasped.

"If you say so," she returned evenly, ignoring the Miss instead of Deputy.

"No, I mean, I don't know their name or anything to identify them by. The man I've been working for is a nameless, faceless entity. I get messages, and I act on them. I don't keep my job if I don't act on them."

Laurel whirled on the admission. "So this has something to do with the mine?"

Mr. Adams sank into a chair, rubbing his hands over his face. "Yes. I guess. I was just told to get rid of some papers. To cover some things up. When Jason started poking around…" He looked up at her plaintively. "I didn't kill him. I don't have anything to do with this except paperwork."

"I need to know everything about the paperwork. I need a list of anyone who is above you and would be affected if the information you destroyed got out. I need everything you know, Mr. Adams. For Lizzie's sake."

He swallowed audibly and nodded. "My office is upstairs. I don't have anything specific, but I can write down some things. They took Lizzie because she's been…" His voice broke and he cleared his throat. "I don't know why, but she's been poking around my work. Asking me questions about the mine, about Jason, and I didn't know what was going on. I figured she'd get bored of it, but—"

"Delaney," Hart called from above. "I found a license plate number written on a scrap of paper."

Laurel met Hart at the bottom of the stairs, glancing at the looping scrawl of what had to be a license plate number.

"Call it in. Have someone check it out," she said.

Hart nodded and started talking into his radio.

Laurel turned her attention to the man behind her. A man who'd clearly done some illegal things, but was scared sick by his daughter's disappearance and his worry for her.

"Show me your office."

He started walking and she followed him up the stairs while Hart stood in the entryway, relaying his information to dispatch.

Mr. Adams led her to a small room at the end of

the hall. It was nicely decorated, dominated by a huge desk. There was a recliner in the corner and everything was neat as a pin.

"I don't bring anything home, and everything I was told to destroy, I destroyed, but I... Lately I've been getting nervous, what with the murder and all, so I started keeping a list." With shaking hands, Mr. Adams opened up a drawer, then reached toward the back, popping something that turned out to be a false bottom.

But instead of a piece of paper or anything innocent, there was a gun. Clear as day. Mr. Adams gasped.

"It isn't mine," he whispered, his voice sounding strained. "I don't own a gun. I don't."

Laurel pulled rubber gloves out of her utility belt and put them on. She picked up the weapon. It was exactly the kind of gun that could have killed Jason Delaney. She closed her eyes for a minute because she wasn't stupid.

Mr. Adams wasn't the murderer, but someone sure wanted her to think he was.

"My notes. They're gone," Mr. Adams gasped, pawing around the false bottom. But it was empty save for the gun. "Oh, God. Oh, God."

"Hart," Laurel barked.

After a few seconds, the deputy appeared. His eyes widened when he saw what Laurel was holding.

"I need you to run the serial number on this gun." She rattled it off to him and Hart relayed the number to dispatch. She racked her brain for a reason to take in Mr. Adams so they could have him in custody while they ran ballistics on the weapon, because as long as his daughter wasn't safe, neither was he. Neither were Clint and Hank, for that matter.

The radio squawked and everyone in the room heard the results clear as day. "That gun has been reported as stolen."

Laurel glanced at Mr. Adams, who looked panic-stricken. "Stolen? I don't own a gun. I haven't stolen a gun. That isn't mine! My notes are gone!"

"Hart. Arrest him."

"No. No! I didn't do anything. Please, understand. I didn't… They're making this…"

"Mr. Adams," Laurel began firmly so he'd stop blubbering and listen. "You have a stolen weapon in your home. I have to arrest you. We'll need to run ballistics on it, and if it comes back as the murder weapon in the Jason Delaney case—"

"What have I done? Oh, God." Mr. Adams began to cry, and Laurel almost felt sympathy for the man, but he'd gotten himself mixed up in some ugly business.

"Consider this the best thing for you right now, Mr. Adams. You'll be safe, and this might be leverage we can use to get Lizzie released. If whoever has her is worried about being linked to the murder, having someone arrested for it might lower their guard. If it's the murder weapon."

He calmed a little bit at that.

"Hart, I want you to arrest him and take him to the station, and get a recording of everything he can remember about the documents he destroyed. Along with anyone he might want to implicate."

Hart stepped forward and went through the steps

to arrest Mr. Adams while Laurel continued to look through all the drawers. She sat down at the desk as Hart led Mr. Adams away. She didn't know what she was looking for, but she could confiscate the computer along with the murder weapon.

She wasn't sure she believed Mr. Adams was completely ignorant of who was behind all of this, but a trip to the station and videotaped questioning might help jog his memory. If nothing else, she truly believed it would convince the real killer they weren't still looking for him.

"I thought we decided he wasn't the murderer."

Laurel glanced over her shoulder to find Grady taking up the entire doorway. "You shouldn't be in here," she said, though the words were a waste and she knew it. "I don't think he's the murderer, but someone wants us to think he is. I don't have any proof he's *not* the murderer. A stolen weapon in the house is enough to bring him in."

She turned back to the desk. "I have to search everything. Once I'm done, and I've compiled all the evidence I've found, we'll drop it off at the station, then head over to the hospital and see if Clint remembers anything."

"You have to sleep at some point, princess."

Her shoulders slumped and the wave of exhaustion she'd been fighting off with sheer adrenaline threatened to topple her. "Yeah, at some point. But not yet." A few more steps and then she could think about sleep.

Grady's large hand covered her shoulder, squeezed. She looked up at him with a million snippy responses she knew she needed to give him. But all she wanted to do was lean into him. Rest against him.

Which wasn't something she could allow herself. "Wait downstairs. Don't touch anything. I'll be down as soon as I'm done."

He didn't remove his hand. Instead, the other came up and cradled her cheek, gentle as could be. Something like a lump lodged itself in her throat at the sheer *wanting*. Wanting him. Wanting sleep. Wanting to just *rest*.

"I'll go downstairs. You've got half an hour to finish up. Then you'll drop off anything you need to at the station. After that, you're heading straight for bed."

"Is that an order?"

He grinned that horrible, lust-inducing grin. "Yeah, I think it is."

It was the simply *kind*, almost caring way he said it that made the lump in her throat impossible to swallow. "Decided you're my caretaker now?" she asked through a tight throat.

"I think we mutually decided that for each other. Get to work, Deputy. I'm tired, too."

On a deep breath, Laurel pulled out of the grasp of Grady's rough hands and did just that.

GRADY'D HAD HIS fill of waiting for people. He'd also had his fill of Laurel looking like she was about to keel over, and then pressing forward as if her sheer force of will could keep her awake for years.

Hell, maybe it could. She walked out of the sheriff's department looking with-it and strong no matter that legions of shadows existed under her eyes. So much so he could see them even in the parking lot lights.

"How's Clint?" she asked.

"Hospital released him. Ty's taking him back to the ranch and him, Noah and Vanessa will keep him out of trouble. I gave him your number in case he remembers something important."

She nodded. "Good."

He hopped off the hood of her car, where he'd been sitting and waiting. "I'm driving."

She rolled her eyes. "You can't drive my county-issued vehicle, Carson."

"Why not?"

"It's against the law. Plus, you've had a concussion."

"I believe that was something like twenty-four hours ago. Which means I'm okay to drive now."

"God, has it been twenty-four hours?" She raked her hands through her hair, which had come out of its band at some point between finding Clint and now.

"Heck of a twenty-four hours."

She huffed out something close to a laugh. "I suppose." She pulled her keys out of her pocket. "If anyone asks, you put a gun to my head before I let you drive my car."

"Got it." He took her keys, trying to tone down his self-satisfied smirk a *little* bit.

She slid into the passenger seat, her eyes already drooping, and he turned the keys in the ignition.

He didn't bother to talk. He let her lean against the window by her side as he drove them away from the sheriff's department and toward Bent. The long way.

Because he had a bad feeling that wherever he stopped, she'd pop back up into Deputy Delaney mode and never get any real rest.

So he drove through the glittering late night, enjoying the peace and the stars, and only finally heading to Laurel's place when he started to come perilously close to dozing off himself.

As he drove Laurel's car up the smooth, curving drive that led to her cabin on the fancy Delaney spread, he couldn't help wondering at this *thing* inside of him.

He'd been bred to hate Delaneys. Told stories of their wrongdoings over the centuries. He'd reveled in that. Being the underdogs, the dangerous ones. He'd used it to excuse the things he'd wanted to excuse in his life.

But Laurel had never fit with all that fiction he'd allowed himself. Something vibrant and good with this odd tug between them he'd always known was there, but had sought to avoid.

But there was no more avoiding. It was here, stronger with every passing hour as they tried to solve this mystery together. The fact of the matter was, a fact he wouldn't likely admit to anyone possibly ever, he cared about Laurel Delaney.

Not just attraction, or that teenaged desire of something that was off-limits and too good for him besides. Not just this lifetime of a wait, the anticipation, the holding himself back since he was a kid and believing he could control that tug.

This was more, and that was what had made the wait endure all those years. That he knew her and understood her. That he *liked* her. That her work ethic made *his* pale in comparison and he'd never met anyone who'd come close.

He parked on the little square of gravel and looked over at her sleeping form in the dim glow of moon and starlight filtered through the car windows.

Even as his body hardened, because she was gorgeous, his heart did some painful twisting thing. That care lodged far too deep to ignore anymore, to avoid, and he was very afraid burrowed too deep to ever be mined out.

"Wake up, princess, or I'm going to have to heft you over my shoulder," he said, far too gruffly. Because truth be told, he didn't know how to do care without a lot of gruff to cover it up. To hide the softness. Ward off the inevitable attack. Wasn't that what dear old Dad had taught him?

Laurel blinked her eyes open, staring out the windshield and then at him. "Oh. You brought me home." She frowned at the clock. "That was a heck of a drive."

"I figured it ensured you at least got an hour."

She pushed out of the car into the frigid night air and took a deep breath. "Feel like a new woman." She grinned over the hood of the car at him. "Now I don't need to sleep at all." But that confidence was underscored when she yawned.

"Uh-huh," he replied, rifling through her keys until he found one that looked like a house key. He tried it in the lock and it worked.

She stepped inside, yawning again as she flipped on a light. When she turned to face him, she frowned.

"Where are you going?"

"To the saloon."

"You can't be alone. You really can't be alone in my car."

"What do you suggest, then?" It was something of a challenge, one he probably shouldn't have laid down when they were both exhausted and no real breaks in the case had been made.

Her gaze held his, unwavering and potent, that thing always between them crackling with a new kind of electricity. Because they'd both acknowledged it now, because they were both operating on less than full capacity. Or just because it was *time*.

"I guess I suggest the inevitable," she said quietly, yet in that self-possessed, certain way she said everything. She stepped forward, as if she had no doubts or concerns, and slid her arms around his neck.

"Is that what it is?" he asked, his voice a rough rasp as she stared up at him, her mouth parted and *right there*. "Inevitable?"

"It feels that way," she replied, her tall, lithe body pressing to his, those brown eyes never leaving his gaze. As if one hour of sleep had given her all the power she needed. "But maybe I just want to." Then her mouth slid against his, soft and hot.

It felt like centuries of waiting even though he'd just kissed her the other day. Her mouth insistent, determined, so *her*, and he wanted to taste every contour of it until it was etched in his very bones.

He didn't seem to be alone in that desire. Her tongue moved against his, her arms clamped around his neck as if she could keep him there, devouring her mouth.

More, his mind chanted. *More, more, more*.

"Grady, I *want* you," she murmured against his mouth. "Now."

He kicked the door behind them closed before moving her toward her bedroom, their arms still wrapped around each other.

"Consider it me taking advantage of your exhaustion," he gritted out, backing her toward the bed. "Then you can pretend you regret it in the morning."

"I won't." She met his gaze then, her brown eyes dark and serious. "I won't." She pulled his mouth back to hers as they tumbled onto the bed together.

Chapter Fifteen

Laurel had never been all that concerned with sex before. When she was in a relationship, it was nice to have, certainly. A kind of physical comfort, two bodies coming together.

There was nothing easy or particularly comfortable about Grady on top of her, pushing her into her mattress, his mouth unrelenting and perfect against hers, his hands molding to every curve of her body as if he couldn't stop himself. Not because it hurt or she was in an awkward position, but because there was this desperate ache inside of her, growing and growing without getting any closer to being fulfilled.

This was not the precursor to sex she knew. This was wild and desperate and she felt like if she didn't feel Grady's naked skin against hers and soon, she might simply combust and turn to ash. Or, worse, beg.

She could feel his erection against the apex of her thighs and it made her wonder if all the minimal sex she'd been having in her life had just been bad. Or if not bad, adequate. Decent and all, but not…this all-encompassing, reason-killing thing.

She pawed at his shirt, wanting to see the grand expanse of his chest, wanting to feel it under her fingertips or pressed against her body.

She'd had a lifetime of occasionally catching glimpses of Grady without a shirt on, but here in her bedroom, in her *bed*, it was, well, it was something else as he sat up and pulled off his T-shirt.

She could see every fine line of his tattoo that took up most of his shoulder and weaved its way down to his elbow. She could reach out and touch the delineation of each impressive muscle, and she could truly absorb and enjoy just how *big* he was. She didn't have to fight that or prove she was just as strong or could take him down. She didn't have to be Deputy Delaney here. For a little while she could just be Laurel.

He reached out and jerked her shirt off her in one quick pull. There was a jolt of self-consciousness that lasted all of five seconds, because his gaze was hot and blazing on her as if he could eat her alive.

She could recognize it in him, because she felt the same way, and that was the thing about whatever it was that existed between them. Maybe it had never made sense, and they'd certainly both ignored and avoided it, but they had always both *felt* it.

He reached forward and palmed her breasts, still clad in her bra, but then he jerked the bra down, not even bothering with the clasp. His hands rasping against the sensitive skin there as his mouth descended onto her mouth, kissing down her neck to her breasts. His beard scraped against her skin everywhere he kissed. It was abrasive and harsh and somehow that made every feeling deep inside of her sparkle brighter and higher.

Abruptly, Grady's mouth left her and he got off the bed. She tried to formulate a question, but she was breathing too hard as he yanked his phone out of his pocket and tossed it as if he didn't care if it landed on a hard surface and broke apart. His keys were next, but when he got his wallet, he flipped it open and pulled out a condom.

She exhaled harshly and maybe she should have been put off by the fact he had a condom, but she didn't care. She flat-out didn't care how or why or how long, as long as he used it with her.

"Take off your pants," he ordered.

Laurel gladly scrambled to comply as he undid the button and zipper on his own pants. As she kicked off her khakis and her underwear, she watched all of Grady come into view. Everything about him strong and broad and beautiful.

There was some dim part of her mind reminding her this was Grady Carson and she wasn't supposed to be getting involved with him. Certainly not like this.

But every other part of her didn't care. Because Grady, for all his swagger and outward appearance and sarcastic jokes, was good and kind and he might not want to ever admit it, but he cared about her. The same way she cared about him. An indelible fact they'd both spent too long trying to falsify.

He was standing there at the foot of her bed, completely naked and impressive. She sat on her bed, naked save for the bra he'd pushed down to her waist.

He flicked a glance at it. "Get it off."

She didn't even hesitate to do as he demanded. To do anything he demanded. Because she had always been in charge in life. She'd never cared for following anyone else's moral compass or rules. She had her own strident ones. She knew how she wanted to live her life, and she did it. Always.

But she'd never felt wild. She'd never been consumed by need or desire, and so why not follow his every order? He was the expert after all.

Grady put one knee on the bed, looming like an incredibly sexy conqueror. She would gladly be conquered. Exhaustion and feuds be damned. All she wanted in this moment was Grady.

He opened the condom wrapper, rolling on the latex before covering her body with his. And she was completely covered. Being flattened into her mattress was a delicious feeling. To live in this world that was only Grady, hard and hot and demanding on top of her.

His hands explored her body, and she smoothed her hands down his expansive, smooth back. His mouth nuzzled against the curve of her neck until she was sighing with pleasure, arching herself against him, desperate for him to enter. Her body somehow both relaxed and coiled at the same moment.

When he finally slid inside of her, there was a moment where they both paused. Holding on to each other, watching each other. Connected. As though she could see over a century in his eyes and vice versa.

Inevitable. That word kept repeating itself in her mind. Because this felt nothing short of inevitable.

This was where she belonged. He was everything she needed. She didn't believe in feuds. She didn't believe in curses of Carsons and Delaneys commingling. But she understood in this moment it was not for the faint of heart. This joining, this meeting. It was only for those strong enough to handle it.

It was a very lucky thing she was strong enough. And so was he.

Grady surged inside of her in a long, slow, inexorable glide as if he felt it, too. The inevitability. The strength it would take and how much they were made for it.

His mouth claimed hers as he moved against her, over and over again, bringing her to a blinding kind of climax she'd never experienced before, shattering around him and chanting his name as he brought her to that peak again.

Her name from his lips against her mouth as together they tumbled off the edge of something that felt nothing short of perfect and meant to be.

GRADY FIGURED HE must be dreaming when a repeatedly shrill noise sounded and he was all wrapped up in a very naked Laurel. Surely this was an alternate universe he found himself in. Because there was no way the things he remembered from the night before could be real. Just no possible way.

In this dream, she was as perfect as he might have imagined. And in this dream, it felt as though no possible outcome of his life could be anything other than Laurel in it. In his bed. Always.

Yes, it had to be a dream.

But Laurel's sleepy voice was very real as it murmured a hello next to him. Her warm and very naked body next to him making him instantly hard again absolutely happening in the present.

He opened his eyes, noting the room was still dark. Which meant at best they'd scored one or two hours of sleep. They both definitely needed more.

Laurel's hand slapped against his bare chest and he winced.

"Where?" she demanded into her phone receiver. "She's all right?" Laurel covered the receiver with one hand. "They found Lizzie," she whispered. "A little beat-up but mostly okay."

"Does Clint know?"

She shook her head, so Grady got out of bed to find his phone. It was somewhere on Laurel's side of the room so he walked around. Her floor was neat as a pin except where their discarded clothes and his tossed phone, keys and wallet dotted the hardwood.

Laurel was barking demanding questions into her phone and clearly getting at least some of the responses she wanted. Grady picked up his phone and typed a text to Clint that Lizzie had been found and was okay.

He watched Laurel as she picked up a pen and notepad from her nightstand and balanced it on her lap. The sheet covered her legs, but her upper body was completely bare, and Grady wanted nothing more than to crawl back into bed and toss her phone and notes away.

But this was her job, and he was an intuitive enough

man to know she would not compromise her priorities. He wished he didn't admire that so much about her.

There was something like panic beating in his chest because he wanted… Well, for the first time in his adult life he wanted something that was out of his control. He could fight for his name, for Rightful Claim, for Bent, but what lay before him with this woman wasn't a fight.

It would be something like a give-and-take, and sometimes he wondered if deep down inside he was just his parents—all take.

But he wasn't a coward. Wouldn't allow himself to be. Panic didn't rule him, and neither did fear. If he wanted to give and take, he damn well would.

Laurel finished writing something down, then clicked off her phone and set it neatly on the nightstand.

"They haven't found who took her. Apparently she was dumped back at the same gas station she was taken from. She doesn't have a description, but they did find that the license plate Lizzie had written down in her room was a Nebraska plate, and Nebraska plates are yellow, which means the plate we have and the car that took her are probably one and the same."

"You think this is all the work of one man?"

"I'm not sure. But one man has the answers and I need to find them. Apparently Lizzie knew her father was in trouble and had been doing her own poking around—mostly with the help of Clint. She's been pretty tight-lipped about what happened while she was kidnapped, so I'm going to go question her. Maybe she'll feel more comfortable with a woman." Laurel was already out of bed, pulling on a T-shirt.

Belatedly she noticed it was his. She shook her head and moved to take it off again, but he stopped her, putting a hand to her abdomen.

"And if she gives you a tip-off to who did this? What are you going to do?"

She looked up at him, then blinked as if to focus herself. Her gaze slid down his naked body, which he had to say he didn't mind.

She shook her head as if to clear it. "I'll follow procedure to bring whoever it is in for questioning. We both need to get dressed and I'll drop you off at the Carson Ranch."

Grady bit back all the jumbled worry inside of him. It had only been a few days of working side by side with her, and she'd been a cop for a long time, but he didn't like... Well, the idea of not being there when she went up against a man capable of murder.

"I need to check on things at the bar," he forced himself to say. "When Vanessa runs things, I tend to find myself a mess. Drop me off there."

She chewed on her bottom lip for a second before reaching out and touching his bare chest. "Just because we have a lead doesn't mean you're not still in danger. You should be somewhere protected, and with people."

"You're in danger all the time. Just by being a cop, right?" he said quietly, because he knew it was true. He *knew* that. He understood that. He just wanted her to understand... Something.

She absorbed those words, seeming to take in their weight. She didn't brush that statement off, she considered it. Which meant something, maybe something more than it should.

It was another layer. They didn't necessarily have to talk every step through for them to understand each other.

"There is a slight difference," she said carefully.

"Rationally, I get that."

"And irrationally?"

"Irrationally, I want you by my side always so I can know you're safe. *I* want to keep *you* safe."

She stared up at him, her fingertips on his chest, and it was like a moor to this world. She was his anchor to this world. This Delaney cop. Somehow it made all the sense. Because she was the last thing he should ever want, of course she was the only one who fit.

She got up on her tiptoes and brushed her mouth across his. "I don't..." She took a deep breath and squared her shoulders, all the while looking him in the eye. "I don't want last night to be a one-time thing."

"Good, because it's not," he returned gruffly.

"And I don't just mean the sex."

"I know what you mean."

"You feel the same way?" she asked him directly, so brave and certain and good.

It grated somehow, because he wasn't all that good, and she probably deserved someone better, but he'd be damned if he let her have another man. He took her mouth with his, the opposite of her sweet little peck. He kissed her long and hard and hot. "You are mine, Laurel Delaney. End of story."

Her mouth curved, almost as if she was indulging

him. "And you are mine, Grady Carson." She patted his chest. "I'm surprised you're not being a baby about it."

"Maybe once I've had a good night's sleep I'll work up a good tantrum."

She smiled at him, but it didn't ease this feeling inside of him. Separate from all the being each other's.

"I don't think we should separate right now," he said, even knowing it was a losing battle to go against what she needed to do.

"I need to question Lizzie alone, and I need a few hours to concentrate. Besides, they let Lizzie go of their own volition. Things are de-escalating. There might still be danger out there, but I think it's weakened. Besides, you have work to do as much as me. You know it."

Grady grunted, irritated she was right. "Something doesn't feel right. Just like the other night when Clint didn't show up. Something doesn't... Something isn't adding up."

"I agree. That's why I need a few hours at the station. Talk to Lizzie. Look at some documents Hart found. I need my concentration on this case for a good two hours. And I can't do that with you around."

"You flatter me, princess."

"Get dressed. I'll drop you off at Rightful Claim, as long as someone can be there with you. I don't want you being alone. I'll put in my few hours at the station, and then..." She chewed on her bottom lip again.

"And then what?"

She trailed the fingertips over his beard. "I'll come and find you."

"You had better." He kissed her, meaning for it to be soft, subtle, just to prove he could. But it evolved somehow, as it always did with her. Wildfire and need. "We both need showers before we go, don't you think?"

"We are not both going to fit in my shower," she said with a breathless laugh.

"But we could give it the old college try," he returned, tugging her toward a door that had to lead to the bathroom. And when she went with him willingly, laughing and naked, he figured things might just be all right after all.

Chapter Sixteen

Laurel drove toward the Bent County Sheriff's Department after dropping Grady off at Rightful Claim, not exactly feeling rested. She was still tired, because she'd grabbed maybe just three hours of sleep. But it had been good, heavy sleep. And something like giddiness was keeping her going.

She was a little embarrassed at that. How much excitement and drive this whole Grady thing had given her. She should calm down. She should be rational.

She and Grady were in some very odd circumstances and it was likely causing heightened feelings… or something. The reality of themselves was possibly a little different outside of the bedroom.

Which was all her fear talking, actually. Because last night and this morning had been good. The kind of good that was overwhelming. The kind of good you had to work for and sacrifice things for. In equal-ish measure.

She blew out a breath. She didn't have time to really work through all that. She had to question Lizzie, and see if the ballistics report had come back yet. Her focus had to be the job, and then she could figure out her personal life.

Because that was the priority list of her life. Always had been.

Why did it suddenly feel like a weight?

She shook her head, focusing on the sun rising behind her. Which was when she realized the same car had been following her for a while now. The same kind of car Clint had mentioned when describing the man who'd taken Lizzie.

The car was far back enough she couldn't make out the letters and numbers on the plate, but she could tell it was yellowish. Just as Clint had described.

She inhaled, then slowly breathed out through her mouth, focusing on being calm and following procedure.

What if they've been following you since before you left Rightful Claim? What if someone is following Grady?

She couldn't focus on *that*. She had to focus on what to do in her here and now. Because she'd left Bent city limits, and the sun was only just beginning to rise. The highway out of town was deserted, and the current stretch she was on was at a high enough elevation that the shoulder was mostly guardrail to prevent cars from going off the slight rocky cliff.

Taking a glance in her rearview mirror as often as she could, she grabbed for her radio without looking at it.

"Dispatch. 549. Rush traffic," she said as calmly as she could manage.

"Go ahead 549."

Before she could get the next words out of her mouth, an engine roared close—too close. She flicked a glance in the rearview mirror just in time to see the black car plow into the back of hers.

She jerked forward, her face smashing into the airbag as she felt her car skid forward and then sideways, metal screeching against the guardrail. That noise reminded her of how precarious her situation was. Because if this car succeeded in pushing her over it, she'd be tumbling down a pretty steep, rocky drop.

She ignored the pain in her head and focused on her grip on the wheel. She jerked it as far to the right as the airbag would allow, braking as hard as she could while she did so.

She had to get out of the car. While it offered some protection, she could be more agile on foot. And possibly run down the steep ravine without plunging to her death.

She couldn't see anything with the airbag in her vision, but the screeching of the guardrail had stopped and so had her movement. She imagined the attacker was reversing to plow into her again, so she had to act fast.

She pushed hard, opening the door open and scrambling out of the car as she disentangled herself from the airbag and seat belt. She grabbed her gun out of her belt as she looked around, trying to find the other car.

It had indeed reversed and was now speeding toward her. Laurel didn't have time to think twice—she ran and jumped over the guardrail, half running, half stumbling down the rocky hillside.

If she drew him into a chase, she could shoot him. Of course, he likely had a gun himself, but at least she'd have a chance to fight back. She glanced behind her—nothing but rocks and bent guardrail.

She surveyed the landscape in front of her. It was mostly open, though there were a few swells of land she might be able to hide behind with enough of a head start.

The biggest problem was she didn't have her radio or her cell. All she had was her gun. So, she kept running, checking over her shoulder every few minutes for signs of someone following her.

She was maybe halfway to a decent cover of rocks and swell of land when a figure appeared, stepping over the guardrail. He was wearing all black, including a ski mask, just as Clint had described the man who'd taken Lizzie.

Well, he was not going to take her. She raised her gun, tried to aim, only to realize her vision wasn't clear. Blood was dripping down into her eyes. Blood? Where had that come from?

She tried to blink it away, finally becoming cognizant of the fact her head was throbbing and burning. In the adrenaline of the moment, she hadn't realized she'd been hurt, but some of that reality was getting through to her now. The world tilted, but she breathed through it and fired off a shot in the direction of the man in black.

She didn't even try to see if she'd hit her target. She

started running again, trying to figure out where she was. If there was somewhere she could go. She was injured and isolated, but she wasn't outnumbered, probably, and just because she was hurt didn't mean she was witless.

After another scan of the area, and remembering where she'd been on the road, she realized she was close to the back entrance to the Carson Ranch she'd dropped Grady off at the other day.

She didn't want to lead this man to the Carsons, but she didn't have a choice. She needed a phone. She needed help. If she at least got to the property, she might get hurt, but maybe someone would find her before she was killed. Maybe.

A shot rang out and she winced at how close it sounded, but nothing touched her. Still, it was too close for comfort, and proof the man was armed with a deadly weapon.

Lungs burning, everything in her body a painful, aching throb, Laurel tried to pull up her shirt and wipe away the blood that was impeding her vision as she ran.

But even without blood in her eyes, her vision was getting blurrier. She felt dizzy and sick but she knew she had to keep running. Someone was after her. The man who'd killed Jason, who'd kidnapped Lizzie. It had to be him.

She got to the back entrance of the Carson Ranch without the man catching up to her or firing off another short. She just had to get to the house, or maybe Noah would be out somewhere close working. Someone who would hear something, do something. She had to hope and pray for that, because she knew her time was running out.

Her legs buckled and the world around her was suddenly dark instead of the picturesque fall morning. She didn't quite realize she'd fallen until her shoulder hit the hard ground.

She tried to get up, but her body wasn't listening to her mind. She could hear approaching footsteps closing in on her.

Dimly she hoped Grady was okay and at Rightful Claim, working and giving Vanessa a hard time. She swallowed at the nausea threatening, praying she'd left enough clues and wreckage for whoever found her to figure out who this man was and where he'd come from.

Somewhat belatedly, she realized she still had her hand on her gun. The gun. She placed her finger on the trigger and when it sounded like the man was right on top of her, she managed to roll onto her back and shoot.

GRADY FROWNED AT his phone with growing irritation. He'd been patient all morning and not called Laurel to see what was going on. But it was nearly two o'clock and there'd been no word from her. Not to him. Not to Clint.

Grady tried to convince himself she'd found a lead and was following it. He tried to convince himself she was doing her job. If something had happened, wouldn't he have heard something? If not from Laurel herself, from *someone*.

Then again, why would anyone think to tell him about the goings-on of Laurel Delaney?

When Dylan Delaney stormed into the bar before they'd officially opened for the day, everything in Grady went cold and still.

The Delaneys did not come into his bar.

"Where is she? What have you gotten her messed up with?"

Grady stood behind the bar, willing his temper to behave. He'd never cared for Laurel's brother the slick, arrogant banker who only'd ever looked down at any Carson in his bank. But Dylan *was* her brother, and maybe he knew something that Grady didn't. It'd grate more if he wasn't so worried.

"What do *I* have your *cop* sister mixed up in?"

"She might be a cop, and this might have more to do with the case she's working on, but when Carson property is involved, so are you. I know it."

"What are you talking about?" Grady demanded, keeping himself unnaturally still. He couldn't *react* yet. First he needed facts.

"My sister disappeared. They've traced footsteps and blood to *your* property, and there's a lot of talk about how you left the station with her last night. So I want to know what you did to her."

Grady pushed out from behind the bar, ignoring Dylan's demands. He pulled his phone out and dialed the ranch. No answer. He dialed Noah's cell, which went straight to voice mail. Ty was in the back, and if he'd heard anything, he would've told Grady by now.

"Ty," Grady called, already to the door. "Lock up.

Meet me at the ranch." He didn't wait to see if his cousin would listen. He called Vanessa. Nothing.

He took his keys out of his pocket as he swung out the front doors.

"You don't walk away from me, Carson," Dylan threatened, hot on his heels.

"I'll fight you after your sister's been found, if that's what you're gunning for. But I've got more important things to do right now than deal with you." He got on his motorcycle.

"I'm following you," Dylan shouted over the roar of the motorcycle's engine, as if that was some kind of deterrent. Grady didn't even respond.

He took off, breaking every possible traffic law to get to the ranch. There was a cop car parked at the front of the house, but he didn't see anyone in it. He scanned the land, heartbeat thumping painfully in his chest.

Blood. Blood. She was bleeding somewhere, and he couldn't do a thing about it.

Except she'd gotten here. His property. There had to be something he could do. Had to be.

Dylan's car pulled up next to him, windows down. "I don't know what you think you're going to do."

"I'm going to find her," Grady replied. Some way. Somehow. There was nothing else *to* do.

"Why are *you* going to do anything? The police are searching for her, and if you had anything to do with—"

"I don't have anything to do with it. I love her." Which was not exactly a *surprise* admission, just an uncomfortable one.

"That's... You're a *Carson*."

"Yeah, I'll worry about that some other time." He scanned the area again, trying to figure out where to start. He had to stop jabbering with Dylan and actually think. Formulate a plan.

"They're at the back entrance," Dylan offered. "What's the quickest way?"

Grady frowned at the sleek sports vehicle Laurel's brother drove. "That car isn't going to make it over this hard terrain."

"It will," Dylan said, everything about him severe and determined. "Now, what's the quickest way?"

"Follow me." Grady took off, narrowly missing wrecking out when he went over a swell of land too fast, but it didn't matter. Nothing mattered aside from finding Laurel.

When they reached the back entrance, there was a whole area taped off with caution tape. The deputy who'd searched the Adams's house with Laurel the other day frowned in his direction as Grady swung off the motorcycle and stormed toward the tape.

"You're going to have to stay back," Hart said firmly.

Grady only did so because he knew the guy was trying to do his job. He glanced at the crowd. Three deputies. And Noah.

He went to stand next to his cousin. "Tell me what you know."

"No signs of a vehicle," Noah said. "But Laurel's car was found crashed into a guardrail on the highway. Someone rear-ended her, but the car that caused the accident is nowhere to be found. The cops found a trail of blood that led here."

"That's a mile at least."

Noah nodded grimly. "Vanessa's with Clint and another officer at the house. I've offered to search the higher elevations on my horse, but they're still making a decision."

"Screw that." Grady looked at Noah's horse tied to a tree, placidly standing a few yards off. "I'm going."

"There's the old stone church up on the ridge. It's the only kind of place to hide anywhere near here," Noah said quietly, angling them away from the deputies gathering evidence and talking earnestly. "Unless someone picked her up on the road, but the cops don't think so. I told them about the church, but—"

Grady shook his head. "They've got their procedure, but we don't. I'm not waiting around. I'm going to take your horse up there. You and Delaney go back and get more horses, rifles, whatever you can. We search for her ourselves."

Noah looked suspiciously at Dylan. "You really want to take him?"

"I'm her brother," Dylan interjected. "Finding Laurel is all that matters."

Noah nodded at that. "All right."

"Wait until I'm gone, then take my bike. It'll be quickest to get back to the barn." Grady handed Noah the keys. "I'm going to ride Star right up the property line to the stone church. You cut up from the barn the opposite direction. Got your cell?"

Noah nodded.

"You see anything, anything comes up, call. I'll do the same. Something big happens, 911, cops, whatever. The only important thing is finding her safe, and keeping yourself out of harm's way. Got it?"

"What about keeping *your*self safe?"

Grady didn't bother to lie. "I'll do what I have to do. Whatever it takes."

"Grady—"

But he was done arguing and standing around. He strode over to Noah's horse and untied the reins from the tree. He mounted Star and gave her neck a quick pat before leading her away from the group and tape.

Once he had a little space, he urged her into a trot. Straight toward the ridge that would lead him up to the old stone church that had been abandoned probably a century ago, and sat just off Carson property, owned and tended by no one.

"Hey, where are you going?" one of the deputies shouted.

Grady didn't bother to answer. He was going to find Laurel. One way or another.

Chapter Seventeen

Laurel heard voices. Unfamiliar voices. She knew she had to open her eyes, but she couldn't seem to manage it. Her head hurt, with so much pain she could barely think past it.

But there were voices, and even though everything hurt and jumbled together, something inside of her knew she had to listen to those voices.

"What kind of idiot are you? There's no way out of this. You've screwed everything up," a man's voice hissed, all restrained fury.

"We could kill her," the other voice suggested, as if he were suggesting getting dessert at a restaurant.

"*You* could kill her," the man retorted. "She did shoot you, after all. We could call it self-defense, perhaps."

"I've done all your dirty work," the second man returned, clearly not happy about it. "All of it."

"That's what I pay you for, and this… You've made this an irreparable mess. You should do all the dirty work when you were the one to muddy it all up. A simple job."

"Simple? Kill two guys and kidnap a girl?"

"You failed at one of those, and the girl was safely returned. You're in the clear there."

The second man laughed bitterly. "I'm not doing another thing for you until I get my full compensation."

"No full compensation until we take care of this problem."

Nausea rolled through Laurel, but she tried to breathe through it. Some of the confusion in her mind cleared, even with the constant ache in her head. The fact they hadn't killed her yet meant *something*.

She had a chance. A chance to live. A chance to escape. If she could only act.

Breathe in. Breathe out. Focus.

She thought she could maybe open her eyes now, but figured it would be best if she gathered her wits before she gave any indication she was conscious. Formulate a plan. Obviously they had weapons. There were two of them, and only one of her.

She blew out a breath, willing herself not to throw up. She was sitting on the cold floor, and her arms were behind her back. Which meant they were tied together. She catalogued the rest of her body as much as she could with her eyes closed and her brain still scrambled.

There was something around her ankles as well. Something hard and cold behind her back. She was cold. So cold.

Focus.

Except she must have said that out loud, or moved, or something.

"She's conscious," the angrier man muttered.

Laurel blinked her eyes open. The man all in black was pulling his mask back down, and she missed any identifying markers. The other man wasn't anywhere she could see, but she was afraid to turn her head to fully search the room.

"Where am I?"

The man in black laughed. "Jupiter, sweetheart."

Dark eyes glittered behind the ski mask and Laurel knew without a shadow of a doubt she had to escape quickly. Even if the other man didn't want to kill her, this one did.

"I'm going to throw up."

He rolled his eyes, turning to somewhere just outside Laurel's vision. She tried to turn her head but pain pierced her skull.

"Just kill her," Angry Man was saying. "*You* this time. So we're both in this and I know you're not going to try and pawn this all off on me."

"Take her outside until she's done. Then bring her back. If we decide to kill her, we need to make sure we have everything we need first."

Angry Man grumbled, but he walked over to her. Laurel was shaking, and no amount of breathing helped that. When two rough hands grabbed her and pulled her to her feet, she swayed and closed her eyes.

He pushed her back roughly against the wall, and she leaned against it, trying to make the world stop spinning. She realized somewhat belatedly he'd untied her legs.

"Walk," he ordered gruffly.

Weaving and swaying, Laurel began to walk. She didn't make an effort to change her weakened gait. The weaker he thought she was, the better. But moving helped. Stepping outside helped.

Except for the fact nothing around her gave her any clue as to where she was. There were trees and sky and rocky ground.

"Well? You gonna throw up or not?"

Laurel bent forward. "I need my hands. I have to use the bathroom."

The man laughed harshly. "Like hell. Stop talking and start retching or we're going back in there right this second." He waved his gun in her face. "If I wasn't trying to prove a point, I would've blown your brains out hours ago."

Hours. Had it been hours? She didn't recognize this place, though it still looked like Wyoming. But maybe it wasn't. Maybe she was far away from home and help.

She bent over, pretending to gag, trying not to cry. Slowly she raised her gaze, trying to find…something. Anything. A place to run and hide. A clue as to where she was.

"You run, I'll only shoot you. Somewhere that'll take a long time to bleed out so you can die a long and terrible death."

She turned her head to look at this man. "Why?"

He shrugged. "Why not?"

Something rustled behind them and the man pushed her down. Since her hands were tied behind her, she couldn't stop the fall. She could only turn her head and brace her body for impact. The sound that came out of her when she hit the hard, cold ground was loud and involuntary.

"Shut up," Angry Man said, giving her a swift, painful kick to the leg. "And don't move."

Laurel sucked in a breath and tried not to sob as she blew it back out. She tilted her head to see where Angry Man had gone. He was slinking around the side of the building, gun held at the ready.

Laurel couldn't help but think it was a squirrel or raccoon or something. Who would stumble upon this...

She looked around her as best she could in her prone position. It was a clearing, the building behind her stone and clearly abandoned for a long time. Windows gone, any clue to what it could have been completely gone.

Except the cross at the very top of the roof.

Oh, God, she knew where she was. She and Vanessa had snuck up here once as kids and spent the night telling each other ghost stories. One of the few times she'd been convinced breaking the rules wasn't the worst thing in the world.

That time was long past, but that church was Wyoming. It was home. She was so close to the Carson Ranch she still had a chance, a real chance, to escape. As long as Angry Man didn't shoot her first.

But he'd disappeared around the corner of the building. And yes, he could likely outrun her in her current injured and tied-up state, but maybe...

A shot rang out, jolting her. She rolled herself onto her side and managed to leverage herself up to her knees. Her vision blurred, but she pushed through it and up onto her feet. She had to... She had to...

When a figure rushed around the corner of the building, Laurel thought for sure she was hallucinating. She had to be. Maybe she'd died. Or was unconscious and dreaming.

Grady stopped short, then swore roughly. Before she could blink, he was in front of her, gingerly touching her shoulder.

"Are you all right?"

"There's another one, Grady," Laurel said, surveying the stone church. They were like sitting ducks out here, and the man inside had to have heard the gunshot.

Except in the next moment, a man was stepping out of the church. He didn't wear a mask or all black and she didn't even see a weapon on him.

"Thank God. Thank God. I was so scared," he said, moving toward her and Grady.

Grady pushed her behind him, holding his pistol up. "Don't come any closer," he ordered the man. "Hold on to me," he whispered to her.

"Please, you've got to help me," the man implored.

Laurel frowned, holding on to Grady's shirt. From everything she'd heard, this man was the leader of the whole debacle. But maybe in her jumbled head she'd been confused.

"That man you shot was holding me captive, much like you." The middle-aged man looked imploringly at her. "Thank God we're both all right."

"Laurel?" Grady asked.

It didn't feel right, but everything was so topsy-turvy and she couldn't trust what she'd heard and what she hadn't.

"The police are on their way. They can sort out whether or not that's true," Grady said firmly, his aim of the gun not wavering from the man's chest.

"Something isn't right," Laurel whispered, more to herself than to Grady.

"What isn't right?" he returned, as quietly and under-his-breath as she'd spoken.

"I don't know." She just didn't know.

GRADY WASN'T ABOUT to lower his weapon on this guy, no matter what he said. Or Laurel said, for that matter. While he wasn't dressed like the man he'd shot on the other side of the church—no mask, no weapon—he was still here. Unharmed, while Laurel's entire face was streaked with blood.

He couldn't think about that, though. If he did he might sink to his knees at the sheer pain of it. That she'd been this hurt, and was somehow still alive. Still here. He had to get her safe.

"I'd feel so much better if you put the gun down," the guy said with a nervous chuckle.

Grady didn't move. "I wouldn't."

"Then maybe I should just go back inside until the police—"

"Don't move."

Something about the guy's expression didn't sit right with Grady. Something about this whole thing didn't sit right, and if the cops didn't get here soon, he'd be forced to act. Because he wasn't going to make Laurel stand through much more of this.

"Why don't you sit down," Grady said. When the man started to bend his knees, Grady rolled his eyes. "Not you. Her."

"Oh," Laurel breathed behind him. "I better stay standing."

"Laurel!"

If Grady wasn't mistaken, it was Dylan's voice, which meant Dylan and Noah had arrived. The cops couldn't be too far back.

"Someone call an ambulance," Grady barked. "Noah, can you ride Laurel out of here without banging her up any more?"

Noah dismounted, about five seconds after Dylan. Both men charged up the hill, taking in the scene around them.

"I'll take her myself," Dylan said hotly.

"I don't know if a horse ride would be the best thing for her in this condition," Noah said calmly. "Head injury—"

"She'll be fine. She needs a doctor fast."

"If all the men could stop posturing and listen to what *I* have to say," Laurel interjected, but she was leaning against Grady and shaking.

"I'm sorry, are any of you a police officer? Or someone who could convince this man to stop pointing his gun at me?" the man Grady hadn't taken his eyes off said.

Grady exchanged a look with Noah, but Noah didn't

seem too keen on the idea, either. "How'd you get up here?" Noah asked.

The man tugged at the collar of his shirt. "I... I don't know. I was brought here against my will."

"How?" Laurel asked from behind Grady.

"W-what?" the man said.

"How did one man bring you and me here against our will?" Laurel asked, her voice sounding stronger and clearer than it had.

"I'm not sure how you arrived, but I was brought here yesterday. Now—"

"Why weren't you tied up?"

The man stood stock-still, everything about him frozen. "I...was."

"No you weren't," Laurel returned, and she moved from where she'd been leaning against Grady's back, to stand next to him. She leaned on him for support, which was certainly a concern, but she stood there, determined. "I saw you. I heard you."

The man's eyes darted around where they all stood in the clearing.

"There isn't anywhere to go," Grady said fiercely, noting that Noah and Dylan had raised their rifles to aim at the man as well.

"And even if you got out of here, I'd find you," Noah said calmly. "I can find anything in these mountains."

The man licked his lips nervously. "I... I don't know what you're all talking about. I don't... I'm a victim. And I haven't done anything wrong. If you do anything to me, I will sue you."

"And who will I sue for paying that man to run me off the road?"

"I did no such thing—" he smirked a little "—that you'll be able to prove."

"Do you own a black sedan, Nebraska license plate 85A GHX?"

The man visibly paled, and it was Grady's turn to smirk. "I think you might be on to something, Deputy," he offered cheerfully.

"I'm going to go out on a limb and say you're employed by the company that runs Evergreen Mining."

"I don't see what that has to do with anything."

"But I do," Laurel said. "I heard your conversation with the other man, and I've got so much evidence built up. All I needed was the man behind it, and here you are."

"You can't…" He shook his head, looking around more desperately. "You're lying."

"I guess we'll find out how much when the police arrive. Noah or Dylan, will you walk around and see if you can find the car?"

"Gladly," Dylan said, sounding about as lethal as Grady felt.

The only thing that kept Grady in place was Laurel leaning against him. Otherwise he'd be more than a little tempted to beat this guy to a bloody pulp.

"You can't do this. My lawyers will have a field day with this. None of you know what you're talking about and…and… This is ludicrous. I'll take you for everything you're worth."

"That supposed to be scary?"

"You have nothing to hold me on. Nothing."

"Cops are here," Dylan called from the other side of the stone church. "And I found the car. Just as Laurel described."

The man darted for the woods, but Grady fired his weapon, hitting him in the upper thigh. The man fell to the ground with a howl. And again, Grady would have gladly gone over and gotten a few kicks in, but Laurel was leaning, saying his name.

"Grady."

He glanced down at her. Her eyes were drooping, and underneath the awful blood all over her, her complexion was gray.

"Open your eyes, baby."

She shook her head almost imperceptibly. "Can't."

"Come on, princess. Stay with me here." He moved the arm not holding a gun around her waist, holding her up. She clutched his shirt, but it was as though her legs didn't hold her up. Her legs buckled.

"I really don't feel well."

"Laurel." But her eyes had rolled back, her body going limp. Grady looked up wildly, heart beating with panic against his chest. "Hart," he barked when the deputy came into view. "Get your car up here now."

Grady had to hand it to the young deputy—he didn't balk at taking orders from a civilian. Hart turned and ran back down the hill, shouting orders to the other deputies with him.

Chapter Eighteen

Laurel wasn't a fan of waking up from unconsciousness not knowing where she was or what had happened. She vaguely remembered the stone church, something about the man who'd been responsible for all this.

She definitely remembered Grady. He'd held her up and kept her safe.

"Grady?" Whatever sound that came out of her mouth certainly didn't sound like his name. She cleared her raw throat and tried again. "Grady?" She tried to open her eyes but it was all too bright.

"Shh. We're right here." Jen's voice. Her sister.

"Jen. Where's Grady?"

"I can't believe she's saying that Carson's name. She must be delirious."

"Hello to you, too, Dad." She felt a large hand on her arm. She imagined it was her father's, and despite all his blustering she was sure he was worried sick. "Can someone dim the lights."

"That should be better," another male voice said.

Laurel's eyes flew open. "Cam." Her brother closest in age to her had been deployed for a while and she hadn't seen him in over a year. But here he was, in her hospital room.

Hospital. Why was everyone here?

"Oh, God, am I dying?"

Jen took her hand. "No, but you certainly gave us all a scare. You lost a lot of blood and needed a lot of stitches. Collapsed lung, bruised ribs and a broken nose." Jen let out a shaky breath. "And Dylan said it could have been so much worse."

Laurel looked around at her family in the hospital room, and she knew she should want this and this alone. She was healing and her family was here because they loved her.

"I need to see Grady." She turned to Jen, imploringly, figuring Jen would be her best, softest-hearted bet. "Please. He saved me, you know." She looked around at her stone-faced father and an even stonier-faced Cam. "He saved me. I need to speak with him."

"I'll get him," Dylan surprised her by saying.

Dad sputtered, Jen soothed him, and Cam ushered all of them out of the room, pausing at the door to look back at her. "I didn't expect to come home and find you looking like hell, sis."

"Are you home to stay?"

"Yeah."

"I'm very glad," she said, feeling overly emotional. She'd blame that on whatever machines she was hooked up to or whatever was in the IV.

"Me, too." And then he disappeared, and only seconds later, Grady stepped in. He was big and strong and she wanted to *weep*. Because he was here, and he'd saved her. "You're here," she managed to rasp.

"Where else would I be, princess?" he asked gruffly.

"What happened?"

"You were hurt—"

"With the guy. The head guy. It's all a blur after I told him I had evidence and—"

"He made a break for it."

She squeaked in outrage.

Grady's mouth curved grimly. "I shot him."

"Oh. I don't remember that. Is he dead?"

"No. Fared better than you. Other guy's in critical. The leader of this whole thing has a million lawyers crawling all over the place, but you built a pretty tight case against the guy. Evidence all over his car that he had Lizzie. And while the other guy may have been driving the car, it's registered to the main guy. Not quite the criminal mastermind he fancied himself."

"So who was the not-head guy?"

"Hired muscle. Basically a hit man he was using however necessary to try and cover all this up."

"Was he really doing all this for EPA violations?"

Grady shrugged, still standing near the door. "We don't know. He's got enough lawyers to block every cop in America, I think."

"Why are you standing all the way over there?" she demanded.

"Because I want to touch you so bad it hurts," he said, hands jammed in his pockets, something like but not quite fury vibrating off him.

"You can touch me."

"You look terrible, princess."

"I'll heal. Come here."

Slowly, he took a step forward, and then another, until he was standing over her, looking at her face as though she'd jabbed a knife in his chest.

He put a fingertip to her collarbone, she assumed since it wasn't bruised or scraped.

"You gave me quite the scare," he murmured, his fingertip warm and gentle on her skin.

"It wasn't exactly roses and unicorns from where I stood, either."

"Laurel." He looked so grim, so serious. Like he was about to deliver the most terrible news on the face of the planet. With her actual name to boot. "I love you."

She blinked. "What?"

"You heard me," he returned grumpily, shoving his hands back in his pockets.

"But…"

"And I'm not prone to saying that, so don't expect me to repeat it."

"Grady," she reached out for him, but he stepped away from the bed.

"Oh, fine," he grumbled. "If you're going to be that way about it."

"What wa—"

"I love you," he blurted as if she'd somehow *forced* the admission out of him, and she was to blame for all of it. "I love you. Grady Carson loves Laurel Delaney. Are you happy?" He raked his fingers through his hair.

She wanted to laugh. He'd lost his mind, and he loved her. Really. "Grady."

"And don't think you're getting out of this," he said, pointing at her. "You started it. You're stuck with me now."

"Come here," she said as forcefully as she could manage. "And calm down."

He looked at her with that same desolate expression he'd used to say he loved her. "You could have died."

A lump clogged her throat, but she spoke through it. "So could you. You came in guns blazing, all by yourself."

"Hours," he said, his voice breaking just there at the end. "You were gone hours before we found you."

"Grady."

"What?" he snapped.

She cupped his face with her hands, reveling in the sharp spikes of his beard. "I love you," she said, looking directly into those beautiful blue eyes, knowing without a doubt that whatever crazy Bent feud nonsense was thrown their way, no matter how many murder investigations went awry, they would make it through together.

He kissed the spot on her collarbone he'd touched earlier. "You're darn right you do, princess."

Two weeks later

When Laurel Delaney sauntered into Rightful Claim on a snowy day, dressed in a drab Bent County PD polo and baggy khaki pants, with her badge attached to her hip, Grady Carson wondered how he'd ever thought he could fight the feeling in his gut he got every time she walked into his bar.

A century-old feud hadn't stood a chance against this wave of possession. Love. She was his. He was hers. Beginning and end of story.

"So, the doctors clear you?" he asked casually.

She slid onto a barstool. "Desk duty," she said disgustedly, some of the cuts on her face still red and a terrible reminder of that day not so long ago. "I can work in-house and lose my marbles."

"I'm guessing that's wise."

She made a rude noise. "I'm fine."

"That's not what you said last night."

She wrinkled her nose. "You just hit my ribs the wrong way. I don't plan on getting naked and sweaty with anyone I'm investigating."

"Good to hear."

"I did get some good news today," she said leaning forward on the bar, then wincing.

He winced right along with her. He thought it had been bad enough seeing her bloody and passed out, or in that horrible white hospital bed, but watching her *heal* and push herself too hard was a new pain he'd never known.

"What's that?" he asked, sliding her a Coke.

"The muscle woke up yesterday. Lawyered up, but he made a plea bargain. Looks like he's going to turn on Mr. Head Guy."

Head Guy. Aaron Zifle. The head of the mining corporations safety department, drowning in safety violations and trying to keep his pretty young wife sparkling in diamonds. Apparently he'd been about to lose his job and so desperate to keep the well-paying position he'd decided the only way to deal with Jason Delaney's accusation had been to kill.

At least that was Laurel's theory after her nonstop investigating while she'd still been forced to spend most of her days in bed. Grady was inclined to believe her since he spent most of his days at her bedside, listening to her chatter.

Vanessa had nearly run his bar into the ground, at least in his estimation, but it still stood, and he was back to work, and Laurel was trying to be.

"That is good news. Make his trial airtight, won't it?"

"Yes. They'll likely up his bond with that information, too. The chances of him getting out of what he's done, even with his team of lawyers, is pretty slim."

"We should celebrate."

"How?" She rubbed at her rib. "I'm not sure I'm up for any serious celebrating."

"How about this. After I close up, I pack all my things up and move them to your cabin."

Her eyebrows furrowed together. "Move. Into my cabin. You?"

"Yes, I believe that's what I meant."

"But… We… We've barely dated," she said, her eyebrows furrowing deeper.

"True."

"My family… A Carson living on Delaney land? The town might have us tarred and feathered."

"Could be."

"And the bar." She gestured around to encompass all of Rightful Claim. "Don't you have to be here at all hours?"

"Not *all* hours. I was thinking about giving Vanessa more control, and the apartment—she's been angling for it for months."

Laurel blinked at him, beautiful and strong and absolutely everything he wanted to wake up to. Go to bed with. Build a life with.

"This is crazy," she said, shaking her head.

But she hadn't said no, and he knew her well enough. "Absolutely insane. So, what do you say?"

Her face broke out into a grin. "How soon can you close up?"

When he leaned across the bar and gave her a nice, hard kiss, a few cheers went up around them. A few mutters. One boo he was pretty sure came from Ty.

But Grady Carson didn't care much, because Laurel Delaney was his. Like it was always meant to be.

* * * * *

LET'S TALK
Romance

For exclusive extracts, competitions
and special offers, find us online:

■ facebook.com/millsandboon

■ @millsandboonuk

■ @millsandboon

Or get in touch on 0844 844 1351*

For all the latest titles coming soon, visit
millsandboon.co.uk/nextmonth